LOUISIANA!

The sixteenth new adventure in the WAGONS WEST series—bold new enterprises by America's most courageous heroes ready to carry their fight for justice into the streets of an exotic city and into the heart of an inscrutable foreign land.

WAGONS WEST

LOUISIANA!

A GROWING NATION'S DESTINY SWEPT THEM FROM THE SOUTH'S MOST IMPORTANT PORT TO THE SHORES OF A FAR AWAY LAND

TOBY HOLT—

No man could best him in battle, no temptation could sway his heart . . . until a secret mission thrust him into the embrace of a treacherous enemy, too beautiful to resist, too clever to escape, and perhaps too deadly for even Toby Holt to survive.

PRINCESS TA-LIEN—

A rare Oriental loveliness made her a living China doll . . . but a ruthless criminal heart made her a lethal woman to love.

KARL KELLERMAN—

Hunted by men on both sides of the law, his uncanny luck keeps him one step ahead of death and determined to repossess the money and the woman he lost.

MILLICENT RANDALL GAUTIER—

A vile scheme would take her from a dream marriage into a nightmare of degradation she might never escape.

★★★★★★★★★★★★★★★★★★★★★★★★★★★★★★★★★★★★

CINDY HOLT—
Now a daughter of the famous wagonmaster Whip Holt inherits the instincts and rare courage that will make her seek out a danger that she must either destroy . . . or die.

HANK BLAKE—
A proud West Point cadet who must choose between his own ambitions and a friend in trouble.

DOMINO—
Boss of bosses who walks the wild side of New Orleans, an obsession may threaten his empire . . . and his life.

MARTHA—
A mysterious and magnificent woman, she does Domino's bidding . . . but the man she dreams of is named Holt.

CH'IEN MING-LO—
Unbeaten champion in the Empress's court, as an enemy he could be Toby Holt's final downfall; as a friend he could be an invincible ally.

★★★★★★★★★★★★★★★★★★★★★★★★★★★★★★

Bantam Books by Dana Fuller Ross
Ask your bookseller for the books you have missed

INDEPENDENCE!—Volume I
NEBRASKA!—Volume II
WYOMING!—Volume III
OREGON!—Volume IV
TEXAS!—Volume V
CALIFORNIA!—Volume VI
COLORADO!—Volume VII
NEVADA!—Volume VIII
WASHINGTON!—Volume IX
MONTANA!—Volume X
DAKOTA!—Volume XI
UTAH!—Volume XII
IDAHO!—Volume XIII
MISSOURI!—Volume XIV
MISSISSIPPI!—Volume XV
LOUISIANA!—Volume XVI

LOUISIANA!

DANA FULLER ROSS

Created by the producers of
White Indian, Children of the
Lion, Stagecoach, and Saga of the
Southwest.

Chairman of the Board: Lyle Kenyon Engel

BANTAM BOOKS
TORONTO • NEW YORK • LONDON • SYDNEY • AUCKLAND

LOUISIANA!
A Bantam Book / Book Creations, Inc.
Bantam edition / January 1986

Produced by Book Creations, Inc.
Chairman of the Board: Lyle Kenyon Engel.

ISBN 0-553-25247-X

Published simultaneously in the United States and Canada

Bantam Books are published by Bantam Books, Inc. Its trademark,
consisting of the words "Bantam Books" and the portrayal of a
rooster, is Registered in U.S. Patent and Trademark Office and in
other countries. Marca Registrada. Bantam Books, Inc., 666 Fifth
Avenue, New York, New York 10103.

PRINTED IN THE UNITED STATES OF AMERICA
H   0 9 8 7 6 5 4 3 2 1

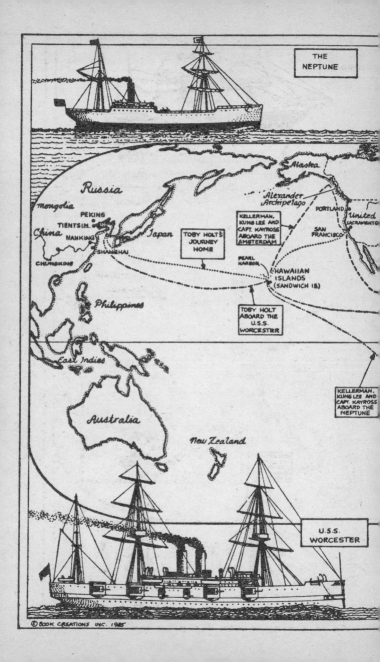

THE
NEPTUNE

Russia

Mongolia

PEKING
TIENTSIN
NANKING
CHUNGKING
SHANGHAI

China

Japan

Alaska

Alexander
Archipelago

PORTLAND

United
SACRAMENTO

KELLERMAN,
KUNG LEE AND
CAPT. KAYROSS
ABOARD THE
AMSTERDAM

SAN
FRANCISCO

TOBY HOLT'S
JOURNEY
HOME

PEARL
HARBOR

HAWAIIAN
ISLANDS
(SANDWICH IS.)

Philippines

TOBY HOLT
ABOARD THE
U.S.S.
WORCESTER

East Indies

KELLERMAN,
KUNG LEE AND
CAPT. KAYROSS
ABOARD THE
NEPTUNE

Australia

New Zealand

U.S.S.
WORCESTER

© BOOK CREATIONS INC. 1985

THE
AMSTERDAM

Russia

Missouri R.
ST. LOUIS   Illinois   Ind.

WEST POINT
NEW YORK
PHILADELPHIA
WASHINGTON

Missouri   CAIRO   Ohio R.   Kentucky

TOBY HOLT
ABOARD THE
U.S.S.
SAVANNAH

Tennessee
MEMPHIS

Arkansas

South
America

PARAISO

KELLERMAN
AND CAPTAIN
KAYROSS
ABOARD THE
AMSTERDAM

Mississippi   Ala.

BATON
ROUGE

Louisiana

NEW
ORLEANS

Gulf of Mexico

U.S.S.
SAVANNAH

RON TOELKE '85

★ ★ WAGONS WEST ★ ★

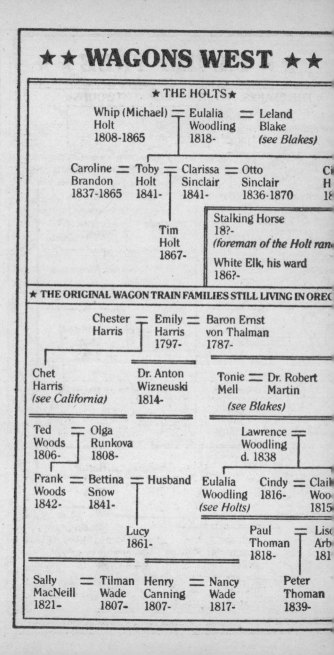

★ THE HOLTS ★

Whip (Michael) = Eulalia   = Leland
Holt   Woodling   Blake
1808-1865   1818-   *(see Blakes)*

Caroline = Toby = Clarissa = Otto   C
Brandon   Holt   Sinclair   Sinclair   H
1837-1865 1841- 1841-   1836-1870   18

Tim
Holt
1867-

Stalking Horse
18?-
(foreman of the Holt ran

White Elk, his ward
186?-

★ THE ORIGINAL WAGON TRAIN FAMILIES STILL LIVING IN OREC

Chester = Emily =   Baron Ernst
Harris   Harris   von Thalman
          1797-   1787-

Chet   Dr. Anton   Tonie = Dr. Robert
Harris   Wizneuski   Mell   Martin
(see California) 1814-   *(see Blakes)*

Ted = Olga   Lawrence =
Woods Runkova   Woodling
1806- 1808-   d. 1838

Frank = Bettina = Husband   Eulalia   Cindy = Clai
Woods   Snow   Woodling   1816-   Woo
1842-   1841-   *(see Holts)*   1815

Lucy   Paul   = Lis
1861-   Thoman   Arb
                             1818-   181

Sally   = Tilman   Henry   = Nancy   Peter
MacNeill   Wade   Canning   Wade   Thoman
1821-   1807-   1807-   1817-   1839-

★ ★ FAMILY TREE ★ ★

★ THE BLAKES, MARTINS, AND BRENTWOODS ★

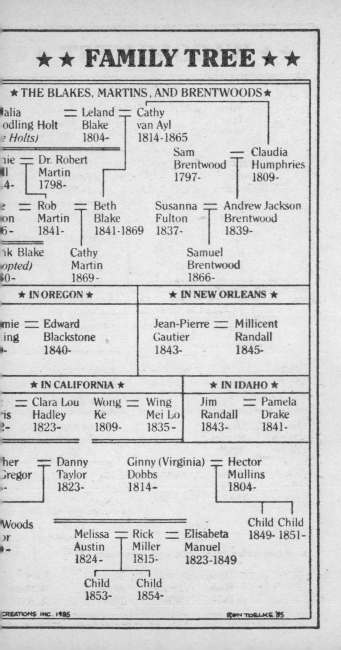

...alia   ═ Leland ─ Cathy
...odling Holt   Blake   van Ayl
...e Holts)   1804-   1814-1865

...nie ═ Dr. Robert   Sam   ─ Claudia
...ll   Martin   Brentwood   Humphries
...4-   1798-   1797-   1809-

...e ═ Rob ═ Beth   Susanna ═ Andrew Jackson
...on   Martin   Blake   Fulton   Brentwood
...6-   1841-   1841-1869   1837-   1839-

...k Blake   Cathy   Samuel
...opted)   Martin   Brentwood
...0-   1869-   1866-

★ IN OREGON ★   ★ IN NEW ORLEANS ★

...mie ═ Edward   Jean-Pierre ═ Millicent
...ing   Blackstone   Gautier   Randall
...-   1840-   1843-   1845-

★ IN CALIFORNIA ★   ★ IN IDAHO ★

...ris ═ Clara Lou   Wong ═ Wing   Jim ═ Pamela
...2-   Hadley   Ke   Mei Lo   Randall   Drake
    1823-   1809-   1835-   1843-   1841-

...her ═ Danny   Ginny (Virginia) ═ Hector
...regor   Taylor   Dobbs   Mullins
...-   1823-   1814-   1804-

                              Child Child
...Woods   1849- 1851-
...or
...-

    Melissa ═ Rick ═ Elisabeta
    Austin   Miller   Manuel
    1824-   1815-   1823-1849

       Child   Child
       1853-   1854-

CREATIONS INC. 1985   RON TOELKE '85

LOUISIANA!

I

The distinctive shape of the peak, Diamond Head, loomed in the distance. Resembling the profile of a crouching lion, it was the most commanding feature of Oahu, in the Sandwich Island group, later to be called the Hawaiian Islands. When he saw it, Captain Robin Kayross, master of the *Neptune*, a steam-powered freighter, knew he was on target after a tiring voyage from New Orleans, around South America, and partway across the Pacific. He was looking forward to a brief layover in Honolulu before sailing on to the port of Tientsin, China, where he would sell his cargo of American manufactured goods and grain.

In Tientsin the *Neptune*'s legitimate cargo would be replaced by a quite different one for the return trip to the United States. Coolies, hoping to find a better life in America, would jam the hold of the ship, then secretly disembark in San Francisco in defiance of immigration laws. Any remaining space in the ship would be filled with cases of opium. Though still valued for its medicinal effects, this drug was far more widely used by those addicted to its euphoric effects—and public health officials in both the United States and China were attempting to control the international distribution of it.

Glancing along the deck, the grizzled captain studied two men leaning on the rail at the far end. Though standing shoulder to shoulder, they were not talking. One of them, a sixty-year-old Chinese named Kung Lee, was the head of the most vicious of tongs in North America. These Chinese gangs were involved in illegal immigration, the dope trade, and numerous other criminal activities. Kung was the right man for the job: He was utterly lacking in sentiment, compassion, or sympathy for any human being. Results, no matter how cruelly achieved, were his goal in all his shady business dealings. It was impossible to guess how many murders, how much mayhem he was responsible for. Even the unscrupulous Kayross was appalled at Kung's bloody record.

Standing beside Kung, elbows resting on the rail, was an impressively large man. Well over six feet and broad-shouldered, Karl Kellerman was once a St. Louis detective sergeant, but was now a hardened criminal. He was aboard the *Neptune* to keep an eye on certain transactions, which he expected would net him one third of the profits from this voyage. But in spite of their temporary partnership, it was obvious that Kung felt only contempt for his associate. The feeling, shared by Captain Kayross, who also was a partner in the venture, was fostered by Kellerman's habit of recklessly making enemies.

Kellerman's most dogged foe was a New Orleans gang leader. Known as Domino, he was an urbane, well-mannered, and thoughtful man with a surprisingly soft heart for anyone he particularly liked. But anyone who crossed him quickly earned his enduring wrath. His most violent hatred was reserved for Karl Kellerman, who had once wounded him in an attempted double cross. No fate would be too horrible for Kellerman, in Domino's opinion.

An equally dangerous opponent of Kellerman's was the renowned Toby Holt, who had taken on the assignment of trying to track down both Kung Lee and Kellerman. In addition, Kellerman's former partner, Wallace Dugald, had vowed vengeance after being betrayed by him. Kellerman's motive, then, for sailing on the *Neptune* was to drop out of sight for a period of time.

Kung Lee turned and sauntered the length of the deck to join Captain Kayross. "Instead of berthing in the Honolulu port," he ordered, "continue on to Pearl Harbor. We will be better off there."

Sailing parallel to the island coast, Kayross maneuvered the freighter past Honolulu toward the more distant port. Kayross did not question the order. He knew that Kung Lee never acted on impulse.

The *Neptune* was close enough to the shore to enable its crew and passengers to discern objects on land clearly. Graceful royal palm trees and fruit-bearing coconut palms towered above low, pastel-painted houses. Occasional breezes filled the air with the unmistakable odor of the tropics, a not-unpleasant combination of blossoms and decaying vegetation. In the distance the pink sandstone palace of King Kamehameha V, the reigning monarch of Hawaii, was visible. Beyond it were larger structures housing the little kingdom's government. Hawaii's national flag flew above the royal palace and the government buildings, but actually the country was under the protection of the United States. It was a relationship that severely cramped the efforts of Great Britain and France to annex the lush islands.

As they sailed, the skyline of Honolulu gave way to an extended tropical rain forest. At last the sheltered basin of Pearl Harbor came into view. Used by Hawaiians for many years, it was protected by land spits on all approaches from the Pacific. Its docking area was much in demand by commercial shippers.

Slowing down, the *Neptune* chugged into the harbor basin. Kung Lee, who had been watching silently, spoke again. "Put in at the dock to your left, next to the Dutch freighter," he told the captain. "The dock and the ship are both mine." Kung's expression revealed satisfaction that the Dutch vessel was on hand just as he had expected, though he had been out of touch with its schedule for months. A large sailing ship that carried auxiliary engines, the *Amsterdam* flew the flag of the Netherlands.

As the *Neptune* approached its berth, Captain Kayross was surprised by the appearance of a dozen men, heavily armed, on the wharf. Most appeared to be Chinese. All wore pistols in holsters and carried high-powered rifles. After a single look at the tong chieftain's stern face, however, Kayross decided not to question Kung about the men.

With a meaningful toss of his head toward Kellerman, who had suddenly appeared near them, Kung quietly mouthed, "Later!" to Kayross.

"As you can see, Kellerman," the captain said easily as a distraction, "we've reached this stopover port, more or less on schedule. We will be here for a few days. You're free to go ashore and explore Oahu if you wish. Do I need to advise you to keep out of trouble?"

Kellerman smirked and asked, "Exactly how long is a

few days, Captain? I don't want to be left behind. I'd miss your delightful company."

"You'll be safe enough," Kayross told him, "if you're back on board in, say, seventy-two hours."

"Add another day, and make that ninety-six hours," Kung Lee amended.

Kellerman, looking intently down at the dock, sucked in his breath. A quartet of prostitutes had appeared and were waiting for the crew to come ashore. Two were Oriental, one was a dark-haired woman apparently of Mediterranean extraction, and one who stood out from the others was a native Hawaiian. She wore flowers in her dark brown hair, and a lei set off her bare shoulders. Tall, with a ripe, full figure, she immediately attracted Kellerman's attention. She caught his eye and smiled lazily.

Kellerman chuckled softly under his breath, then waved and winked. A moment later he was gone. When the gangway was lowered, he was the first ashore. He exchanged a few words with the Hawaiian, and they strode off, arm in arm.

"Kellerman could be valuable in an operation," Kung Lee said quietly. "But that weakness for women makes him too vulnerable. Every time he sees a pretty face he loses his head."

"I was angry when we left New Orleans," Kayross rejoined. "Just think of it! We had the great Toby Holt on board on a snooping expedition! We nabbed him, and if we had thrown him overboard when we hit the Gulf, that would have been the end of him." His voice became bitter. "But Holt escaped—because of Kellerman."

"Yes, thanks to Kellerman," Kung Lee added, his voice still soft, "Holt is alive, knowing that the *Neptune*'s return cargo is to be immigrants and opium. I hold him responsible for this change in our plans."

Kayross raised an eyebrow, asking a silent question.

"The *Neptune* and the *Amsterdam*," Kung explained, "will seem to hold to their original schedules. But not quite! The *Neptune* will carry this cargo to China, where she will pick up our return cargo. We'll worry later about her return voyage. What is important to you and me right now is returning to the States without detection. By being aboard the *Amsterdam*, we will be totally unexpected. As for the *Amsterdam*, having come from the Orient, she is to proceed to New Orleans with her own cargo of coolies and opium. But effective immediately, you and your crew are to leave the *Neptune* and take over the *Amsterdam*. We are exchanging crews."

"Why is that?" Kayross was perplexed.

"Because," Kung replied forcefully, "the authorities will not be on the lookout for us on the *Amsterdam*."

"My crew will be glad enough that we are not going on to the Orient," Kayross said. "I'd like to give them leave before we sail."

"You know I never interfere in such matters." The owner smiled, his words belying his behavior. "When the transfer takes place, today's guards will be augmented by a dozen more. Be prepared to keep clear of them, and step smartly."

"I gather," Kayross said, "that they are to prevent any interruption in our, ah, dealings here. And perhaps," he added, "to keep the coolies in line. Am I correct?"

Kung Lee's smile was chilling. "Completely correct, Captain. You and I understand each other as usual. That's more than I can say for that oaf Kellerman. I'm sorry that we took him on as a partner."

Kellerman, in fact, had a surprise in store for his partners the following day. He had been looking after his own interests in Honolulu, as well as enjoying himself. He strolled into the master's cabin as the pair were sitting down to a light noonday dinner. His manner jaunty, he asked, "How much of a profit are you expecting on that cotton-weaving machinery in the aft hold?"

"If we can dispose of it in the Canton region where cotton is grown," Kung answered without deigning to look at him, "we will double our money."

"You don't think you could possibly get three times what we paid for it?"

"That's virtually impossible. I don't know of any cotton people in Canton who would pay that high a price."

"I found someone last night who will pay us triple," Kellerman said triumphantly. "An Englishman who heads a group of cotton growers on the big island, Hawaii."

"If he can pay the price, the merchandise is his. And welcome to it."

"Sold!" Kellerman crowed enthusiastically.

"You can use the space," Captain Kayross interjected, speaking to Kung Lee, "by taking on coconuts, for which there's always a demand."

"You have a new choice to make, Kellerman," Kung said briskly. "You can continue on to China aboard the *Neptune*, as you have intended. Or you can return with me to the mainland on the *Amsterdam*."

Kellerman's pale-blue eyes widened in surprise. "If it's safe," he said, "I'd much rather go back to the States, instead of spending more weeks crossing the Pacific."

Kung Lee stared at him indifferently.

"If you do consider it safe, as you appear to," Kellerman

added after a moment's thought, "I guess it'll be safe for me. I'll go back with you."

"Very well," the tong leader said, and returned to his meal, signifying that the discussion was over.

The dinner-table atmosphere was festive in the Fort Vancouver home of Major General Leland Blake, commander of the army in the West, and his wife, Eulalia. Laughter echoed through the house. He was in fine spirits, as he invariably was when Eulalia's children and grandson joined them.

The immediate cause of the merriment was three-year old Tim Holt, who was insisting on trying to slice his own portion of meat. He was being encouraged by his doting grandmother, his titian-haired mother, Clarissa, and his young aunt, Cindy Holt.

General Blake, a trim, distinguished-looking man in his late sixties, sat back in his chair at the head of the table and enjoyed the spectacle. Sometimes it was hard for him to believe that his lovely, dark-haired wife could have a daughter with sandy-blond hair like Cindy's, though Cindy had her mother's slim figure. Eulalia's son, Toby, also had sandy hair, and the older he grew the more his tall, lean frame resembled that of his late father, Whip Holt, the famous hero of the West. Toby, whose reputation as a man of dauntless courage was also beginning to rival his father's, winked at the general and smiled.

But his smile faded when Eulalia urged, "Timmie, let Grandma cut your steak for you before it grows cold."

"You're spoiling him, Mama," Toby protested.

Eulalia was one of the few people who dared contradict Toby. "Nonsense!" she declared blithely. "I cut your meat for you until you were six. And you certainly don't

8

seem any the worse for it. At least, I don't *think* so," she added with a note of false uncertainty.

Cindy's laughter sounded above that of the others.

Toby looked at his sister in mock indignation. "Quiet, child," he said, deftly changing the subject. "It has come to my attention that you are eager for an excuse to pay a visit to your betrothed." He was referring to Hank Blake, Lee and Eulalia's adopted son, who was enrolled in the United States Military Academy at West Point. "Just remember that the only way you'll cross the country is with me chaperoning you. Otherwise, it's back to your college for you, no matter how impressed the dean was about your opportunity to make an 'educational' trip."

Cindy returned his direct gaze with pretended innocence. "Did you hear that, Clarissa?" she demanded, turning to her sister-in-law. "Toby says *he's* going East, too! I thought that the trip you and I are to make to West Point was the important event for the future."

Clarissa declined to join in the teasing game. "That's enough, you two," she said. "I get my share of silliness every day from Tim."

She beamed at the little boy, who was devouring the beef that Eulalia had cut into small pieces.

"Look at him eat!" Toby said in awe.

"That's because he takes after you in everything, Toby—and after your dad, too," General Blake said. "He's a real male animal. I can see he's going to be quite a fellow in a few more years. He should be perfect material for the class of eighty-nine at the academy."

"You hear that, Tim?" Toby asked him. "Grandpa has your whole future mapped out already. Since he's such a soft touch for you, maybe you can find out from him the

9

real reason I'm being summoned to Washington. He's awfully wary of saying very much on that score."

General Blake quickly sobered. "That's not at all the case," he objected. "I've told you everything I know. President Grant wishes to see you. Clarissa, too. The President intends to award you a citation. I assume it may have to do with your work in exposing the tong's importation of illegal aliens and opium from China."

"Living in the White House must do strange things to a man," Clarissa said. "President Grant could have sent the citation here to Fort Vancouver and ordered you to present it to Toby, Papa, instead of requiring Toby and me to travel across the United States, just to receive a piece of paper."

"I don't mind such a trip at the President's pleasure, if that's what's bothering you," Toby assured her quietly.

"No, that's not it," Clarissa said, sighing. "I'm distressed at being separated from Tim for weeks. Oh, I know it wouldn't be convenient to take him on such a long journey, and certainly nobody could be better able to look after him than you, Mama. After all, you've had more years of experience than we've had!"

"We'll both miss him very much," Toby interjected, "but I suspect the separation might be healthy for him. He's old enough to begin learning some lessons in self-reliance."

"When you start packing for your trip, Cindy," General Blake said, "we'll have a few small packages for you to take to Hank."

"Of course, Papa," she replied. "May I ask what you are sending him?"

"For one thing, a few books on military strategy and tactics from my library. He'll find them useful in a course he's just about to start. And your mother has a tin of those hard candies he loves."

"In this family," Toby asserted, "*everybody* is spoiled. But when you stop to think about it, why not? Hank ranks first in his class, so a treat of a few chunks of candy isn't going to turn his head. It would take more than that," he said laughing, "like having his special girl come clear across the United States to see him for a few hours."

Just as another presidential citation won't turn your head, Toby, the general thought. *This is a remarkable brood!*

Little Tim was so sleepy that his parents bundled him up to take him home as soon as supper ended. Cindy hurried upstairs to get her suitcase, as she was going to accompany Toby and Clarissa, spending the night with them at their ranch house in Oregon, across the Columbia River from Fort Vancouver.

A short time later, when the Blakes were alone in their living room, the general selected a book and started to read. Eulalia sat down opposite him and looked at him quizzically.

Becoming aware of her gaze, he put down his book. "You want to talk?"

She smiled. "That's the general idea," she replied. "I have a notion that you know more than you told Toby and Clarissa about their trip to Washington—either because you've divined it or you've been told. I believe the President has sent for Toby for some reason other than presenting a citation."

The general laughed. "You never cease to astonish me!"

"I know you well enough that I'm sometimes able to

read your mind," she replied. After a moment she asked, "Well?"

"President Grant," he said, "didn't honor me with his confidences. What I know was contained in a personal letter that I received from a West Point classmate of mine. He's a brigadier general who serves as the liaison officer between the War and State departments. He said that the President intends to send Toby on a very important mission that would take him out of the country for as long as a year."

"Oh, dear!" Eulalia murmured in distress.

Her husband raised an eyebrow as he studied her.

"You've forgotten, apparently," she went on, "that Toby promised Clarissa that he wouldn't leave her alone again. He told her that he has accepted the last assignment that would separate them, and that from now on he intends to stay at home with her and with Timmie."

"Indeed, I haven't forgotten," the general assured her. "And, for that matter, the President even appears to know about Toby's promise. My friend emphasized that Grant deliberately included Clarissa in his invitation because he wants to meet her. Apparently, he's intending to try to persuade her to release Toby from that promise."

"Toby is a Holt!" Eulalia exclaimed, worry evident in her voice. "When he gives his word, he regards it as a solemn, binding oath. He'll allow nothing to change his mind. President Grant will need to be enormously persuasive—or, I assure you, Toby will not budge!"

Under the watchful eyes of Captain Kayross and Kung Lee, the crew of the *Neptune* changed places with that of the *Amsterdam*, an older vessel that had been built in a Dutch shipyard ten years earlier. Then the two vessels resumed their voyages.

Kellerman, kept in the dark about Kung's and Kayross's plans, became confused when the *Amsterdam* sailed north by northeast—far off the expected course for California—and finally anchored outside a little port town in Alaska's Alexander Archipelago.

No one on board the *Amsterdam* except the captain was permitted ashore. Kayross conferred at length with customs and immigration authorities, and Kellerman guessed that some under-the-table deal was reached. Twenty-four hours later, the captain, with an expression of smug satisfaction, gave the order to pull up anchor, and the ship slipped down the west coast of the North American continent to San Francisco.

A few hours before putting into the port, Kung at last called Kellerman into his cabin following many days of silence. Smiling and at ease, the tong leader leaned back. "I will be quitting the *Amsterdam* here, so we'll use this opportunity for a final business meeting."

"I assumed you might be leaving us," Kellerman replied with equal terseness. His gnawing annoyance with his partner was coming close to the surface.

Kung did not reply directly. "The *Amsterdam* will discharge her cargo," he said, "and will take on another. Thanks to the generous and shortsighted policies of the United States government, my agents have been able to purchase, through intermediaries, a large quantity of surplus military equipment—rifles, artillery, and a great deal of ammunition. In South America, where wars are in progress or civil strife is occurring, they want all of the munitions they can get. The sale of our little arsenal can add a great deal to your profits. And mine."

"How are you going to unload your present cargo?" Kellerman demanded, exhibiting in words and manner his customary crude bluntness. "In spite of your efforts to keep this from me, I know for a fact it is coolies and opium, as we had expected the *Neptune* to carry on her return."

Kung looked pained at this lack of tact and finesse. "When I accepted you as a partner," he said with a show of exasperation, "you agreed to never ask questions, much less expect answers from me. Our cargo will be disposed of in ways that my organization deems wise and profitable. As you may have gathered, our transferring ships should put the U.S. Customs and Immigration Bureaus off their guard. They have no reason to be looking for us on the *Amsterdam*. Now, as to *your* own future plans. You have a choice: You may leave the ship in San Francisco, too. Or you may stay on board and sail with her to New Orleans. You should have no difficulty in going ashore in either port."

Kellerman needed little time in pondering his alternatives. "I've never set foot in San Francisco, and I don't know anyone in the city," he replied. "But I do have many friends and associates in New Orleans—as well as an enemy or two, of course. But I'm able to function well there. Given the choice, I prefer to continue on. Furthermore, I can keep my eyes and ears open so that my chances will be better of getting all the money that will be due me."

"You dishonor me by intimating that I might try to cheat you out of your fair share of profits," Kung Lee said in a level voice. "Ordinarily, I would take grave offense at this insult, and you would pay a heavy penalty for it. Since I have come to know you, however, I expect nothing better from you. You may do as you please. I have done you the favor of informing you of my plans. And that is final." He pointed to the door in dismissal.

Kellerman wanted to hear a great deal more, but he knew better than to arouse Kung's antagonism any further. Instead, he rose to his feet, clicked his heels, bowed stiffly, and took his leave in what he believed was a suitably dignified style.

A harbor pilot came on board an hour after nightfall, and the freighter threaded her way slowly into the busy port, a difficult and hazardous maneuver. When she tied up at a dock, customs and immigration officials came aboard. Now the purpose of the seemingly unnecessary detour to the Alaskan territory became clear. Captain Kayross blithely produced papers saying that the ship had been in Alaska. These papers had the desired effect: As far as the authorities were concerned, the *Amsterdam*, since last visiting an American port, had traveled only as far as Alaskan territory, and a new examination was not needed. Consequently, the *Amsterdam*'s cargo was safe. The deception was simple but highly successful, and at a cost of nothing except some extra days at sea. Watching from the slightly opened door of his cabin, Kellerman marveled at the cleverness of Kung and of Captain Kayross in carrying out the devious plan.

The officials left, and no sooner did they disappear into the shadows than Kung Lee appeared. Behind him were two crew members, carrying his luggage. He shook hands with Kayross, exchanging wishes for good fortune in days to come. Then he hurried down the gangplank, where he was immediately surrounded by a band of tong members. They moved quickly along the dock together and vanished.

The *Amsterdam* was berthed some distance from the

center of port activities. After a time the area grew very quiet and deserted. Then suddenly several dozen tong workers, clad in the billowing black garb of Chinese laborers, appeared silently as if out of nowhere. They created no stir. Crew members hauled crates of opium up from the hold and handed them over to the newcomers, who removed them. Two men carried each crate with mechanical efficiency, disappearing quickly among the huge warehouses that lined the shore.

Next came the most delicate part of the operation. Scores of miserable coolies were brought up from the bowels of the ship. Lured from their home villages with lies about the bright future that awaited them in the far-off land of America, they had been promptly made prisoners by the tong as soon as they were away from their villages.

Emaciated and frightened, weak from the lack of food and air and from seasickness, the coolies staggered up onto the deck, each secured to a man ahead and one behind by a rope looped and tied around the neck. Crewmen watched their every move, and the tong's men, weapons at the ready, awaited them ashore. Several dozen closed carriages were crowded into an area at the front of the dock. Herded into the vehicles, the coolies would be transported to a farm owned by the tong in nearby Oakland. There they would be fed and exercised until they gained the weight and muscle they would need to do the work of unskilled laborers; then they would be sold as slaves.

After the last of the coolies was ashore, Captain Kayross ordered the hold scrubbed and aired. No evidence of the human cargo remained. Once again, the authorities had been deceived.

The captain left the bridge for his own quarters.

There he summoned Kellerman. "I thank the Lord that's finished!" he exclaimed when his partner arrived. "I always breathe easier after we get rid of opium and Chinese. It's a lot easier to pick up arms and munitions and sell them in South America." He sipped a strong drink gratefully, looking at Kellerman across the rim of his glass. "I gather you're going with me?"

"I certainly hadn't been planning on it," Kellerman replied, his deep voice steady, "any more than I was intending to return to the U.S.A. so soon. That business of sailing to Alaska in order to avoid customs inspection here was as clever as they come. So here we are, and what am I to do about it? I don't know anyone here, so I've decided to risk going back to New Orleans."

He took a sip of the drink the captain offered, and coughed. "As a matter of fact, Kung disappeared so fast tonight that I had no chance to discuss an idea of great importance. I wanted to sound him out on my working regularly for the tong."

"Don't waste your time or your breath," Kayross advised. "You don't know the tong or the way those cutthroats operate. Stay away from it."

"I'd like to hear more."

"This is the sixth job that I've done for them over the years. I do my best, I get my money, and then I go on to the next assignment, whenever and wherever that may be."

"As for me, I know the ins and outs of every enterprise in every town on the Mississippi," Kellerman said. "Without boasting, I swear to you I know every trick of any trade that's practiced there."

"The tong has its own experts," Kayross told him, "men who can match you step for step, every inch of the

17

way. If the tong finds itself short of men to carry out an assignment, Kung Lee hires an expert. He knows now what you can do, what your strengths are—and your weaknesses, too. He'll act accordingly. If and when he wants you, you'll hear, all right."

"But—"

"You'll be well advised to mind your own business. Forget you ever had any dealings with him and don't mention them to anyone. If they find out you're talking out of turn, they'll be gunning for you. Be satisfied that Kung knows enough about you after spending weeks with you on the high seas."

"Is that what you're willing to do?" Kellerman asked incredulously. "After you've peddled the guns and ammunition, you're able to walk away and wonder when Kung will have work for you again?"

"Sure," Kayross said easily. "But this won't be my last job for the tong."

"And you're sure," Kellerman persisted, "that you'll be paid your share of the profits?"

"Absolutely! Kung Lee has never owed me a copper that he hasn't paid."

"And I'll be paid what's owed me from this voyage?"

"I'm not so sure of that," Kayross replied quickly. "In my opinion, if Kung and his tong want to keep your goodwill, they'll pay what they owe you, without any fuss. But if they don't like you, they'll try to cheat you. You've come up against situations like that over the years, and you know how to look out for your own interests. Nothing much I could teach you."

"You can be sure I'm prepared to do whatever is necessary to protect my interests," Kellerman growled, his face growing dark and his voice ominous. "And you can pass the word to your friend Kung as to that!"

II

The eastbound Union Pacific train from Sacramento picked up speed after it crossed the Rockies and descended to the plateau of eastern Colorado. By the time it reached the Great Plains country of Nebraska, in the eyes of its fascinated passengers it almost seemed to be flying. Whenever the engineer sounded the whistle for a remote crossing, the plaintive, lonely cry echoed across the prairie.

One passenger, Toby Holt, rated the best accommodations. A former employee of the railroad, he had helped to lay out the route across the mountains from Colorado to California. And then he had supervised much construction along the westerly route. Now his reward included quarters for his family that included not only three sleeping rooms but also a sitting room, which made the long hours of travel more pleasant.

Seated in a comfortable chair beside a large window, Toby tried to read but found himself frequently looking out at the fields of grain and the endless prairie beyond. Nearby, Clarissa and Cindy were playing double solitaire on a table that neatly fitted into the wall.

While Cindy was shuffling the cards, Clarissa, gazing out a window, became pensive and silent. "Toby," she called. "Look!"

"I've been watching," he said. "It's really awe-inspiring, isn't it? All that land, and it goes on and on and on."

"Think of the courage and the daring," she mused, "of the Holts and the Blakes and the others on that first wagon train when they crossed this continent."

"It's difficult to imagine what they went through in those days," Cindy put in. "Mama has told us stories about their experiences and those of their friends. But I just can't put myself in their shoes. How often have we heard about the dreadful time that Mama was captured and actually enslaved by hostile Indians before Papa came to her rescue. I wonder if we would be up to it. I even found the stagecoach trip from home to Sacramento to be tiring."

Toby continued to study the passing scene. "I think we're still pretty strong," he remarked. "We're still facing up to insurrections by various Indian nations. I think our record is good in dealing with what must be done. We can handle trouble."

"*You* can, is what you mean," his sister objected. "You're a true throwback, Toby Holt. You should have lived in Papa's time."

"Maybe so," he admitted cheerfully. "I sometimes envy him and the others who were like him. I often think of how glorious an adventure it would have been, leading a wagon train to Oregon across unknown territory and uncharted mountains."

"I might have enjoyed it, too—provided you were there with me, Toby," Clarissa said loyally.

"You're too much, you two!" Cindy exclaimed. "Hank and I live today and look forward to tomorrow. But you have your feet securely planted in the past, even though you're only a few years older. That's partially because you were grown by the time of the Civil War, I suppose. You have a different set of values than I have. I'm grateful to all those who crossed the country by wagon train, but I wouldn't change places with them, not for a minute. Life is difficult enough in eighteen-seventy without turning the calendar back and struggling again through thirty-five tough years. I much prefer a comfortable, safe train to bouncing in a covered wagon that's creating its own road across the wilderness."

"No, I doubt that anyone would choose a covered wagon instead of a train," Toby agreed. After a moment's thought, he added, "But I do think that if it proved necessary, our generation could cross the continent by wagon train. Just because we think that the country is becoming more 'civilized' doesn't mean that we all are soft. Successive generations have kept the pioneer traditions alive in the nation. That same spirit will one day transform us eventually into a world power. Mark my words!"

Cindy looked at him slyly. "What do you expect to do, Toby," she teased, "about making certain that the next generation has enough strong men and women to carry on the traditions you prize so much?"

In response, Toby reached across and, with a broad grin, tousled her hair.

Further train travel was in store for them. In Omaha, they changed to the Chicago, Rock Island, and Pacific line, and at Chicago they changed once more to the Baltimore & Ohio. They were tired by the time they finally reached Washington via a subsidiary line of the B&O from Baltimore.

On the morning after their arrival in the nation's capital, Clarissa and Cindy accompanied Toby to the executive mansion. They were almost overwhelmed by its impressive exterior and magnificent furnishings as well as by the cordiality of the staff.

President Ulysses S. Grant, his stocky figure erect in a soldier's military bearing, entered the East Room almost as soon as they arrived. His casualness put them at ease.

Toby was surprised and pleased to see high-ranking officials among the two dozen guests. He particularly recognized the secretary of state, Hamilton Fish, and the secretary of war, William Belknap, as well as General William T. Sherman, the chief of staff.

The President beckoned to Toby, then walked to a lectern at the far end of the long room. Toby, who disliked public attention and praise, was red-faced as he reluctantly followed.

Ulysses Grant, never renowned as a public speaker, kept his speech brief and to the point. "This distinguished group has gathered here to honor Colonel Toby Holt, who has made a name rivaling his father's among our leading citizens." The President cleared his throat before continuing. "Colonel Holt, your contributions to the welfare of the United States are too numerous for me to enumerate. We have gathered here to recognize your invaluable assistance to our country. Most particularly, I have in mind your role in exposing a vicious gang of criminals, banded together in a so-called tong, who threaten to disrupt the well-being of our people. The organization that you confronted so courageously was not destroyed, but you crippled it, thus hindering future attacks on our citizens. As a symbol of the appreciation of all the people for your efforts, I am pleased and honored to present you with this commendation."

He handed Toby a framed citation. Embarrassed, Toby was scarcely able to stammer his few words of thanks.

The guests applauded, and the ceremony came to an end. Everyone crowded about Toby to shake his hand. Prominent among the guests were senators Williams and Corbett and Representative Smith from Toby's home state of Oregon.

The President, asking Toby to accompany him, led the way out of the East Room and down a corridor to his office. Meanwhile, Clarissa and Cindy were invited by Mrs. Grant to accompany her on a visit to the family's private quarters upstairs.

At his office door, the President was handed a list of callers who awaited him. He glanced at the roster, then told his secretary that he did not wish to be disturbed while meeting with Colonel Holt. Toby was impressed, in spite of his misgivings.

They entered the office, where President Grant sank into an easy chair and motioned Toby to a seat opposite him. "I remember how I felt," he said, "in this very room, when President Lincoln asked me to take personal command of the Army of the Potomac for the campaign that finally brought the Civil War to an end. I felt as though a mule had just kicked me in the stomach, and I begged him to reconsider. I'll never forget his words to me: 'General,' he said, 'if you can name someone who can do a better job than you will, by all means he should be appointed. But unless you can get a better man, do it yourself!'"

Toby smiled politely but wondered why the President had elected to tell this particular story. He quickly found out.

"I have a request to make of you, Colonel Holt," the President said, "an official request. I ask it in the same vein that Mr. Lincoln put the matter to me."

Toby stiffened involuntarily.

"What do you know of Tz'u Hsi, the dowager empress of China?"

"I've read very little about her, Mr. President," Toby answered. "I know virtually nothing of her reign or her as a person."

The President stepped to his desk and picked up a sheet of paper. He studied it briefly. "Officially," he said, "she is co-regent of the country. Beyond that, and unofficially, she wields great power. She is, in fact, the single most powerful force in all of China. Her unrestrained use of that power has fostered rebellion in China for several years and has created conflict with every major nation. She's tough and stubborn. And like many members of the ruling class in China, she combines an incredible sophistication with ignorance and barbaric cruelty."

"She sounds like a fascinating person." Toby was silent for a moment, pondering the implication of the President's statements. Then he asked, "Why are you telling me this, sir?"

"I want you to perform another mission for the United States," President Grant said forcefully as he resumed his seat opposite Toby. "I want you to deliver a personal letter from me to the dowager empress."

Toby hesitated again for a time before he answered.

"Surely you have couriers in the State Department who are capable of delivering a letter for you, Mr. President?"

A fleeting smile crossed President Grant's serious, square-jawed face. "It's more than delivering the letter, which I've already written," he said. "Let me paraphrase it for you. I described the serious problems created here by the tongs, which smuggle poverty-stricken Chinese into this country. The tongs, I pointed out, are also flooding the United States with opium. I asked for the help of the dowager empress in eradicating the tongs' activities. I suggested that she make use of your services, and I told her of your credentials. I also said that you have incurred the personal enmity of Kung Lee, the head of the most powerful and vicious of the tongs in America."

"I'd gladly oblige you if I could, Mr. President," Toby replied. "I'd like nothing better than to serve my country in this matter. I know of no organization worse than the tong, and certainly no other criminal at large in the United States who is as depraved as Kung Lee. However, for the past several years, I have spent a great deal of time in government service, and for most of that time I've been separated from my wife and son. Recently I made a promise to her that I regard as a solemn pledge—I told her that I would refuse any assignment that would take me away from home. I cannot possibly violate my word."

The President frowned. "I'm sensitive to your promise, Colonel Holt. But I'm sworn to look out for the welfare of all our people. Like you, I regard the tong as a curse, a stain on the name of the United States. With that in mind, I must ask: Will you permit me to speak with Mrs. Holt?"

"Certainly, Mr. President, by all means do so," Toby promptly assented. "But, meaning no disrespect, sir, anything that you might say to Clarissa could not relieve me of the burden of my promise."

Ulysses Grant smiled almost smugly. "I've been married for twenty-two years, young man," he said. "I suspect I may have a fairly good understanding of the art of persuasion and the place of obligation." He then changed the subject, proceeding to outline some of the travel arrangements for the proposed mission, to which Toby listened dutifully but reluctantly.

Finally, the President rose. "Come along," he said, smiling. "The ladies are probably having a cup of tea in our private sitting room, and we'd best rejoin them. No time like the present to solve our problem."

As he had suggested, he and Toby found Mrs. Grant entertaining Clarissa and Cindy at tea. After no more than the most cursory of greetings and compliments, the President bluntly announced that he wished to confer privately with Mrs. Holt. He hurried her off unceremoniously to a small study that opened off the sitting room. Left alone with Julia Grant and Cindy, Toby experienced difficulty in trying to keep up a pleasant conversation without permitting himself to stare rudely at the first lady's badly crossed eyes. Cindy did her best to keep a light exchange going.

In the study the President's manner was stiff as he held a chair for Clarissa, then seated himself on the edge of a settee. "You and I have a problem, Mrs. Holt," he said without preamble. He launched quickly into an explanation of his request to Toby and of Toby's hesitation to accept his offer.

"It's not easy, and perhaps not possible, Mrs. Holt," he went on, "to find another person as well qualified for this mission. I know of no one else who could perform the task as ably, as conscientiously, and as thoroughly. I can predict that he will win the dowager empress over to his side and gain her confidence. Then, I am sure, he'll find it possible to find some method of killing the tong's roots. When that has happened, the American branch of the tong will wither and die. And the people of the United States will be spared an abominable curse, thanks to your husband's services."

Clarissa was able to be blunt, too, even with the President of the United States. "What is it you want from me, Mr. President?" she asked, though fearing that she knew the answer full well.

"Release your husband from his promise!" he urged. "His country desperately needs him. What more can I say?"

"I've been married long enough to understand what it means to be a Holt and to feel like a Holt," Clarissa said proudly. "I've learned to recognize the need to give up personal wishes for the good of the country. My father-in-law lived that way, and though I had the pleasure of knowing him only briefly, I never have heard a single complaint from his wife. Toby lives according to that same principle. And now I, too, have the opportunity. If I decided in favor of my own happiness at the expense of the country's welfare, I hardly would be worthy of the name of Holt, would I? Naturally I will release Toby from his promise; Mr. President!"

Ulysses Grant mopped his face with a large linen handkerchief. "Shall I tell him, Mrs. Holt?" he asked softly.

"If you don't mind, Mr. President, I prefer to do that myself," Clarissa said firmly. "Toby gave me his pledge, and I see it as my place to release him from it. The matter will be resolved this very day, I assure you."

*   *   *

In their quarters later, Toby listened to Clarissa's account somberly, half expecting the outcome. She told of the President's conversation and how he finally asked her, point-blank, to release her husband from his promise. And she described her own answer.

Toby felt dismayed. He could sense the loneliness that would engulf each of them for many months to come. The feeling of pride in being requested by the President of the United States to undertake a mission that he would entrust to no other American could not overcome the disappointment in having their life together interrupted once more.

For several hours, his downcast state prevailed. He was unable to express his disappointment to Clarissa, much less reveal the depth of his anger at having been tricked into breaking his promise to her.

At last, Clarissa could stand his morose silence no longer, and she confronted him. "Listen to me!" she commanded sternly. "When I told you that I released you from your pledge to me, you found the whole subject so painful you couldn't discuss it, and I understood. But now you're unhappy, and I think it's unfair to send you off to the Orient with such a cloud hanging over your head. I want you to understand one thing. As I told President Grant, I'm a Holt, too. You are not the only Holt who can make sacrifices for your country. In some ways, staying at home as part of one's duty seems even more difficult than being able to leave. At least you'll be active. All I can do is wait for word that you're all right and will be coming home quickly."

"You have no idea how much I value the sacrifice you're making," he told her.

"It's enough, I think," she replied smiling, "that we *both* are making a sacrifice. Each of us in our own way. Let's always remember that, shall we?"

Clarissa reached out her hands to him. He took them in his, then leaned forward and kissed her. The barriers that had separated them melted, and for a long moment, they took renewed comfort in each other's presence and nearness. Then, as they reluctantly drew apart, Toby forced a smile.

"I'll be traveling in high style, after all," he said. "The navy is providing a new, all-metal ship to take me as far as the Isthmus of Panama. I'll cross the isthmus by the new train that links the Atlantic and Pacific coasts. And another navy ship will be waiting for the voyage to China. The President himself told me all this, though I could barely bring myself to listen."

Clarissa was impressed. "You'll be the only passenger?"

"Apparently so. The navy is tying itself in knots to hurry me to China. When Mr. Grant speaks, action follows promptly—as you yourself found out."

He fell silent for a time. "I was tempted at one point to ask the President," he finally said, "if you could come as far as Tientsin and wait for me there. But I could see that really wouldn't be possible. Navy regulations prohibit all civilians, except those on official business, from sailing on any of its ships. But for whatever consolation it may be to you, I'm sorrier than you'll ever know that that idea couldn't work out."

"Oh, Toby," Clarissa exclaimed, "I'm certain you'll be so busy you won't know whether I'm there or not."

"Not *that* preoccupied," he protested. "There will be some free time occasionally, you may be sure, and I imagine that I'll be occupied with diversions like—using chopsticks!"

"If you do master chopsticks," she replied with forced gaiety, "you'll have to be ready to teach me the art, too, when you come home."

"Only on condition that you wear the *cheongsam* I'm planning to have made for you. I will ask Cindy for your, um, measurements."

"Don't you dare, Toby Holt!" she protested, though actually pleased.

His smile broadened. "There's no telling what I may do," he answered, his tone equally bantering.

In a sudden change of mood, she became serious. "Do what you please, Toby," she pleaded, "as long as you don't stop loving me."

His own smile faded, and he gripped her hands fiercely. "Never! One promise I could never break, no matter what, is that I will love you as long as we both live. That's a fact for forever. I don't know how I could have been lucky enough to find you or how we're fortunate enough to be together, but I thank the Almighty every day of my life. There's one thing you can depend on, whatever else may happen in the world: I'll be coming home to you, if it's the last thing I ever do—which it won't be!"

The President's own carriage, pulled by a team of matched bays, transported Toby and Clarissa from their hotel to the Baltimore & Ohio depot. Toby was en route to Baltimore, in order to board a naval vessel for his long voyage to China; Clarissa would go by train later to New York with Cindy.

In Toby's inner coat pocket, protected by a leather

case, was the letter from President Grant to the dowager empress. He kept a tight grip on a valise that contained the President's gifts to her: a turquoise and silver necklace made by the Navajo Indians and a set of six magnificent, matched tomahawks. Toby had tested those himself for sharpness and balance. Small turquoise nuggets studded the handles, making the tomahawks as decorative as they were practical.

The couple made certain that their parting at the depot was short and unemotional. They avoided a lingering farewell that would only have resulted in tears and melancholy. After giving Toby a quick kiss and a fond hug, Clarissa turned and walked briskly away from the platform. Toby looked after her for a long moment, then stepped decisively and fatefully into the waiting day coach for the hour's ride to Baltimore.

There, he found a carriage to transport him to the teeming dock area. He had no difficulty in directing the driver to his ship, the U.S.S. *Savannah*, a light cruiser that had a displacement of six thousand tons. Steam propelled and all metal, she was among the navy's newest vessels. Formidable cannon were mounted on the fore and aft decks.

As soon as Toby's carriage rolled to a halt alongside the *Savannah*, a young officer and two sailors appeared. As Toby stepped out of the carriage, the officer saluted him. The sailors stood by to help transfer Toby's suitcases.

"Colonel Holt? Ensign Tucker, sir," the officer said. "Captain White's compliments, sir. The ship has worked up a head of steam, and we're ready to sail as soon as you give the word. The gangplank is only a few steps forward, sir." He saluted again and stepped back respectfully.

With the gifts for the empress firmly in hand, Toby

mounted the gangplank behind the ensign and was taken directly to the bridge, where Captain Peter White, the boyish-looking commander, awaited him. "Welcome aboard, Colonel Holt," the captain said cordially, grasping his hand and pumping it. "We're pleased to have such a distinguished 'passenger list' for this voyage. It is our honor to transport you toward your destination, as the President and secretary of state direct."

The ship's deck vibrated as her engines throbbed, and she began to inch away from the dock. The whole operation had been extremely efficient thus far, Toby reflected.

A yeoman led Toby to his cabin, which proved to be more than adequate, though hardly luxurious. Later, he learned that the cabin ordinarily was that of the ship's executive officer.

The *Savannah* lost no time in threading her way out of the harbor into Chesapeake Bay and heading southward for the Atlantic beyond.

Four days later, the ship dropped anchor at the port town of Colón in Panama. After saying his good-byes to the captain and other officers, Toby was rowed ashore.

As he stepped onto the pier there, he was further reminded that the officials who had arranged his mission were determined to avoid any risks to him. A State Department representative was on hand to greet him, accompanied by two stalwart guards. Toby had the impression that they kept as close a watch over the bag of gifts as they maintained over its bearer. Escorted to a railway station, he boarded a narrow-gauge car that would transport the party across the isthmus to the Pacific port of Panama City.

Aware of the countless difficulties and hazards of building a railroad under such primitive conditions, Toby reflected that laying this line through the thick tropical jungle and over the steep inclines of the isthmus must have been a major task and a notable triumph comparable to building rail lines across the Rocky Mountains.

A carriage was ready for the party at an open-air station in Panama City and carried them to the waterfront. The State Department man, seeing the end of his assignment drawing near, seemed to breathe more easily as they caught a glimpse of the U.S.S. *Worcester*, which was to carry Toby to China. As for Toby, he felt a new and unexpected thrill of excitement. The final phase of a long and complicated journey was about to begin.

Clarissa and Cindy's train from Washington to New York left very early in the morning. They sat in reasonably comfortable parlor-car chairs, leaving them just for breakfast and lunch in the handsome dining car. They were to arrive in New York in the afternoon. They planned on spending one night at a hotel, then leaving for West Point by train in the morning.

Clarissa felt that she already had been separated from Toby for months, and she couldn't help sighing as the train halted in the Baltimore station to take on passengers.

Cindy looked up from her reading.

"I do miss Toby something awful," Clarissa confessed.

"I know what you mean. It's like that with Hank and me. It may sound silly, but the sun shines brightly when we're together. But the minute we separate, it seems as though the sky goes dark. Whether we're apart for minutes or months, it stays dark until we're together again."

"I should behave better," Clarissa said, peering gloomily at the new passengers on the platform. "Toby and I have been separated so often. But somehow I never grow accustomed to the sensation, no matter how often we're parted. This time I feel even worse than usual because he's going halfway around the world."

"You could try pretending that he's merely tending to business in a city not far away," Cindy suggested, smiling.

"What makes it all so difficult for me, I suppose," Clarissa continued, as if she had not heard, "is that I can't picture what he'll be doing in China. That is, assuming that the President's offer of Toby's services in fighting against the tongs is accepted. Will he merely give advice? Will he work in an office, directing others' activities, or will he actually seek out tong members and destroy them? The uncertainty upsets me."

"I realize this is easier said than done," Cindy told her, "but if I were you, I'd try to stop speculating. You'll find out when Toby comes home exactly what he had to do. You'll gain nothing by worrying."

"I can see your point," Clarissa admitted.

"For the present," Cindy went on, "isn't it enough to know he's completely competent to look after himself under any conditions or any circumstances? How many times has he crossed the mountains with Indians lying in wait to kill him? More often than we'll ever know, I'm sure. Yet he always has escaped. Time and again he's turned the tables on his enemies."

"I—I suppose you're right," Clarissa agreed uncertainly.

"I know I'm right!" Cindy answered emphatically. "Don't forget he's Whip Holt's son. He thrives on adventure. He needs it in order to survive the way ordinary men need bread and cheese. I don't believe Toby can be happy unless the odds are against him in the battle of survival. He needs a challenge. If he knew you were worrying so about him, he'd want to laugh at you, no matter how he might try to understand and console."

Clarissa was silent as the train started to move again, and she did not speak until it had resumed full speed. "Thank you, Cindy," she murmured at last. "I needed the help that you've given me. Don't worry; I'll be fine now. I was feeling sorry for myself, and I needed your kind of common sense to wake me up. You've given it to me. Until Toby returns home, I'll do my very best to live up to what he should expect of me."

When the freighter *Amsterdam* passed the breakwater of the large Chilean port of Valparaiso, its passengers could see the city rising above the waterfront. First came the manufacturing plants that were making Valparaiso one of the most important cities of South America. And high in the hills above were many private homes; a substantial middle class was established there, and the presence of the country's naval academy meant that many of them were navy officers, including those of the ordnance and procurement divisions. These officers were, in fact, the reason for the *Amsterdam*'s arrival.

The port call was the sixth for the ship since leaving San Francisco. At previous stops in Mexico, Central America, and the upper coast of South America, she had put in so that Kayross could do a lucrative business either with beleaguered governments or antigovernment agitators, depending on which side reached him first with the best bid. Here, according to word that he had received during the last deal, he should try to contact the Chilean government's representatives, particularly the navy, where the focus of power appeared to reside at present. Captain Kayross, whose safe was bulging with the gold of a number of countries, was delighted at the prospect. And the voyage was not yet half over.

After picking up a pilot and threading its way through the busy harbor, the *Amsterdam* slid into a berth.

There, customs officials visited the freighter, and to them Captain Kayross let it be known that he was interested in interviewing a high-ranking procurement officer of the navy.

"As you can see, I am carrying cargo that should be of particular interest," Kayross said. "Pass the word that I'm in a position to offer some of it at a reasonable price. No questions asked, no answers required."

Karl Kellerman was eager to go ashore, his interest increased by the appearance of several women who were parading on the dock. His eyes gleaming, he moistened his dry lips repeatedly as he watched them strolling in their tight-fitting dresses and high-heeled shoes. He was pleased that he had only recently shaved off his mustache, believing that he now would look younger and more virile.

"The women will wait, Kellerman," Captain Kayross told him dryly. "We have business to take care of first."

"When?" Kellerman demanded, continuing to stare steadily, paying particular attention to one tall, shapely brunette who seemed to be posing for his benefit.

"After an officer from their navy chooses to visit us," Kayross replied sharply. "We're in no position to set the pace. Just remember, business comes before pleasure. The women will still be here hanging about on the dock, I assure you, no matter what the time of day." Kellerman was a perpetual trial to him, but the captain thought it prudent to cause his partner to feel as though he were involved in the business activities, thus avoiding possible suspicions and arguments about how the captain had acted to his own advantage and not to Kellerman's.

As for Kellerman, he knew he could not argue with the captain's position, and he assented, grumbling under his breath.

The navy showed no interest in the *Amsterdam*'s merchandise for several hours, but Kayross, an old hand at such dealings, showed unusual patience and only smiled, shaking his head each time Kellerman suggested that, since nothing was happening, he might as well go ashore.

"Wait," the captain told him. "The bees have sniffed the blossom. They will require time to fly to it from their old hive."

In midafternoon, a white uniformed junior officer, resplendent in the gold braid of an aide-de-camp, appeared at the ship and saluted smartly as he was escorted to the bridge. "Captain," he said, "I bring you the greetings of Comandante Garcia, the director of naval procurement for the Valparaiso district. He hopes that you and any colleagues who may be traveling with you will be free to accept an invitation to dine with him this evening at the Valparaiso Club."

"I have a partner, whom I shall allow to accompany me, and we shall be delighted to meet Comandante Garcia this evening."

"Very good, sir. The comandante's carriage will pick you up here at eight o'clock tonight." The young officer again saluted and then withdrew.

Promptly at eight, the carriage arrived, and the two men climbed into it for the drive up the face of a cliff in the heart of Valparaiso. It proved to be one of the most harrowing experiences of its kind that Kayross and Kellerman had ever known. The road was so steep that the workhorse pulling the carriage had to struggle all the way, and occasionally the turns were so sharp that the driver dismounted and blindfolded the animal, then led it around the curves.

At last they came to a handsome, three-story stone building, the Valparaiso Club. Waiting in the lounge for them was an imposing, heavyset naval officer with three gold stripes on each sleeve of his immaculate white uniform.

Comandante Garcia introduced himself and then led the way to a private dining room. There, to Robin Kayross's surprise and the delight of Karl Kellerman, three women also were waiting. In his element at last, Kellerman promptly and boldly laid claim to Carmen, the youngest of them, whose blue-black hair, dark eyes, and trim figure immediately attracted him.

Comandante Garcia proved a generous host, and one dish followed another. He was equally free in dispensing whiskey and gin, as well as wines and brandies.

Kellerman concentrated all his attention on Carmen, encouraging her to drink with him and flirting outrageously with her. The more they drank, the more Carmen responded to his flirting and the more uninhibited his own conduct became. Carmen made no objection when he draped an arm around her shoulders or caressed her leg. Ignoring the presence of the others, he kissed her passionately between swallows of gin and wine. Becoming increasingly intoxicated, they sang off-key songs together and embraced repeatedly.

In contrast, Kayross's conduct was correct, formal, and precise. He ate moderately, took occasional sips of wine, and treated the women on either side of him with grave courtesy. But he was far more interested in Comandante Garcia.

Garcia was clearly in no hurry to direct the conversation toward the subject that had brought them together. He dawdled over each course, offered innumerable toasts, and frequently inquired after the comfort of his guests.

When he finally grew tired of the game he was playing, as Kayross was hoping he would, he told the two women sitting on either side of Kayross to move away, and he himself pulled his chair closer to the captain's. He launched into a sharp discussion on the price of muskets and Gatling guns. They argued over the price of gunpowder and lead bullets and haggled over reductions in prices for purchases in large quantities.

At last Garcia and Kayross struck a bargain, agreeing on immediate delivery and instant payment.

"Ladies," Garcia said to the two young women who were sitting apart whispering together, "I now thank you for your company, and I take pleasure in presenting this token to each of you. Also, an extra payment is yours if you will be good enough to take Carmen home."

"I shall need some assistance," Kayross said, "to get Señor Kellerman into the carriage." By this time, Kellerman had passed out, his head on the table. Carmen was in somewhat better condition.

The officer snapped his fingers for a steward, who then summoned other of the club's staff to carry Kellerman to the carriage. He was so sound asleep that he missed the terrors of the drive down the cliff.

When they reached the waterfront area, Comandante Garcia paused at a navy office to arrange for transportation of the munitions. They were followed to the *Amsterdam*'s dock by two teams of horses pulling oversized carts.

Even though it was now past midnight, Captain Kayross

put his crew to work unloading. They were accustomed to working at odd hours of the day or night and didn't question the order.

The wagons quickly were filled with muskets and light cannon, ammunition, and bags of gunpowder. Envelopes of money were slipped into the captain's pockets, and the transaction was complete.

Only then did Kayross remember Kellerman. He summoned several members of his crew, who unceremoniously picked Kellerman up from the dock where he had been dumped, carried him onto the ship, and placed him in his bunk.

"I regret any inconvenience he has caused you," Captain Kayross said to Garcia, "but he's hopeless. Only because he is my partner did I allow myself to be persuaded to include him in your kind invitation. He has once more made a fool of himself. He cannot or will not learn."

"You waste your time trying to teach a jackass, my friend," Comandante Garcia replied. "He is one of those creatures to whom the delights of the flesh always will mean more than appreciation of finer things, such as our successful transaction this evening."

"And sometimes," the captain added, "silent partners are preferable to those who are awake and alert to every move."

By the time the *Amsterdam* reached the Gulf of Mexico en route to New Orleans, she had visited a dozen South American ports on both coasts. Everywhere, Captain Kayross sold guns and ammunition. He could have disposed of much more than he had on board.

Consequently, the captain was in an expansive frame of mind as he sat in his cabin with Karl Kellerman. They were drinking metaxa, a Greek after-dinner beverage. "I have to hand it to you, Captain," Kellerman said admiringly. "When I went down into the hold today, I couldn't see a single rifle, cannon, bullet, or bag of gunpowder. You sold every ounce of the cargo."

Kayross was irritated to hear of the man's snooping in the hold, but because he apparently had done no harm, the captain let the reference pass. "I was lucky, I guess," he said modestly.

"You made a sale in every port," Kellerman continued. "If we had been carrying twice as big a load, you could have disposed of that, too. One hell of a lot more than luck was involved."

Kayross sipped his drink. "Well," he said, "we happened to have been in the right place at the right time. Little wars are erupting everywhere in South America, so naturally everybody wants arms and more arms. The most important result, though, is that we earned a very satisfactory bundle for ourselves."

Kellerman smacked his lips greedily and rubbed his hands together. "How big is your share of the profits and what's mine, after you put aside what's owed to Kung Lee?"

"I haven't had an opportunity, as yet," the captain answered cautiously, "to divide the money."

"No time like the present!" Kellerman said boldly.

Kayross was trapped. Advised by Kung Lee to delay paying Kellerman anything at all, he no longer could avoid an accounting. To prevent a violent scene, he would have to go through the motions of figuring out the overall profit, which he already had worked out to the last penny, and then prepare to divide with Kellerman. All Kayross could hope was that Kung Lee would not be angry when

41

he found out what had happened. And Kayross had good reason to fear the results of the tong leader's wrath.

Kung Lee was not in a happy frame of mind as he sat in his inner sanctum at the tong headquarters above a curio shop in an old building in San Francisco. He reread a hurried letter from Captain Kayross.

Dispatched at one of the layover stops of the *Amsterdam*, the letter predicted it might prove necessary to give Kellerman as much as twenty-five thousand dollars as his share of the profits. Both men regarded such a payment as outrageous.

Kayross held out one slender hope: Kellerman was afraid that authorities in New Orleans would learn of his prospective return to the city or, even worse, that Domino would know that he had come back. In either case, his life would be in jeopardy. Kayross expected that Kellerman would hide out on the ship for a while, thus offering the chance that the payment could be retrieved.

Kung Lee sat, staring into space, for a few minutes. Then, reaching a decision, he picked up an exquisitely etched brass bell and rang it sharply four times.

Within a few moments, the door opened silently, and a young Chinese man entered. He was wearing the traditional Chinese garb of jacket and voluminous trousers. "You rang, Lord Kung?" he asked.

"I rang," Kung replied brusquely, and pointed to a chair.

"You are to go at once, by the fastest means available, to New Orleans, Chang," Kung directed. "Draw the necessary funds from the paymaster. When there, you will go to the port and search out our freighter, the *Amsterdam*. Do you understand so far?"

"Yes, Lord Kung."

"If you find it useful," Kung Lee went on, "identify yourself to Captain Kayross and seek his assistance. But it will be far better if you function without his knowledge, much less his consent. Search the quarters of Karl Kellerman for the sum of twenty-five thousand dollars. If you do not find it in his cabin, then ask Kayross about it. But I fear the money will be in Kellerman's possession. When you have it, you will silence Kellerman with a knife between his ribs in the approved manner, and make sure you dispose of the body so that it looks as though he just disappeared and no blame can be attached to the ship."

"Very well, Lord Kung."

Kung dismissed him by lowering his gaze to papers on the desk before him.

Chang backed toward the door but before reaching it sank to the floor and touched the edge of the rug with his forehead in a deep kowtow. Then he rose and silently departed.

Kung chuckled softly. Lighting a perfumed cigarette with a sulfur match, he inhaled deeply and stared at the ceiling for a long time. Occasionally he smiled and nodded in satisfaction.

Having arrived in New Orleans, Kellerman had one final confrontation with Captain Kayross. His threatening presence intimidated the captain, who sighed and withdrew a stack of bills from a strongbox. He tossed it to Kellerman. "Count it!" he instructed. "Twenty-five thousand is there. Let me tell you that I consider this a very generous settlement. Under the circumstances, I will let you use it pending a final reckoning, on the basis of later word from Kung. And his word goes! I hope you understand that."

Kayross was prepared to steal the money back. Toward that end, he added a bit of advice. "You'd better leave it on the ship as long as you're here," he urged gruffly. "You wouldn't be very safe with it in this town, now would you?"

Kellerman, having counted the money, retreated from the captain's quarters and hurried to his own cabin, where he secreted it behind a chest, reasonably sure no one would come across it.

Now, feeling flush though still annoyed that he had not pressed Kayross for more, he peered out his cabin porthole and examined the dock. It appeared deserted.

Not satisfied, he grabbed a pair of binoculars, left his cabin, and went up to the ship's bridge where, concealing himself in shadows, he studied the shore. Most members of the crew were on shore leave, so even the prostitutes who inevitably appeared when a vessel put into port were missing. As nearly as he could tell, no authorities were keeping watch on the ship. Nor were any of Domino's gang on the lookout. He concluded it might be safe for him to venture to land.

Transferring his gaze to the area beyond the wharf, he raised the binoculars to his eyes. He examined each warehouse in turn, concentrating on the entrances. He could see no sign of anyone loitering or in a position to keep watch on the freighter. Apparently, neither the government nor his enemies, including Wallace Dugald, his betrayed partner, had any idea he was on board.

Two seamen, armed with cutlasses and single-shot .50-caliber pistols, patrolled the main deck near the gangplank. A third was stationed near the hatch that led to the ship's hold. Otherwise, Kellerman could see no sentries on the ship. Even the captain and his officers were ashore.

Kellerman longed for a good meal, but the ship's cook did not even light the galley fires when in port, and Kellerman was living on cold slabs of meat, stale bread, and tasteless pudding. More urgently, he wanted a woman, but Kayross forbade prostitutes on board. Having in mind the possibility that a review of the records might bring him more funds than he already had received, he was reluctant to antagonize the captain.

He put aside his caution and hesitancy at last and started back to his cabin to leave his binoculars and take enough money to assure a good time in the city.

The door to the cabin was ajar. He could have sworn that he had closed it securely. Nevertheless, he pushed it open and suddenly froze.

On the far side of the cabin, rummaging in a chest of drawers, was a man so engrossed in his search that he failed to hear Kellerman enter.

Kellerman cursed himself for having been so busy looking for Domino's gang and government agents that he had failed to even consider that the head of the tong might try to double-cross him. He could see enough of the intruder to identify him as Chinese.

The only way they'll get a penny is over my dead body! Kellerman vowed.

Chang seemed to feel, rather than hear, him at last. He whirled, a long knife glittering in one hand.

Kellerman quickly reached for the knife in his own belt. Before he could draw it, however, the Chinese sprang, blade upraised. Using all his strength, Chang struck downward.

Kellerman barely managed to deflect the blow by

catching Chang's wrist and halting the motion of his arm in midair. Simultaneously, he was able to pull his own blade from its sheath.

Chang freed his arm and struck again. But he was a fraction of a second too late, and Kellerman caught his wrist again, then attacked with his own knife, the six-inch blade of which had been exactingly honed. Chang knocked the thrust aside with a smart forehand block.

Both men fell back several paces, glaring and breathing hard. Only one could emerge alive from the deadly encounter.

Kellerman was about to rush his opponent but decided instead to adopt a defensive pose. He realized how unlikely it was that he could wield a knife as cleverly as or with the fitness of a Chinese trained and practiced in such combat. His best chance, he reasoned, might come if Chang let down his guard for a second.

They circled warily, each with his right hand upraised. Twice Chang inched forward, then struck, but both times Kellerman leaped backward and managed to avoid injury.

Chang was irritated by the refusal of his opponent to seize the initiative. His mood made him reckless and lessened his usual caution. Impatient, eager to end the battle, Chang suddenly hurtled at Kellerman, his right hand raising the knife high over his head.

This was the chance for which Kellerman had been hoping. Before his foe could lower his arm, he struck. He drove his blade into the left side of Chang's chest, his blade aimed up and in.

As the double-edged blade cut deep, Chang's body stiffened in shock, and by the time he collapsed onto the floor, he was dead.

Kellerman quickly dragged the body up to the main deck, where he searched and found a toolbox. After checking Chang's pockets to make certain that he had not discovered the money, Kellerman tied a rope securely to the man's ankle and then to the toolbox, and heaved the body overboard. It dangled below the level of the deck until Kellerman picked up the box and dropped it overboard, as well. He heard a resounding splash and could see that the box's weight pulled the body far below the surface. With any luck, Kellerman thought, the box would remain attached to the ankle until the body no longer was recognizable.

He took the precaution of searching the deck and the floor of his cabin for bloodstains, wiped up the traces he found, and then washed off his knife. Satisfied that the police would find it impossible to connect him with the crime, he made sure that his money was still securely hidden and removed a hundred dollars for what he thought of as "walking around money." Then he changed his clothes, put on a suitcoat and hat, and ventured jauntily down the gangplank.

III

Riding at anchor in the waters of the Pacific off Panama City, the U.S.S. *Worcester* was a new type of war vessel, a heavy cruiser, made completely of iron. Her displacement was in excess of ten thousand tons. She looked bulky and clumsy, but her armor plate was thick, and she carried twice as many cannon as the U.S.S. *Savannah*. Waiting at a dock beside a gig manned by seamen was a commander in a white uniform, the three gold stripes of his rank shimmering in the tropical sunlight. As Toby approached, the commander raised his right hand to the visor of his cap. "Colonel Holt?" he asked. "Sterling is the name, Niles Sterling."

"Glad to know you, Commander," Toby said, and was impressed by the other's firm handshake. After bidding farewell to the State Department diplomat and to the security men, Toby preceded Commander Sterling into the gig.

While they were being rowed out to the cruiser, Commander Sterling smiled as he said, "I hope you're prepared to make this a working voyage to the Orient, Colonel Holt. We have quite a regimen planned for you."

"I'm completely at your service, Commander," Toby assured him. "What activities do you have in mind?"

"I'm assigned," Commander Sterling said, "to be with you until we reach Tientsin. I am to teach you the rudiments of the Mandarin dialect. As you may know, that is only one of nine Chinese languages, but it is the one used exclusively by the upper classes. I am to teach you, additionally, the basics of Chinese tradition and culture. We're to find our relief in physical exercise, specifically in the martial arts, known in China as kung fu. In Japan, a version of it is called judo."

"It sounds," Toby answered, "as though we're going to be busy."

The navy officer smiled again. "Very busy, Colonel Holt," he replied. "I spent more than twenty years in the Orient. The navy, on orders from the President, is expecting me to teach you all I know in the few weeks that it will take us to reach China."

Kellerman went first to a waterfront bar, had several drinks in succession, then picked up a prostitute and went off with her.

As the evening wore on, he abandoned her and found a café that catered to seamen and served meals at any hour.

After a meal of roast beef, he lighted one of his favorite long cigars, and sitting back and sipping coffee, he reviewed his situation.

The fact that a Chinese had tried to rob and kill him

proved that his fear of Kung Lee was justified. The tong leader was ready to deny him his rightful share of the profits of their joint venture. Further, Kellerman realized that he might be regarded as having learned too much about the tong's operation; therefore, Kung would again seek to do away with him.

Perhaps killing the robber would give him a respite, but he could not even be sure of this. Everything depended on whether or not the Chinese had been operating alone.

Kellerman realized, too, that he could not depend upon Kayross and his officers. Kayross, in particular, had been associated for too long with the tong. Consequently, in a showdown he would be loyal only to Kung Lee.

It now seemed to be even more dangerous, Kellerman recognized, to remain on the *Amsterdam*, the property of the tong, than to take his chances in New Orleans. His first move, then, would be to find a place where he could not be traced by the tong or located by Wallace Dugald, if in fact his one-time partner was still alive and in the city.

After leaving the café, Kellerman stopped at the home of a merchant whom he had known for a long time and obtained an excellent wig of gray hair and a matching false mustache to replace the one he had shaved off on the *Amsterdam*. Then he returned to the freighter, where his luck was good: Captain Kayross, his officers, and crew had not yet returned. Hurrying to his cabin, he retrieved and counted his money. It was all there. Then, after storing it securely in an inner pocket, he packed his clothing in a single valise.

Carrying the valise, he hurried ashore, and within the protective shadow of a warehouse, he put on the wig and mustache. Then, convinced that no one would recognize him, he walked boldly into the heart of town to an old French mansion converted into a fashionable bordello. He tapped insistently at the door.

A dignified-looking, rather plump woman opened the door. Her high-necked, full-skirted dress was severe but in the latest fashion. She wore no makeup, and her dark hair was pinned at the nape of her neck.

"Good evening, Madame Gayley," Kellerman said politely.

A puzzled expression appeared in her dark eyes. "Do I know you, sir?" she asked in a voice thick with a New Orleans accent.

Instead of replying, he turned away and quickly pulled off his mustache before turning back to her with a smile.

"Well, I do declare," Madame Gayley murmured, "if it ain't Kellerman. I haven't seen you for so long that I assumed New Orleans was rid of you."

"I was out of town for quite a spell," he admitted, "but I'm back now. I just arrived tonight and need a place to stay."

She looked at him clearly, her eyes shrewd as she took particular note of the valise. "Y'all been mixed up in some of that funny business of yours, and so it just ain't healthy for you to go to a hotel now. Am I right?"

Kellerman nodded. "I'm not asking for a handout," he said. "I'm willing to pay my way. In fact, I'll pay handsomely."

Madame Gayley contemplated his statement. "Would you go as high as twenty-five dollars a week?"

"Gladly, ma'am," he replied promptly.

Giving him no chance to change his mind, she turned and called sharply over her shoulder, "Joseph!"

After a brief wait, a dark-skinned, middle-aged man

appeared from inside the house. "Ma'am?" he asked deferentially.

"Take the gentleman's luggage up to room twenty-four on the second floor," Madame Gayley directed.

In the seconds before Joseph had appeared, Kellerman had found time to slip on the mustache again. "I'm grateful to you, Miz Gayley," he said, "for not mentioning my name."

Madame Gayley sniffed audibly. "Really, sir!" she said indignantly. "What do you take me for? I'm hardly new at this business!"

As Kellerman closed the door and entered the house, he was observed from within the sitting room's sliding doors by a caller whom he did not notice. Before he started up the broad staircase behind Joseph, he was obliged to stand aside for two girls who were descending together, chatting. Both were dressed only in strapless corselets of revealing black lace. Fastened to attached garters were stockings of sheer black silk. High-heeled black mules completed their outfits. When they saw the stranger, they stopped their chatter and smiled.

Kellerman instantly regretted having satisfied his sexual desires earlier. In any event, more urgent matters required his attention. Returning the smiles, he continued up the stairs.

"Joseph," he said at the door of his new room, "go down the street a block to the French Quarter and turn left there. You know the liquor store near the corner, and the nearby news dealer will still be open, despite the hour. Bring me a bottle of good corn whiskey and all of today's newspapers that they have in stock, both this morning's and this evening's. Here's two dollars, and if you'll hurry, you can keep the change."

Kellerman looked around the ornately furnished chamber, dominated by a four-poster bed that had pillows heaped on the coverlet. He went to the french windows, opened them, and noted with satisfaction that they overlooked an inner garden. He should be as safe there as anywhere in New Orleans, he reflected.

Within a few minutes, Joseph returned with a bottle of liquor and several newspapers. Pouring himself a stiff drink, Kellerman piled up the papers beside him and began to scan them, looking only for local items, each of which he read intently. He was pleased to see a familiar name on the society page of one paper.

"My luck is still good!" he exclaimed aloud. The article mentioned the name of Mrs. Jean-Pierre Gautier, wife of a prominent young citizen of French descent. She was chairwoman of a concert being given by a string quartet from New York on behalf of a charity.

Kellerman had known her as Millicent Randall, a Baltimore heiress whom he had first attracted when she was still under the influence of mind-altering drugs administered by another admirer. The memory of their association stirred the passion he had once felt for her. He wanted her back, although he realized it would be a difficult goal, for her husband was a man of means who could provide her with anything she wanted.

Now his mind raced. If Kellerman coveted anything more than a beautiful woman, it was money. Millicent had inherited a considerable fortune and had married well. A wave of envy swept over Kellerman. He not only wanted Millicent, he also badly wanted her money.

Finishing his drink, he poured another and sat staring out at the garden, trying to devise a plan. Finally he decided on an action that was bold, full of risks, and sufficiently imaginative that no one would be able to connect him with it. Chuckling softly, he rose to his feet and circled the gaudy bedchamber, lifting his glass in a silent toast to himself.

Wallace Dugald was in luck. He had wandered aimlessly for days in the waterfront area of New Orleans, and at last his good fortune had materialized; he had seen Karl Kellerman. He had watched the man don his strange disguise. Then, filled with an obsessive desire to eliminate his sworn enemy, he had followed Kellerman to Madame Gayley's. Now he waited across the street in the dark, hidden from the entrance by the trunk of a large tree.

Time had not dimmed Dugald's memory of the events that had given rise to his hatred of Kellerman. Formerly Dugald's partner in a New Orleans waterfront bar, Kellerman had callously turned on his associate, delivering him as one of a number of shanghaied men to the Greek sea captain, Robin Kayross. Held aboard Kayross's ship, the *Diana*, Dugald had escaped only because another of the prisoners—a resourceful Englishman named Edward Blackstone—had had a knife with him, with which he had cut the ropes binding him and the other captives. Then the prisoners had overcome the ship's crew in a pitched battle. Many of the latter had sought safety by jumping overboard, only to meet death in alligator-infested waters. Karl Kellerman, the instigator of all the trouble, had disappeared—some said to the Far East. But now he was back—why or how, Wallace Dugald did not know. The only thing that mattered was that Kellerman, at this very moment, was not fifty feet away.

All Dugald had to do now was wait. When Kellerman emerged from Madame Gayley's, Dugald would follow him. With all the stealth and patience of a stalking panther, he would watch his prey by day and by night, if necessary. Then, when the time and circumstances were ideal, he would strike. He would call out to Kellerman, and when the man turned, he would shoot him with the nickel-plated pistol that he carried in his jacket pocket.

Dugald's fingers opened and closed convulsively on the handle of the pistol. At last he drew out his hand and wiped the moisture from his palm. He was shaking, his whole being consumed by his hatred for the man who had ruined his life.

He reached into his inner coat pocket and pulled out a bottle that he had taken from the saloon he operated near the waterfront. Drawing the cork, he took a long swallow of the harsh-tasting whiskey, then another, before recorking the bottle and returning it to his pocket. The fiery liquor gave him courage.

It would be easy to obtain the vengeance of which he had dreamed. All he had to do was call out Kellerman's name at the right time, point the pistol, and fire it. That would be the end of the matter, and from then on, Dugald would be able to rest easy. The vengeance he sought would be his at last, and Kellerman would burn for all eternity in the hell that he deserved.

Many people speculated as to the identity of Martha, the beautiful red-haired woman who lived in the headquarters of Domino, leader of New Orleans's most powerful criminal gang. Was she Domino's mistress, as most of the curious believed? Or was it more likely that she was merely a business associate? That was possible, certainly, because it was clear her authority over the members of the organization was second only to Domino's. A very few were convinced that she and he were related; knowing nothing of his well-hidden past, they could only hazard wild and romantic guesses.

Very much at home under Domino's roof, Martha sat now in his library, dressed in a stunning white silk dressing gown. Suspended on a gold chain hanging from her neck were two miniature dominoes of jade with diamonds denoting the numbers on each. She and Domino were sitting at his desk, engrossed in playing Domino's favorite game, and occasionally as they played, they sipped from tall drinks.

Finally Martha broke the silence with a quiet, triumphant laugh. "Damnation!" Domino exclaimed. "That's the third game in a row you've taken from me."

Reaching into a pocket, he peeled several bills from a large wad and handed them to her. She demurely tucked the money into the top of a stocking. "Don't feel badly," she said. "I happen to know how your mind works, that's all. Whenever I win a game, my victory owes very little to luck."

"I'm well aware of it," he replied. "Actually, Martha, I feel uncomfortable that anybody should know me that well."

She smiled. "Be glad that I'm the one, rather than any of a lot of people we could mention."

"Oh, I'm very grateful for it, believe me," he said comfortably. Sitting back in his chair, he took a long swallow of his drink. It was evident that he was completely relaxed, completely at home with her.

A dark-haired, hulking giant of a man appeared in the open doorway. "Excuse me for interrupting, Domino."

"What is it, Samson?" Domino asked crisply.

"Eddie Neff is here. Says he has to see you right away. Claims it's very important."

"Then, by all means, show him in."

Martha started to rise, but Domino waved her back to her chair.

An intense, young man with strong features and trim blond hair and mustache hurried into the room.

"Evening, Eddie," Domino greeted him. "What's up?"

"He's back in town, Domino!" the young man burst out, without even saying hello or acknowledging Martha.

Domino remained relaxed. "Who is?"

"Karl Kellerman!"

Jerking himself bolt upright, Domino smashed his fist onto the polished surface of his desk. "Tell me everything," he said. "Don't leave out any details."

"Yes, sir," Neff replied, and calmed himself with a great effort. "I was making the rounds of our houses tonight, checking on them. I thought I'd stop in at Madame Gayley's. She's an independent operator, of course, but I know you're thinking of taking over her place. I wanted to see what kind of business she's doing. Anyway, a fellow is renting a room from her and paid a week's rent in advance. He was wearing a wig and a mustache, but he didn't fool me for a second. I recognized Kellerman right off. I just happened to be in her parlor near the door when he arrived."

"Are you sure?" Domino asked sharply. "You couldn't be mistaken?"

"No, sir!" was the emphatic reply. "Matter of fact, I checked Gayley on his identity as soon as he went upstairs. It's Kellerman, all right. You know how Gayley is—anything for money. I gave her a sawbuck. She confirmed it's Kellerman, but she begged me not to let him know that she told me. He's trying to keep it a secret that he's in New Orleans."

"I'll just bet he is," Martha said, and laughed.

Domino saw nothing amusing in the development. "So he's going to be at Gayley's for a week, is he?"

"No, sir. I didn't say that. I said he rented a room for a week. We have no way of knowing how long he's actually going to use it."

Domino had regained complete control of his emotions. "Quite so," he said with quiet menace. "I stand corrected. He'll probably be there for at least a day or two, but we'll take no chances. I want you to go back to Gayley and rent the room next to the one Kellerman is in. Make it worth her while, as usual."

"I doubt it's available," Neff told him. "One of her girls may be using it."

"Then instruct Gayley to move her elsewhere," Domino ordered coldly. "Keep a close watch on him. The next time he leaves the room, drill a peephole in the wall so we can really keep an eye on him—and get the goods on him for sure. I'll assign several of the lads to join you. You will be in charge."

"Yes, sir!"

"This is one time," Domino said sharply, "that Kellerman will not escape from the net we're going to spread for him!"

Superintendent Thomas G. Pitcher of the U.S. Military Academy and his officers took pains to welcome Clarissa and Cindy Holt, daughter-in-law and stepdaughter, respectively, of Major General Leland Blake. As this was Clarissa's first visit, the two women received a tour of the grounds, followed by tea with Mrs. Pitcher.

After they returned to their accommodations at the West Point Hotel, Clarissa and Cindy were relieved to be alone again in the privacy of their room. Then Cindy exploded.

"Why do they think we came here, all the way from the West Coast?" she demanded. "To tour the entire academy with the commandant of cadets? To take tea with the superintendent's wife? Hardly! I came to see Hank, and we have yet to set eyes on him. I would have asked to see him, but I was afraid that if I made any fuss, he would suffer for it."

"I see no need for you to be so upset," Clarissa replied calmly. "Superintendent Pitcher told us that the whole corps of cadets is in class and won't be free until after four o'clock. It's just past four now."

"All the same," Cindy said, "I'm going to fall apart and die if I have to wait much longer to see Hank."

No sooner had she spoken than a knock sounded at the door. "One moment!" Clarissa called.

Cindy became flustered. "How does my hair look?" she asked. "Oh, dear! I can't remember if I unpacked my comb and brush. And whatever has become of my lip rouge? May I borrow yours, Clarissa?"

"Of all the cosmetics that are made," Clarissa answered, smiling, "I suspect you'll have less use for lip rouge than for anything else. I suggest that you answer the door, Cindy. I'm going out to see the view from our balcony." She withdrew from the room, walked out to the balcony, and closed the door.

The tap at the door was repeated.

"Just a second!" Cindy called, and was surprised to find that her legs were trembling so that she had difficulty in walking across the room. At last she pulled the door open.

Cadet Henry Blake stood there, dashing in his gray uniform.

He and Cindy just looked at each other for a long moment before they embraced and kissed. The pain of long months of separation was swept aside in the joy and passion of the reunion.

At last they separated, both short of breath. "You look exactly as I've pictured you all these months," Hank exclaimed.

Cindy smiled. For a hard-bitten and realistic young man, his statement was as close to poetic as he possibly could come.

As the room gradually righted itself, Hank became more aware of his surroundings. "Where's Clarissa?" he asked, knowing that Cindy had been accompanied by her sister-in-law.

Cindy giggled and nodded toward the balcony. "She's out there. She's being discreet and letting us be alone while we—say hello to each other."

He strode at once to the doors to the balcony, opened them, and kissed Clarissa. As soon as they had exchanged warm greetings, Hank returned to Cindy's side and put an arm around her shoulders.

"To think that I was quietly cursing the top brass of the academy," she said. "I was sure you hadn't even been told we'd arrived."

"I've done even better than you know." Hank laughed. "Since I now rank first in my class, I've been given a whole weekend's leave. I can go down to New York City with you and Clarissa. And I won't have to be back here until Sunday night."

The room reverberated with Cindy's shriek of delight. The gifts she had brought from General and Mrs. Blake were overlooked until much later.

United States warships that visited Hawaii used commercial dockage in the Honolulu harbor, not yet sharing Kung Lee's discovery that the facilities at Pearl Harbor were superior. Consequently, the ironclad carrying Toby Holt and Commander Sterling to the Orient tied up at a wharf in the Honolulu harbor usually reserved for a freighter.

"We'll be here until tomorrow, taking on provisions, water, and fuel," Commander Sterling said, "so you and I might as well go ashore for dinner. It'll give us a welcome break from ship's fare."

"Sounds fine to me," Toby replied. "Where do you want to go?"

"Officers of the American and British navies have access to a private club organized by a Hawaiian duke," Sterling said. "The food is said to be first-rate, and the atmosphere thoroughly Hawaiian. I expect we'll enjoy the place."

They went ashore an hour later, wearing civilian clothes and leaving their firearms behind. "The navy is very strict on this subject," Commander Sterling said. "We are to wear uniforms ashore only on official business, and only then are we to carry arms. Relations with the royal family here in Hawaii are very friendly, and our government is determined that they remain so. We are therefore about to station four or five American warships in port here for every one that flies the British flag."

At the end of the dock, Commander Sterling hailed a pedicab, a wicker passenger seat mounted on three wheels, propelled by a bicyclelike contraption pedaled by a single operator. This type of locomotion, the commander explained, had originated in the Dutch East Indies, where it had become the favorite form of transportation in the cities.

"Look yonder," Sterling said in disgust as he pointed toward a number of young women. "Less than a hundred years ago, prostitution was unknown on these islands. Then the Americans, British, and French arrived. First came the missionaries, and after them came the men of business. Now, as civilization has come to the islands, crimes multiply. In fact, so many assaults and armed robberies occur here that a number of officers have petitioned the navy to change its regulation prohibiting personal weapons ashore."

"It's a damned shame," Toby said, "but what can be done about it? Every civilization pays a high price as it advances."

At their destination in downtown Honolulu, Commander Sterling showed his credentials, and they were admitted at once. They were seated at a table on a *lanai*, an open porch located at the rear of the establishment. There, in the balmy night air, they enjoyed dinner in comfort.

The meal had been simply prepared, cooked over an open fire, and Toby found it reminiscent of food served in Oregon. He felt very much at home, even though the exotic surroundings were alien.

Since they had eaten more than they had intended, after the meal they decided to return to the ship on foot. As they started off through the downtown district of Honolulu, they passed two Hawaiian natives in feathered capes, carrying long bamboo poles. Toby looked questioningly at his companion.

"They're members of the royal constabulary," Commander Sterling said. "Their feathered coats are symbols of their power and authority. So are the poles. They're made of bamboo, which is regarded as a royal wood. I can understand why. Bamboo may be light in weight, as woods go, but those sticks, if used properly, can be very effective in a fight."

The district of shops, offices, restaurants, and other public buildings gave way to small homes. The streets were narrow and very dark, relying on only the moon and stars for illumination. Street lamps appeared to be unknown.

Suddenly three men appeared from behind a house at an intersection ahead and blocked their way. They were all tall and brawny, dressed in shirts, pants, and sandals.

"I reckon we're going to have a chance to work off our dinner," Toby observed quietly.

"I'm none too sure of their intentions," Commander Sterling replied, "but they look as though they're spoiling for a fight."

"I assume they're interested in our wallets," Toby said, flexing his hands.

"Not necessarily," the officer told him. "A patriotic movement has been under way here for some time now. A new political party has been created to advocate the throwing of all foreigners out of the islands. I wouldn't be surprised if these thugs are from that party."

"Well," Toby muttered grimly, "I don't mind getting out of their homeland, but I need to be asked to leave. If they try to throw us out, I'll react rather strongly to their lack of hospitality."

The two groups were sufficiently close now that the Americans saw that they were outweighed by all three of the natives, who had spread across the street and stood with their legs apart, waiting.

"One is carrying a bamboo baton," Sterling warned. "Be wary of it."

Toby saw that one of the Hawaiians held a four-foot length of bamboo in one hand, and he nodded. He could see that such a weapon would be a nasty instrument in a hand-to-hand battle.

A faint smile crossed his lips. "In spite of the odds, Commander," he said, "why don't you let me take on these boys by myself? I'd like to see just how well I've learned your lessons."

"I can't approve of that," the commander replied, frowning. "You could get seriously hurt."

"There's no telling what I'll face when I get to China," Toby rejoined. "Better I should find out now how good I am at Oriental ways of fighting."

"All right, if you insist. But I'll be ready to jump in the minute you get into real trouble."

"Fair enough," Toby replied. Leaping forward, he aimed a straight-legged kick at the nearer one of his opponents. His toes caught the man directly under the chin, and the blow knocked the Hawaiian to the hard clay of the bare road, stunning him. For a moment at least, he was removed from combat.

Toby wheeled toward a second of his adversaries, and holding the fingers of his right hand together stiffly, he drove them, tips forward, into the cavity directly below the man's rib cage. Commander Sterling had emphasized in his instructions that this was one of the most sensitive and vulnerable parts of the human body. The Hawaiian gasped, and turning pale, he collapsed onto the ground.

Only one man was left, which meant that Toby could

now face an enemy on equal terms. He soon realized, however, that the terms were far from equal. His opponent still carried the bamboo stick. Toby feinted with his left hand, then brought his right forearm down in a semi-circular chopping motion and with his forearm struck the Hawaiian's hand that grasped the bamboo rod. The blow was sharp, its delivery precise, and the rod fell from the Hawaiian's grasp to the ground. Toby kicked it, sending it spinning down the road.

Then Toby began to circle, and the Hawaiian followed. He moved inch by inch as he kept his opponent directly in front of him. He realized that he had very little time. The Hawaiian's two comrades were out of the fight only temporarily, and either could soon recover and rejoin the fray.

Toby chose now to rely on a type of fighting with which he had been familiar for many years, rather than on martial arts, where he was still feeling his way.

Balancing his weight on the balls of his feet, he moved toward his foe, both fists flailing. Before the startled Hawaiian had an opportunity to protect himself, Toby had landed a number of hard lefts and rights to the man's face, head, and body. He continued to pound the larger man without mercy, each hard-driven blow taking its toll. Soon the Hawaiian was groggy and, unable to defend himself properly, let his arms fall to his sides.

Trying to end the battle swiftly, Toby concentrated his blows on the Hawaiian's face and head. His fists smashed repeatedly into the other's eyes, nose, and cheekbones until the man sank to one knee. Grasping his head in both hands, he swayed and appeared to be on the verge of losing consciousness.

"I reckon this is enough damage for one night," Toby said. "Let's get out of here."

He and Commander Sterling began to walk rapidly up the street. The Hawaiians were beginning to recover but had no desire for further combat with the demon in human form who had trounced them so severely.

"One way or another," Sterling said, "you're a handy partner in a brawl. I'll make you a special deal, Toby. I'll continue to teach you how to protect yourself in the Oriental martial arts if you show me how to use my fists the way you do!"

IV

Carefully and cautiously putting his plan together, Karl Kellerman went from the Gayley house in his disguise and rented a sturdy, closed carriage and a team of black horses. Then he went shopping and bought a large, lightweight blanket and a ball of stout twine. Having acquired from another shop an outfit suitable for a prostitute, he went to a third store to purchase a considerable supply of cosmetics. He was ready now for the next step.

He spent two days acquainting himself with the location of the home of Jean-Pierre and Millicent Gautier, and with the roads in its vicinity. Meticulous in his surveys, he even timed the comings and goings of the members of the entire household. At last, he was ready to begin.

Kellerman had no idea that he was under close observation and that everything he did was reported in detail to Domino. During his first absence, Eddie Neff had drilled a peephole that was now in continuous use by several men.

On the fourth morning after his arrival, Kellerman went out for an early breakfast at a nearby restaurant. His time of waiting was ended. Driving the rented carriage, he headed for the home of the Gautiers.

When he reached it, he noted to his satisfaction that Jean-Pierre already was departing in his carriage for his office, leaving Millicent with her servants. He could not tell exactly how many servants might be on hand, but he had already figured out a way around that problem.

Driving to a thickly wooded area less than a half mile away, he concealed his carriage and the horses behind the foliage and waited near the road. When he heard a horse approaching after an hour, he hoped that it might be Millicent going out as she seemed to do at this time on the days he had been watching. His vigil was rewarded. She was seated in her light carriage, looking prim in a severe, navy blue dress and a beribboned bonnet.

Millicent's horse was moving at a sedate pace. Kellerman quickly sprang from his cover, grabbed the reins, and dragged the animal to a full stop.

Millicent opened her mouth and started to scream for help. Kellerman immediately leaped into her carriage and clapped a hand over her mouth. "Quiet!" he commanded. "Shut your mouth and you won't be hurt!"

Helpless in his grasp and unable to cry out further, she recognized him as the debased man she once had known only too well. Her eyes grew wide in terror, and she became limp.

"That's the way," he said, assuming that she was giving in. "Easy does it." He had counted on her shock of recognition to deprive her temporarily of her ability to resist, and he had been right. Before she could recover from her stunned astonishment, Kellerman stuffed a gag into her mouth, bound her wrists securely behind her back, and tied her ankles together. Then he threw a lightweight blanket over her and wrapped her securely in it.

After placing her on the floor of his own carriage, Kellerman turned her horse and carriage around and then struck the animal sharply on the rump. The horse reacted to the clapping sound, as well as to the blow, and started off at a lively clip. With any luck, Kellerman reasoned, the horse would return with the carriage to the Gautier stable, and in that way the household would learn that Millicent must be missing.

After a hurried but uneventful ride, Kellerman arrived at Madame Gayley's establishment. He turned the horses and carriage over to an attendant. Tipping him lavishly and warning him to forget this incident, he instructed the man to return the horses to the livery stable. Looking around to determine that no one else was watching, he carried the bundle containing the helpless Millicent to his room, almost running.

Then, unaware that he was being observed through the peephole, he took the blanket off her at last, then removed the gag, and slashed the bonds at her wrists and ankles.

"What's the meaning of this—this outrage?" Millicent asked in a choked voice.

"Why, Madame Gautier, I thought you'd be glad to see me," Kellerman replied in the taunting tone she remembered well. "You should be as glad to see me as I am to see you." Reaching out suddenly, he pulled several combs from her head. Her dark brown hair, released from its bun, tumbled down her back.

In almost the same motion, Kellerman, still grasping

the knife used on her bonds, slashed at her dress and then cut away her underclothing. He tugged at it with his other hand until she stood before him, almost completely nude. He now slashed all her clothes to ribbons so that they couldn't be worn again.

"Get rid of those awful stockings," he instructed harshly, "and throw away those old-lady shoes."

Conscious of her naked vulnerability, Millicent hastened to obey, although she was trembling. This indeed was the man with whom she had once shared a tempestuous affair but then had come to loathe. Seeing him again under such dreadful circumstances was a nightmare come true.

"Here, put these on in the bathroom," he told her, handing her a bundle containing a corselet like those worn by the prostitutes, a pair of net stockings, high-heeled shoes, and a thigh-length garment of transparent silk with long sleeves. It could not hope to conceal her bare bosom, shoulders, and arms. "You'll find a couple of scarves in the bundle," he told her. "One is to be wound around your neck, the other you use in your hair so it looks attractive."

Snatching the bundle, she retreated hastily into the bathroom and closed the door, grateful for any respite from this madman.

Humming, Kellerman poured himself a stiff, tall drink. As he waited, he wandered aimlessly around the chamber, hands jammed into trouser pockets.

Meanwhile, the adjoining room was a beehive of activity. When they saw Kellerman reappear with a woman, Domino's men had first sent a messenger to inform Domino. Until Domino gave orders, they could do nothing but watch and await developments.

Eventually a white-faced Millicent emerged timidly

from the bathroom, her attire leaving nothing to the imagination. Yet, despite the vulgar clothing, she looked lovely and strangely vulnerable.

"Hold still!" he commanded. "Just stand there while I look at you!"

Shivering, Millicent submitted to his orders. As she stood there, he picked up a slender, supple birch rod and experimented by cutting through the air with its length. It made an ugly, swishing sound. She knew full well the significance of that birch rod: He would beat her with it if she dared to disobey. In fact, he might decide to slash her with it several times just for the sheer pleasure of hurting her.

"Put these on," he said, handing her a pair of frilly, ornamental garters. "I forgot to give them to you. And while you're at it, for God's sake, add some makeup to your pretty face. You've grown too pale—like all the so-called society women. Plenty of it! You'll find all you need in the bathroom, and don't spare it. You know how I want you to look." He emphasized his words by slashing the birch rod through the air again.

Humming softly, he finished his drink and poured another. His plan was succeeding without a hitch.

When Millicent returned from the bathroom, the change in her appearance was remarkable. Now she bore a striking resemblance to the prostitutes. Her thick, shiny hair tumbled in waves over her shoulders, and its appearance was further enhanced by a small, scarlet scarf pinned to the crown of her head. Her eyes looked enormous as they were rimmed in kohl, and her lashes were heavy with mascara.

Kellerman inspected her at length, enjoying not only the sight of her but the prospect of humiliating her further. "You can make every tart in this place look cheap," he remarked. "Your marriage sure as hell hasn't hurt the way you look. Once you get fixed up right, that is." Moving closer, he began to caress her with both hands. Millicent shrank back from him.

"Damn you, woman! Hold still when I come near you!"

Millicent finally dared to take a stand. "I can see you're up to new deviltry now!" she said hotly.

Kellerman was undisturbed by her anger. "You and I," he said, "are going to enjoy a cozy little adventure together. Just do what you're told, relax, and have a good time. I know what you like and what you don't. But if you try to run away, you're going to be in trouble."

"Tell me more," she sneered acidly.

"This house," he told her, "is a bordello. You're now dressed just like all the other women. In fact, you look exactly like them. If you try to get away, you'll be caught. And turned over to the first available customer."

She shuddered and rubbed her arms.

"The only way you can avoid that," he said, "is to stay here with me."

Millicent put one hand on her hip and looked up at him mockingly. "Don't tell me," she said, "that you went to all the trouble of abducting me simply because you want to go to bed with me again. I'm sure you had a good time in those months we spent together. But I was too naive and unsophisticated for your tastes. I still am. You need women of far greater experience. And you also need variety. You may know me, Karl, but I know you, too."

"You don't know me nearly as well as you think you do," he retorted. "For the present, let me just say that you're here because I want you. You'll stay right here in this place, and you'll be available to me anytime I feel like taking you. I've warned you what'll happen if you try to get away. You can imagine for yourself the sensation you'd cause if you appeared on the street looking the way you look right now. Well, believe me, you're not going to have any more clothes than you have on at this second. So get used to your lot! If and when I have other ideas in mind for you, you'll learn about them. I have no intention, as of now, of using force to make you do what I say. You're too intelligent to need that. You just think about what I've said while I go out and attend to a few errands. And when I come back, we'll have us a stirring reunion." He reached out, patted her insultingly across the buttocks, and took his leave.

When Millicent was certain she was alone, she began to explore the room and the view from the window overlooking the garden. Noticing Kellerman's whiskey bottle, she recklessly poured a drink. When she saw herself in a full-length mirror, she stared at her reflection for a long time, uncertain whether to laugh or weep.

During the time she had lived with Kellerman, she had learned never to take his word for anything. Her first need, therefore, was to find out whether or not he was telling the truth when he claimed that she was being held in a bordello. Opening the door to her room and pushing the bolt so the door wouldn't close behind her, she walked rather timidly toward the main staircase.

As she approached it, a brassy blonde of about her own age, wearing an identical corselet and net stockings, was walking down the corridor from the rear of the house, her hips swinging. "Hello, there!" the blonde called.

Millicent belatedly realized she was being addressed. "Uh—hello," she replied faintly.

"You're new here, ain't you? I'm Carole. Who are you?"

"I'm Millicent—" she said hesitantly.

"Millie, huh?" Carole interrupted. "Who brought you here?"

Millicent looked blank for a moment.

"It don't really matter," Carole said impatiently. "The way you look, you'll get along. There's not a dame in the house with a figure as good as yours."

Millicent stirred uncomfortably under the other woman's critical gaze.

"You could make yourself a real bundle," Carole told her. "You're sure to be one of the most popular girls."

"All I want," Millicent said emphatically, "is to get out of here as fast as I can."

"Don't pull any funny business, whatever you do," Carole advised in alarm. "Just go along and do whatever you're told. That's the only way you can survive in one piece. Kick up your heels and start saying what you will or won't do, and Gayley will have it in for you, for sure. You'll get a beating for your pains. You'll be so black and blue you won't work for a week. Believe me, honey, there's only one way you can come out even and then get ahead of the game. Do as you're told, take good care of your customers, and never complain. After about six months, they'll buy you a street outfit. In time, you'll get a day off once in a while. Meanwhile, you'll have a good-sized nest egg building up for your future. I've been here for more than three years now, and believe me, I'm telling you the only way you can get along. Try anything else—*anything*—and you'll be cut down to size fast!"

She reached out, patted Millicent's cheek sympathetically, and went on her way downstairs. Her wriggling walk became even more pronounced as she neared the first floor. Heartsick and despairing, Millicent turned back to her own room. Safely inside, she bolted the door. She had heard men's voices from the parlor below, and she wanted to take no risk that she might be recruited as a partner for one of them. Clenching her fists so hard that her fingernails dug into her palms, Millicent began to pace the room in helpless fury. Only Kellerman could have dreamed up a depraved scheme that made her his prisoner in a bordello. She knew that Jean-Pierre would never think of coming to such a place in search of her. Anytime she rebelled against Kellerman, he could turn her over to the proprietress of the bordello, and she could expect even more degrading treatment.

Why, she wondered, *have I been subjected to such a disgusting fate?* She wanted only to bury her head in her hands and cry herself to sleep, but she knew she could not afford such a luxury. She needed to stay alert to face whatever might lie in store for her.

As Millicent pondered her dismal future, she had no way of knowing that every move was being observed through the peephole in the adjoining room.

Fourteenth Street in Manhattan was the most fashionable thoroughfare in New York City. Several popular theaters were located there, as were restaurants with international reputations. There were a number of department stores in the area.

Clarissa Holt insisted on taking Cindy and Hank to dinner at the most renowned of the restaurants, Delmonico's. After a delicious meal, they emerged onto Fourteenth Street. Performances were still going on at the nearby theaters, so the street was relatively free of pedestrians, and Hank had no trouble in making his way to the curb to hail a passing carriage that would take them back to their hotel. Concentrating his attention on the traffic as he searched for an empty carriage, he did not see four men in nondescript clothes approach Cindy and Clarissa. One, apparently the leader, reached inside his short coat and pulled out a pistol.

Cindy gasped. Hearing the surprise and distress in her voice, Hank turned, saw the pistol, and sprang forward toward the group. He recognized the weapon as one of the original Colt repeating pistols, made some thirty years earlier. A legitimate six-shooter, it was a cumbersome weapon none too easy to handle, even though fairly reliable. Hank was wearing the gray uniform of a cadet but carried no weapons except his dress sword. Its thick-edged ceremonial blade rendered it useless in combat. Nevertheless, he drew it.

The gang's leader was amused. "Don't try to be a hero, soldier boy," he sneered, "or you'll end up with a bullet in your chest. Just hand over your money peaceful-like, while we help ourselves to the money and jewelry of these dames. Then we'll be on our way, and you can be the hero some other time."

Hank reacted instantly. As a member of the West Point fencing team, he was experienced in swordsmanship. He thrust his sword in a violently sharp move toward the thug and knocked the pistol from his hand. It clattered harmlessly to the cobblestones.

The robber leaped forward and bent down to retrieve it. But Hank was too fast and agile for him. Reaching the weapon first, he brought a knee up sharply and caught the man under the chin. The sharp blow toppled him backward onto the street, and his head struck the cobble-stones, stunning him.

Hank scooped up the pistol before any of the other members of the gang could reach it. As they neared him, he was able to hold them at bay.

"Get your hands into the air, all of you! And keep them there!" he commanded. "Higher! Still higher!" He turned to the leader sprawled on the pavement. "On your feet! Get your hands up high and be quick about it. I have an itchy trigger finger, and I'll fill you full of holes unless you do what I tell you. In a hurry!"

The groggy leader scrambled to his feet and feebly raised his hands above his head.

"Clarissa," Hank instructed, "start looking for a policeman. Cindy, see if you can find a mounted constable on Fourteenth Street. Take your time. These birds and I will wait right here. . . . You, there! Don't start dropping your hands. You make me nervous, and I might pull the trigger! That's it, as high up as you can reach!"

A small crowd was gathering, and the women pushed their way through as they hastened to do Hank's bidding. Hank continued to hold the quartet at bay, his expression grim, his manner unyielding.

After several tense minutes, Clarissa reappeared with two policemen. Both were carrying their pistols, but they quickly saw that the situation was under control.

"Glad to see you, gentlemen," Hank said quietly. "These thugs had the audacity to try to hold up me and the two ladies I am escorting. I'll be pleased to come to the station house and bring charges against them."

He continued to hold the men helpless until the officers had handcuffed them to each other. One officer stepped from the curb and blew sharply on his whistle. In the distance, other officers heard and acted. Within several minutes, a large wagon with barred windows pulled by four horses arrived, and the criminals were herded inside. Hank turned over the pistol to the constables, to be used later as evidence.

"The station house is on Fifth Avenue, just north of Fourteenth," one of the constables told them.

"The ladies and I will walk," Hank said. "We'll meet you there presently."

With Cindy on one side of Hank and Clarissa on the other, they began their walk to the police station. But as they left, someone in the crowd started to cheer. Soon a dozen voices or more were raised. Embarrassed, Hank raised a hand to the visor of his hat in salute.

At the station house, the lieutenant in charge of the night shift greeted them and asked that they sign statements describing the assault and the roles they had played.

But if they thought that would end the incident, they were mistaken. Several newspaper reporters awaited them outside the station house as they left, and they were interviewed at length. Dozens of questions were put to them before the reporters allowed them to depart in a carriage that was on hand to take them back to their hotel.

Not until they entered the living room of their suite did Hank finally relax. "This town," he said, "is an extraordinary place. People here are ready to make a fuss over you for the darnedest reasons."

Clarissa laughed aloud. "You really don't know why the reporters made a fuss over you, Hank?"

He shook his head. "Out West," he said, "nobody would think a blamed thing about what happened tonight. Here, they make too much of it."

The following morning, when they went down to the

dining room for a late breakfast, they were nonplussed to find that word of their role in the incident had preceded them, and employees and other guests were exclaiming over them. Every newspaper in the city had printed an article about their adventure.

Still self-conscious after they had taken a long stroll about the city, Cindy and Clarissa accompanied Hank to the railroad station, where he was to board an afternoon train for his return to the academy. He and Cindy did not know exactly how many months might pass before they saw each other again. They consoled themselves with Clarissa's observation that Hank's time at the academy was passing rapidly and that no matter how difficult their separation, it was temporary.

Hank arrived in West Point shortly before the expiration of his leave. When he reached his quarters, his roommate, who was studying, dropped his book and saluted. "You certainly had quite a time in town last night. Congratulations!"

Hank smiled sheepishly. "You heard about last night?"

"Heard about it? The superintendent threw away his notes and delivered a special lecture at chapel this morning. You'll even find a letter from him on your desk."

To his astonishment, he found a note of warm commendation for his behavior, together with an added notation that the report was to be included in his permanent personnel file. The incident had assumed an importance far greater than he could have imagined.

Extremely distressed, Jean-Pierre Gautier nervously paced the length of his handsomely furnished living room. Hours earlier, one of his horses had returned home pulling an empty carriage. Millicent had left with that horse and carriage on her way to attend to some errands, and that was the last that anyone had seen of her. In the carriage, Jean-Pierre had found a shawl Millicent had left behind.

According to the servants, whom he had questioned closely, Millicent had driven off in midmorning, as soon as her carriage was made ready for her. Dusk would be falling shortly, and as yet no word concerning her had arrived, nor any suggestion of her whereabouts. He was greatly worried but had not gone to the police because he felt he had nothing of significance to tell them. If she failed to appear soon, however, he intended to go to the authorities and report that his wife had vanished. Meanwhile, he was torn by a feeling of need for support from his parents, with whom he always had been close, and by a contrary recognition that it would be kinder not to cause them undue concern. He decided to postpone consulting them, hoping that it wouldn't be necessary.

He heard a knock at the door, but he continued to pace, paying no attention. Some moments later, a maid entered the room, bearing a letter on a silver tray. "Excuse me, sir. This was delivered to the front door just now."

Jean-Pierre saw his name in crudely printed capital letters on the envelope. Snatching it up, he walked to a window in order to take advantage of the remaining daylight.

IF YOU WANT TO SEE YOUR WIFE
ALIVE, WELL, AND RETURNED TO YOU,
PUT FIFTY THOUSAND DOLLARS IN CASH,
WRAPPED IN OLD NEWSPAPERS, UNDER
A BENCH IN LOOKOUT POINT ON THE

RIVER ABOUT TWO MILES NORTH OF
YOUR HOME.
    OBEY THESE ORDERS EXACTLY
AND SAY NOTHING TO THE POLICE!

Feeling as though he had been kicked in the stomach,
Jean-Pierre now paced even more rapidly.

The bad news sickened and frightened him, and he
didn't know what to do. Should he obey the instructions?
Or get in touch with the constabulary despite the warning? Or, perhaps, even try to mount a counteroffensive of
some kind? His worst fears for his wife's safety had materialized, and they left him unsure as to how to proceed. An
hour passed while he brooded uncertainly and paced incessantly. Deep in his confused thoughts, he ignored the
knock at the door. A moment later the maid once more
came into the room. "A lady is here to see you, sir," she
announced.

At this time of crisis he was in no mood for a social
call. "Who is she?"

"She would not give me her name, Mr. Gautier," the
maid said. "But she is a lady, all right," she added.

"How can you tell that?"

The serving woman drew herself up to her full height.

"In all kinds of ways, sir," she told him with dignity.
"The way she looks. The way she dresses. The way she
talks—among others."

"Show her in," he said wearily, making up his mind
to be rid of the visitor as soon as he politely could.

In a moment, an exceptionally pretty woman with
flame-colored hair came into the living room. As the maid
had suggested, she was well dressed. Her only jewelry
was a pair of miniature dominoes suspended from a necklace.

"I regret intruding on you at such a critical time," she said in a cultured, well-modulated voice. "But I am here on a matter directly concerned with your current problem. I represent Domino."

Jean-Pierre's surprise turned to bewilderment. "I've heard of him," he said. "But what could he possibly have to do with me or my wife?"

"He happens to be more important to her well-being than you can possibly imagine. In fact, he is important to all of New Orleans, far more than any other person in this city," she said with a charming smile. "Perhaps you will recall the newspapers' occasional reference to him as leader of an organization that controls certain underworld activity. But no matter how powerful an individual may be, he can't exert complete control, as the disappearance of your wife illustrates. It was, unfortunately, a kidnapping engineered by one man."

At the word "kidnapping," Jean-Pierre had started violently, and his behavior became even more agitated. Martha continued without a break.

"Domino believes he can be useful in recovering her safely. He knows the identity of the man who perpetrated this vicious act. He wants to meet with you. And to work out, if possible, a plan with you for her safe return."

Jean-Pierre stared at her. "I can imagine," he said bitterly, spitting out each word, "that I then shall be indebted to him in some way I could never hope to repay."

"Not at all," she replied quickly. "He will want no money whatever from you, or anything else in return. What he's doing, he intends mostly as a favor to himself. His reason is that the perpetrator happens to be a personal enemy whose extermination Domino is committed to bringing about. Now, will you come with me?"

Jean-Pierre gripped the anonymous letter even more tightly. "Why not?" he asked rhetorically. "Apparently I have little to lose."

"I am pleased that you see it our way," she told him coolly, and held out a hand. "Allow me to introduce myself. I'm called Martha." She was obviously declining to identify herself fully and ignored his raised eyebrows.

They walked together to her waiting carriage in the driveway. Jean-Pierre was impressed by the coach's luxuriousness, by the driver and footman in livery, and by the matched white horses. As they were driven toward the heart of the city, Jean-Pierre showed Martha the letter and peppered her with questions: Did Domino really know the identity of his wife's abductor? Was Millicent safe, and would she be returned unharmed? Where was she being held? Was the ransom request legitimate? Should he pay?

"I'm unfamiliar with the details, so I'm in no position to answer your questions, Mr. Gautier," Martha responded. "But I am authorized to tell you one thing. Your wife undoubtedly will be recovered this very evening!"

He moistened his lips and asked eagerly, "She'll be removed from her kidnapper's possession?"

"Apparently so."

"I want to be a member of the party that rescues her!" he insisted quickly.

"I don't blame you," Martha said smiling slightly. "In your position, I'd feel just as you do. Unfortunately, I can't authorize you to join in the rescue efforts. You must take that up with Domino."

When they reached Domino's headquarters, Martha ushered Jean-Pierre into the library. There they were joined a short time later by Domino; never had the gang leader looked gentler than he did at this moment, dressed as he was in a dark suit, starched white shirt, and midnight blue cravat. His expression was placid, his demeanor amiable.

"You are familiar with a man named Karl Kellerman?" Domino asked after they were seated in easy chairs.

"I certainly am," Jean-Pierre replied instantly. "He's nothing but despicable scum."

"That's one of the milder descriptions applicable to Kellerman." Domino chuckled. "It won't come as news to you, then, that it is he who abducted your wife." Considerate of the younger man's feelings, he refrained from adding that Millicent was being held in a bordello.

Jean-Pierre silently handed over the ransom note. Domino read it without surprise. He decided not to voice his opinion that even if the ransom were paid, no one could guarantee that Kellerman would not welsh on the deal.

"I think we can handle this," was all that Domino said.

"I want to join any rescue party," Jean-Pierre announced firmly. "It's my right!"

"Setting her free," Domino said quietly in response, "is a task that requires the services of professionals—men who know what they're doing, who can handle firearms expertly. You mean well, Mr. Gautier, but you're an amateur. Your inclusion in the group would place your wife in greater danger. I shall be obliged if you wait here. Dine with Martha, if you will, and enjoy yourself. By the time you're having a cordial after your dinner, your wife should be happily reunited with you."

Domino repeated his explanation three times before

Jean-Pierre Gautier reluctantly accepted it. After Gautier was shown into an anteroom, Domino spoke in a low, intense voice to Martha. "Use any and every means at your disposal to prevent young Gautier from trying to follow us," he instructed. "Tie him to the table, take him to bed—do anything to keep him out of our way while we do what's necessary to take care of Kellerman and rescue Gautier's wife!"

V

The U.S.S. *Worcester* crept forward under reduced power as she entered the busy harbor of Tientsin in northern China. The Stars and Stripes flying from her masthead dipped in the direction of a thousand-year-old fortress guarding the entrance to the harbor. Eleven cannon boomed in an official welcome that was not too well timed, but for the inexperienced Chinese it amounted to a gallant effort.

Commander Niles Sterling smiled ruefully at Toby Holt. Speaking in Mandarin, as he often did, in order to give Toby practice in the language, he said, "The gunners have improved since the last time I entered this harbor. They are now firing more or less at regular intervals."

Toby frowned, concentrating on the words in order to understand Sterling, then smiled and replied in his own Mandarin. "It is astonishing, you know," he answered, "that although the Chinese invented gunpowder, they can still put on a sloppy show like that. They must have been outstripped in most respects by almost every other civilized nation."

"Indeed they have," the naval officer replied, now reverting to English to convey a more complex thought. "As I've been telling you, they are relatively advanced in some areas, but almost incredibly backward in others. Their civilization remained closed for so long that the world caught up and passed them in most areas. Only thirty years have passed, remember, since the British fought the Opium Wars here. They forced the doors open to Western civilization. As a matter of fact, most Chinese, particularly in the interior of the country, have never seen a white man or a black man."

"That's hard to believe," Toby agreed.

"I've been surrounded in the street in towns here by curious people who just gaped at me. Most of them regarded me as a white devil. You will find the same curiosity."

"Not at the court of the dowager empress, surely!" Toby protested.

"You'll be surprised," Niles Sterling told him. "The empress and members of her immediate staff deal with whites, of course. So do a number of the eunuchs who head government departments. But most soldiers are peasants from the interior, and they have never seen any white men. Neither have the majority of the nobles. You have some rare experiences in store for you."

The *Worcester* dropped anchor in the inner harbor. Within moments, a curious craft made its way across the water toward her. Eight oarsmen on each side of this high-prowed vessel were in uniforms resembling those of the British navy. The boat's forward progress was aided by a large, bulbous sail. Located amidships, it was tended by a pair of seamen. Seated aft, high on a mound of cushions, was a diminutive man wearing horn-rimmed glasses and a long queue. The tarnished gold braid on his uniform cuffs showed him to be a rear admiral in the virtually nonexistent Chinese navy. "He undoubtedly is the commander of the port," Sterling explained. "We should join the captain for the welcoming ceremonies so I can attend to the translations."

The admiral, speaking in Mandarin, made a flowery address on behalf of the dowager empress, welcoming the officers and men of the *Worcester*. Toby was pleased to find that he could follow it well enough to get the general meaning.

Not to be outdone, Commander Sterling extended the greetings of President Grant to the entire harbor garrison.

These amenities completed, Toby was presented to the admiral as a special American envoy en route to Peking on matters relating to the mutual security of the United States and China. Commander Sterling begged permission to escort his associate across ninety miles of open country to the Chinese capital so that he could present his credentials to the dowager empress. They would be accompanied by a squad of U.S. Marines, Sterling added. They were eager to get under way on their four-day journey that same afternoon. He also inquired whether they could borrow or buy four packhorses.

The Chinese official made no reply, but he appeared dubious.

Toby was astonished to see Niles Sterling reach into a pocket. He pulled out a gold coin, which he handed to the admiral—a blatant bribe.

After another exchange of excessive compliments, the

admiral returned with his staff to their boat and rowed ashore.

"You should have seen your face when you watched me slipping the admiral a gold piece," Sterling said, chuckling. "That's lesson number one, my friend. You're in the Orient now, and don't forget it. Almost everyone here accepts bribes, except the dowager empress and perhaps the key members of her personal staff."

"It's hard to believe any government can be so corrupt," Toby replied.

"You mustn't judge these people by the standards you'd apply at home," Sterling cautioned. "Money, jewelry, and other items of value are routinely given here, in order to obtain results. Of course, you must be careful to whom you offer a gift. Some officials would not accept one and would be mortally insulted if one were offered. So you need to feel your way. You'll have to spend more than a little time in the country before you know whom to reward. And, likewise, whom to ignore."

Toby removed his broad-brimmed hat and ran a hand through his thick blond hair. "I have so much to learn here that I wonder if I'll ever catch on," he observed.

"You will," Commander Sterling assured him.

Early in the afternoon, the pair went ashore, together with the eight marines of their escort. The four packhorses were ready, as they had hoped. After signing a cumbersome registry in the immigration office within the ancient waterfront fortress, they started out on their journey to the capital of China.

Making their way through the busy streets of Tientsin en route to the open countryside beyond, they followed a tortuous path on the worn stones. Toby was sure that he had never seen so many people walking in one small area.

"This city has about one million persons, though it is virtually unknown to us in the West," Sterling informed him.

Toby laughed wryly. "It seems the entire million are out on this one street."

Pedestrian traffic was so heavy in all directions that it was impossible for them to proceed quickly. Most men and women on foot were dressed alike in the traditional black cotton. On their feet they wore socks that separated the large toe from the rest of the foot, and over this they wore sandals with loops that slipped onto the large toes. Almost without exception, the men wore single braids down their backs.

Here and there, rickshas were pulled by sweating Chinese. The occupants of the chairs were well-to-do men of business, judging by their expensive ankle-length gowns of black, dark gray, and midnight blue silk.

Sterling explained that farm people, both men and women, could be distinguished by their pagodalike hats of black straw. Younger women were distinguished by their *cheongsams*, the tight-fitting dresses with mandarin collars and slit skirts they preferred to the loose jackets and baggy trousers of their elders.

Occasionally, a younger man stood out in the shapeless, gray-green uniform of the imperial army. These soldiers carried muskets, which looked as though they weren't in any condition to be fired.

When Toby stared incredulously at a musket, Sterling chuckled. "I decided to let you see them for yourself without explaining in advance," he said. "Now perhaps you can understand why the imperial army is virtually useless. And why a thousand bandits or rebels can cause a military force ten times as strong to flee for its life."

"If they don't manufacture modern weapons in this country," Toby said, "surely they can buy them abroad!"

"They make progress one step at a time," the commander replied. "When I first came to China, the armed forces of the emperor carried only double-pronged spears. Many of them still do, but after the dowager empress took power, they also acquired firearms, albeit primitive ones. The empress seems to be doing her best to modernize the country, but she faces a tremendous task. For example, most people here speak the dialect of the north, which is also used in Peking. Travel south, even as far as Nanking, and you find a completely different dialect. Go west, into the interior, and you will find still another. The only universal language is a Mandarin dialect, but among the million inhabitants of Tientsin, I doubt if more than a couple of thousand of the educated class can understand it and speak it. If you hope to understand Chinese civilization, you must have an open mind as to how people can exist in such bleak circumstances."

"I'm reaching that conclusion," Toby said.

"At the same time that they seem so hopelessly behind the West," the commander reminded him, "they have been far ahead of us in many things. They invented the printing press, as well as gunpowder. Our debt to China is almost endless."

"Apparently so," Toby agreed.

They were in the center of town now, and conversation was becoming impossible. They had to devote their attention to pressing forward through the extraordinarily thick throng or risk being knocked off their feet.

The crowd thinned somewhat when they left the area of offices, public buildings, and eating places and arrived in the residential district. Here, a sea of one-story buildings, most of them little better than huts, stretched out toward the horizon. Some were fashioned of stone, but most were of clay or of rough bricks, crudely put together by incompetent masons. It was evident that these dwellings could consist of no more than single rooms, where entire families slept, ate, lived, and died.

China's poverty was indescribable, Toby thought. Without having personally witnessed the wretched living conditions, he never would have believed that such circumstances actually existed.

At last they came to a high stone wall, five feet thick, marking the outer boundary of Tientsin. Imperial troops were stationed at an iron gate set in the wall. Other troops were sitting on the ramparts at intervals of some thirty yards. Rather than relying on their uncertain muskets, these men carried swords shaped somewhat like scimitars, and also the curious spears with double-pronged points that Sterling had described. The soldiers stared at the white men, but by now Toby was becoming accustomed to being an object of curiosity.

When the party moved into the open countryside, Commander Sterling took the lead, followed by Toby. Then came a pair of marines leading the packhorses. The remainder of the detail followed. Toby and Sterling carried modern six-shooters and short, double-edged swords; the marines were armed with postwar rifles.

Commander Sterling relied on a small nautical compass as he set the course for Peking. Increasing their pace after leaving the city, the members of the group crossed open terrain. Toby saw wheat, barley, and oats being grown, planted closer together than at home. Land was precious, he understood, and many more mouths needed to be fed.

As they continued to move through open countryside, Toby turned to his companion. "How does it happen, Niles," he asked, "that there is no major road to Peking?"

"One of the many peculiarities of China," the commander replied, "is that no roads worthy of the name exist here. You might think that Tientsin and Peking, each with a population of one million people, would be connected by a real highway, but we'll find hardly any road at all, and no signs to indicate the location of each city. Land for farming is too much in demand to allow much of it for roads. Anyone who damages the foliage and nearby crops by trampling on them is required to pay a very heavy fine. As a result, people travel between the cities by walking between fields, finding fallow ones whenever possible."

Something else struck Toby as peculiar: No matter which way he looked, in any direction, not a tree was in sight, though crops and other vegetation were plentiful. He questioned Niles about this.

"Forests are a major part of our American heritage," the commander said, "and, like you, others who come to Cathay notice the lack of trees. You'll find them elsewhere in China, but not in this part of the country. Any that grew here disappeared long ago. The need for firewood, furniture, and arms was simply too great. The Chinese never bothered to replace them."

The party pressed on until dusk, when they halted in a relatively flat spot on the eastern slope of a long hill.

"Never make camp in a bivouac area that has a western exposure," Niles observed, "at least in this part of China. The prevailing winds blow from west to east. And they carry huge quantities of sand and dust from the deserts of Mongolia. Sometimes the dust clouds become so thick it's almost impossible to breathe. You will find that is one of the hazards of living in Peking. It is particularly true during the winter."

Toby picked up a handful of dirt and allowed it to sift through his fingers. The black loam was topped by a layer of fine sand an inch thick. "What about the rainfall here?" he inquired.

"Only fair. In these parts, the peasants pray regularly for enough rain to bring in a decent harvest."

Life in China, Toby concluded, certainly could not be said to be easy.

The marine contingent had brought a small amount of firewood, and with a portion of it, a fire was built to cook the evening meal. One marine doubled as a cook, and he quickly served up a decent stew of beef, potatoes, onions, and carrots, all from the *Worcester*'s stores.

Their sleep that night was in half tents, erected so as to protect them from the wind from the west. By early morning they breakfasted on bacon and sourdough biscuits, a meal that reminded Toby of countless meals he had eaten in the American West. As they prepared to push on, he smiled to himself, thinking how far from there he had come in order to have an identical breakfast.

So far, he had seen nothing to indicate where the farmers who tended the crops could live. His question was answered when they passed a series of four walled villages, self-contained communities of stone huts housing approximately three hundred peasants. The buildings were enclosed behind stone walls high enough to discourage raiding criminals and other possible invaders. The peasants took turns standing guard duty, as Commander Sterling explained, three or four at a time around the clock. Horns were mounted for emergency summonses to the defense of the village.

As for the people themselves, they regarded the Americans curiously but without hostility. "The Chinese are a peaceful people," the commander remarked, "and become aggressive only when they're threatened."

On the third night, the party halted beside a small stream, once more on the eastern side of a slope. Toby noted that there were several clumps of pine trees in the area, the first he had seen. After refilling their canteens and watering their horses, the men prepared their overnight camp. A cooking fire was lighted, and Toby sat down near it with the commander. Niles unfolded a rough map of the area, pointing out their location and estimating how much farther they had to go.

Suddenly his voice broke off in midsentence. He toppled backward. A crimson stain was spreading on his white tunic. A steel shaft protruded from his chest. And on his ashen face was etched a surprised expression. Toby knew his companion was dead by the time his body fell backward to the ground.

Instantly drawing his six-shooter and cocking it, Toby threw himself, facedown, to the ground and called out sharply, "We're under attack! Spread out and take what cover you can find! Protect the packhorses as best you can!"

There were no rocks or trees near the marines' position, so finding cover was difficult. They spread out as Toby had directed, then lay flat on the ground, their rifles ready.

There were no further shots from the enemy, so neither Toby nor the marines could return the fire. Toby surveyed the upper slope of the hill behind him in the half light of dusk. He discerned a slight movement behind two evergreens standing close together. Grimly aiming between the trees, he squeezed the trigger.

The sound of his shot, echoing across the hills, was followed immediately by a high-pitched scream. He had found his target.

Almost simultaneously, two marines fired their rifles. Instantly a shower of steel arrows sang overhead.

"Keep your shots low," Toby shouted in a brief lull in the firing. "Make every one count!"

Paying no heed to the lethal crossbow arrows that whizzed past, Toby coolly analyzed the situation. As his father had been, he was at his best in a crisis. Noting that the heaviest fire was coming from a small clump of evergreens near the crest of the hill, Toby realized that at least two archers were hidden there. If he could break up that concentration of fire, the pressure on him and his comrades would be greatly relieved.

He could not see his target clearly but brushed that aside as irrelevant. Directing the marines to concentrate their fire at the clump of trees, he again cocked his pistol and put his second shot into the center of the trees. The marines sent a volley of rifle fire in the same direction.

Suddenly a diminutive figure plunged forward out of the trees and rolled wildly down the hill, his weapon falling after him. He somersaulted, then turned over and over sideways before rolling to a halt a few feet from Toby. His weapon, which landed just a short distance away, resembled a medieval crossbow. His face was hidden by a mask that covered his entire head, with holes cut for his eyes and nose. Toby assumed that he was part of a gang of bandits that preyed on the unwary in the countryside, as Niles had related. It was their mistake to have attacked this heavily armed party of professionals.

Once again Toby scanned the ground ahead. "I see another nest," he called out. "About three quarters of the way up the hill!" He sent a bullet toward the newly discovered hiding place, and the marines fired a volley in the same direction. All became still in that sector.

As nearly as Toby could judge, only one active sector remained. Crossbowmen appeared to be located directly below the crest of the hill. From there, they could take refuge by slipping over the top and hiding on the far slope. They were too distant now to aim their crossbows accurately. They could, nevertheless, potentially cause damage with a lucky stray shot or two.

Toby felt a strong desire to punish all the attackers for their senseless murder of his friend. He fired repeatedly toward the crest of the hill, and the marines immediately followed his example. Within minutes, the skirmish came to an end. The hillside was quiet.

Gesturing to the marines, Toby began to climb toward the summit, keeping low and moving slowly. Two of the detail remained to guard the horses, but the others joined him. They discovered the bodies of five bandits. A sixth was alive but severely wounded. A marine put him out of his misery with a pistol shot into his forehead.

They could find no sign of any other surviving bandits. All the rest had scattered and fled, their number unknown.

At the base of the hill, Sergeant Ed Flynn, leader of the marine squad, supervised the digging of a grave by a somber team.

Toby removed his friend's wallet and sword in order that they could be forwarded to the commander's family. And after the body was laid in the grave, he fetched a small Bible that Clarissa once had given him and that he made a point of carrying at all times. Opening it to the Book of Psalms, he bared his head and read aloud the eighth psalm, a favorite of his family's:

"O Lord our Lord, how excellent is Thy name in all the earth! who has set Thy glory above the heavens.

Out of the mouths of babes and sucklings hast thou ordained strength because of Thine enemies, that Thou mightest still the enemy and the avenger.

When I consider Thy heavens, the work of Thy fingers, the moon and the stars, which Thou hast ordained;

What is man, that Thou art mindful of him? And the son of man, that Thou visitest him?

For Thou hast made him a little lower than the angels, and hast crowned him with glory and honor.

Thou madest him to have dominion over the works of Thy hands; Thou hast put all things under his feet:

All sheep and oxen, yea, and the beasts of the field;

The fowl of the air, and the fish of the sea,

and whatsoever passeth through the paths of
the seas.

O Lord our Lord, how excellent is Thy
name in all the earth!"

Toby held his hat over his heart, and the marines
stood at attention as two of their group filled in the grave.
Then a volley was fired over it, and the sad ceremony
came to an end.

Reflecting on the death of Niles Sterling as he forced
himself to eat a few mouthfuls of supper, Toby thought it
tragic that he had died so needlessly and so far from
home. Using the light of the cooking fire, he wrote a
sentimental letter to the commander's widow, whom Niles
had lovingly mentioned frequently in the past weeks. After he had signed and sealed the message, he handed it to
Sergeant Flynn, along with the commander's possessions.
Flynn would be returning to Tientsin from Peking with
the marine detail. Months might elapse before Mrs. Sterling received the letter, but he hoped it would offer her
some comfort.

Early the next morning the journey was resumed.
Toby used the commander's compass as a guide. By midafternoon, they could see the high outer walls of Peking
looming ahead.

Arriving there, Toby showed his credentials to the
military guards at the entrance gate. After the party gained
easy admittance, he realized that the soldiers undoubtedly
were illiterate and unable to understand the documents he
presented.

Peking was as populated as Tientsin but geographi-
cally larger. Everywhere were huts of plaster or stone,

homes for large families. The narrow streets were as crowded as those in Tientsin. But one difference was noticeable. Because the legations of a dozen Western nations were in Peking, residents were more accustomed to seeing white-skinned people. Toby and the marines attracted no unusual attention.

Remembering what Niles Sterling had told him about Peking, Toby pressed ahead slowly through the throngs and reached a forbidding inner wall. Soldiers on duty at its gate summoned an officer of the guard. Apparently unfamiliar with Mandarin, he spoke in a dialect that Toby could not understand. The man could read, however, and inspected the Americans' credentials before admitting them to this sector of Peking, known as the Imperial City.

Private homes here were built inside high walls, and there were approximately ten in an area roughly equal to a square block in American cities. But most of the buildings were huge structures of stone, four to eight stories high, and occupying entire blocks. They housed offices of many of the twenty-seven major departments of the Chinese government. Here its affairs were administered; from here the daily lives of the people in the most populated nation on earth were supervised. Because no accurate census had ever been taken, all that could be assumed was that China had hundreds of millions of citizens.

In every government department, all the executive positions were filled by members of an organization unique in the world: the Corps of Eunuchs. Poor boys who showed intellectual promise were taken before their twelfth birthdays and emasculated. Brought to Peking, they were enrolled in the corps and spent a decade learning the intricacies of governmental administration. Thereafter, another five years were devoted to study in such specialized subjects as economics, farming, and foreign affairs. At the end of that time, each recruit was assigned to a position in the government bureaucracy. Then began his active service, though only under highly competitive conditions. Those who successfully competed remained in the government until they died. If they reached the advanced age of eighty years, they became advisers to their successors.

Below them in the hierarchy and in status were other men, not eunuchs, and these constituted the overwhelming bulk of the government's staff. These males, forbidden to marry, lived in vast dormitories near their offices. And also close by were government-owned brothels reserved exclusively for these employees.

Meals, clothing, and other necessities, as well as the housing, were provided free to all in the employ of the imperial government. The theory behind this extraordinary procedure, as Niles had explained to Toby, was that, relieved of all material concerns, these employees could better devote their entire time and efforts to their work and thus bring greater glory to their vast country.

At last the travelers came to a third high wall, boundary of the innermost circle in Peking, the Forbidden City. The extensive premises inside the wall were guarded by an elite corps of troops, the imperial guards, who wore tailored uniforms of wool and silk and carried the only modern weapons owned by the Chinese army. All the guards were required to read, write, and speak two dialects and to understand Mandarin well enough to obey orders given in that tongue; on duty, they could speak only Mandarin.

For the first time, Toby and his escort were subjected to an exhaustive inquiry to certify their identity and establish their reasons for approaching the Forbidden City.

Only when they had satisfied the person in command were they admitted. An individual was then assigned to act as their guide.

Here, the atmosphere bore little resemblance to other parts of Peking. Foot traffic was far lighter. Only an occasional horseman—an army officer, a bearded scholar in a long robe, a government official in a green silk uniform—rode past. Otherwise, the streets appeared almost deserted.

Ornamental lakes dotted the district, and on their banks stood pagodas, lacquered in deep black and a shimmering red. Numerous large, imposing structures, many of them individually walled, were described by the guide as the homes of the royal family, government ministers, and other officials of the highest rank.

Dwarfing all else in the Forbidden City was the imperial palace, half concealed behind more thick, high walls. Here lived the little boy emperor and his all-powerful grandmother, the dowager empress, in whose hands rested ultimate power in the nation. Most key members of her personal staff also lived and worked in the palace.

According to what Niles Sterling had related to Toby, one of the world's foremost collections of jade, ivory, porcelain, and gems was housed in the imperial palace. Emperors had been collecting these precious objects for five thousand years. Neither the queen of England nor the sultan of Turkey could boast possessions worth as much as the dazzling array owned by the dowager empress.

Unusually large fruit trees provided ample shade in the immediate vicinity of the palace, and the lawns were lush, constantly tended by an army of expert gardeners. Exotic flowers of every color of the rainbow were arranged in formal gardens that were decorated with miniature bridges crossing tiny streams.

The captain of the guard brought them to a special district, in which each city block was subdivided by a low wall into thirds. Inside each wall was a complex of buildings consisting of private homes, offices, and barracks. The entrance to the area was dominated by a large barracks. From it flew the blue and white flag of China. Two companies of immaculately attired troops, stationed in front of the building, assumed the present-arms position when the visitors approached, then stood at parade rest. A higher officer who appeared examined the group's credentials once again before admitting Toby to the street beyond.

"This is Legation Row," the escorting captain explained as he and Toby started down the avenue. Toby already was discovering the truth of Sterling's remark about the dusty conditions that prevailed in Peking. "On this side, you see the British, Russian, and Portuguese compounds. Across the street are the embassies of France, Spain, and Sweden. The American compound is in the next block."

The national flag of each country flew at each compound, and sentries in uniform were posted at the main doors of the legations.

The two marine guards stationed at the entrance of the United States legation were wide-eyed when they saw eight of their colleagues approach, grinning broadly. They exchanged sharp salutes; these would be followed by all the camaraderie the circumstances permitted. Soon after the greetings, Toby's loyal escort would depart, returning to Tientsin.

Toby entered the building alone, after thanking Sergeant Flynn and the others. In a few minutes, he was closeted with the American minister to China, Simon Mc-

Clellan. His full, dark beard helped to create a close resemblance to President Grant.

The diplomat sighed as he listened to Toby's description of Commander Sterling's murder. "In this part of the world," he said harshly, "human life seems to have no value, no dignity, no meaning. It's cheap. People here are killed as quickly and as easily as we at home invite each other to dinner. It's a shameful situation. You will need to acclimate yourself to it if you hope to survive, Colonel Holt."

In response to a question from Toby about starting in on the next phase of his mission, McClellan went on.

"I have prepared the way by explaining your mission to the empress and to a number of key persons on her staff. But the major effort is up to you. Either you will produce results, tangible results they can see and feel and know are real—"

"Or?" Toby prompted.

"Or the Chinese won't hesitate to do away with you. I am not indulging in rhetoric. Either you will do as you are mandated to do, and make substantial progress in ridding China and the United States of these infernal tongs, or the empress may well order you executed as a 'lesson' to others who may need a new incentive to do their best for her."

Toby could not understand why his own government wouldn't act to protect its emissary in such circumstances. He was about to make a caustic reply when McClellan said, "Of course, we'll do what we can to protect you—but the Chinese are crafty, and if the empress takes sudden action against you, it's possible we might not be able to reach the scene in time.

"You come to China with a dazzling reputation, Colonel Holt," McClellan concluded. "Believe me, you need all of whatever prowess you can muster, plus all the good luck that may come your way. You are about to meet a woman who demands perfection—and is never satisfied, even when she gets it!"

The loneliness on the Holt ranch was all-encompassing after a busy morning. The entire crew had gone off on various chores under the direction of Stalking Horse, the elderly Cherokee who had been the Holts' resident foreman for many years, and Clarissa Holt was alone at the ranch house. That is to say, she was alone for all practical purposes. Her little son, Tim, was taking his afternoon nap, and White Elk, the ten-year-old Indian boy who was Stalking Horse's adopted grandson, sat at the kitchen table.

White Elk ordinarily divided his time between his grandfather's home and that of Pamela Randall, a friend of the Holts' in Idaho who had also adopted the boy and for whom he held great affection. But with the consent of all concerned, he had extended his stay in Oregon, and Clarissa found she was glad for his presence.

She had also learned that at times like this, the best way to avoid feeling the absence of her husband too deeply was to keep very busy. By attending to her regular chores, and taking on some additional ones, she was able to pass the time relatively rapidly and with a minimum of pain.

She washed the noon dishes, then went outside and cleaned the grill where the ranch hands had cooked and eaten their meal. Then, intending to wash the kitchen floor, she carried two buckets to the pump outside the kitchen door. Pumping rapidly, she filled one and was starting on the other bucket when she heard the sound of approaching horses. Two riders appeared on the trail that led to the front gate.

As they approached, Clarissa noted they were Indians. However, they were dressed in nondescript shirts and trousers that looked like white men's castoffs. Although they looked rather grubby, they were smiling politely, and nothing in their attitude could be interpreted as menacing.

Nevertheless, Clarissa felt uneasy. The ranch hands were scattered over many miles, and she was alone. Something about the two Indians struck her as being amiss; they definitely did not resemble Stalking Horse or any of the hard-working Indians in the area.

One of the men tipped his hat. "Please, lady," he said, "we want water."

His request was harmless enough and easy to fill. Breathing a little easier, Clarissa pointed to the bucket that she had already filled. "There it is," she said. "Be my guests."

The pair dismounted slowly and helped themselves to the cool water, which they drank from a dipper that rested in one pail.

As they continued refilling the dipper, they eyed Clarissa. They exchanged no words, but stared at her boldly. Feeling her uneasiness returning, Clarissa unconsciously took two backward steps toward the kitchen.

The taller and more heavily built of the men wiped his mouth on his sleeve and followed her. "Water is good," he said, "but we want real drink. Whiskey!" He leered at her.

Clarissa tried to take another step toward the kitchen, but the man was too quick for her. He placed himself between her and the kitchen door.

Now she was sure that they meant trouble, and her heart hammered against her rib cage.

"Your man's not here," the second Indian said. "Your Indian boss-man's gone for day. You're alone here."

Clarissa needed no reminders of her isolation. She thought of the rifle hanging in the kitchen, where it did her no good. There was no way she could get to it without forcing her way past the burly Indian who blocked her way.

"You get whiskey," the second man said, "and we all drink."

Clarissa knew she had to stall for time. "All right," she said, "you wait here while I go in the house and get a bottle." Once she got her hands on the rifle, the situation would be changed drastically.

The two Indians exchanged a glance and laughed. "You go in house," he said. "We go too!" Then he and his companion laughed uproariously.

Clarissa felt she had nothing to lose by trying, so she attempted to duck around the burly Indian and run toward the kitchen door. The man stopped her, however, by taking hold of her shoulders and pulling her out of the path.

Clarissa struggled in an attempt to free herself, and he, enjoying the game, grasped her more tightly. Putting an arm around her, he tried to pull her close.

Suddenly the roar of a weapon fired close by startled the trio. Clarissa looked up to see little White Elk standing outside the kitchen door, holding her rifle, which was as long as he was tall. He had fired one shot into the air and now was aiming the weapon at the second Indian, who was standing a few feet away from the Indian holding Clarissa. The boy's expression was devoid of any emotion.

The renegades were completely surprised by his appearance, and the rifle spoke for itself. Having no desire to contend with a child who obviously intended to shoot first and discuss the problem later, the brave who had hold of Clarissa let her go, and he and his companion raced to their ponies.

Laughing and weeping, Clarissa snatched the weapon from White Elk and raised it to her shoulder. There was one bullet remaining in the chamber, and she fully intended to fire it.

The renegades gave her no opportunity to prove her marksmanship, however. They spurred their horses and quickly disappeared down the path that led to the end of the property, both of them crouching low in their saddles and riding at top speed, their heels digging into the flanks of their animals.

Aware of her inability to hit a moving target, Clarissa lowered the rifle and laughed aloud. A moment later, she was returning White Elk's ferocious hug.

"No-good Indians," the boy said, his tone remarkably calm. "They give all Indians a bad name."

VI

Toby took up temporary residence at the American legation. Less than twenty-four hours after his arrival, he accompanied Simon McClellan to the imperial court. None of the many extravagant descriptions he had heard had prepared him for the reality of the place.

The walls of the large, marble-lined audience chamber were almost completely covered by exquisite tapestries, depicting China's history, emphasizing the virtues of the rulers. Alabaster and marble statues stood against the walls and in niches; they represented gods in the Chinese pantheon. These immortals appeared to be conferring with emperors, who seemed to be their equals.

Officers of the personal guard to the empress, in blue uniforms, were armed with pistols and curved scimitarlike swords.

At the far end of the chamber was a two-tiered dais. Two of the four seats on the lower level of the dais were occupied by elderly men in the black gowns of scholars. The third occupant was a military officer wearing the shoulder boards of a general.

And the fourth was one of the most beautiful young women Toby had ever seen. Her shimmering, blue-black hair framed her face and cascaded down her shoulders. Barely visible were three-inch silver earrings. Toby's superior eyesight enabled him to discern that they contained some of the symbols for good luck that he had heard described by Commander Sterling. Beneath a high forehead and thin, shapely brows, her almond-shaped eyes were fringed with exceptionally thick lashes. High cheekbones contributed to an aristocratic appearance, and her nose was straight and small. Her lips, lightly rouged, were full and moist. Her chin was firm, her swanlike neck graceful.

She was wearing a high-necked *cheongsam* of a silvery fabric. Its skirt was slit above the knees to reveal her slender, long legs. She had a high, full bust and a very tiny waist. She was wearing open, high-heeled slippers, and her toenails and inch-long fingernails were painted a startling black.

As Toby would discover shortly, this was Princess Ta-lien, interpreter for the dowager empress. Though the empress spoke several foreign languages, she preferred to rely on an interpreter, possibly because that arrangement allowed her more time to consider how to respond to visitors.

Above the lower dais, on a jade chair known as the Chrysanthemum Throne, Tz'u Hsi, co-regent and dowager empress, sat in omnipotent splendor. She ruled with an iron hand and was as suspicious as she was autocratic. In her thirties, she was grossly overweight. This, together with her perpetual scowl, caused her to appear considerably older. Her *cheongsam*, made from the cloth-of-gold that was forbidden to all but the empress herself, was unique. Its color was the "Imperial Chrysanthemum" reserved by decree for the imperial household. The garment fitted loosely to help hide the empress's folds of flesh, and to Toby it made her seem dowdy compared to the impeccably gowned interpreter.

Minister Simon McClellan walked forward with Toby across the Oriental rugs. In accordance with instructions, they halted fifteen feet from the upper dais and bowed.

McClellan said in a respectful tone, "Your Imperial Majesty: I have the honor to present to you Colonel Toby Holt as a representative of President Grant of the United States." They had agreed that Toby's title in the army reserve would impress the empress.

Princess Ta-lien swiftly translated the envoy's words into Mandarin.

Again, Toby bowed, a gesture unfamiliar to him, with the result that he performed it rather awkwardly, though in essence it was simple and dignified.

The empress responded in a high-pitched, penetrating, and thoroughly unpleasant voice. Toby realized that he could understand some of her words but diplomatically waited to answer until the princess had translated them.

"You do not kowtow before me, Colonel Holt?" The kowtow involved touching one's forehead to the floor three times before being told to rise.

Toby and McClellan had discussed the question of what he should do when confronted with the empress's requirement that everyone abase himself before she would consent to hear business discussed. "I do not, ma'am," he replied quietly but in a firm manner. "I do not kowtow to the President of the United States or, for that matter, to anyone else. As a free, independent American citizen, I believe that every human being is born the equal of anyone else on earth. I have great respect for the exalted office that you occupy, and I am prepared to extend great respect to you as an individual."

The dowager empress studied him closely, her shrewd eyes narrowing. Gradually, a change took place in her manner. At first, her face was flushed as anger suffused it. Slowly, her vexation gave way to reluctant admiration, and now she looked at the American with a new expression. He was blunt, straightforward, and, above all, courageous, and for those reasons she decided that perhaps she could like him, after all.

While she underwent her change of heart, silence prevailed in the chamber. Minister McClellan stepped forward now and read aloud the letter in which President Grant offered the services of Colonel Holt in eliminating the tongs that threatened to spread a blight over America. Then the letter went on to describe the President's reasons for Colonel Holt to oppose the tongs.

Notorious for her hatred of foreigners, the empress, who previously had heard Minister McClellan's explanation of Toby's mission, habitually refused to credit any information of a foreign origin, no matter how factual. No sooner had Ta-lien finished translating President Grant's letter than the empress was on her feet, her fists clenched and her eyes glazing in fury. "I refuse to believe," she said stubbornly, "this preposterous allegation that our subjects are transported to a foreign land and forced against their wishes to serve American masters there!"

One of the elderly scholars on the lower bank of thrones dared to interrupt the imperial diatribe. "I humbly beg Your Majesty's pardon," he said, "but the statements made in President Grant's letter are factual and true."

Her rasping voice rose still higher. "You have the temerity to tell me now that this is so? Why have you not told me of this previously, if you are so well informed?"

"The information, I believe, is prepared regularly in the state of the nation bulletins written exclusively for Your Majesty's perusal."

The empress had no intention of admitting either that she did not read such material or that she knew the truth and was only overreacting to hearing it verified in President Grant's letter. Instead, she sat down again and looked inquiringly at the general, who also was seated below her.

As a rule, he took pleasure in disagreeing with the scholars, but that day he had no argument with them. "I must state, Your Majesty, that Dr. Wu is accurate in his assessment," he said. "It is true that each year thousands of your loyal subjects are being transported across the Pacific Ocean to work as menial laborers in the United States, having been lured there by attractive, false promises. As soon as they leave their homes, they become prisoners of the tong, and upon arriving in America they are impressed into servitude, sold for the tong's benefit."

An overweight eunuch with a gold link necklace that identified him as a cabinet member, standing in the first rank of the audience, dared take a step forward. "It is also true, Your Majesty," he called, "that large quantities of opium are being boxed and smuggled out of our country for sale in the United States. As you will no doubt recall, four of Your Majesty's major government departments are engaged in an all-out campaign to stop this traffic, but so far we have been thwarted. The criminals anticipate our every move and are clever beyond compare. They are so brazen they even disregard what they must know are the stern wishes of Your Majesty."

Once again the empress glanced at the general, Lin Lo-yuang. He shook his head with evident regret. "I need not point out to you that the army is one of those four government departments, Your Majesty," he said. "We have tried our best to halt the production of opium and to prevent it from being exported. But our efforts have been unsuccessful. I am convinced, Your Majesty, that a mastermind is at work on behalf of the tong. No matter how many traps we set or in how many ways we try to track these devils, they invariably escape the nets we throw out for them. They continue their activities unharmed and undiminished."

The empress grimaced and tapped a forefinger on the arm of her throne. "It appears," she said loftily, "that because of the inefficiency of my own government I shall be forced to intervene personally and take charge of this matter myself. . . . Colonel Holt, I now take under advisement your offer. If I accept it, I will expect you to report directly to me on the conduct of your efforts."

Simon McClellan had positioned himself in such a way that Toby could see an expression of wry sympathy on his face. He previously had made it clear that he felt sorry for anyone required to be associated closely with the empress.

Toby was interested in the reaction of Princess Talien, who seemed to have amusement in her eyes as she glanced from him to the empress.

Toby recognized that although his mission still had to be accomplished, he had passed the first test. To help seal the agreement, he took a package from McClellan and bowed again. "I bring you two personal gifts, Your Majesty," he said in Mandarin, deciding on the spur of the moment to discard reliance on the use of the interpreter. He had, in fact, rehearsed this little speech. "This is for you with the highest compliments of President Grant." He handed her the box containing the necklace.

Like a child opening a gift, the empress tore away the wrappings and opened the box. She gasped with pleasure and fastened the turquoise and silver necklace around her throat. "Please express to your president my gratitude for this gift," she said. She could not, however, resist the opportunity to insert a barb. "Unfortunately, the turquoise is not nearly as handsome as that which we have available."

Her actions belied her unkind words, for even as she spoke she patted and stroked the necklace, greatly pleased with it.

"This next gift," Toby now told her, "is presented to you on behalf of the people of the United States with their warmest respect."

The empress opened the second box and found herself looking at a set of six American Indian tomahawks, each studded with turquoise on the handle to enable a user to obtain a better grip. The burnished blades were honed to razorlike sharpness.

"Thank you," the empress said in a flat tone. It appeared that she was unwilling to admit that she had never seen such weapons and was ignorant of their use. Adopting one of her favorite tactics, she quickly provided a diversion. "Perhaps," she said in a tone that conveyed a command rather than a suggestion, "you would be interested in a display of martial skills?"

Without enthusiasm, Toby agreed politely. General

Lin called for an aide to fetch two soldiers who would put on the exhibition.

Princess Ta-lien surprised Toby by asking him to sit beside her. By sliding over, she made enough room for him to squeeze onto the thronelike seat and was insistent in her request. Toby realized that it would appear rude to refuse in view of the audience, so he accepted her invitation, very much conscious of her stunning beauty and of the jasmine scent of her perfume. As they waited for the soldiers to arrive, he could sense her dark, liquid eyes regarding him. Uncomfortable, he began to feel as though they were burning into him. She was flirting openly, even brazenly, but he did his best to ignore her overtures. Soon becoming aware of his lack of response, Ta-lien withdrew, but she gave no sign that she was annoyed by the rebuff.

When the two soldiers appeared, each carried a large board bearing a life-sized figure of a man.

The two boards were placed facing each other thirty feet apart near the dais. After kowtowing to the empress, one soldier stood beside each board. Members of the audience who were standing in the vicinity of the boards prudently moved aside.

Producing knives with sleek silver handles, each soldier started to throw at the opposite board. They threw in clusters of four knives, one cluster aimed at the forehead of the target, a second at the heart, and a third aimed at the torso. Both men proved quite proficient. Once Toby was satisfied that they were superior marksman, he lost interest in their activity and suddenly had to stifle a yawn. Ta-lien pounced instantly. "Don't tell me, Colonel Holt," she murmured in English that conveyed irony, "that you are bored by the imperial exhibition being staged in your honor?"

Chagrined, Toby stammered a reply. "I—I'm sorry, it's just that I'm tired from my journey."

"I see," the princess said, in a mocking tone. "Well, in that case, I'm only sorry that our little display did not succeed in reviving you. But then, perhaps you feel you can do better? If so, now is your chance to speak up!"

On the long voyage across the Pacific, Toby had been reminded frequently by Commander Sterling to avoid the worst fate in the Orient: a loss of face. If that should happen, he had been told, allies would desert, enemies would multiply, and respect would vanish.

He had carelessly maneuvered himself into a position where he would have to prove himself. After applause for the soldiers had subsided, he stood, bowed to the dowager empress, and addressed her in Mandarin. "Your Majesty," he said, "perhaps you will allow me to try to make a contribution to your entertainment and that of your court."

The empress was startled. "Whatever you may have in mind, Colonel Holt," she replied, clearly nonplussed, "would be acceptable to me, I believe. But perhaps you will be good enough to inform us further."

"Allow me to borrow, if you please, the American hatchets, which we call tomahawks." The box was handed to him, and he waved the soldiers away from their targets.

The audience watched in silence as he tested one of the tomahawks with a thumb and briefly studied a target.

Then, raising his arm, he hurled the tomahawk. Spinning end over end, the weapon flew toward the target, where it knocked four knives to the floor and embedded itself in the board.

The court applauded politely. Prominent among those clapping quite enthusiastically was Ta-lien, who was making little secret of her admiration for Toby. The dowager empress remained motionless, her face showing neither approval nor disapproval.

Adjusting his stance so that he faced the second target, Toby grasped another tomahawk with his left hand and repeated his approach. He succeeded in equaling his achievement; all four knives dropped from the lower portion of the other target as the tomahawk displaced them. Again the applause was polite.

He asked that the targets be moved so that they were adjacent. Now varying his procedure, Toby grasped two tomahawks simultaneously, one with each hand. Raising them, he let them fly simultaneously. His double blows proved remarkably accurate, and the knives in the middle of each target clattered to the floor.

Now the applause, led by Princess Ta-lien, was unrestrained. Even the reserve of the dowager empress was broken, and she clapped for nearly a minute. Her elaborate rings of diamonds and jade made sparkling circles in the light as she applauded.

Toby no longer felt even slightly apprehensive about his skills. Reassured that he had not lost his talents despite a long period in which he had not seriously used them, or even practiced, he picked up the last two tomahawks. Then he deliberately turned his back toward the targets, glancing at them briefly over his shoulder.

As the ladies and gentlemen of the court became aware of the daring feat that he intended to attempt, they fell silent. A deathly hush pervaded the throne room. The dowager empress even rose to her feet in order to obtain a better view. Several of the spectators crowded forward but were impatiently waved back by Ta-lien.

Toby showed no awareness of the stir he was creating. Concentrating only on the task at hand, he threw both tomahawks backward over his shoulders.

The two blades landed at the same instant amid the highest clusters, those in the heads of the figures as drawn on the board. Eight knives clattered onto the tiles, but the two tomahawks remained in the boards, after having almost miraculously found their marks.

No one had ever witnessed such superb marksmanship, and the spectators applauded loudly.

Smiling modestly, Toby moved several paces to the side of Simon McClellan. "I was wondering if I might be able to retrieve the pistol that I had to deposit at the door of the palace," he murmured.

"You would need the personal approval of the empress for that," the diplomat replied. "I'm not certain the request would be wise. Why do you want it?"

Instead of answering the question directly, Toby walked to the foot of the dais and called out above the applause, "Your Majesty, in order to complete my exhibition, I would like to regain possession of my firearm, which I was obliged to leave with the sentry when I entered."

The dowager empress interrupted her applause long enough to instruct a servant to oblige the visitor's strange request. Her attitude of skepticism and remoteness had disappeared completely.

A few minutes later, an aide brought the pistol. Toby checked it quickly to assure himself that all six chambers were properly loaded.

As the court realized that in their midst a stranger armed with a deadly weapon was close enough to the empress to kill her if he wished, the assemblage grew still once more.

"Would you please be good enough," Toby asked

Princess Ta-lien, "to instruct the knife throwers to take their places and to direct their knives to their targets again?"

Though startled by this unexpected turn in the strange event that was unfolding, the princess, overcome by curiosity, issued the instructions to the knife throwers. While they were retrieving their weapons and returning to their previous positions at opposite ends of the dais, where the targets had been placed again, Toby retreated as far as he could from them. The audience stood aside as he advanced; when he finally took a stand, he was some sixty feet from the dais. As it became evident that he was intending to shoot at the knives, the spectators promptly cleared all the intervening space, elbowing one another to the side.

The empress quite naturally displayed apprehension, even though she had given permission for this foreigner to regain his weapon and hold it in her presence. She gestured to General Lin Lo-yuang, who rose and took a position between her and Toby.

Toby was paying no attention to her, to the general, or to Ta-lien, who seemed to be trying to conceal a disdain for the empress and her fears. He was annoyed with himself for taking a needless risk. He had felt it necessary, when challenged, to demonstrate his skill with the tomahawks. In so doing, he knew his prowess had impressed the dowager empress. Having already accomplished that goal, he had nothing to gain by further exhibiting skill with weapons. If he were to fail now, he would be taking the edge off his achievement; even if he succeeded, he would add little luster to the reputation he was establishing. In brief, he knew now he had a great deal to lose and little to gain. He had committed himself, however, to a renewed display of his talents, and he had no choice but to make the best of it.

Someone audibly drew a breath, then held it. The mood of the assemblage was expressed so clearly that a number of the courtiers giggled nervously.

Slowly Toby raised one arm to shoulder height. The click of his pistol's hammer echoed in the silent chamber.

At his signal, the two knife throwers went into action, hurling their blades with great force and precision. The knives were only shining blurs as they sped to the targets.

The bark of Toby's pistol startled everyone, even though they had been awaiting it. The pistol sounded five more times, but after he had emptied its six chambers, no one really knew what he had been firing at.

Ta-lien was among the first to see what he had done. She gasped aloud, then pointed a forefinger. Six knives had never reached their targets; they lay shattered on the tile floor. Each had been struck by a bullet that bent it out of shape. General Lin picked them up, gave two to the empress, and distributed the others on the lower dais.

Colonel Toby Holt had succeeded in achieving the impossible: shooting down, in six consecutive pistol shots, six knives thrown at great speed.

General Lin shook his head repeatedly, Ta-lien was openmouthed, and the empress showed that she again was deeply impressed by the American's accomplishments. Unpredictable as ever, she peered at Toby and called out a challenge. "Are you willing to meet the imperial champion of champions in combat?"

The American minister tried to warn his fellow countryman by shaking his head emphatically, but Toby didn't see him, even though the diplomat was openly discouraging. Realizing only that he was being challenged, Toby rose to the bait and instantly agreed.

The dowager empress smiled coldly. "Send at once for Ch'ien Ming-lo," she ordered. "He will offer a worthy opposition to this proud visitor." She turned now to Ta-lien. "Prepare him!" she instructed.

The princess rose to her feet at once, beckoning to Toby as she backed away from the dais and toward an exit from the chamber. He followed her, remembering not to insult the empress by turning his back on the Chrysanthemum Throne.

When they reached a corridor outside the chamber, Ta-lien looked up at him and smiled as she walked rapidly along. "You may be foolhardy," she remarked, "but I admire you as a man of real courage."

Before Toby could reply, they entered a small, private room and were greeted by two middle-aged serving maids wearing the style of jacket and trousers that marked them as members of the imperial household. As they kowtowed before the princess, she addressed them rapidly in a dialect that Toby did not understand.

To his alarm, they promptly began to remove his clothing.

Ta-lien seated herself in a chair with ornately carved dragon's head arms. Preparing to enjoy a spectacle, she addressed Toby in English. "Submit gracefully to the ministrations of these serving women of the empress," she advised, smiling. "They know what they are doing, and they will soon be finished."

Toby's face felt fiery as the two women stripped him before wrapping him in a diaperlike loincloth. His distress was greater than it otherwise might have been because of the way the princess Ta-lien was enjoying herself. Finally, the maids covered him from head to toe with a thin coating of a perfumed oil that presumably would make it difficult for an opponent to grasp him in combat.

Ta-lien made no secret of her admiration for his appearance. "Regardless of what may happen," she said teasingly, "you do have a handsome body—I hope it does not become disfigured." Standing, she moved to the door and motioned for him to join her to walk back to the audience chamber.

As they reentered the chamber to the accompaniment of an expectant murmur, Toby saw an awesome-looking man. Clad also in a loincloth, the giant was almost a full head taller than Toby, and he seemed to weigh as much as three hundred pounds. He was thick-necked and barrel-chested. His hands, arms, and legs exuded power. His massive weight clearly was concentrated in muscle without a pound of fat. Ch'ien Ming-lo, the gladiator the empress called the "champion of champions," seemed powerful enough to break an ordinary person in two.

Toby was confident he was in prime condition, and thanks to the many hours of tutelage he had received in practice with Commander Sterling, he was thoroughly familiar with the martial arts of the Orient. But whether or not he would be a match for this gigantic opponent was a question he hardly dared ask himself. In any event, although the contest made no sense, he had left himself with no alternative but to go ahead. He was obliged to fight China's champion for the pleasure the spectacle would give the court as it awaited the foreigner's downfall, humiliation, and possible destruction.

The empress very evidently was prepared to enjoy herself. Her eyes gleamed, and she smiled in anticipation. Princess Ta-lien, although less obvious than the empress, also seemed ready to enjoy the contest. Spots of color appeared in her cheeks, and her eyes looked feverish. A holiday atmosphere, in fact, permeated the entire court. Only Simon McClellan looked out of sorts and pessimistic, resigned to the inevitability of the forthcoming match.

Toby was briefly reminded of what he remembered reading about gladiatorial contests in ancient Rome. At the very least, he understood how the gladiators must have felt. Wrenching his mind back to the present, he stepped up onto a quilted mat that had been spread out for this combat and that covered the better part of the open floor in front of the dais. He studied his opponent intently.

Ming-lo stood unmoving, his heavy arms folded across his bare chest as he stared with expressionless eyes at his opponent. It was impossible for Toby to gather what he might be thinking; he offered no air of either hostility or softness and amiability.

Without intending it, Toby couldn't help smiling at him. The giant's face remained wooden; his expression did not change in the slightest.

General Lin explained the terms of the combat. No holds were barred, no tricks forbidden. He raised an arm and called for the combat to begin.

The spectators, exhibiting both civilized and barbaric behavior by Western standards, cheered, stamped their feet, and whistled. Toby was determined to block them from his consciousness as he concentrated on this most dangerous of foes in a contest the likes of which he had never experienced.

With surprising speed and agility, Ming-lo lunged. Toby managed to twist out of harm's way just in time. As the heavyset Chinese hurtled past, Toby reached out one foot and tripped him. Ming-lo crashed to the mat.

Throwing himself onto the giant with all his strength, Toby was able to push him over onto his back and grasp his shoulders, intending to pin him to the mat.

But Ming-lo, far from beaten, used his powerful arms to envelop Toby in a bear hug. Slowly he began to squeeze the breath out of his opponent. His lips were close to Toby's ear. *Am I dreaming?* Toby thought, when he heard Ming-lo speaking in a dialect so close to Mandarin that he was able to understand almost every word.

"I have been ordered by the dowager empress herself to defeat the white devil," Ming-lo was whispering. "But I want you to know that I carry no grudge and I wish you no harm. I heard of your skill with the throwing hatchet and with the little musket, and I envy your great talents."

"I wish you no harm, either," Toby replied. "I can best explain my feelings toward you by illustrating them." He grasped the man's burly shoulders and went through the motions of trying to pin them to the mat. He actually exerted too little pressure, and his attempts failed.

A hint of a smile appeared at the corners of Ming-lo's oversized mouth. "This is far better," he said in his low voice, "than a fight in which one of us dies."

Toby was quick to agree. "Yes, life is usually better than death."

"I will regain the lead for a time now. I will knock you to one side with a fierce blow to the head." Ming-lo raised one hand and, swiping Toby across the head in a move reminiscent of a bear's angry gesture, caught him on the head. Toby pretended to be staggered, fell to the mat, and Ming-lo promptly pounced on him. Belatedly, it occurred to Toby that perhaps his foe was trying to trick him.

As if reading his mind, Ming-lo shook his head and

said softly, "Have no fear, my friend. I have given my word to you that I would feign the battle, and that is what I shall do. I expect the same from you in return."

For the next quarter of an hour they engaged in a mock fight that left the onlookers exhausted. Ostensibly beating at each other unmercifully, they knocked one another about, using one wrestling hold after another as, in turn, they repeatedly almost achieved the victory that invariably eluded them. At last, their theatrics exhausted them both. "I have had enough of this," Ming-lo muttered, drenched in perspiration and breathing hard. "Let us call an end to our 'battle.'"

So weary that he had to call on all his remaining strength in order to stand upright, Toby said, "Agreed. Enough is enough."

They stood side by side facing the empress. Ch'ien Ming-lo was the first to speak. "Your Majesty," he said with difficulty, "with great regret I must tell you the duel of skills must end in a draw. I lack the strength and skill to defeat the white devil. His ability is as great as mine, our cunning is equal."

"Ming-lo and I are well matched, Your Majesty," Toby added. "We both tried our utmost, yet victory has eluded his grasp, as well as mine. We stand here as equals in your sight."

Though the outcome might have represented a loss of face for the dowager empress, she was far too clever and immediately turned the indecisive battle to her own advantage. "Both of you are truly fighting men beyond compare," she announced. "Colonel Holt, having decided to accept the offer of President Grant, I now further appoint you as head of the force that will undertake that responsibility."

"May I ask one favor in return, Your Majesty?"

The empress, surprised, tilted her head questioningly.

"I request that you please designate Ch'ien Ming-lo as my deputy to assist in my efforts to successfully carry out your wishes and those of the President of the United States."

The empress agreed, and the assemblage erupted in a storm of fresh applause.

Ming-lo kowtowed before the empress, Toby bowed to her, and together they backed out of the chamber. When they reached the corridor, the Chinese said softly, "After a fight such as we allegedly had, we are privileged to swim in the imperial lake. Come." He led the way to a good-sized ornamental lake. At one end was a large, black pagoda with a scarlet roof. Partially submerged in the water was a huge stone sculpture, a barge rowed by forty oarsmen.

He and the giant dove into the lake's cool water and rinsed off the remains of the oil from their bodies. When they were thoroughly refreshed, they swam back to shore. A servant handed each of them an enormous towel. Wrapping the towels around themselves, they went to an auxiliary building behind the pagoda and there found clothes laid out for them. Toby was surprised to see, instead of his own clothing, silken trousers and jacket. He was pleased to find a new Colt repeating pistol, loaded and in its holster, beside the clothing. Ming-lo had a huge curved sword with a double-edged blade, resembling a Turkish scimitar, which he promptly buckled around his girth.

When they were dressed and ready to return to the palace, they exchanged quick, intimate smiles. "You are responsible," Ming-lo said, "for winning me the post of your assistant in the campaign against the tongs. I swear that I will be faithful to the trust you show in me."

"You already have demonstrated your friendship, as I have in return," Toby replied.

"We must be strong and vigilant and wise," the Chinese continued. "I know an old story that my people often tell of the many-headed dragon that lived in the mountains beyond Chungking and defied all efforts to kill it. Brave warriors were summoned from every part of the empire. But no matter how hard they tried, the dragon flourished. Why? Why should this be so?" He lowered his voice dramatically. "Whenever a warrior tried to cut off one head, the others rallied to its defense, and the warrior was defeated. The dragon continued to flourish and do evil until finally, one clever warrior caused the heads to quarrel and fight among themselves so that he could conquer them all. The empire was saved. So it is with the tongs that spread fear through our land. Only if you and I are vigilant can we cut off all its heads and save the people of this mighty land."

Touched by his new friend's story of the dragon, Toby stretched enough to place an arm over his shoulders. "All we can do," he declared, "is our very best. We will do no less!"

VII

Painfully aware of her seminude, provocative appearance, Millicent became seriously concerned for her safety when she heard a tap at the door. Hoping that whoever was outside had made a mistake and had approached the wrong room, she reluctantly went to the door, moved the bolt, and opened it a crack.

To her consternation, a young man pushed it wide open with such force that he knocked her aside as he burst in. He closed and bolted the door in a single, swift motion. Then he stepped close to her and began to murmur in her ear.

"Don't be afraid," he told her. "I mean you no harm. I work for Domino, the sworn enemy of Kellerman. Domino knows who you are and means to save you. Your safety comes first, even ahead of our capturing Kellerman, which we intend to do."

She refused to be reassured and tried to squirm from his grasp.

Eddie Neff remembered what Martha had told him before he had started out. "Domino," he whispered, "is a friend of Toby Holt's."

Millicent stopped struggling. "Toby is a party to your plan?" she asked.

"Not exactly," Eddie admitted, "but that's only because he is not in New Orleans at the moment. He's very close to Domino, my boss. If he were here, he'd join in the party to rescue you. Now please cooperate, in your own interests!"

"What can I do?" Millicent asked. Her panic was subsiding gradually, in part because the man was not trying to take any advantage of her, as he easily could have done.

"In one way or another," he said, "when Kellerman returns, try to distract him—get him so involved that he neglects to take precautions. If necessary, entice him into making love to you. Most important of all," he went on before she could respond, "is that Kellerman be separated from his weapons. If at all possible, work it so that he'll leave them on one side of the room while you and he are on the other side. In that way, he'll be all but helpless when we move in."

Sheer astonishment was etched on her face.

"Don't worry," Eddie assured her. "You won't need to actually go through with any lovemaking. We'll have a very close watch on Kellerman, beginning the very moment he enters this room. As soon as you've succeeded in separating him from his weapons, we'll strike. He once found you irresistible, I understand, and no doubt he still is strongly attracted to you. You should have a safe and fairly easy session with him. I give you my word that your ordeal will be brief and that we'll end it quickly and decisively."

Millicent's doubts crystallized in a single question: "How do I know I can trust you?"

"You don't," he answered. "But please have faith in us, and you soon will be safe, and Kellerman will be taken care of, too—in another way."

Millicent hoped that his advice was sound, because if she were to escape from Karl, she had to put her trust in the man called Domino and in his associates.

Holding her at arm's length, Eddie examined her critically. "You look," he remarked, smiling, "like a frightened little girl dressed up for a wicked masquerade. I'm sure you can do better." Letting his arms fall, he quickly went to the door. "Good luck," he told her as he disappeared. "We'll meet again shortly."

Millicent, now alone, saw her reflection in a mirror above the bureau and laughed nervously. The man's description was distressingly accurate.

Recalling vividly what Kellerman had liked in their previous life together, she went into the bathroom and began to apply additional kohl, rouge, and other cosmetics, using a liberal hand. By the time she had finished she bore even less resemblance to a proper young matron who graced New Orleans society.

As she heard a key turning in the lock, she returned to the bedroom and posed seductively on the chaise longue. Placing her hands behind her, she leaned back against her arms and stretched her long legs before her.

When Kellerman came into the room, he was so astonished he forgot to bolt the door behind him. "Well!" he exclaimed huskily. "Damned if you don't look like the Millicent I knew."

Her alluring smile was steady, unwavering. Never one to reflect at length on unexpected good fortune, Kellerman wasted no time now. Instead, he walked to the bureau, picked up his bottle of whiskey, and poured liberal quantities into two glasses. Handing one to Millicent, he chuckled as he leaned against a wall near her. "Everything is working out exactly as I planned it," he announced smugly. "By now, your husband has received my ransom demand."

"How much are you asking for me?" she inquired archly.

"Fifty thousand," he told her curtly.

She laughed in pretended relief. "Oh, that will be just fine," she said with an effort at lightness. "He'll pay fifty without a murmur." She paused, seemingly lost in thought. "You know," she said softly, "no law says I've got to return as soon as Jean-Pierre pays up."

Kellerman became rigid, his eyes narrowing. "What do you mean?"

"You and I," she said in little more than a confidential whisper, "could go somewhere—together—and with fifty thousand dollars, make a fresh start."

Kellerman appeared doubtful. "Are you serious?"

"I've never been more in earnest in my life," she told him. "Jean-Pierre is a sweet boy, but you—well, you're a man, Karl. And I'm afraid you spoiled me for anyone else." She sighed convincingly, then extended her arms and beckoned to him.

Kellerman was unable to resist her appeal. He went to her, pulled her to him, and kissed her long and hard.

At last, Millicent was able to avert her face slightly. Lowering her thick lashes, she murmured, "Your pistol. It's pressing into me. It hurts me."

Cursing impatiently under his breath, he unbuckled his holster. He removed it and its pistol and placed them on the bureau. Then, kissing her again, he lifted her off her feet and carried her across the room to the bed.

Millicent hoped desperately that her rescuers were as alert as promised and were ready to intervene. Previous experience with Kellerman made her certain he was thoroughly aroused already and would pull off her corselet within seconds and promptly take her.

He dropped her on the bed; within a moment his large hands were fondling and caressing her half-nude body.

Millicent used all her self-control to keep from crying out and rolling away from his groping, insistent hands. All too conscious of the crudeness of his touch, she began to experience an old nightmare once again. She thought she had buried it for all time, but it came alive now and threatened to overwhelm her, leaving her sickened and spent.

What can be delaying Domino's men? she wondered, totally panicked. Cringing, sickened by the enforced intimacy, she became increasingly frantic. Suddenly, at the exact moment when she knew within her that she was able to tolerate no more, the door burst open. Five of Domino's men poured into the room.

Kellerman, cut off from access to his weapon, was enraged, but his mind continued to function clearly. He had no intention of wasting a second trying to guess the identity of his enemies. Leaping to his feet, he dragged Millicent upright and held her by the arms in a grip of iron. "You filthy bitch!" he muttered. "You did this! You double-crossed me!" He seized her and shoved her violently in the way of the intruders, who were crowding toward him.

In the same motion, he turned and leaped out the window into the soft soil of a garden below.

Eddie Neff reacted quickly. "Joe! Don!" he called. "Follow him out the window and stop him, if you can, before he gets away through the garden. Bill! Charlie! Head through the dining room downstairs, into the garden, and try to prevent him from doubling back! I'll be here with Millicent."

His four companions obeyed at once, and the chase was on.

Eddie turned to speak to Millicent but was shocked to discover that she was unconscious on the floor a few paces from him. A bruise was swelling near her right temple. When Kellerman had shoved her, she had stumbled and fallen, hitting her head hard against the wall.

Eddie tried to revive her but to no avail. He decided that all he could do would be to take her to Domino's house as soon as his companions returned from trying to capture Kellerman.

A quarter of an hour passed, and Millicent appeared to be sleeping deeply on the bed, where Eddie had placed her. When the other four members of Domino's team returned, they were crestfallen. "That Kellerman is as slippery as a sewer rat," one reported angrily. "He vanishes, slick as you please, and he doesn't leave a trace. He's gone, and no matter how we may search, he's going to stay gone."

"Domino will decide what's to be done," Eddie said. "He'll have to take charge of this poor woman, too. We'd better take her to him while she's still breathing." He was not so distracted by her condition, however, that he neglected to search for Kellerman's money and remove it—almost twenty-five thousand dollars as it turned out, when it was counted later in Domino's headquarters.

Simon McClellan was waiting at the entrance to the royal palace when Toby and Ming-lo returned from their swim. He grinned when he saw Toby wearing the yellow garment. To Ming-lo he courteously extended an invitation to visit the legation with him and Toby. As they walked across the manicured lawns of the Forbidden City, he brought Toby up to date. "As you saw, Holt," he said, "the empress is very sour on all foreigners. Many of my colleagues in the diplomatic corps believe that she has a phobia on the subject, and I'm inclined to believe they're right. But you turned her upside down today. The exhibition with the tomahawks and the pistol stunned her. And your combat with Ming-lo finished her off."

Toby smiled in appreciation but made no reply.

"Now," McClellan went on, "you're about to receive an unprecedented honor. At least, I've never heard of anything like it. You are to be the principal guest at an imperial banquet. Many of the country's renowned men—generals, scholars, cultural leaders—are to gather at the palace to meet you. At this moment, an epic poem is being composed extolling your virtues. The company of royal dancers is commemorating your accomplishments by committing them to a special dance. All this you will see and hear at the banquet."

Toby's laugh was forced. "When is this function to be held?" he asked. "I must say I wish I didn't have to go."

McClellan looked at him in surprise, shaking his head. "This very night! When the empress is enthusiastic, she wastes no time. The diplomatic corps will be present to a

135

man, in full dress. By the way, I hope you brought evening clothes?"

"No, indeed," Toby answered. "And since the empress gave me this outfit, I expect I'm going to be stuck with it. For now, Ming-lo and I have some things to do while you and Mrs. McClellan get ready for the evening."

"What kind of things?"

Toby's face relaxed. "We have a great deal of work ahead of us. For one thing, I must teach Ming-lo how to handle firearms."

When they reached the legation, Toby and Ming-lo retreated to the garden behind it. Toby drew his pistol. "By the time we're through, my friend," he said, presenting it to him, "you'll be the best shot in all China."

Ming-lo proved an apt pupil. In the short time before sundown, they fired an entire box of ammunition. By the end of the lesson, Ming-lo had gained a creditable proficiency as a marksman. He promised to teach Toby the subtleties of using his scimitarlike sword.

When the time arrived to return to the palace for the banquet, Toby and Ming-lo were required to ride with McClellan and his pretty wife in a padded carriage of state.

Several servants were waiting, and they promptly whisked Toby off to the long chamber in which the banquet would be held. There he bowed to the empress, who wore a dazzling diamond and jade necklace, and greeted Princess Ta-lien. The empress instructed him to stand on her left, with Ta-lien between them, as guests lined up to be presented to this new royal favorite.

Of the women who stepped forward, many hobbled on tiny feet, and Ta-lien explained in an undertone that they came from families that bound the feet of girl babies in order to hamper their growth, an ancient practice gradually being abandoned, especially in sections of the country in contact with Westerners.

By far the best dressed of the Chinese were the imperial viceroys. Their silken capes were trimmed in ermine, with diamonds, emeralds, rubies, sapphires, and pearls sewn to the fabric.

Like all the other Chinese officials present, even the highest-ranking viceroys kowtowed before the dowager empress, touching their foreheads to the floor as required. Only the small diplomatic corps was exempted from this practice. Minister McClellan had explained that the nations of the West had won this right.

The ceremonies seemed interminable to Toby, but at last even the dowager empress grew weary of the pageantry. Clapping her hands sharply three times, she marched to a long table facing the assemblage and took a seat at the right end. Virtually everyone else present seemed to know his or her proper place and went to it. Toby was guided by Ta-lien, who took him by the arm and led him to the far left end of the head table. As they seated themselves, he saw that he was the only foreigner at the table.

From his vantage point he looked out and discovered that practically everyone in the dining hall seemed to be covertly studying him. These upper-class Chinese were so polite, however, that they refused to meet his gaze and averted their eyes whenever they realized he was looking toward them.

The banquet began with whole carp sizzling on a pewter platter. Ta-lien told him the heads were considered a great delicacy. A series of other dishes followed, most consisting of bite-sized chunks of beef, pork, chicken, and shellfish, each accompanied by sauces and chopped vegetables unfamiliar to Toby. He couldn't be sure of what he was eating much of the time, but each dish seemed to be more delicious than those that had preceded it.

Ta-lien undertook to teach him to use chopsticks, and after practicing for some minutes, he became rather adept at the art. There was no single right or wrong way to manipulate chopsticks, the princess told him. Every individual used a technique that seemed the most comfortable and the easiest.

Toby's thoughts went quickly to Clarissa and his lighthearted promise to teach her how to use chopsticks effectively. He forced himself to concentrate on the banquet.

Bowls of a rare Chinese specialty, bird's nest soup, ended the meal, after which small silver cups were placed in front of each diner.

"We now are to have toasts," Ta-lien told him. "We drink them in *mao-t'ai*, a liquor distilled from millet and wheat."

The empress offered the first toast to Toby Holt, so he was spared the need to touch the drink of *mao-t'ai* in front of him.

After Ta-lien pointedly whispered that he was expected to return the compliment, he offered a standing toast to the dowager empress, speaking out clearly in understandable Mandarin. He raised his glass to his lips and immediately felt as though he were strangling. Everyone else was sitting again after the toasts and paying no attention, so only the princess was aware of Toby's extreme discomfort.

"I'm sorry," she murmured. "I should have warned you that *mao-t'ai* is very potent. You will be expected to drink much of it this evening." She clapped her hands once sharply to summon a servant, and in a moment Toby was given a cup of tea, which he sipped gratefully. Thereafter, as successive toasts were offered, he confined himself to tiny swallows of the strong liquor, followed by the soothing tea, as needed.

"Thanks to you," he told Ta-lien, "I have survived intact the drinking of toasts."

Much to his surprise, her leg pressed against his beneath the dining table. Her gesture was as intimate as it was unexpected. Not sure of what to do, Toby pretended that nothing out of the ordinary was taking place. Eventually Ta-lien drew back, making no effort to conceal her irritation at his lack of response.

His attention was diverted when two men and a woman, dressed in chrysanthemum-yellow garb, came forward and took turns reading a long poem in free verse that extolled the virtues of the empress, the greatness of China, and, incidentally, the good deeds that the young stranger from America would do for the country. Toby found that the recitation exceeded his grasp of Mandarin.

As the reading went on, a team of dancers appeared, their faces painted chalk-white, their costumes representing dragons and other mythical beasts. The dances they performed to the rhythm of the poem were stylized, stiff, and strangely formal. Toby, keenly aware of his ignorance of Chinese culture, failed to understand the dance, but he nevertheless applauded heartily when it was finished; in a sense, the dancers had dedicated their night's efforts to him.

The readers of poetry and the dancers were succeeded by a group of gorgeously costumed singers, who were accompanied by musicians playing flutelike instruments, guitars, and cymbals.

Together they staged an excerpt from a Chinese opera. Toby was bored and bewildered by its seemingly tuneless music.

He began to feel depressed by the thought of how very far from home he was, far from customs that he knew and ways of life he understood. He was alone among strangers at the far side of the earth, saddled with an almost impossible mission that he did not know how he was going to fulfill.

Noticing Ming-lo seated at a table, Toby thought how he and his partner faced overwhelming odds in their coming struggle against the tong. The leaders of the criminal band undoubtedly were clever, highly intelligent people. What chance did a Chinese strongman and a total stranger to China and her ways have against them?

Flattering as it was to be honored at a banquet given by the empress, Toby knew that, in the long run, only results mattered. Searching for phantoms, he had no way of knowing when one might appear. Considering a place to start his mission, he decided to gather all the information he could from Simon McClellan, unlikely as it was that the diplomat could provide much information on the tong's operations. Perhaps he could approach Ta-lien for help; she had made it clear that she sympathized with him, although again the extent of actual assistance was doubtful. It was possible, however, that through her he might meet people victimized by the tong, who would be willing to offer information that could lead to the heart of the problem. At least, such an effort seemed worth a try.

Martha had her hands full with Jean-Pierre Gautier in the living room of Domino's quiet home. Increasingly frantic, he paced the room, pausing every minute or two to pull his watch from a waistcoat pocket and consult it. Occasionally he took a sip from a drink that Martha had given him. He lighted a cigar, puffed absently, then snuffed it out. Martha abandoned her attempts to calm him. Impervious to her charm, he did not hear her when she tried to talk to him sensibly, and she eventually stopped trying. Maintaining surface calm, she sat and watched him pace, quietly hoping that their travail soon would end.

The door opened, and Domino came in, looking, as always, as complacent and confident as a highly successful businessman. Jean-Pierre immediately began to shout. "Where is my wife? You said she would be returned to me here, but time goes on and on and on, and there's no sign of her!"

Domino exchanged a quick glance with Martha, whose expression confirmed the young husband's unstable condition.

"Some of my men should be arriving with her at any moment now," Domino said soothingly. "They never have failed me on a mission, and Eddie Neff, who is in charge, is especially reliable. I'm sure your wife is safe, in good hands, and on her way here."

"Where did they find her?" Jean-Pierre demanded.

Unwilling to tell him in his upset condition that Millicent had been secreted in a bordello, Domino replied smoothly, "As I'm sure Martha has told you, Kellerman hid her away in a house near the French district. Obviously you can dismiss from your mind the thought of paying his absurd ransom demand. You won't have to pay a penny."

"That's good," Jean-Pierre said tersely. "But I won't be really satisfied until I see him behind bars."

"Or dead, perhaps," Domino amended diplomatically.

He had no intention of revealing that his men expected to kill Kellerman rather than turn him over to the authorities.

Martha quietly poured Domino a drink and topped the contents of Jean-Pierre's glass. Suddenly she raised her head. "I think I hear a carriage pulling into the courtyard!"

All three ran into the adjoining dining room and hurried through the french doors to the courtyard. A large carriage was just pulling to a halt. Eddie Neff was the first to descend. "Kellerman got away again, damn his soul!" he called. "He jumped down into the garden and was gone by the time we could follow. Easy with the lady there, fellas!"

Jean-Pierre gasped.

Domino immediately took charge, fighting off his own rage. "What happened to her, Eddie?"

"Kellerman banged her head on the wall while he was escaping."

"Take her to the guest bedroom on the second floor—down the corridor from Martha's room," Domino instructed. "Eddie, run to Dr. Gregg's house and get him here in one almighty hurry!"

Martha led the way up to the second floor, with the man who was carrying Millicent close behind her. Jean-Pierre, ashen-faced, and Domino brought up the rear. He could not take his eyes from his unconscious wife in her provocative costume and heavy makeup. The thought flashed through his mind that his parents must never know of this dreadful occurrence. He was relieved beyond words that he had not turned to them earlier in his distress.

"Everybody out now!" Martha ordered. "Except you, Jean-Pierre. You stay with me—and Millicent."

Domino and the other man obediently left. Jean-

Pierre stood at the foot of the bed gaping at his wife. "My God!" he muttered. "She looks like a—a trollop!"

His naivete annoyed Martha. "You of all people should know she's not!" she exclaimed. "Can't you see that Kellerman dressed her this way to keep her cowed and helpless? Use your head! Now put any evil thoughts out of your mind and help me!" With his assistance, she removed the offensive clothing from Millicent's body and dressed her in a nightgown.

In the meantime, a maid had brought a basin of warm water and a container of soft, perfumed soap. Using a washcloth, Martha gently removed the heavy layers of cosmetics from Millicent's face.

"Now she looks better," Martha said at last.

"At least," Jean-Pierre agreed, "she does look more like herself. It's really her condition that worries me."

A short time later, Doctor Hilary Gregg hurriedly arrived and was conducted straight to the patient. One of the city's leading physicians, who long had numbered Jean-Pierre's parents among his patients, he also was clearly on familiar terms with the notorious gang leader.

After shooing Martha and Jean-Pierre from the bedchamber, Doctor Gregg examined Millicent thoroughly. At last, he walked downstairs to join the waiting group in the living room.

"Mrs. Gautier appears to have had a nasty experience," the doctor reported soberly. "She seems to have suffered a concussion. She responds, I am glad to say, to various tests, so I can say that her reflexes are normal. As for when she can be expected to regain consciousness, I am not yet ready to state."

"But she will be all right?" Jean-Pierre asked eagerly.

"I wish I could give you a satisfactory answer to that

question," the physician replied wearily. "Her recovery depends first and foremost on her getting complete rest and quiet for a considerable period of time. She can't possibly be moved again. It is regrettable that she had to be disturbed by being brought here. I can see that it was necessary, but it was done at great risk to her well-being."

Jean-Pierre was severely disappointed. "You mean I can't take her home?"

"That's exactly what I mean. Do I assume correctly that it will be no hardship, Domino, to keep the young lady here?"

"No hardship at all," was the immediate reply. "We shall be delighted to cooperate in every possible way."

"Good! See to it that she remains quiet. Jean-Pierre, say nothing and do nothing to get her unnecessarily excited. I have no way of predicting whether she will be lucid or out of her mind when she wakes up. If she's lucid, there's no guarantee that she will remain that way. We may find that she slips back and forth between reality and a dreamworld. That occurs frequently in cases like this. If she does slip in and out, it's no cause for alarm. She should stabilize, and with the proper care and treatment, she'll ultimately be her old self again."

"Thank you, Dr. Gregg," Jean-Pierre said, looking dazed. Then he added to Domino, "And I'm grateful to you, sir, for your hospitality. I just wish I could repay you in some way."

"The only way," Domino told him, "is to restore your wife to good health."

"I'll come by every day and check on her progress. You could help by keeping note of the changes as they occur," Dr. Gregg said as he shook hands all around. "If there's anything you think she needs or any questions that you may want answered, I'll always be available."

As soon as the physician departed, Jean-Pierre returned to take up a vigil beside his wife's bed.

"He has a tough row to hoe, Martha, much tougher than he realizes," Domino said in a voice lower than usual. "If you will, stand by him and offer him help whenever he needs it."

"I will," she assured him quietly. "You know you can count on me."

"In the meantime," he added, "I'm going to turn the whole organization loose in a hunt for Kellerman. He's eluded us once too often. This time when I get him, I'm going to really nail him to the wall!"

Dawn was breaking over the Mississippi, and daylight seeped through the blinds into Millicent's sickroom. She stirred for the first time. As she surveyed the strange room in surprise, she saw the figure of a man sprawled in a chair beside her bed. Her vision was blurred, and it was too dark for her to recognize Jean-Pierre.

"Karl?" she asked tentatively.

Jean-Pierre struggled to sit upright and managed to open his eyes.

"I know you, Karl," she said. "You can't fool me by remaining silent. Are you going to set me free, or must I go to bed with you first?" Suddenly she laughed. "Oh, yes! I'm wise to you! I know you, Karl—better than you know yourself. And I realize you dressed me up like this because you're anxious to take me again. In all the months we lived together, you went to bed with me dozens of times, but you never had your fill of me. You told me again and again how badly you wanted me. I thought you were just talking, but I know better now, Karl. I know you really do want me, so I'm willing to strike a bargain with you. Take me and do as you please with me!"

Millicent flung out her arms dramatically. "That's my half of the bargain. Your half is that once you've had me and are satisfied, you will let me go, and I'll be free to rejoin my husband."

Jean-Pierre, horrified, tried to speak, but the words caught in his throat, and he was unable to utter a coherent sound. If he had been less upset and startled, he might have realized that she was indulging in a bit of playacting for the benefit of the man she believed was Kellerman. But instead he accepted every word literally, and his horror increased as she went on.

"You're the best lover I've ever had, Karl." Her voice was reduced to a husky, seductive whisper now. "Poor little Jean-Pierre is so young, so inexperienced. He's simply not in your class, Karl. You can't know how I've missed you in all these months that we've been separated. So take me now—quickly—before you set me free!"

Jean-Pierre could tolerate no more. The thought of his lovely young bride being manhandled and being the object of Kellerman's lovemaking was bad enough, but hearing Millicent denigrating his own lovemaking was enough to make him feel ill. He was aware of the dangers of exciting or upsetting her, but he could not control himself any longer. Too many questions crowded into his mind, and he wanted answers. "I have the right to know the answers to some questions," he said stridently. "It's your duty to me as your husband to answer me truthfully. How did you get together with Kellerman in the first place? How did you happen to be wearing a trollop's clothes? Surely Kellerman didn't hold a gun to you and force you to dress for him. What happened that you willingly took the part of a trollop for him? And what did you do once you were dressed up? Did you go to bed with him? What happened between you?" He was so overwrought that he had no idea he was shouting.

Millicent frowned as she stared at him, her eyes round with wonder. Apparently she had been mistaken. This man was not Kellerman after all. In fact, he bore a remarkable resemblance to Jean-Pierre. Actually, he sounded like Jean-Pierre. Finally, the truth dawned on her, and she began to weep. He *was* Jean-Pierre!

Her tears became heavier, and gradually she became hysterical, sobbing loudly. Her husband was horrified by what he had done and tried to undo the damage, but it was too late. She was incapable of listening to his stammered apologies, and she didn't hear him when he tried to offer her a lame explanation. Her sobbing grew louder, tearing Jean-Pierre apart. He tried desperately to shut out the sound but could not.

Finally, her hysteria wore itself out, and her tears subsided. Leaning back against the pillows, she closed her eyes and soon drifted off to sleep. Jean-Pierre could only stare in numb confusion.

An hour later, when Martha came into the room, she found him red-eyed and haggard, still looking intently at his wife, who was sleeping peacefully.

Martha needed all her skill and tact to find out what had happened. When she finally heard what Millicent had said and how Jean-Pierre had reacted, she realized the seriousness of the situation.

Tightening the sash that held her silken dressing gown closed, she said lightly, "I don't see the problem that you're creating for yourself. What's important is that Millicent woke up and actually spoke. Judging by what the doctor said, it isn't important that she's not yet in her right mind, that she temporarily assumed you were Kellerman. Naturally you reacted strongly to that idea, which upset her, but I'm sure no permanent harm was done. The next time she wakes up, or perhaps the time after that, she undoubtedly will be herself again, and you can put everything right."

A sympathetic smile touched the corners of her mouth. "Come downstairs with me and have some coffee," she urged. "You've been on guard all night, and you certainly could stand something to bolster you. Then I'll take over here, and you are to get some rest."

Reluctantly Jean-Pierre joined her. She took his arm as they started down the stairs together. "Your trouble," she remarked, "is that you don't understand women. Just put yourself in Millicent's place. Kellerman had abducted her and was holding her for ransom after forcing her to dress like a prostitute. She was thoroughly familiar with the man, unfortunately, and understood his greatest weakness, his vanity. So she was trying to play up to that weakness by flattery, which she hoped would get her out of his hands. You can rest assured she didn't mean a word of what she was saying. When she tore you down and built Kellerman up, her one desire was to protect herself."

They reached the dining room, and Jean-Pierre held Martha's chair for her as she seated herself at the table. She wanted only grapefruit and coffee, but when a maid came into the dining room, Martha insisted that Jean-Pierre eat a full breakfast of scrambled eggs, ham, buttered biscuits, and hash-browned potatoes.

When they were alone again, he sighed. "You are very kind," he murmured, "but I can't quite believe you.

I'll grant you that Millicent was out of her mind. I'm sorry, too, that I let myself get so upset with her, while she's in a weakened condition. But if you'd been there and heard the ring of sincerity in her voice, you would have to believe that she meant every word she said against me. She actually does prefer that monster to me, her husband." His distress was growing, and his voice broke.

Martha recognized that nothing she might say would convince Jean-Pierre that his conclusion was wrong. Therefore, she abandoned her efforts and instead engaged him in small talk. To open his eyes to what she herself saw as the truth, she knew she must speak some other way.

Jean-Pierre ate mechanically, scarcely tasting the food. He briefly answered her comments, hardly seeming to hear a word she said. His gloom was all-pervading, and Martha could see it was about to submerge him into suicidal panic.

After breakfast they climbed the stairs together, and Martha guided Jean-Pierre to a room opposite the chamber in which Millicent was sleeping. "I owe you an apology," she said lightly. "We were so concerned about your wife last night that we completely forgot about providing you with a suitable room. Here it is, and you will share my bathroom, if you don't mind. My chamber is on the other side of it. You will find a razor and shaving soap, I believe. And we have one of the new bathtubs that you can fill with hot water just by turning on the faucet. Do help yourself."

Alone in the bathroom, he shaved and then enjoyed the luxury of bathing simply by twisting the tap and filling the tub with water. It was the first time he had ever used such newfangled equipment, and he knew that Domino must be very rich if he could afford to install such a tub in his house.

Clad in an oversized towel, which he wrapped around his middle, Jean-Pierre returned to his bedroom. There he stopped short.

Seated in the room's easy chair was Martha, still wearing her dressing gown, her face freshly made up and her shining red hair tumbling down her shoulders.

She smiled at him. "Are your spirits improved?"

"Not really," he said, forcing a wan smile of his own. "I still feel as though Millicent has kicked me in the teeth."

"I've had time to give more thought to your dilemma," she told him, "and I now realize that nothing I can say will change your mind."

"I'm afraid not," he replied, lowering his gaze.

"Perhaps," she said, "I can do something, however, to change your perspective." Giving him no chance to respond, she deftly removed her dressing gown in a single movement and revealed herself, stark naked. Catching hold of one end of the towel wrapped around his waist, she unwound it swiftly, so that he, too, was nude.

"We're going to find out whether Millicent was exaggerating for Kellerman's sake, as I believe, or whether you really are a failure as a lover, as you think she accused you of being. Make love to me! Now!" she commanded, curling her arms around his neck.

He was too startled to reply in words, but her nearness spurred him, and his reaction was purely physical. Placing his arms around her slender waist, he drew her to him, and they kissed. Martha's lips parted, and from the onset, he took the lead in their lovemaking. Before Jean-Pierre quite realized what was happening, their bodies were pressing close together. The next thing he knew, they were side by side on the bed.

From the beginning, Martha simulated a greater passion than she felt: moaning and squirming, crying out in delight and acting as though her self-control was slipping. She went through the motions of achieving a climax with the same breathless show of sincerity. Her performance was so smooth that Jean-Pierre had no idea she was pretending.

After they simmered down, Martha kissed him and then murmured casually but distinctly enough so that he wouldn't miss a single word, "That was wonderful! And how much better you must be with Millicent, whom you really love. I envy her!"

Jean-Pierre tried to shrug off her compliment, but Martha persisted. "Don't ever let me hear again that you're inadequate," she admonished. "I suspected I was right when I learned that Millicent, in her confusion, thought you were Kellerman. I was convinced that she was merely acting in order to protect herself. Now that I've known your lovemaking, I am sure beyond any question that I'm right. Dismiss from your mind the little incident that took place earlier, and just be glad your wife's condition is improving."

Jean-Pierre felt greatly in her debt for having used the simplest, most direct means of persuading him that his perception of Millicent's behavior was wrong. "How can I ever thank you?" he asked. Only later did he begin to feel embarrassed as he considered how easily he had played Millicent false, regardless of his motivation.

Martha climbed out of bed and slipped into her dressing gown. "I want no thanks," she told him. "Just be courageous and exercise patience in dealing with her problem. Above all, show sympathy and understanding for the suffering she has undergone. Do those kind things, and I shall be amply repaid."

Smiling, she left the room, giving Jean-Pierre a wink and an intimate smile.

Before he dropped off to sleep, Jean-Pierre marveled that Martha, who clearly was closely associated with Domino, had unhesitatingly sacrificed her own virtue for his sake and Millicent's. Though he had no idea of Martha's actual identity, he wished her well, and he fell asleep hoping that she would gain all that she wanted out of life.

VIII

Hoping for information that would lead them to the tong, Toby and Ming-lo had waited impatiently in the headquarters that the dowager empress assigned them in the imperial palace. Now, as it became clear that nothing would happen without prodding, Toby persuaded the empress to offer suitable rewards for any useful leads. It was announced officially that pieces of carved ivory and green jade would be awarded to anyone who provided such information. Within twenty-four hours, a court eunuch in his robes of office appeared at Toby's door.

Remaining calm on the surface, Toby waved the visitor to a seat. His face revealed none of his sudden tension. Ming-lo, lounging on a window seat, made no move but was instantly alert.

Although the day was cool, the eunuch snapped open a fan with an ornately carved handle and waved it vigorously. "I want to be quite certain," he lisped, his manner imperious, "that the prize is worth my time and the risks that I would be taking."

Toby did not choose to reply in words. Instead, he opened a drawer of his ornate desk and removed a piece of pale green jade about six inches long, perhaps half as wide, and three-eighths of an inch thick. On it were carved figures of a formal garden with a stream running through it, with a handsome pagoda in the background. He handed it over to the official, who examined it eagerly. It was beautifully carved, the work of a master craftsman, and the jade itself was extremely valuable. His eyes glistened behind his spectacles, and he moistened his fat lips. "How can I be sure," he asked, "that no one will know I have given you information?"

"You'll have to take my word and that of my colleague," Toby informed him brusquely, as he nodded in the direction of Ming-lo. "I do require you to tell me, however, how you came to possess the information that you would pass on to us."

The eunuch sighed, pursed his lips, and then said reluctantly, "I hold the position of deputy commissioner in the Department of Roads. My seal is needed to authenticate travel by any party that consists of more than ten persons. The leaders of any party traveling without appropriate authority can be caged for a period of thirty to sixty days. The entire group can be fined."

Toby nodded slightly but said nothing.

"This very morning," the eunuch went on, "there crossed my desk a request for a party of pilgrims to make a journey from Peking to Tientsin for the purpose of visiting the shrine of the god of the sea. The entire group will include one hundred and seventy-five people, even as many as two hundred. Why, I asked myself, should so many residents of Peking show an interest in a god of the sea, who is worshiped in Tientsin? It makes no sense. I issued the seal that authorizes this journey, but I am convinced that most of the travelers are peasants who have no business in Tientsin. The whole thing is very suspicious."

"It does sound that way," Ming-lo said quietly. "I suspect that this really might be a party of illegal emigrants."

Toby's eyes narrowed. "You say they will leave from here for Tientsin?"

"Their permit to leave the vicinity of this city becomes effective at the sixth hour after midnight tomorrow," the official elaborated, "and may be put into use up to two days and four hours later. Further, they are permitted to spend eight days in travel, until they reach their destination."

"Do you have any additional information you can give us?"

The eunuch shook his head a trifle impatiently.

Toby took the jade from him and locked it in the desk drawer. "Return in fourteen days' time," he instructed. "If the information leads to the apprehension or dispersal of a group of migrants, you shall be paid the jade prize."

He and Ming-lo rose to their feet and exchanged deep bows with the eunuch, who departed hastily.

Sitting again, Toby glanced at his associate. "What do you think?"

Ming-lo curled a huge hand into a tight fist. "I think we are about to catch some rats," he said. "The eunuch's information can be regarded as accurate, I think, because he was fearful in coming to you. If he were peddling a story, I doubt that he would have dared come. I propose that we leave tonight and take ourselves to an appropriate place on the trail to Tientsin. There we will await the party and deal with them when they approach."

"Do we ask for assistance from the imperial army at this time?"

"I think not," his companion said after consideration. "Before the military will take us seriously, we must capture one band ourselves, unassisted. The wages of the officers are low, and the common soldiers have little beyond their uniforms and food. As a result, they are all open to bribes by the tong. Not until we confront them with a solid success will the military take us seriously."

"Very well," Toby assented. "We'll take care of this matter ourselves, even though the odds against us may be, let's say, one hundred to one."

Under their shirts, Toby and Ming-lo each wore two belts with places for twenty throwing knives. Over their shirts, they carried Colt repeating pistols with additional ammunition in their holster belts. Finally, they carried American rifles, of the latest design, manufactured by the Winchester Company.

Keeping their departure secret from everyone, they left at midnight, mounted on two large, sure-footed horses, with small packs tied behind their saddles. By morning, when they surmised the peasants were just setting out from the area near Peking, they had traveled at least twenty miles.

Ming-lo, familiar with the tong's probable route, chose a rock-infested, steeply hilly region to establish their bivouac. After tethering their horses behind massive boulders, they chose a secluded spot in which to hide their camp. There, they unrolled their blanket packs.

Ming-lo prepared a simple meal swiftly, using Chinese implements. Toby found the meal delicious. But, looking around him, he found the countryside alien and forbidding. Though now feeling more at home in China, he nevertheless experienced difficulty in acclimating himself to a region devoid of trees or even large bushes.

They began to plan for their reception of the captured peasants and the men who would be guarding them. "We have no way of knowing," Toby said, "how many armed men will be accompanying the poor devils. Armed guards don't come cheap, of course, so we can guess there won't be many of them."

"It is true, too," Ming-lo concurred, "that one man with firearms can control many who are cowed. Would you estimate as many as fifty guards accompanying the procession?"

"Frankly, I'd be astonished to see that many," Toby told him. "As a guess, I'd say between fifteen and twenty-five men."

"That is good," Ming-lo said cheerfully. "Not too many for us to handle, then."

His optimism made Toby laugh. "We'll have to see how we fare when the time comes," he replied. "One thing is sure—we have no reinforcements we can count on."

They spent the morning walking over every foot of the ground on the approach to the heights where they intended to make their stand. They examined their own position from various angles below and noted particularly the fact that they would have cover behind various boulders and rocks while their opponents would have none. Their own position would be better protected and far easier to defend than the ground the travelers would be forced to move through. They were going to be perfectly positioned. Also, they would be able to create a diversion by rolling down a boulder on the guards leading the procession, taking them out without harming the peasants. Then, when they threw their knives, they would need to be exposed for only a few seconds at a time. If many of their foes survived, they might then be in grave danger. Risks were necessary, however, with only two against many.

Selecting a boulder that they judged to be in the right spot, Toby and Ming-lo pushed against it, to see if they could move it. They were relieved to find that while it was very heavy and moving it would require all of their combined efforts, the stone could be set in motion.

While Toby swept the horizon with powerful binoculars that Commander Sterling had provided him, Ming-lo hurriedly fixed another meal. Toby found no sign of the approaching tong members and their prisoners, so he joined Ming-lo in the makeshift repast.

Every quarter of an hour, Toby or Ming-lo used the glasses to search, taking care not to let the sun shine into the lenses, which might give a warning flash to betray the ambush. Only in the late afternoon, when the sun was already beginning to set behind hills to the west, could Toby see about twenty mounted men, riding short, sturdy ponies. Dressed in black, the leader and five others fronted the group, and the rest of the guards surrounded a mass of about one hundred and fifty peasants tied together with ropes around their necks. The men were forced to move along because their captors wielded whips or long bamboo poles, to which metal tips were affixed, similar to cattle prods.

"It's so late they may stop for the night before they come this far," Toby suggested.

Ming-lo shook his head emphatically. "I think you are wrong, my friend. They are certain to come at least this far. The ground on which they are now traveling is too low to be easily defended. Those in charge will want to make their camp on the heights, where they can see enemies who may approach from any direction. They are certain to pass this place. In fact, they may have it in mind to make their camp where we are right now."

Toby's mind was racing as he revised his strategy. "I hadn't expected they'd show up this late in the day," he said. "I'd prefer not to use firearms because the gun flashes will give away our positions and show how few we are. Also, an attack that's silent—until we roll the boulder we selected—will be the most effective. I suggest we try it."

"You mean we don't touch our firearms," Ming-lo asked with a smile, "and use only throwing knives?"

"Yes, knives it will be, during the confusion created by the boulder coming down on them. If this fails, we can always use our pistols. The greatest disadvantage we'll suffer is that we'll have to allow the front riders to come relatively close so we can make sure that our rolling stone is effective and yet not hurt the peasants. That will leave us very little margin for error. During the confusion, our aim must be accurate from the moment we start throwing, or we're in extreme danger of being overwhelmed. They could ride us down and destroy us."

Ming-lo's loud grunt of disapproval revealed his reaction to such pessimistic talk. He busied himself in transferring his knife belts to the outside of his clothing.

By the time Toby and Ming-lo were ready for combat, the tong members and their bound victims were plainly visible without binoculars.

As the sun sank steadily, casting longer shadows of boulders and rocks, Toby plucked a throwing knife from his belt, tested it with his thumb, and smiled. This was the hour of day when, according to Chinese superstition, ghosts of the departed, particularly evil spirits, were set free to return to earth to wreak havoc. The time could not have been better for a silent assault.

As soon as the group came within throwing distance, Toby was tempted to launch his first knife at the expedition's leader, who rode slightly in advance of the other guards. But he forced himself to refrain. He required no reminder of the need to make every throw of their knives count. To achieve his goal he could not afford to put them on guard.

As he waited, he noted that the leader was older than he would have expected. He had salt-and-pepper hair, his long mustache also was liberally sprinkled with gray, and deep lines were etched around his mouth.

Silently Toby and Ming-lo waited, hidden behind the boulder. Then, at a signal from Toby, who was watching the progress of the approaching party, both men started to push against the huge stone. As they had expected, the stone moved forward—but then it stopped and could not be budged further. Dismayed by this unexpected snag in their plans, Toby and Ming-lo looked at the base of the stone for some clue as to what had happened. Immediately they observed that the stone had rolled onto a patch of soft, sandy soil, and because of its great weight, it had created in the soft ground a hole from which it evidently could not be moved.

Frantically looking around the stone and seeing the relentless advance of their enemy, Toby and Ming-lo desperately pushed against the stone again. Still it stood, as if rooted to the ground. Again, summoning the last reserves of their strength, they gave the stone one more mighty heave. This time, to their vast relief, it started to inch forward. Toby and Ming-lo were able to push the stone out of the depression in which it had been caught, so that it would roll, as they had intended, down the slope toward the tong members.

The leader, seeing the boulder rolling down upon him and his men, seemed petrified. Then Toby let fly his first knife. At the same instant, Ming-lo threw the first of his also and aimed at a guard riding directly behind the leader.

Both victims died silently and swiftly, slumping in their saddles. The eerie part of the experience was that no sound was uttered except for the noise of the giant boulder rolling down and the cries of those first seeing it.

The guards halted their ponies and began to mill around frenziedly, trying to get out of the path of the juggernaut bearing down upon them.

Toby realized that the foe could not identify where the attack was coming from, much less how it was being launched. He and Ming-lo had a decided advantage. Drawing a second throwing knife, Toby let loose at the head of another rider, who succeeded in getting out of the path of the stone that had already crushed three of those guarding the group of captives. Again his aim was true, and the tong member fell sideways from his saddle and toppled to the ground, where his frightened mount trampled his already lifeless body.

Ming-lo threw his second knife, which found its mark also.

Luckily, the boulder rolled right by the captive peasants, who were huddled together like so many lost sheep and offered no resistance to anyone. They were thoroughly bewildered by the unexpected developments and seemed not to realize that a battle to the death was raging and that an opportunity for escape had been opened to them.

The surviving tong members finally figured out that the assault was coming from the crest of the hill. Now, though they could not see their attackers, they banded together in an attempt to drive them into the open. Using their old-fashioned muskets, they sent volleys crashing into the boulders. Thanks to their uncertain aim and the fact that they really could not see their enemies, the tong members sprayed a wide area, and Toby and Ming-lo were untouched. Careful to keep concealed except for the few moments when taking aim, Toby and Ming-lo fought furiously. They realized that continued success depended entirely upon their speed in keeping up the action with their knives while they had the advantage. Meanwhile, the fire from the surviving tong members was becoming considerably more infrequent.

Suddenly, to Toby's surprise, the fighting ceased. The surviving tong members simultaneously seemed to reach the decision to run for it. One moment they were pumping shots in the general direction of the boulders; in the next, they were in full flight, escaping from the battle scene by digging heels into their horses' flanks and sending them into wild retreat at top speed.

Toby and Ming-lo meanwhile hurried down the slope to the former field of action. The dead tong members lay where they had fallen. Their horses were wandering farther and farther afield, but Ming-lo paid them no more heed, observing that they would be picked up by grateful farmers.

Disappointed when he found no identifying documents or other papers in the pockets of the tong leader, Toby accepted the advice of Ming-lo to let the bodies rot where they fell, as a warning to other Chinese not to deal with the tong. He and Ming-lo did, however, take the time to retrieve their throwing knives.

The peasants were still in a totally confused state. Toby and Ming-lo passed among them, cutting the ropes around their necks that bound them together. They neither understood nor spoke Mandarin, so Toby was not able to communicate with them. Ming-lo, however, assured them that their trials were at an end. If they accompanied him and the white man back to Peking, he told them, they soon would be returned to their homes by soldiers in the employ of the empress. Many of the peasants, however, seemed unable to grasp what they were being told.

Each man carried a pouch containing several handfuls of boiled rice, and Ming-lo cautioned them to stretch their rations as best they could because he did not know whether or not additional food would be available on the return journey.

A campsite was established for the night on the eastern slope of the highest nearby hill. The following morning, Toby began to understand more fully the frustrations of dealing with the peasants. At least a dozen had wandered off during the night, even though far from home with no knowledge of their present location. Of those who stayed behind, some had ignored Ming-lo's advice and had eaten all of their remaining rice rations. No food was available, and they would have to go hungry until they returned to the city.

Toby and Ming-lo rounded up the remaining peasants

and started them on the journey toward Peking. At first, they seemed recalcitrant, as if they still had no comprehension that they were being restored to freedom and to their families. But gradually, as the march back continued at a slow pace, some of them observed that they were indeed retracing the route of their enforced march the previous day. These individuals spread the news to others, and soon there was a hubbub of conversation followed by exclamations of joy and a marked increase in the rate of march. Toby and Ming-lo were overjoyed to see that their charges were now eagerly pressing their steps toward the capital.

In midafternoon they overtook a government buying agent in the midst of acquiring rice for the imperial storehouses. Toby and Ming-lo succeeded in purchasing several sacks of rice and some pots from him. Shortly thereafter, they located a stream and proceeded to boil the rice and feed the peasants.

As the sun set, Toby and Ming-lo decided that they were close enough to Peking to continue on to their destination. A full moon had arisen to light the way, and it was obvious that the peasants were by now desperately eager to reach home.

At last, the city walls were sighted, and a spontaneous cheer arose from the marchers. They pressed forward, and it was difficult for Toby and Ming-lo to keep the peasants from breaking into a run toward the city gate.

Once inside the city, Toby sought out General Lin Yo-luang. Toby requested, and the general agreed, that troopers be assigned to escort the peasants to their home districts. Toby saw to it that each of the peasants was given a large silver coin worth ninety cents in American money. None of the peasants had possessed that much money in all their lives, and they went off to their families praising the empress and hailing the "foreign devil" as their savior.

Though the hour was late, Toby and Ming-lo were received at the imperial palace by the dowager empress, and congratulated at length on their exploit. As a sign of her pleasure, she invited them to dine with her the following evening. Toby was fatigued, and in the absence of an interpreter and other members of the court, he was less than cautious. "Your Majesty," he said, shaking his head, "I think you are rejoicing too soon."

No one ever contradicted the dowager empress to her face. She could only stare at him. "What do you mean?" she demanded, her annoyance plain.

"It is true," he said, "that Ming-lo and I killed a handful of tong ruffians and prevented the dispatching of a number of peasants to America. But what we have done is hardly a cause for celebration. We haven't seriously crippled Your Majesty's enemies, nor have we made it impossible—or even more difficult—for them to recruit other laborers as volunteers before they brutalize them. In my opinion, we haven't even scratched the surface in our efforts to unearth the enemy, learn his identity, and destroy him."

The dowager empress laughed. "You are too modest."

"I'm only being realistic," he said. "And I must tell you right out that winning a battle is not the same as winning the war. We have a long way to go. And a great deal of blood will be shed before we achieve a real victory over the tong!"

Over the years, the old palace of stone and marble directly behind the Pagoda of Purple Jasmine in the Imperial City had been used for many purposes. With only forty-three rooms, it was too small to serve as an official residence or to be used as an office building by the eunuchs, so it had been employed principally as a library housing some rare literary manuscripts, as well as other documents. Gradually, its very existence had been forgotten in the welter of the larger and more imposing buildings that surrounded it. Its use as a private dwelling had been reintroduced slowly. The main gate and entrance were never used, and its present occupants entered only by doors that opened onto the walled garden at the rear of the structure. Here, another door gave occupants and the infrequent visitor access to the adjoining pagoda.

So it happened that only a short distance from the imperial palace in the Forbidden City was a building that served as headquarters for the tong, which in many ways was the rival, in influence and power, of the imperial headquarters itself.

Those who served the tong labored in silence, but their power, octopuslike, stretched out to include every major city in China, as well as dozens of other cities in countries where large numbers of Chinese lived. Branches of the tong were to be found in a score of cities in the Orient, in Central America, the Caribbean, and most recently and viciously in the United States.

Force and terror were the weapons commonly used to enforce obedience to the tong's will. Each cell of its management consisted of three persons, none of whom knew those in the unit above. In this way, the identity of the tong hierarchy was protected. Practically no one, in or out of the tong, knew that the supreme leader of the organization was a woman, just as the dowager empress was the leader of all China.

She made her headquarters in a suite located on the third floor of the old palace, overlooking an isolated garden. Although she still maintained an official apartment in the imperial palace, she preferred to spend as much of her time as she could in this older palace. She came and went by way of a hidden staircase.

Even the servants, the tong's security guards, and other palace personnel in the small palace were unaware of the woman's identity. She habitually dressed in one of a number of cloth-of-gold *cheongsams*, worn in defiance of the imperial order that no one except the empress could wear a dress of that material. Her face was covered at all times by a mask of gold metal that extended from her forehead to the tip of her nose. This covering perpetuated the mystery and the legends that inevitably grew up among the few who even were aware that a woman headed their organization.

Although various responsible members of the palace staff wondered occasionally if she was the leader of the tong, most were sure she was merely the mistress of the head of the organization. No mere woman with a figure that attractive, they argued, could possibly be the sole director of the far-flung illegal activities. The fact that they knew even less of her supposed lover, much less ever saw him, was dismissed as irrelevant.

Well aware of the dispute that split her staff, she was secretly amused by it. She continued to live mysteriously. Among the tiny handful of her subordinates who knew her identity, all were sworn to secrecy. The chiefs of various departments, each an imperial viceroy in his own right, knew that they would be sealing their own death sentences if they revealed her identity.

So far, then, Princess Ta-lien's secret was safe. Her

top lieutenants sometimes speculated on her reasons for playing such a dangerous game, and none quite knew the answer. She was wealthy, held the highest possible position at the imperial court, and was a blood relative of the dowager empress and the boy emperor. No one realized that she fretted incessantly over the accident of birth that had deprived her of the supreme place in the nation. If she had been a decade older, if her father had been an older rather than a younger brother, she would now be on the throne. Unknown to the rest of the imperial family, she had quietly taken over a lesser residence that no one else wanted. It proved to be invaluable for her clandestine needs.

The tong, operating outside the law and defying the basic decencies of civilization, fulfilled Ta-lien's need for the power she craved. The money the tong earned meant nothing to her. All that mattered was that she reigned supreme and that her word caused instant obedience.

On the morning after Toby Holt's triumphant return to Peking, the princess met with an aide in a secluded office in her small palace. He gave her a full report on the unequal battle fought on the way to Tientsin.

"Two guards who survived the fight came back last night. I interviewed them myself," the aide reported. "They lived only because they were frightened and hid themselves behind a boulder during the fighting. From there they could see the white devil, Holt, performing miracles with his knife throwing, and inspiring Ch'ien Ming-lo to outdo himself. Together they destroyed and completely routed our men, and they now are having the peasants returned to their home regions. The dowager empress is highly pleased. And I understand she is giving a banquet tonight in Holt's honor."

Ta-lien's eyes gleamed behind her gold face mask. "It is no wonder," she said softly, "that Toby Holt is so highly regarded in the United States. He is proving himself to be a man of many accomplishments and unsuspected skills."

"In this instance," the lieutenant said harshly, "he has deprived us of a very large sum of money. As you know, an American railroad stands ready to pay us one thousand dollars in U.S. funds for each coolie we provide them. That money is lost to us now."

"Not at all!" Ta-lien replied swiftly. "Send word to Shanghai at once and let our associates there recruit the same number of coolies. Let the ship that will carry them to America be sent from Tientsin to Shanghai to pick them up, and the deed can be accomplished quickly and easily."

"It shall be done as you command," the aide said, bowing.

"It is equally important," she continued, "to ensure that Holt does not interfere with our plans again. Let him be brought here before me after the banquet tonight."

The aide, startled, hesitated for a long moment. "It will not be easy," he pointed out, "to obtain the services of men willing to make Holt their prisoner and bring him before you. Even the most courageous of our band now believes that he enjoys supernatural powers conferred upon him by the gods. They will prove unwilling to risk their necks and their lives in a confrontation with him."

Ta-lien sighed impatiently. "Does no one in the tong use his brains, no matter how high his rank?" she demanded. "Must I alone do all the thinking for the entire organization? I shall attend the banquet tonight, and it should be an easy matter for me to contrive to sit beside Holt at the meal. Before the banquet ends, I will drop a potion into his drink that will assure his sound sleep. Your minions should have little difficulty in quietly removing a sleeping man from his quarters, spiriting him out of the empress's palace, and bringing him here. They will be perfectly safe. Once he is deposited before me, I shall make him inhale an antidote that I assure you will awaken him. And thereafter I shall deal with him as I intend. You and your fainthearted underlings need not fear that the wrath of Toby Holt will be directed against you. Am I understood?" She gestured angrily, dismissing him.

The man kowtowed before her, then quickly withdrew.

Gradually Ta-lien's good humor was restored. She changed into a cloth-of-silver *cheongsam,* her customary court attire, and removed the mask. Studying her reflection in a full-length mirror, she was thoroughly satisfied with what she saw: She was endowed with a rare beauty that few other women on earth could match.

Laughing lightly, confidently, she walked down the secret staircase and emerged into the garden behind the old palace. From there she needed to walk only several paces to the street, where her sedan chair and its bearers, wearing her own livery, awaited. Seating herself as the bearers closed the door and hoisted the chair onto their shoulders, she was carried serenely to the imperial palace.

IX

When he found Princess Ta-lien seated beside him at the banquet that evening, Toby was pleased, even though it meant that he and Ming-lo would be separated. Her beauty was stunning, and she was the most intelligent person he had met in China. They discussed many subjects as they were served the numerous courses, and finally, acting on impulse, Toby asked, "I'm wondering if you might happen to know anything about the tong, with which I had a run-in the other day?"

"I believe I may know a little on the subject," she admitted, her voice bland, her face registering no surprise. "If you would like, perhaps we could discuss it at leisure after the banquet."

"I would like that, very much," Toby told her.

Ta-lien confirmed the engagement with a nod and then smiled smugly. She would have no need to put a sleeping potion in Toby's tea. With almost no effort on her part, he had agreed to the private meeting for which she had been scheming. Fortune was favoring her, as it so often did, and the princess was in high spirits when the banquet ended and they took their leave of the dowager empress.

A ricksha with a sliding roof and closed curtains to guard the traveler from inclement weather awaited Ta-lien at the main gate of the imperial palace. Inviting Toby to ride with her, she closed the flaps, even though the night was warm and pleasant. She wanted to take no chances on his seeing where the liveried servant pulling the ricksha would take them.

When they arrived at the old palace, Ta-lien led her guest up the private stairs to her personal quarters. There, she poured two cups of *mao-t'ai* and urged Toby to make himself comfortable on the mound of cushions piled high on the floor.

She sank to cushions opposite him and took no apparent notice when her tight, slit skirt rode high above her knees.

Unburdening himself as he cautiously sipped his drink, Toby explained that he could not regard his victory over the tong as significant and that he fully recognized the struggle ahead. "I was lucky enough," he said, "to intervene in time to prevent the exportation of one load of peasants. But the tong has infinitely greater resources than I can command. And for every load of contraband that I can halt, they can squeeze twenty or more out of China. It's an unequal battle, one that I can't possibly win. I am seeing that now much more clearly than before, and I'm unsure as to what to try to do about it. I don't expect to break and run, the way the tong did under fire. But I'm in the position of being under fire myself—and badly, hopelessly outnumbered."

"I am glad you are realistic enough to recognize the danger that awaits you at every move," Ta-lien said. "You also need to take into account the fact that many people believe the empress to be omnipotent. She herself accepts that myth, and most members of her court believe in it, too. It seems to me that they succeed only in fooling themselves. You will hear it said in many places that the tong's roots sink deep into the consciousness of our people and take hold because of what is increasingly regarded as the unfairness of our social system. The few in China who are wealthy live according to standards that do not exist elsewhere. Even I will admit that. I have studied the customs of many lands, and I have to concede that only here are the rich endlessly presented meals with one magnificent course following another. As you have seen for yourself, it doesn't matter how much of the food is actually eaten and how much is thrown to the pigs. Rather, what counts is the variety and color and beauty of the meal's presentation.

"I am unhappily aware, as are many others, of the disgraceful contrasts among our people. Our wealthy live in great pagodalike dwellings. We wear clothes made only of the finest silk. We are never required to exert ourselves or to engage in a day's honest work. We live sheltered dream lives from the moment we are born until we die at a very old, pampered age. I am ashamed to include myself in such privileged circumstances. But most of our people— millions upon millions of them—exist in the most abject poverty that it is possible for human beings to imagine. I have seen their homes, mud hovels that lack even the basic comforts of civilization. Their clothes are thin cotton that clings to them in summer and allows the wind of winter to blow through. Fruits and vegetables are unknown to them. I throw up my hands in despair that their only food staple is rice and that the only times they eat meat is when they are fortunate enough to catch a rat or a mouse, which they throw into the stew pot.

"These are the conditions that understandably can breed the men who make up the tong. I am sure they are desperate men, made desperate by their circumstances. They will undertake any risk in order to acquire their ill-gotten gains. And it seems obvious that a superior intelligence is guiding them. The Chrysanthemum Throne is far from invincible!"

"Are you suggesting," Toby asked, "that the United States could reach an accommodation with the tong?"

"Perhaps that would be a wise course," Ta-lien replied. "America is a great land, founded on the ideal that all men are created equal. When you return home, go to your president. Perhaps you could make clear to him the origins of the tong and the need to recognize how such conditions must be faced realistically."

Toby wanted to protest that tong members were criminals. He realized, however, that his hostess's sentiment in support of what the tong stood for would make it unlikely she wanted to hear any such arguments; wisely, he decided to say nothing more.

The princess construed his silence as a sign that he was favorably impressed by her relatively guarded comments. This mistake led her to assume that the time was ripe to consolidate her apparent gains and to win Toby permanently to the side of the tong, as unlikely as that had seemed.

Ta-lien had her own way of handling such a situation.

Rising to refill their *mao-t'ai* cups, she turned her back to Toby for a few moments. In so doing, she touched a hidden spring beside the stone of the ring that she wore. The stone sprang up, revealing a tiny hollow filled with a white powder, an odorless, tasteless hallucinogenic drug. She poured it into the *mao-t'ai*, in which it dissolved. Pouring herself another drink, she returned to the cushions, reclining, as if by chance, far closer to Toby than she had been.

Toby's drink no longer had a noticeably bitter taste, and as he sipped it, he began to feel a sensation of floating through space. The fog settling around him was rather thick, but through it he was able to recognize his wife, Clarissa. "We have been separated for a long time," she was saying in a low, barely distinguishable voice. "But our separation has ended, and now we are together again."

As Toby reached for her, he was overjoyed to realize anew the perfection of her figure. This woman he took to be Clarissa slid her hand inside his trousers and began to caress him.

Pulling her close, he murmured, "I love you, Clarissa," as he stroked her. Then he kissed her, and the world dissolved in a wild explosion that left both of them shattered.

Their lovemaking more became frantic. They removed their clothing and pressed their bodies closer together.

In spite of the primitive desires that filled him and threatened to engulf him, Toby was strangely comforted. Whenever he murmured, "I love you, Clarissa!" she replied in a whisper, "I love you, Toby!" It had been so long since they had been together that his very soul was involved.

They quickly reached a memorable climax. Toby could scarcely breathe. Clarissa was gasping for breath, too, and they lay in each other's arms for a long time, panting as they tried to recover their equilibrium. Toby closed his eyes and felt a serenity that he had not felt since he had left Clarissa in Washington.

A feminine voice, soft but insistent, sounded in Toby's ear. "Clarissa is removed from you by half the breadth of the world," it said. "But Ta-lien is very near. Ta-lien gives you all that Clarissa can give you. Ta-lien offers you constancy and love."

As the insistent voice went on, Toby grew increasingly drowsy. The voice in his ear became more strident. "You will be true to Ta-lien," it said. "You will be faithful to her. You will do nothing to harm her or to hurt her interests. You will put her first among all the women in your life."

The strong odor of incense filled the air, and Toby breathed deeply. Nevertheless, he could hear Ta-lien's words coming to him, as if from a distance. All at once he raised his head slightly. "Clarissa," he murmured groggily, "Clarissa, are you there? Where are you?" With that, he let his head fall back on the pillow, succumbing at last to the full effect of the drug.

Ta-lien listened for a moment to the sound of his steady breathing. Clearly, she thought, this man, for all her temporary power over his mind and his body, was not one to be easily led astray, and she was chagrined at her lack of complete success. Flinging herself from the bed, she quickly dressed Toby in his chrysanthemum clothing. Donning a cloth-of-gold kimono and settling her mask of gold mesh over her face, she tugged a bell rope. Then she unlocked the door and waited.

After a few moments, two burly retainers entered and kowtowed.

"Take this creature to the imperial palace and deposit

him in his bed there, in his own chamber," she directed. "Let no one see you entering. And let no one see you with him!"

The retainers followed orders and removed the unconscious Toby from the room.

Ta-lien was restless. She uncovered the grillwork from the small metal bowl in which incense had been burning, and after assuring herself that the fire in it was extinguished, she opened a window and hurled the burned-out ashes into the garden below. Then she stood at the window for several minutes, her fists clenched as she breathed the night air in and out in a deliberate attempt to calm herself.

Realizing that she had first befuddled and then fooled Toby Holt, she told herself she deserved congratulations because she had managed to seduce him, but the memory of that act gave her no feeling of pleasure. In fact, she was thoroughly frustrated, her pride shattered. She felt naked and exposed to the elements of scorn.

She had been forced to rely on hallucinogenic drugs in order to persuade Toby Holt to go to bed with her. He had made love only because he believed she was his wife. Had he known her actual identity, he would have turned from her, just as he had done when in his right senses. She could feel no elation, no sense of having won a victory.

The few people at the imperial court in the Forbidden City of Peking who were well acquainted with Princess Ta-lien realized she was a creature of moods. She could be violently angry one moment, cool and calculating the next. The anger and frustration caused by her inability to establish a truly intimate relationship with Toby gradually gave way to a far deeper, far more primitive emotion. She yearned for revenge, a revenge that would suit her long-term purpose of attaining the goals she sought for herself and her tong. She realized again how she could not only use Holt to gain her own ends, but simultaneously show him up as impotent and incompetent.

As she drew this picture for herself, her anger faded, replaced by a tranquillity behind which only a tremor of doubt remained. But she knew from experience how to get rid of it.

Ta-lien walked to a corner of the room, and picking up a stick, one end of which was padded with felt, she struck a large gong twice. She was soothed by the sound that reverberated through the building. Then she walked to a chaise and stretched out on it in anticipation, waiting for an answer to her summons.

After a time a hearty knock sounded at the door. "You may enter," she called.

The door opened, and a naked man with bulging muscles came into the room. His features marked him as Mongolian, rather than Chinese; his head was shaved. He wore broad bands of a shiny metal on his upper arms and the calves of his legs. Ceremoniously, he handed Ta-lien a whip with a pearl handle, and then he prostrated himself on the floor at her feet.

Her face expressionless, she gazed for a time at the husky man who was abasing himself before her. Then slowly, with great deliberation, she stood, raised the whip, and brought it down sharply. It sang through the air, and the leather thong left an ugly welt on his back. He shuddered involuntarily as the blow creased his skin.

The knowledge that she had inflicted pain on a man strong enough to break her in two gave Ta-lien great pleasure. She had no desire to inflict real injury on him or to incapacitate him, however, so she put aside the whip and clapped her hands together sharply as she sank back onto the chaise.

The Mongolian, who had been pressing his face into the thick rug at her feet, raised his head. The princess gestured abruptly, summoning him, and he obeyed instantly, stepping close to her.

Raising herself on one elbow, she began to fondle him, taking her time and amusing herself by seeing how light a touch she could maintain. Accustomed to her routines, the man tolerated her ministrations as best he was able, standing motionless, his face revealing nothing of his feelings.

Ta-lien knew it would be self-defeating to procrastinate now, so she reached up and drew him down beside her. The Mongolian began to make love to her brutally, violently, using all his strength.

Ultimately giving in to him, finally allowing herself to be conquered, Ta-lien succeeded in putting her encounter with Toby out of her mind.

Toby awakened in bed in the palace quarters assigned to him by the dowager empress. Yawning and stretching, he felt unaccountably lazy, and although he usually was wide awake the moment he opened his eyes, that morning he took a long time to rise to the full surface of consciousness.

Oddly, he couldn't remember going to bed. Now that he thought about it, his whole evening after the conclusion of the banquet seemed to be a blank, too.

The strange thought crossed his mind that he and Clarissa had made love during that evening, but he promptly dismissed the idea as nothing more than wishful thinking.

Nothing on earth would have given him greater satisfaction, but the unhappy truth was that he and his wife were separated by half the globe.

A manservant stationed in the corridor outside his room heard him stir and brought a large mug of strong tea. As Toby sipped, he allowed his mind to drift back over the events of the evening. An inexplicable feeling of well-being swept over him. He remembered sitting beside Ta-lien at dinner, and he reflected that he always enjoyed her warm and sympathetic company. He told himself that of all the people he had met in China, she and Ming-lo were the best friends he had made. In fact, he actively looked forward to his next meeting with her. He did not recall having accompanied the princess out of the imperial palace, and he had no memory of sharing intimacies with her.

After he bathed, shaved, and dressed, Toby went off to the main dining hall, where meals were served throughout the day. No sooner was he seated at a small table than Princess Ta-lien came toward him, dressed in her customary silver *cheongsam*. His broad smile indicated his pleasure at seeing her.

"If you are not to meet someone," she said, "perhaps I could join you for breakfast?"

Ta-lien had been tarrying outside the hall, waiting for him to arrive. She had resolved to make certain that he did not recall that anything untoward had happened the evening before. She would try another tack in her scheme to subvert this man who represented the greatest single danger to the tong. Perhaps where her own charms, aided by drugs, had failed, a show of reasonableness and friendliness would prevail. These Western devils were strange creatures, she thought, and it was a tactic worth trying.

"I'd be delighted to have breakfast with you," Toby said to her.

She took charge of ordering their meal, speaking to their waiter in a dialect Toby did not understand.

Her choices were superior to the meal he would have ordered. They began with large portions of broiled fish, as thick and tender as North American cod. This was followed by turtle eggs, basted and served with strips of pickled pork. They finished the meal with bowls of iced litchis, a fruit unlike anything Toby was familiar with in the West.

Throughout the meal, they chatted amiably. Toby was pleased and mildly surprised to discover how much at ease he was in Ta-lien's company. Ordinarily, he was reserved in the presence of even relative strangers, but he realized that he no longer regarded the princess as a stranger. He was able to relax completely in her presence.

After they ate their fill of litchis and were drinking hot, fragrant tea, Ta-lien looked at Toby and spoke softly. "I do not quite know how to say this to you," she said, "but I want you to know that I admire what you are doing for the empress. If I can be of any assistance in stamping out the tong, please let me know. I am familiar with much that relates to the customs and ways of our people. Perhaps I can be of help to you in finding shortcuts through the maze of our complicated bureaucracy."

"Thank you," he said, "but I really would not wish to impose."

Ta-lien placed a hand on his arm and let it linger there. "It is never an imposition," she said, "to extend help in an important cause. In China, the purpose of friendship is much like it must be in America. Friends stand together, forming united fronts in opposition to their common enemies."

Heartened by her words and conscious of her touch on his arm, Toby smiled broadly.

With great attentiveness, Ta-lien searched his face, which showed no sign that he remembered what had happened during the night. Judging from his present behavior, she might yet succeed in winning him over. She cautioned herself, however, that he had already displayed hidden reserves of fortitude and a steely resolve in carrying out his purposes. The conflict between them might well be tested by force of arms before she had a chance to gain his confidence. She could be sure of only one thing: In this man, she had more than met her match, and she would have to proceed very carefully.

Toby and Ch'ien Ming-lo occupied adjacent offices. The door between was invariably open, on Toby's insistence, as a sign to associates and visitors that he had no secrets from his companion and that the war against the tong was being conducted completely as planned. Consequently, a rumble of voices could be heard in Toby's office whenever Ming-lo had a caller.

These sounds never disturbed Toby. At the moment, he was deeply immersed in reading a translation of a report from an imperial agriculture inspector stationed in the far southwestern provinces. According to his report, he had come across a field of one thousand acres where, in defiance of the law, opium poppies were growing. The farmer had offered a bribe to the inspector to look the other way. But the inspector had not been moved, and as a result, the unlucky farmer had been beheaded and his property forfeited to the empress. The net result was a clear-cut victory for the forces attempting to control distribution of opium in China.

Toby looked up to find Ming-lo in the open doorway. Several paces behind him and to one side was an old woman with a deeply wrinkled face, wearing shapeless cotton clothes that had been washed so often that the color had faded.

Ming-lo gestured over his shoulder. "This is Po-ling. I want you to hear what she has told me. You might not be able to understand her, but I will interpret." The old woman painfully lowered herself to the floor and started to kowtow before Toby.

"Here, now, we'll have none of that!" he muttered, speaking English in his agitation. Leaping forward, he grasped her by the elbows and lifted her to her feet.

Po-ling was angry and disturbed, but she caught a glimpse of the humor in the white devil's eyes and ended by smiling at him shyly. Toby smiled in return.

When the old woman started to speak, the words came pouring out in a torrent. She was using an unfamiliar dialect, however, and he could not make out the meaning of a single word.

"Po-ling," Ming-lo explained, "has lived for more than eighty years in Peking. In that time, she has seen from afar emperors and empresses. This is the first time in all her days that she has ventured into the Forbidden City. She has dared to come here only because she feels it is necessary for her to tell her story. She wishes to make a contribution to the cause of opposing the tongs, as is the aim of the revered dowager empress."

Toby gestured toward two broad visitors' stools covered in leather. Po-ling and Ming-lo seated themselves. As she spoke the old woman steadily tugged at an already shredded remnant of what once might have been a handkerchief.

"The husband of Po-ling," Ming-lo translated, "worked for many years in the tin mines in the region north of Peking. He was granted a holiday of four and twenty hours at the end of each month. He always visited his wife on these occasions. They were very poor, but they never stole, and they never begged.

"Po-ling's husband died of the miners' disease thirty-six winters ago. The grief that opened in her heart at that time has not healed to this day."

The old woman dabbed ineffectually at her eyes.

"Then it became the turn of Po-ling's son to support his mother, which he did, even though he had his own life and, eventually, a child of his own to support. He was a man of great strength who went from house to house carrying large buckets of water. These he sold to the people of the city. He earned a meager living, but like his father, he was always honest."

Po-ling shuddered, took a deep breath, and then went on with her tale, with Ming-lo, deeply concentrating, providing a quick translation.

"When he, too, died at an early age, it became the duty of her grandson, Teng Liu, to become the main support of the family. Like his father, he possesses great physical strength, but unlike his father and his grandfather, he has no morality. He has had many opportunities to obtain honorable employment, but instead he chooses to work for the tong. He uses threats to make people do the bidding of the tong. If that fails he uses force against them."

The old lady began to speak more stridently, but Ming-lo lowered his voice and translated very softly. "All who live in Po-ling's neighborhood fear the strength and the temper of her grandson. They do his bidding because they are afraid he will do them serious injury if they displease him.

"He brings his grandmother large sums of money, but she will not use it; she will not spend it. It is tainted money."

The old woman reached inside her faded gown, took out a threadbare purse, and after fumbling in it, drew out a shiny coin, which she pressed into Ming-lo's hand.

"Recently Teng Liu went to Hong Kong with some comrades on a business trip for the tong. His grandmother doesn't know what he did there, but she is certain that he broke the law. The money that he gave her when he returned is by far the largest sum that Po-ling has ever seen at one time in her life."

The old woman's voice sank to a whisper, and then she drew herself up proudly and spoke more forcefully.

"This coin," Ming-lo said, "would buy her much good rice and fat meat. It would pay for clothing she badly needs. It would even pay the rent on the hovel where she lives. But it is tainted money, so she will not use it."

Toby reached for the coin and examined it. It was a gold half-sovereign issued the previous year by the British government. To poverty-stricken Chinese, it represented a fortune. Undoubtedly, it could support Po-ling for a year or more.

Toby returned the coin, and she reluctantly jammed it back into her purse. Then she finished her recital, her voice bitter and defeated, her manner resigned.

"Again, her grandson has been absent from this city," Ming-lo said. "This morning she received word that he has returned now to Peking and that he will be calling on her before the sun sets tonight. She intends to order him to leave her house for all time."

"Before she does anything too drastic," Toby interjected, "it can't do much harm if you and I are waiting at her house and have a few words with her grandson. Perhaps we can talk a little sense into him."

A smile spread slowly across Ming-lo's face. "It's strange," he said, "but I had exactly that same idea myself."

Sitting cross-legged on a tattered mat that faced the door of the mud hovel, Toby marveled that any human being could have spent eight decades living in such a primitive place. Po-ling had not only spent her own childhood there but had lived there with her husband and, over the many years, had raised two succeeding generations. Now she was alone again in a hut that scarcely seemed big enough for one person.

On crude shelves in the corner were piled the gifts Toby and Ming-lo had brought her: sacks of rice and flour, a slab of bacon and a large container of dried fish, a box of tea, an oil lamp, and a sack of sugar. A bolt of wool and one of cotton cloth were enough to make sufficient new clothes for Po-ling to last her for years, perhaps for the rest of her days.

Seeming dazed by her good fortune, she was not inclined to talk now. Toby and Ming-lo were silent, too, as they sat waiting for her grandson's appearance.

Night came, and Po-ling proudly lighted the oil lamp that they had brought. At last, after a wait that seemed interminable, a bulky shadow appeared in the door frame.

"What's this?" Teng Liu demanded roughly in a harsh provincial accent.

Toby and Ming-lo rose to their feet. "We are friends

of your grandmother," Ming-lo said. "We have come to share her grief because her grandson is following the path that will surely lead to the executioner's ax."

The young man, with an incongruous broad-brimmed American hat on his head, stared at the strangers in the light of the oil lamp. Suddenly his eyes glittered. "I know you!" he exclaimed. "The white devil is from America. He has gone to work for the empress to help her against the tong. And he enlisted Ch'ien Ming-lo, who boasts that no man on earth can best him in personal combat. I say that both of you are stupid fools, who deserve all that is going to happen to you before you are finished. You will learn better than to tamper with the power and might of the tong."

He reached for a long, bone-handled knife in his belt. Before he could pull it, he found that Toby had outdrawn him. He was suddenly staring into the muzzle of the American's repeating pistol. "Drop the knife!" Toby instinctively spoke first in English and then repeated the order in Mandarin.

Teng Liu understood neither language, but the meaning was painfully clear. He dropped the knife, which fell to the earth. His grandmother stooped to pick it up. With a flourish, she handed it to Ming-lo.

"If you wish to enjoy continuing good health," Ming-lo said, "I urge you to give up the use of all weapons while in the presence of my companion and me." Reaching out quickly, he relieved Teng of a length of iron pipe and a set of brass knuckles.

The young man cursed in a low, menacing monotone. Ming-lo did not hesitate for an instant. He slapped the youth hard across the face while Toby kept his pistol trained on Teng.

"You will forget at your peril that you are in the presence of a lady," Ming-lo said severely. "I demand that you apologize to her."

The young man was so enraged that he stammered. However, he begged his grandmother's pardon for using foul language.

In the meantime, Ming-lo quickly explained the situation to Toby. The giant then turned back to the errant grandson.

"Those who bear arms on behalf of the tong will end their days together in a common grave," Ming-lo said in a stern voice. "If you would be spared the stain of eternal dishonor in the eyes of your ancestors, turn your back on your present companions. Join the forces of right and good. We offer you this chance, not for your own sake, but for the sake of your grandmother, who has grieved for you."

"If I were to enter the service of the dowager empress," Teng Liu objected, "I might earn in one month of hard labor what I can make in only one day for the tong. Look at the way my grandmother lives." Teng raised his voice. "I was born in this very pigsty, and I grew up here. Through great good luck I managed to escape, and I enjoy a far better life. Do you think I would willingly endure the misery and shame of a renewed existence here? Do you think that I look forward to a life of not enough to eat and clothes so thin that the winds of winter chill my bones?"

The old woman covered her face with her worn, veined hands and wept silently.

"You may swear loyalty to the dowager empress, if you wish," her grandson went on. "As for me, I insist on my freedom. I am no subject of Tz'u Hsi. I swear fealty only to my own kind, and the only law I recognize is the law of might."

As Ming-lo translated rapidly for Toby, they shared a long, significant glance. Both of them realized they could not hope to relieve Po-ling's heartbreak. No matter what happened, her grandson would not reform. Having dedicated himself to the life of an outlaw, nothing would change his mind.

"If you will not improve in your attitude," Ming-lo told him, "leave and be gone for all time. Do not return to the roof of your grandmother again!"

The young Chinese stared at him insolently. "Hand my weapons to me," he said, "and I will be on my way."

Ming-lo, outraged, growled inarticulately, clenching and unclenching his huge fists.

Teng Liu hastily departed, scarcely bothering to nod farewell to his grandmother as he went out into the street. Conscious of having lost face, he made certain that he soon became lost from sight in the gathering darkness.

"I'm sorry, Grandmother," Toby said gently to Po-ling.

The old woman looked first at him, then at Ming-lo. "You are kind," she said. "Both of you have generous hearts. I regret that which cannot be. I must close my mind and my heart and understand that some things are not possible."

They left her staring fixedly into space, her eyes dry, her face composed, her manner calm. Toby knew he would never forget the picture of her at that moment.

He and Ming-lo were silent as they made their way back to the imperial palace. Both were conscious of failing to sway Teng Liu to break his association with the tong.

At the palace they went to a small table in the far corner of the dining hall. Because it was plain that they sought no company, the members of the court left them alone. Neither had much appetite, and they ate sparingly. As they were finishing, a sergeant of the elite guard came into the hall, stood searching the room, and then approached them. He addressed Ming-lo in a dialect that Toby could not understand.

The giant paled, and for a moment he appeared stunned. Then, gradually, an expression of icy resolve replaced the stunned expression. Even though Toby had no idea what was happening, he shivered involuntarily.

Ming-lo rose and buckled on his sword belt and scimitar, which had been hanging on the back of his chair. "I shall return after I attend to a personal matter," he announced shortly.

Toby wanted to ask whether his companion desired or needed help, but he knew he was being deliberately excluded. Whatever Ming-lo was going to do, he intended to proceed alone.

After retiring to his quarters, Toby put everything else out of his mind as he concentrated on more detailed reports submitted by government agencies. The tong was active throughout China, it appeared, and had so many tentacles that Toby wondered anew how it could be possible to sever them.

While he was still pondering the problem, a tap sounded at the door, and he admitted a smartly uniformed colonel of the elite guard. Apologizing for his intrusion at such a late hour, the officer asked Toby to accompany him.

Two large, strong horses awaited them at the main entrance, and they rode quickly through the Forbidden City and the Imperial City to the outer portion of Peking. There, as they made their way through narrow, crooked streets that seemed vaguely familiar to Toby, they stopped at last in front of a mud hut surrounded by many others of its kind. He recognized it as the home of Po-ling. A squad of soldiers armed with old-fashioned muskets to which bayonets were attached held at bay a large gathering of the curious. The colonel, with Toby close beside him, pushed through and halted in the entrance to the hut.

Crumpled on the ground directly in front of Toby was the body of Teng Liu. Blood was everywhere. He had been stabbed at least a dozen times, and his shirt was smeared with blood. His body lay in a pool of it.

"He presumably had a falling out with his comrades," the colonel said. Picking up the oil lamp, he lighted it with a new-style sulfur match. The wick caught, and the flame spread, illuminating the interior of the drab hovel.

Toby caught his breath. On the floor near her grandson was the lifeless body of Po-ling, another victim of the tong's cruelty. Her neck had been brutally twisted, almost dismembering her head, which lolled to one side, touching her shoulder. Her eyes were wide open, and pain filled her face, but Toby could see no reflection of fear. She died as she had lived, with dignity.

"Come," the colonel said, and extinguished the oil lamp.

Toby, badly shaken, followed him into the open, where the silent crowd shrank back as the two men mounted their horses and cantered off.

The colonel led the way to an ancient bridge over a busy intersection. This was the "Traitors' Bridge," so called because in the Middle Ages the emperors had displayed on its posts the severed heads of those disloyal to the crown.

Ordinarily, the bridge was teeming with pedestrian

traffic, no matter what the hour. Tonight, it was virtually deserted.

The shock of the grisly spectacle was overwhelming. Mounted on the palings were three severed heads whose sightless eyes stared vacantly into space. Attached to the paling below each head was a neatly lettered placard saying, "I was a traitor to the empress and a member of the tong."

Toby realized at once that this was the work of Ming-lo, who had obtained vengeance in his own way for the death of Po-ling. China, in spite of its thick veneer of ancient culture, was still a barbarous, primitive land.

X

Karl Kellerman, virtually destitute, could count only ninety dollars in bills and some change in his pockets. When he fled from Madame Gayley's, he had lost his twenty-five thousand dollars, and he knew that he could not return for it, even if a search of his room had not disclosed it. Someone would be certain to be lying in wait for him there, and it would be hopeless to try to elude his assailants. Besides, they undoubtedly had struck a deal with Madame Gayley, promising her a large sum of money if she informed them whenever he turned up. He wandered disconsolately, lacking even a hat and a coat, and with nothing but the gray wig and mustache as a disguise. He needed all his self-control to keep his temper in check whenever he thought of how close he had come to picking up fifty thousand in ransom money for Millicent Gautier. He had been certain that her frightened husband would willingly pay up, but the interference of Millicent's rescuers at exactly the wrong moment had ruined everything.

Bad luck had been dogging his footsteps for too long. He had invested in the tong's venture into Far East trade, but Kung Lee had not repaid a penny of that money. Nor had he turned over any of the profits. He was sure the illegal immigrants the *Amsterdam* brought to the West Coast from China by way of Hawaii would have earned a very large profit, and so would the opium brought in. But Kellerman had not seen any return from that enterprise. The money grudgingly released by Captain Kayross as partial payment on the gunrunning was all he had to show for his investment, efforts, and risk, and now that was gone, too—abandoned when he had fled from Millicent's rescuers. He vowed to retrieve that money ultimately, although he had no idea of how he could do so. For his peace of mind, it was just as well that he could not know that the money was now securely stored in one of Domino's safes.

As a man who took great pride in his ruthless lack of sentiment, he had allowed himself to be fooled and frightened by Kung Lee, whose ruthlessness had turned out to exceed his own.

"I can't afford to wait any longer," Kellerman muttered aloud. "I must act—and act quickly." He promptly decided exactly what he would do: He would go to the dock where the *Amsterdam* was berthed and would demand the rest of his share from Kayross. He was determined that he would not be denied. Then with money in his pockets again, he would be free to make a fresh start elsewhere, far from New Orleans authorities and also Domino, whom he could assume might well be behind the attack on him.

Kellerman's spirits began to revive at the thought of

beginning anew, and on his way to the pier where the *Amsterdam* was docked, he stopped at a saloon for a long drink of gin. Seeing his reflection in a long mirror behind the bar, he grinned amiably at himself and smoothed the creases in his jacket. He had suffered a temporary reverse but was certain he was not beaten yet, and he was no worse off than he allowed himself to feel. For years his greatest asset had been his self-confidence; now, suddenly, that confidence was restored. Nothing could defeat him!

Kellerman's stride was positively jaunty as he resumed his walk toward the docks. Whistling tunelessly, he winked at several prostitutes whom he passed in the streets of the shipping center.

At last he saw in the distance the *Amsterdam*'s familiar superstructure. Quickening his pace, he soon reached the wharf where the freighter was berthed. The dock area seemed deserted, but a seaman was stationed on the main deck, at the far end of the gangplank. In one hand, he held a spar as a handy weapon.

"Evening, Murphy," Kellerman called out. "It's Kellerman."

The boatswain peered at him in the gloom. "Oh, so it is," he said at last. "Didn't recognize you at first. How be ya?"

"Doing nicely. Is the captain on board?"

"Yes, sir, he was in his quarters, last I knew."

"Good," Kellerman replied, boldly moving up the gangplank. "He's the very fellow I want to see." As his feet touched the deck, he breathed more easily. At least, no orders had been issued to bar him from the ship.

He moved forward on the deck, climbed to the bridge,

walked through, and opened a door at the rear that was the private entrance to the master's quarters.

Two lamps were burning cheerfully in the cabin. Captain Kayross was seated in an overstuffed easy chair, a glass within reach on a table. Behind it was a large bottle of ouzo, the Greek liquor for which he had an insatiable thirst.

"Good evening, Kayross," Kellerman said. "I'm back."

"I can see that," Kayross said flatly. "I've been wondering what's become of you." He reached around to his gun belt, which was hanging on a wall peg.

"You have no need for a pistol," Kellerman replied quickly. As though contradicting his reassurance, he dug his right hand into his jacket pocket. Actually unarmed, he seemed to be reaching for a small pistol. Kayross instantly subsided.

"That's more like it," Kellerman said amiably. "You and I have been friends, after all, and I don't see any reason to argue now."

"That's good to know," the ship's master said. "Help yourself to a drink. Glasses on the shelf yonder."

Kellerman reached up to the shelf, took down a glass, and after blowing dust from it, poured himself a drink. Then he settled into a chair opposite Kayross. "Here's to you and me," he said, "partners of the tong."

Kayross eyed him speculatively. He had suspected for some time that Kellerman, having incurred the ill will of Kung Lee, had vanished suddenly from the *Amsterdam* because he was afraid that the tong had ordered his death. Certainly, the man was tense beneath his surface air of good fellowship.

"I imagine that by this time," Kellerman said pleasantly, "Kung Lee has sent you our shares of the profits from the voyage to San Francisco."

Kayross laughed hollowly. Kellerman clenched his fists, then forced himself to speak calmly. "What's so funny?"

"Obviously you don't understand the tong," the captain told him sourly. "Kung Lee has kept those profits for the tong's use. We made money on the guns we sold, and you've got your share from that."

"I was expecting one hell of a lot more than that," Kellerman objected. "After all, I did invest thirty-five thousand in cash with Kung Lee. I haven't seen any of that money. Some partnership!"

"So you have had most of your money returned," the captain told him. "If that isn't good enough for you, complain to Kung. Don't sing your sad story to me."

"But I have more coming to me, whether from him or from you."

"Not from me, I can assure you. You've had it from me, fair and square, even if I wasn't sure I should have paid up so quickly. You have no complaint with me. And as for Kung Lee, let me remind you that when you're playing with the tong, you follow their rules, or you get out of the game. It's a little too late now to quit, so my advice to you is to abide by their rules—and be glad they haven't decided to eliminate you altogether."

Kellerman rubbed his lean jaw. "If you can give me an advance on what I ought to get from the tong, I'll pay you back with interest. How about it?"

"I'm not cutting any fancy deals," Kayross said curtly. "If you're shy of funds, you can stay on board. I won't even charge you anything. Have another drink and think it over, Kellerman. That is all that I'm willing to do for you. It's hardly my fault if you've lost all that I gave you."

*   *   *

Domino's house was as quiet and as well-run as a hospital. People spoke in subdued tones, medical assistance was administered promptly, and meals were served on schedule.

Having appointed herself head of the nursing staff tending to Millicent Gautier's needs, Martha was indefatigable. She kept a sharp watch on the patient, and when she saw Millicent open her eyes for the second time and seem to be aware of her surroundings, she immediately sent for Jean-Pierre.

She met him outside the room, and her instructions, issued in a low voice, were succinct. "Your wife has regained consciousness again," she told him. "She'll know you, I believe, and she will know where she is. Remember the doctor's orders. You are to speak with her for no more than five minutes. Discuss nothing of importance, certainly nothing that will upset or alarm her. At the end of five minutes, you will leave so she can go back to sleep. Do I make myself clear?"

"Very clear," Jean-Pierre assured her with a smile.

"Go in, then," she said. "Millicent is expecting you."

Martha listened to him greeting his wife, then closed the door and went downstairs to Domino's study. She felt a need for a drink after a long day.

As she measured whiskey into a glass, she heard a familiar voice. "Here you are," Domino called. "I've been looking for you."

Turning, she raised her glass in a silent toast.

"I'm worried about you, Martha," he said. "You're spending every waking moment with Millicent. If she's beginning to improve now, you should start paying less attention to her."

"You don't understand, Domino," she said. "You're spending most of your time searching for Kellerman. If Toby Holt were here now instead of being off in China, he'd be doing exactly as you're doing. I'm not constituted that way. If I started a hunt for Kellerman, too, I'd be certain to bungle the job. I feel I must do my duty by doing my part, and in this case, my part is looking after Millicent and making sure that she has a proper recovery."

Before Domino could reply, Eddie Neff came into the room, out of breath. "Excuse me for busting in like this," he panted, "but I just had a report from Tony. Kellerman was seen not fifteen minutes ago."

"Where?" Domino asked sharply.

"Down at the docks. He went on board the *Amsterdam*. Your hunch was right that sooner or later he'd show up again at the ship."

"All right," Domino said in a controlled voice, "we're all set to go. The brewery wagon is in the stable right now with a barrel of gunpowder and four barrels of pine tar. You all know what to do. Take plenty of help. And blow that freighter to kingdom come—while Kellerman is still on board!"

"Yes, sir!" Eddie answered smartly, starting to edge away.

"One minute," Domino added. "Eddie, don't forget that you are fully in charge of this project. Get moving on it. And if you don't succeed, don't bother to come back!"

Boatswain Murphy leaned back against the hatch cover, made himself more comfortable, and closed his eyes. Unless he missed his guess, Captain Kayross and that big lug, Kellerman, were in the captain's quarters, guzzling Greek liquor. Murphy would have exchanged several teeth for even a shot of ouzo, but he knew better than to tempt fate. The captain was death on anyone who drank while on duty. Murphy valued his job, so he hunched lower on the deck and soon dozed.

Suddenly something awakened him—perhaps instinct, perhaps an unusual sound. Whatever it was, he opened his eyes and glanced around the deck. A young man dressed in a black sweater and trousers, and with a black hat pulled low over his face, was directing half a dozen other men in placing several barrels they apparently had brought on board. They made no sound but worked steadily, lowering barrels down a hatch as Murphy stared in amazement.

The boatswain struggled to a sitting position and started to rise. The leader seemed to have eyes in the back of his head. He turned to look at Murphy and snapped his fingers.

Murphy never heard or saw the black-clad figure who crept up behind him and brought a lead pipe down with full force on the back of his head just above the left ear. He crumpled to the deck, blood oozing from his wound.

Robin Kayross refilled both glasses with an unsteady hand. "Karl," he said, slurring his words, "you're a good fellow. But you go too far, and you're likely to end up in serious trouble."

"All I want," Kellerman replied thickly, "is what's due me."

"You're getting as fair a share as anyone is ever paid by the tong," Kayross told him again. "You'll have to be satisfied with that. If Kung Lee turns sour on you, God have mercy on your soul. He'll follow you to the ends of the earth, and you won't know when you're destroyed, but believe me, he'll get to you. Agree with him in all things, don't make a fuss, and accept whatever comes your way. That's the only way you're going to get along with Kung."

He was interrupted by banging and thumping noises from somewhere below the cabin.

While Kayross went off to investigate, Kellerman remained in his chair, and reaching for the liquor bottle, he emptied its contents into his glass. He was still sober enough to know that he would not accomplish his goal. He could see no way to persuade Robin Kayross to pay him at least a portion of what the tong owed him. In disgust, he stepped outside and began to pace the deck.

As he did so, a violent explosion rocked the entire commercial waterfront district. Deafened and stunned, Kellerman was flung through the air like a rag doll. The entire freighter was collapsing around him, and before he realized what had happened, he felt the shock of cold water as he landed in the harbor. The thrust of the explosion, combined with his total immersion, sobered him. As nearly as he could judge, he had not suffered broken bones or been incapacitated in any way. He began to swim, feebly at first, then as the effects of the severe shock began to diminish, he used increasing strength. Bits of timber and other matter that had been propelled skyward by the explosion fell around him. He was aware, too, of the light and heat from the flames that were enveloping the remains of the *Amsterdam*. He had to call on all his great strength in order to swim to a piling that jutted out of the water. It was at a lower level that was used as an entrance to the hold of any ship that was using the dockage space. Since no vessel was there at present, Kellerman was able to haul himself, inch by inch, onto the waterlogged piling, until he was able to stretch out on it. He looked back, panting and exhausted, at the scene from which he had just escaped. The spreading flames leaped high, illuminating the entire interior of the ship. Kellerman was reminded of the illustrations of Hades he had seen as a child in Sunday school.

Captain Kayross and a few members of the crew, apparently the only survivors of the ship's company, were trying ineffectually to battle the flames. Equipped with a hose to which a nozzle was attached and a hand pump that brought up water from the dock area, Kayross and two seamen held the hose while another pair pumped frantically. The captain was dissatisfied with the strength of the stream of water that was being played on the fire, and leaving the hose in other hands, he joined the pair at the pump.

To an extent, Kayross's zeal overcame the lethargy of the seamen, but Kellerman could see their efforts were doomed. The stream of water raised by the pump was too puny to be effective. The raging flames continued to spread, consuming everything in their path.

The heat was so intense that Kellerman, a hundred feet away from the nearest part of the freighter, felt as though he, too, was about to catch fire at any moment. To his surprise, he found his clothes were actually drying.

The interior of the freighter was consumed, and the fire was so hot that in places the metal hull buckled and twisted out of shape. Suddenly the flames jumped thirty feet, and Kellerman became aware of the terrible dilemma of the fire fighters. While Kayross and his men had been fighting the blaze in front of them, the fire had been spreading rapidly at their rear. They were compelled to abandon their attempts to save the ship and instead were fighting for their own lives. The fire pressed closer from both directions. They turned the hose on themselves to delay catching fire, but their respite was only temporary. Their hose was eaten by the fire, as was the wooden pump that had fed it.

Kellerman's blood turned cold, in spite of the intense heat that the fire generated. He swallowed hard, his eyes glassy, as he watched the seamen collapsing one by one, the smoke swirling around them.

The last to survive, fittingly, was Captain Kayross. His shirt had been burned from his back, and his skin glowed a deep shade of pink in the hellish light of the flames. Still, he continued to fight the flame, wielding an ax and fruitlessly trying to batter down what was left of the ship's superstructure before the fire attacked it.

But his efforts were for naught. Suddenly flames swept over him, soaring as they engulfed him. The fire continued its deadly work, consuming the last of the ship's interior as it advanced.

Kellerman was notoriously cold-blooded, but he had identified closely with Robin Kayross, and the captain's cruel death left him weak.

Gradually, he became aware of other sounds and sights—the steady clanging of the fire department's bells, the neighing of the horses that pulled the heavy trucks, and the rush of vast quantities of water being sucked out of the harbor and sprayed onto the flames. The nearby docks were crowded with fire fighters; hundreds of spectators were being held back.

The firemen's efforts were in vain. Nothing would stop the inexorable onward march of the blaze. Not until the ship was reduced to a charred, twisted hulk did the flames begin to subside. Thanks to the efforts of the water pumpers, the last of the blaze ultimately was extinguished.

Still hiding in the shadow of the pilings, Kellerman heard the shout of a fire official. "No survivors!"

"No survivors!" The cry was echoed up and down the suddenly silent waterfront. They were unaware of the one individual who had not died.

Kellerman intuitively assumed that the explosion had not been an accident but rather had been deliberately set by his enemies. Very well, he thought. Let them rejoice, let them assume that Karl Kellerman, as Robin Kayross and his crew, had died tragically on board the doomed freighter. Let the world think he had died. Let his foes believe he had perished—and that they could stop searching for him.

He was free now, and he could be reasonably confident that his enemies would no longer be looking for him. At the moment he was penniless, but a few hold-ups soon would change all that, and he could acquire enough to live while he shook the dust of New Orleans from his feet. His supposed death had given him a new lease on life.

Weary and bedraggled, Kellerman left the safety of the pilings and scrambled up to the street level. There, several hundred feet away, he saw the fire lines and made out the forms of several fire department officials conferring as they studied the smoldering embers. So far as he could tell, no one saw him. Turning, he limped slowly from the scene, conscious that he had a breathing spell now and would be able to take his time in quitting New Orleans.

Though he was sure that his escape was unobserved, one pair of eyes had taken in the strange scene of a creature rising from the disaster scene. One of Domino's scouts, left behind to keep an eye on the destruction of the ship, saw and drew his own conclusions. No one could have survived—but apparently someone had. Domino must be informed promptly. The scout left at a trot.

Wet and cold after his efforts to haul himself to safety following the explosion of the ship, Kellerman staggered down the street. He was exhausted, but his mind continued to function clearly. He stayed on the dark side of the street where he would be protected by the shadows, and he moved slowly to conserve his energy. He occasionally suffered bouts of dizziness, but despite the shock he had suffered he now believed he knew he would survive.

Kellerman had no idea that he was being followed, at a distance, by his former partner Wallace Dugald, who had spent weeks shadowing him and knew the time had come at last for him to strike.

It was easy enough for Dugald, hiding in the shadows and staying close to the walls of the buildings, to determine that Kellerman was in a state of near-exhaustion. He staggered when he walked. Now and again he seemed to lose his balance entirely, and on these occasions he stopped, leaned against the nearest wall, and after breathing hard for several minutes, forced himself to continue. It was a miracle that the man was able to move at all after the experience he had undergone, and Dugald marveled at the stamina of his one-time partner.

An inner voice urged Dugald that the time to attack was now, when Kellerman was ailing and could not strike back. This was the moment that he had awaited for what seemed like an eternity.

All that remained was for him to call himself to Kellerman's attention, so that the man would know justice was being meted out to him by the partner whom he had wronged.

Wiping the moisture from his upper lip and forehead, Dugald dried his hands on his shabby jacket and steadied himself. He opened his mouth to speak, but at first no sound came forth. He had to try several times before he was able to utter a single word. "Kellerman!"

Hearing his name, Kellerman stiffened and slowly turned. He peered hard into the darkness, recognized Dugald, and in his relief a slow smile that more nearly resembled a sneer appeared on his face.

Adhering to his plan, Dugald had taken his nickel-plated pistol from his pocket, and he now pointed it at his tormentor.

A flicker of fear appeared in Kellerman's eyes, and Dugald rejoiced. This was the moment for which he had waited. It would be all the more satisfying now if Kellerman pleaded for mercy and Dugald had the supreme pleasure of refusing. But that was asking for too much, Dugald realized. Instead, his grip tightened on the pistol, and his forefinger squeezed the trigger.

To his horror, the weapon did not fire. Something had gone wrong, and the mechanism refused to function.

Kellerman recognized at once that his foe's plan had gone awry. Suddenly, strength flowed into the big man's body, and he felt invigorated. He had no idea where the energy had originated and did not care. It was now a matter of getting rid of Dugald once and for all. He leapt forward, intent on choking the life out of the little man.

Seeing Kellerman lunging toward him, a sneer of contemptuous hatred on his face, Dugald became panicky. Instead of holding on to the pistol and trying to use it as a club, he hurled it at the bigger man but it missed. The weapon clattered to the street, where it skidded for a distance of about ten or fifteen feet before landing in the gutter. Kellerman reached out and with strong hands took hold of the shoulders of Dugald's threadbare jacket.

The smaller man fought hard, but his blows rained ineffectually on his former partner and in no way deterred him. Kellerman's fingers closed around Dugald's throat, and he began to smash his head against the nearest wall, simultaneously squeezing hard as he tried to choke the life out of the Scotsman.

Then somewhere in the distance—or perhaps as close as a block away—Kellerman heard the shrill piping of a policeman's whistle. He couldn't take the chance of being caught. Cursing under his breath, he struck Dugald's head against the stone wall one last time, then dropped the limp body and fled.

More dead than alive, Wallace Dugald lay in the gutter, sucking in great quantities of air. His head ached, every muscle in his body felt bruised. Worst of all, he knew that the most perfect opportunity he would ever have to obtain revenge against Karl Kellerman had ended in abject failure. Sick and battered, he wept in helpless frustration, the sobs echoing down the empty street.

The academy's entire corps of cadets stood at ease after its regular, formal review on the parade ground. The occasion was the weekly announcement of individual standings in each class. The ratings were read off by the commandant, and interest was particularly keen in the race currently in progress between two of the cadets.

For several weeks, Henry Blake and Reed Kerr had remained tied for first place in their class, a highly unusual situation. Cadet Kerr had been improving his performance sharply and had moved into contention for a place previously held solely by Hank.

Few surprises were in store as the commandant began his reading of the roll. But the tension grew before he reached the names everyone was waiting to hear.

"Again tied for first place in their class are Cadet Sergeant Henry Blake and Cadet Sergeant Reed Kerr," the commandant said.

The entire corps was excited, marveling that not only had one cadet scored so unusually high, but that two had done so over such a long period of time.

Hank Blake stood fast, eyes straight ahead, resisting the impulse to exchange a quick smile with Reed Kerr, who stood in front of his own squad. Amazingly, they were the best of friends and had been close for the better part of three years.

It was strange, Hank often reflected, but he and Reed had been rivals as well as friends ever since they had entered the academy. What Hank found remarkable was that even as their competition had intensified, their friendship had deepened. That they would become brother officers was more important than whatever small difference remained in their relative standings.

The staff officers were well aware of the competition. The superintendent and the commandant of cadets, who were the two ranking officers, declared themselves wholly impartial observers, but everyone else on the faculty had his own favorite, and they occasionally discussed their preferences in the privacy of their own quarters. The academy expected both to produce the highest grades, and both had obliged accordingly.

When the review ended and the cadets were dismissed, many eyes were on the pair. Hank and Reed met halfway between their respective squads, where they shook hands firmly. "I swear," Hank said, laughing, after they exchanged congratulations, "you could feel the tension rise in the ranks as the commandant read off our score."

"I honestly don't care anymore which one of us wins," Reed Kerr told him. "I'd be unhappy, though, if some outsider came along and tried to take our first place."

"So would I," Hank replied. "That first position belongs only to you and to me."

They laughed together, and then Reed said, "By the way, they've announced the coming intramural track meet."

"I know," Hank told him. "I saw the notice this morning. Have you signed up yet?"

"I'm going to compete in only one event. Exams are coming, so I don't want too heavy a track schedule."

"The same for me."

They looked at each other, and both started to laugh. "Don't tell me!" Hank exclaimed. "I signed up for the six-mile cross-country run, so I suppose that'll turn out to be the very event you signed for."

"Correct." Reed grinned. "We're fated to compete with each other once again. Well, I can't say it will be a new feeling."

"I must admit one thing," Hank said after a moment's silence. "At least one of us will emerge with a clear-cut victory and that will affect our respective overall standings. We'll stop chasing shadows for at least one day. That will be a novelty."

They were interrupted by a plebe, one of the first-year men who traditionally were required to run errands. He approached them, halted breathlessly, and saluted. "Sir," he said to Reed Kerr, "you're wanted immediately in the commandant's office."

"Uh-oh," Reed said. "Wonder what I've done wrong! Well, I'll find out soon enough." He turned away and started off down the path that led to the office of the commandant.

"Good luck, friend," Hank called after him, as he continued on his way to their dormitory.

He had just settled down for a session of studying before the next meal when a rumor swept through the barracks: Brigadier General Robert Kerr had been killed in a battle with Indians in southern Dakota Territory.

Cadet Kerr soon confirmed the rumor. He appeared, pale and red-eyed, at the dormitory and hastily packed a valise. Granted leave to attend his father's funeral, he would return in a week.

During the following week, Hank was haunted by the bleak expression on Reed Kerr's face after he had been notified of his father's death. It was all too easy to imagine himself in a similar situation. Members of an officer's family lived with the ever-present possibility that death would take away the head of the family when they least expected it. An officer's life, like his time, was not his own. He had dedicated himself to the defense of the United States of America, and he had to be prepared for any sacrifice that he might be called on to make.

When Reed returned, Hank took the lead in greeting him with a quiet, firm handshake but made no further mention of the tragedy. General Kerr's death had been widely publicized in newspapers, but Hank thought it better to permit Reed to behave as though everything were all right.

Reed gratefully accepted this arrangement. It was part of the West Point tradition to carry on in the face of tragedy; one's duty remained the most important consideration in one's life.

In the days that followed, Hank continued to admire

his friend's attitude and behavior. Wishing that he could find some way to contribute to Reed's peace of mind, he came up with an idea.

He had no doubt that their personal rivalry was every bit as important to his classmate as it was to him. The cadet who ranked first at graduation was the recipient of an honor that would follow him throughout his entire career. Initially, he would be given the best duty assignment available and thereafter would continue to be favored by the War Department. Graduating first in his class would remain a mark of distinction on his record until he retired.

Members of the class still had many months to go before they would receive their commissions and be assigned their first duty posts. In that time, Hank told himself, the lead in class standings might change again and again. The fact that one was first at the moment did not necessarily mean he would emerge as the ultimate winner. He and Reed would continue to battle for first place, and it was always possible, too, that some other classmate might come up fast and sweep both of them aside. For the present, however, he knew that Reed was his principal competition.

One night, when he could not sleep, the emotional dilemma involved in the friendly competition threatened to overwhelm him. He made up his mind that night on his future course of action but said nothing to anyone about his decision. Thereafter, however, he was at peace within himself.

On the Saturday of the track meet, both cadets went at the same time to the locker room of the gymnasium, to change into their running clothes.

"Good luck, Reed," Hank said as he tied the laces of his shoes.

"The same to you, my friend," Reed Kerr replied, and they shook hands. Both recognized the importance of the cross-country race. The winner would take possession of first place in the far more important race of position in the class. They walked together onto the field, and other cadets watched them respectfully, again impressed because their close friendship prevailed in spite of the rivalry. Each represented the very best that the academy had to offer.

XI

As the fourteen contestants lined up for the cross-country run, the athletic director spoke briefly. "Gentlemen," he said, "you undoubtedly are familiar with the course. Take the river road north of the academy and follow it for a distance of approximately three miles before you make a large loop and return. Pickets are assigned to various posts along the way to clock you and to make sure that all of you are on course. Any questions?"

Fourteen cadets shook their heads.

"Very well, prepare yourselves, gentlemen. On your marks . . . Get set . . ." The crack of a pistol marked the start of the race.

Hank broke fast and sprinted down the cinder track that extended the length of the playing field. He headed for the north exit and followed the prescribed route, running in the direction of the Hudson River Road.

Most of the contestants chose not to expend their

energies recklessly by sprinting so early in the race. Only one of them was competing directly with Hank, who heard footsteps pounding a half pace behind. He had no need to look over his shoulder to identify the other runner: He knew that Reed Kerr had accepted the challenge immediately and was keeping pace with him.

The path led through woods before it turned at right angles and emerged onto the palisades high above the river. At that point, Reed decided to take the lead. By putting on a short burst of increased speed, he edged past Hank.

Wasting no breath on words, Hank grinned broadly at him. Reed returned the compliment, raising his right hand to his forehead in a sharp salute.

Reed had accepted his strategy from the start and was running with sufficient speed to increase the distance between them and the remainder of the pack, which was falling farther and farther behind. Stamina was more important than speed in a race of this length, and the other runners were content to let the leaders burn themselves out.

Hank actually had no intention of exhausting himself prematurely, and he was sure that Reed, whose mind functioned in the same way his did, was similarly inclined.

After maintaining the blistering pace for the better part of a mile, Reed slowed noticeably. Then, as they headed steeply uphill, he slowed again. He seemed to be indicating that he was ready to let Hank set the pace.

Sensing his friend's desire, Hank obligingly pulled forward. When he came even with his classmate, he did not forge ahead, and they ran side by side, their strides equal.

Observers at two posts were surprised to see Blake

and Kerr running neck and neck. They were a quarter-mile ahead of the rest of the runners, who would realize too late that they would have to put on a tremendous burst of speed if they hoped to close the gap.

Hank and Reed seemed to amuse themselves by alternating in the lead. First one drew ahead, then the other, but each never fell behind by more than a yard or two. They were running at the top of their form, their gait almost mechanical.

As they completed the large loop and began their return to the academy, their tactics did not alter. They had increased their lead over the field even farther now. Almost no possibility remained that any of the other runners could put on a sustained burst of speed to catch up.

Three miles to go became two, two became little more than one. Hank was aware of an increasing tension in his opponent. He assumed that Reed had figured out his basic strategy. Each would try to call on his reserves of energy and put on a final burst for as great a distance as he could manage, in order to pull ahead of his opponent and be the first across the finish line.

As they left the palisades of the Hudson and swung through the woods, Hank knew the race would end in about one more mile. Now was the time to forge ahead and stay ahead. Not even glancing at his opponent, he sucked in his breath and increased his pace. His feet pounded on the dirt road, and he ran as never before. Gradually increasing his speed, he reached a maximum that would be difficult to maintain, if not impossible.

He did not take Reed by surprise, however. He, too, summoned his reserves and moved forward at a far greater speed than he had been maintaining.

As they came to the cinder track at one end of the

athletic field, they were only two hundred yards from the tape. Gasping for breath, Hank continued to make long strides toward the finish line.

Reed kept pace with him. Those who watched the end of the duel said later they never had seen anything like it. Two young men, both in superb physical condition, were straining every muscle of their bodies in a supreme attempt to emerge victorious.

With only fifty yards to go, Reed pulled ahead by a half pace. Hank made a final effort to catch up and pass him, but Reed clung grimly to the lead and broke the tape as he crossed the finish line, with Hank only a step too late.

Both stumbled and threw themselves onto the ground, gasping as they sucked precious air into their lungs, their hearts pounding. They were so weary they were incapable of sitting upright. Gradually, they began to recover their strength and equilibrium and were able to sit.

Hank held out his hand. "Congratulations, Reed," he breathed. "You ran one whale of a race!"

"So did you, my friend," Reed Kerr replied. "If I won, I didn't beat you by more than a whisker."

Hank could see by the expression in his friend's eyes that the significance of the race was not lost on him. Reed had moved into first place in the standings now, and he intended to stay there. Hank was happy for him, knowing how he would have felt.

Coaches and classmates surrounded the pair, offering congratulations and wondering at the closeness of the race. It was astonishing to them that Reed had won by considerably less than a yard. Never had they seen a closer contest.

After the other contestants staggered to the finish line, they, too, added their praise.

The commandant of cadets, General Cavanaugh, was on hand, and after congratulating Reed and then Hank, he beckoned to the latter. "After you've had your shower, and dress, Blake," he said, "please report to my office."

Only one response was possible. "Yes, sir!" Hank said, and wondered what had happened. The stern commandant was feared by the cadets, and Hank couldn't help wondering if he had done something wrong. He went off to the locker room, where he primed the shower by pouring several buckets of water into the container at the top. And after he had washed up and dressed in his uniform, he went without delay to the administration building.

"At ease, Blake," the general said with a surprisingly genial smile. "Sit down and make yourself at home. I just wanted to have a little informal chat."

"Yes, sir," Hank replied warily. He had never thought the general capable of informality.

"You and Reed Kerr certainly ran one tremendous race," the general said. "It's an event like that that creates legends. Cadets will be talking about that race for years, and the story will be embroidered beyond recognition." He smiled.

Hank responded with a weak smile.

"I assume that the basic strategy that both of you employed—creating a big gap between you and the bulk of the other runners—was devised by you."

"Well," Hank replied modestly, "yes, sir, it was my idea." He paused for a fraction of a second and then inquired, "May I ask how you happen to know that, sir?"

"It took no particular skills to figure that out," the general told him. "I watched you setting a very fast pace and taking the lead, so I figured the strategy had to be yours. That was sound thinking, Blake, not only for the race, but for other situations, as well. I congratulate you on it."

"Thank you, sir." Hank looked down at the faded Oriental rug that had been a gift to a previous commandant by his fellow officers.

"I wonder—strictly between you and me—whether you perhaps felt a muscle twinge near the very end of the race."

Hank's heart pounded hard, but his face remained composed. "No, sir," he said. "Nothing like that happened. My muscles were perfectly fine, everything was, and I lost the race fair and square. I make no excuses for myself."

The general maintained a casual air, but he continued to regard Hank closely. "I wonder if it isn't possible that you may have picked up a pebble that lodged under your foot, or something of the sort?"

"No, sir," Hank replied stolidly. "Nothing like that happened."

"Well," the general said, "I just wondered. You see, it seemed to me, watching you during the last moments of the race, that you faltered almost imperceptibly as you approached the tape. It appeared to be a hint that something had gone amiss for no more than a fraction of a second. In that fraction of a second, Reed Kerr moved ahead of you and won the race by an eyelash."

"He beat me outright, General," Hank insisted. "I was driving as hard as I could toward the finish line, when he went past me and took over first place. It was that simple. He ran a tremendous race. He deserved to win."

General Cavanaugh waved away his explanation as though the whole subject were of no consequence. "That's very interesting. I just wondered idly, that's all." He leaned forward slightly in his chair, and his tone unchanging, he added, "I suppose you realize that Kerr moves into first place in your class."

"I can't say I knew it, General, but I assumed as much," Hank replied, "and I'm glad for him. He has been having the devil's own time, I suspect, since his father was killed in action. This step into first place should be of great help to him."

The commandant raised an eyebrow. "You're pleased for him, even though he advanced at your expense?" he asked quietly.

Hank had not been looking forward to this interview, because of the general's fearsome reputation. Now the man was taking him aback with his obvious human qualities as he prodded almost gently for what he appeared to suspect was a hidden truth behind the race's outcome. He showed genuine interest, too, in Hank as a person, expressing his queries with warmth.

"Certainly I'm pleased for Reed," Hank replied, trying as best he could to meet the general's steady gaze. "But I'll have plenty of chances to fight back and try to capture first place again between now and graduation next year. Reed was in need of a boost, and what he won is exactly what he needed. That's why I'm glad for him."

The general was silent for a moment, then nodded to suggest the subject no longer interested him. Switching to another topic, he chatted with the cadet for several minutes, then dismissed him.

Once he was alone, the general stared up at the ceiling for a time and then reached for a pen and paper and began to write thoughtfully and at length on a cadet personnel evaluation form:

Suspecting that Cadet Henry Blake deliberately lost his race this afternoon to Cadet Reed Kerr, and with it, his standing as first in their class, I questioned him indirectly on the subject, without his knowing my purpose. I asked if some difficulty near the end of the race caused him to lose. Although he vehemently denies this, I have no question in my mind that he purposely let himself slip from the lead.

Cadet Blake's motive was that Cadet Kerr, his friend, who lost his father in an Indian attack in the Dakota Territory only two weeks ago, needed such a victory for morale purposes. Therefore, Cadet Blake purposely sacrificed his own standing in his class in order that his friend, whose need he considered greater than his own, would benefit by it and move into the place that he himself had lost. He took great pains to assure me that he had lost the race fairly, squarely, and above all, honestly.

Cadet Blake's sacrifice was in the best and highest traditions of the military academy. I cannot commend him too highly for this unselfish, farsighted act, and I commend him without qualification to the officers who will read this confidential report on the eve of his graduation from the academy next year.

Regardless of where he may rank in his class standings at that time I will recommend him, with no reservation, for the highest and most difficult post that any second lieutenant in the army can possibly hold. He will be a credit to the

army, to his unit, and to his commanding officer.
Of those facts I am certain.

Major General Leland Blake was making an official
inspection trip to the Presidio in San Francisco and other
key forts under his command. Mrs. Blake was accompanying him, and consequently they were not at home when
Eulalia Blake's daughter, Cindy Holt, came home from
Oregon State College on a brief visit.

Flexibly changing her plans, Cindy decided to visit
her sister-in-law, Clarissa, at the Holt ranch in Oregon.
Lonely during Toby's prolonged trip to China, Clarissa
was delighted to have her young sister-in-law's company.

On their first evening together, after Clarissa had put
young Tim to bed, she brought Cindy up to date on
events in the neighborhood. "You just wouldn't know this
area anymore, Cindy," she said. "We've had wild excitement hereabouts lately."

"Really? I've been convinced for years that nothing of
any significance ever happens around here."

"You're wrong, dear, completely wrong," Clarissa told
her. "We have trouble on our hands—lots of it—caused by
a band of Indian renegades."

Cindy interrupted. "What tribe are they?"

"All that we know for certain is that a number of them
are Nez Percé. Apparently they come from three or four
different tribes. About twenty of them are involved in all,
and they're just plain no good! They're giving all the
Indians a bad name. They're robbing, raping, and murder-
ing. They specialize in attacking ranches at times when
women are alone. I've already had one run-in with two of
them—though I didn't know at the time that they were
part of a larger band." Briefly she told her sister-in-law

about the two men who had threatened her and whom little White Elk had been able to drive away.

"Clarissa, that's terrible!" Cindy exclaimed. "Thank goodness White Elk acted when he did. He's a brave little boy."

"That he is," Clarissa agreed. "And I'm glad Stalking Horse and the ranch hands are here, too—you can be sure of that. The only thing is, they can't be expected to wait around the ranch house, just because something might happen. They have too much else to do."

"Why haven't the authorities been able to catch them?" Cindy asked.

"That's easier said than done," Clarissa replied. "The men have acquired the reputation for vanishing into thin air after their raids."

"I don't believe it."

"Well, it happens to be true, so help me," Clarissa said. "Every time a posse tries to chase them, they can't even find the Indians. No one knows what's become of them. You can even hear talk that they're a ghost tribe. Though that's a lot of nonsense."

"How do you explain it?" Cindy asked.

"I don't!" Clarissa replied. "I'm merely repeating what two or three people who've experienced the 'disappearance' have said about it. It's interesting that all of them report the same thing."

"It *is* confusing," Cindy said, shaking her head. "And sounds as if some people are having bad dreams."

"The robberies and killings and rapes aren't dreams," Clarissa assured her. "Unfortunately, they're very real. The sheriff's office has assigned several deputies to patrol the area, but they can't be everywhere, and these renegades have a genius for striking in unprotected districts."

"Is the army going to intervene?"

"I've heard talk of it," Clarissa said, "but I don't think any final action will be taken until the general gets back and decides what—if anything—he's prepared to do about it."

Cindy drank the last of her after-dinner coffee. "Well," she said, "it's interesting, but I'm certainly not going to worry. That's something I learned when I was very young: Never stew about things you can't control."

In spite of Toby's absence, ranch life went on at its customary pace. The following morning, Stalking Horse, the ranch foreman, was called to the stable when a mare went into the throes of foaling.

Time was hanging heavy on the hands of his ward, White Elk, and the boy decided to go fishing, using the primitive pole and line of his forebears. He rode to a spot just past the far end of the ranch, where there was a small stream, marked by a thirty-foot waterfall. In the dark, deep pools below the falls lurked delicious trout, and White Elk had his heart set on catching enough to make a noonday meal.

Baiting his hook, he cast it expertly, no easy task, since he was using a line without a reel. He threw the baited hook as far as he could and then slowly dragged it toward him. He repeated the process until he had a strike. The technique required endless patience, a quality Stalking Horse was trying to develop in him.

So intent was he that he at first failed to see a procession approach until it reached a point almost directly opposite him on the far side of the river. A party of some twenty Indians, mostly dressed in their own distinctive leather gear, others wearing rough, white-man's attire, were riding single file toward the waterfall. Almost miraculously, none of the men noticed the boy across the stream from them.

As soon as White Elk became aware of the riders, he hauled in his line and pressed himself close to the earth in the tall grass. He recalled having heard Stalking Horse and several ranch hands discussing the band that was robbing and terrorizing the region. Instinctively, he knew this was the gang. Peering out from his hiding place, he was able to distinguish differences among them. He recognized that the braves were from three different tribes, although he was not familiar with their names.

Realizing that the consequences might be serious if the outlaws became aware of his presence, White Elk made no sound but tried to burrow deeper into the grass. Only after he was certain that the party had passed, did he raise himself to one elbow and follow their progress more closely.

To his astonishment, they rode directly up to the base of the falls, where they dismounted. Several of the friskier horses were blindfolded, then the party advanced again. Each Indian led his horse on shortened reins. They walked right into the waterfall and then, one by one, vanished.

White Elk could hardly believe what he had seen. As he thought about it he realized that there had to be an opening of some sort behind the waterfall.

Wildly excited by his discovery, White Elk ran into the woods where he had tethered his horse. He rode as fast as the mount would carry him back to the Holt ranch.

The mare was dropping her foal when he ran into the barn, where Stalking Horse was completely occupied. Unable to concentrate on what the boy was breathlessly telling him, Stalking Horse nodded absently. "I'm very busy right now, White Elk," he said. "Why don't you tell me all about it at supper tonight?" He returned to his duties.

Disconsolate, the boy flung himself out of the barn into the open. Tears stung his eyes, but he blinked them away as he stared miserably at the ground. He had pictured himself as a hero, responsible for the capture of the entire band, but his dream was vanishing as rapidly as the gang itself had disappeared.

Paying too little attention to where he was, he crashed into Cindy Holt, who was on her way to the barn to watch the birthing of the foal.

She caught hold of White Elk, who had stumbled, and prevented him from falling. "I'm sorry, White Elk," she said. "I must have been daydreaming."

"No, it was my fault, Cindy," the unhappy boy said. "I wasn't looking where I was going—and no wonder."

Hearing the misery in his voice, Cindy looked at him more closely. When she saw a tear glistening on his face, she put an arm around his narrow shoulders. "Maybe it would help," she suggested, "if you talk to me about it."

His energy quickly restored, White Elk began to babble about his remarkable discovery. In detail, he told about the Indians he had watched leading their horses through the waterfall and out of sight.

White Elk half expected Cindy to laugh at him, but instead she answered enthusiastically, her eyes bright. "What a clever boy you are!" she said. "I believe you found the answer to the mystery that's been confounding everybody. Can you show me the place where they disappeared?"

"Sure," White Elk told her. "Let's go!"

"I'll get a horse out of the corral and join you," she said. "But hold on a minute." Suddenly she remembered advice that she had heard given to Toby by their father, Whip Holt, when they were children: "Whenever you can, steer clear of trouble. When you can't avoid it, make sure you're properly armed. It's not a good idea to walk into a hornet's nest unless you've got a big enough swatter to take care of the hornets."

"I'll be with you in a minute," she told White Elk. "I'm going up to the house to get my rifle."

Wishing he had thought of that himself, White Elk hurried to the dwelling he shared with Stalking Horse, where he picked up the small-caliber rifle that the old man had given him as a birthday present. Making sure it was loaded and that he had extra ammunition, he returned to the compound, where he mounted his horse and waited for Cindy.

When she emerged from the ranch house and joined him, rifle in hand, they grinned at each other like conspirators. They were sharing an unusual adventure, and the prospect was exciting.

Clarissa spent the morning at a neighbor's property, where Tim had a playmate. When she returned with him to the ranch at noon, in time for dinner, she was mildly surprised that Cindy was nowhere to be seen, but she was not concerned.

After preparing dinner, however, she searched for her sister-in-law and, not finding her, began to be worried. She found Stalking Horse washing up at a pump behind the kitchen, preparatory to joining the hands at dinner in the bunkhouse.

"Have you seen Cindy anywhere?" she asked. "I thought she might have gone into town this morning, but she didn't leave a message. And that isn't like her."

"I have not seen Cindy all morning," he replied. "I have been busy with the mare. At dinner I will ask the men about her."

He paused thinking, then said, "I have not seen White Elk, either." He waved his hands in the air to dry them and then set out for the bunkhouse.

Clarissa went back to the kitchen, where she fed Tim but did not serve her own meal, preferring to wait for Cindy. A few minutes later, Stalking Horse came in. As always, his face revealed no emotion, but his grave tone suggested he was more disturbed than he was willing to admit.

"Cindy and White Elk went off together more than an hour ago," he said. "Two men saw them riding through the pasturelands on the northeastern side of the ranch. The men said that both Cindy and White Elk seemed excited, and," he added portentously, "both carried rifles."

"It does no harm to be armed when you're riding off the ranch somewhere," Clarissa mentioned. "Not these days."

Stalking Horse struck his forehead with an open palm. "I forgot! It is just coming back to me now!"

Clarissa looked at him curiously.

"When I was busy with the mare, White Elk came in and was talking as fast as he could. I thought he was talking nonsense. He said he had found the hiding place of the renegades. He must have talked Cindy into going to see this place!"

Clarissa instantly became aware of the dangers to Cindy and White Elk, but she refused to panic. "What should we do about this?" she asked as calmly as she could.

"First," Stalking Horse said, "I will send one of the

227

men into town to tell the sheriff to send a strong posse out to our northeast section. And while he is doing that, I will take several men with me to see what I can learn."

"I'm coming with you!" Clarissa answered.

At this, Stalking Horse looked at her sternly. "You will do no such thing. You will stay right here at the ranch house."

"You have no right to tell me what to do!" she flared.

"I must take the right," he replied stolidly, "because Toby asked me to keep watch over you. You and Tim will stay here. I will leave some hands here to protect you. If any strangers come onto the property, our men will shoot first—and find out later who the strangers were."

In spite of his advanced years, he darted out of the kitchen and sprinted to the corral to fetch his horse.

Clarissa knew he was right, of course. If Toby were there, he would forbid her to put herself in jeopardy. All the same, she would find it terribly difficult to stand aside, inactive, while the drama played itself out.

With their horses tethered in woods on the far side of a hill, Cindy and White Elk lay prone, keeping their eyes fixed on the waterfall. Its steady, tinkling sound was light and melodious, but it grated on Cindy's nerves after more than an hour. So far, they had seen no sign of activity. No one had appeared through the mist surrounding the falls. She stirred restlessly and sighed. A small hand crept through the grass and touched her arm.

"Don't be impatient," White Elk murmured. "It may be that we shall need to wait many hours before they appear."

Cindy felt ashamed. The boy's mild criticism was

deserved. She felt the sting of being reprimanded by a ten-year-old.

She turned her head toward him, nodded agreement, and pushing her hair in back of her ears, settled down to wait. She was determined anew to see their adventure through, no matter how long they might need to remain in this less than comfortable position.

Suddenly White Elk sucked in his breath. Peering at the waterfall, Cindy became positively giddy with triumph and excitement. Just as the boy had predicted, men were emerging from the waterfall in single file, each leading a horse. Some of the animals were blindfolded until they had reached the bank.

Squinting down the length of her rifle barrel, Cindy whispered, "If we're lucky, maybe they won't see us, and we'll avoid a gunfight. We just need to learn what they're up to—and where they're headed!"

No sooner did she speak, however, than she knew she had voiced a forlorn hope. She saw the sun gleaming on the barrel of White Elk's rifle—and at almost that same instant one of the renegades glimpsed it, too. He pointed to the place in the high grass where Cindy and White Elk were concealed and spoke abruptly to his companions. The next moment, all the Indians spread out. Aiming their weapons, they began to fire at the spot where the men had seen the sun's reflection.

"If that rifle of yours is more than a toy," Cindy told the boy grimly, "now's the time to prove it." She set her sights on the chest of a renegade warrior and pulled the trigger.

That was the beginning of a battle that won Cindy instant fame.

Unaccustomed to the sensitive, modern rifles they

were using, the renegades consistently overshot their target. Their aim was too high, and their bullets went flying well overhead. Cindy, however, had no such trouble. Her training as a sharpshooter was initiated by her father when she had been very young. In recent years, her skills were polished further by General Blake, her stepfather. In a quarter-hour exchange of fire, she demonstrated that she was truly Whip Holt's daughter. She killed three renegade Indians with three shots: two with bullets into their foreheads, and the third Indian in his chest.

White Elk proved that Stalking Horse took second place to no one as a teacher. He quickly managed to wound two of the renegades, putting a bullet into the upper arm of one, just below the shoulder, and inflicting a painful stomach wound on a second.

He and Cindy were so intent on their task that both failed to notice a dangerous development. One of the braves had separated himself from the others and, creeping away by a circuitous route, made his way to the crest of the hill behind Cindy and her youthful companion.

Astonished to find that the foe consisted of a young woman and a small Indian boy, the outlaw immediately assumed that he alone could take care of them. He did not regard Cindy, as a woman, as a serious threat and thus paid full attention to White Elk. His eyes narrowed as he watched the boy raise his small-bore rifle to his shoulder, fire, ride with the rebound, and show the expertise of a veteran as he rammed in another bullet and took aim again. It was evident that the boy knew exactly what he was doing and did it well.

Holding him responsible for the carnage below, the outlaw decided to get rid of the child immediately. Measuring the distance to the boy from the spot where he was crouching, the renegade drew his knife from his belt and tensed himself, ready to leap downward and plunge the blade into the boy's back.

Now Cindy demonstrated once more that she was worthy of being Toby Holt's brother, as well as the daughter of their father, the legendary Whip Holt. Whip had been noted for a unique "sixth sense" that warned him when extreme danger threatened. His son, Toby, was endowed with the same quality, which had saved his life on numerous occasions. And now Cindy, motivated by a strange feeling she would never be able to explain, showed the same quality. Whirling suddenly, she held her rifle close beside her and pointed it to the rear.

As she turned, the renegade sprang toward White Elk.

Not hesitating for even a split second, Cindy squeezed the trigger and fired at the figure in midair. The renegade crashed to the ground, dying before he could get to White Elk.

At this moment, Stalking Horse and a half dozen ranch hands appeared from the woods and thundered down the slope. At Cindy's urgent suggestion, Stalking Horse ordered the men to take cover, and as soon as they were in position, they opened a heavy barrage of gunfire at the renegades.

The arrival of the reinforcements was too much for the outlaws. Their horses, frightened by the heavy firing, tore free and began to disappear from the path along the bank of the stream. The renegades, finding themselves under heavy fire and deprived of their mounts, promptly began to scatter.

Because the Indians had panicked instead of remaining disciplined, it was easy for the ranch hands to round up nearly a dozen. Only three outlaw Indians had succeeded in escaping.

A short time later, Cindy and White Elk approached the waterfall with Stalking Horse. As they came very close to the cascading water, they were amazed to find that a ledge passed behind the falls. Following along it, they emerged on the other side of the falls into a small, hidden valley. Here the outlaws had built several crude shelters. Lean-tos housed large quantities of booty acquired in their raids. While their horses grazed in the valley, the men had lived here openly, away from their bewildered pursuers.

The headlines in the Portland newspaper told the full story:

RENEGADES FLEE! 7 DIE! 11 CAPTURED!
Whip Holt's Daughter
and Indian Boy
Win Battle

XII

The success of Toby and Ming-lo in breaking up the tong's convoy inspired other Chinese government bureaucrats to follow the lead of the eunuch who first came with information and later reaped the rich reward that had been promised. Word of this prize had spread like wildfire.

In the next few weeks, others came forward, bringing tips that led to successful efforts to break up several more caravans of coolies destined for export to America. Three were smashed by Toby and his loyal partner.

The last of these confrontations was significant because it illustrated how far the tong was willing to go in its opposition to Toby and Ming-lo.

The eunuch who acted as their informer told Toby and Ming-lo privately that one hundred and fifty townsmen from Peking, all from the lower class, were going to be marched to Nanking and would be transported from there to the United States. The tong had become wary, the eunuch reported, and therefore was assigning many more guards to keep watch on the recruits. He had no idea exactly how many guards were being added, but the tong presumably had unlimited reserves of manpower available.

"Obviously, we may be facing a large band of armed and ruthless men," Toby said when he and Ming-lo discussed the coming confrontation. "Possibly as many as eighty or a hundred trained killers. I think a change of tactics is called for, so as to surprise the tong."

"You are right, my friend," Ming-lo replied. "The tong has already observed aggressive action on our part. They now begin to fear us as they fear the devils of mythology. If we can keep surprising them, our reputation will be even further enhanced, and eventually the mere fact that we stand in their path will be enough to cause them to surrender."

"We're a long way from reaching that stage," Toby told him, grinning, and then sobered as he concentrated on the problem that faced them. "In previous attacks, we've tried to maintain silence, using knives as much as possible instead of firepower. Suppose this time we reverse that strategy and use firepower to the maximum. And, let us try something a little different. Why don't you get several strings of those firecrackers, the large ones that were used at the display for the empress the other evening. We'll light these strings, placing them in the two or three areas where we won't fire from. This will draw the tong's fire, since the firecrackers will seemingly sound like the heaviest concentration of shooting. Each of us could carry several repeating pistols. Since each gun will fire six shots rapidly, we'll be able to make the tong members think that far more than two of us are in the attacking force. This will be particularly true if we launch our assault after nightfall and if each of us fires from a different location. The sounds will merge with the firecrackers and make what the tong hears more realistic. Hearing rapid gunshots from different angles at night will enhance the guards' illusion that they're being struck by a force equal to their own or even larger. Our shots will not give away our positions because they'll blend with the firecrackers. Of course, we will have to keep moving quickly, but I think it will work."

"I can get the firecrackers, the larger ones that will sound like our handguns," Ming-lo said. "It is an excellent strategy. I agree with you that the chance is worth taking, because we will sound like an army of attackers."

"Good!" Toby replied, smiling with satisfaction. "If I understand the minds of your countrymen—and I'm not sure I do—the success of the tong depends in good part on the belief that it possesses a mysterious power of invincibility. If individuals both inside the tong and outside hold this view, it will tend to reinforce itself, making the tong all the stronger. But if you and I can shatter this myth, proving that two ordinary men and a nonexistent army can defeat the tong, then they will have lost so much face that their future threats will be laughed at by everyone."

Several days later, Ming-lo received another message from the informer:

> They march to Nanking with 173 prisoners. Will begin after dark tonight. Approximately 100 tong members make up the guard force. A halt for the night will be called in the place where no willows grow.

Toby studied the message and was puzzled by it. "What is meant," he asked, "by 'the place where no willows grow'?"

Ming-lo smiled. "Many years ago, an emperor built a retreat directly south of this city on the road to Nanking. Then he went to great expense and brought in thousands of young willow trees, which he planted around it. It was his intention to have a house in a woodland surrounded by willows. But the forces of nature often challenge the authority of mere man, even one who sits on the Chrysanthemum Throne. No trees grew where they were planted —the seedlings all died. It is on that site that the caravan will halt for the night."

"Can you find this place?"

"With ease. It is difficult to miss it. Few travelers stop there because it has reputedly become the home grounds of the spirit of the unhappy emperor, and the superstitious are afraid to pause there after dark. We'll find no expected visitors."

Toby chuckled dryly. "I daresay it will be a dangerous place tonight," he said, "but not because the ghost of an emperor is roaming about the neighborhood. Instead, they'll think it's his army."

Carefully timing their departure from Peking, Toby and Ming-lo rode out of the city an hour before midnight, moments before the gates were closed and locked for the night. No one would be permitted to enter or leave the capital until morning.

The night was favorable for the daring attack they had in mind, Toby thought as he looked up at the sky. Clouds, in which quantities of desert sand and dust were mixed, were blowing in from the plains of Mongolia and filling the sky with deep splotches of gray. The moon could not be seen, nor could the stars; no one could make out anything clearly beyond a few yards. Conditions would be just right for what Toby and Ming-lo had planned.

Ming-lo rode hard for about two hours and then slowed his pace dramatically, so much so that Toby thought that he was merely resting the horses. Finally, Ming-lo dismounted, gestured for silence, and tying his mount to one of the few scrub trees in the area, pressed forward on foot.

Toby followed his example. Peering ahead, he caught a glimpse of sentries armed with muskets. Beyond, large tents had been erected as shelters for the captives and their masters.

Remaining outside the perimeter of the camp, the pair separated, lit a sixty-second fuse on three extra-long strings of firecrackers, and each moved stealthily but rapidly away from the fireworks nearly one hundred yards. Then, figuring the firecrackers were about to go off, they drew one of the three pistols that each carried and, firing more or less in unison, they began to close in as the explosions began to reverberate. Every few yards, they fired another shot. When the ammunition was exhausted in one pistol, they drew a second one; finally, they came to their last. By the time they had emptied its barrels, they had reached a point close to each other. There they busily reloaded all their weapons.

In the meantime, seeing that the tong members were firing their shots away from them, toward the fireworks, they knew they had created precisely the effect they had sought. They had given their foes the impression that the attack was being conducted by a large number of marksmen. In spite of the darkness, Toby's shots had been effective: Several cooking fires had outlined the tong members, and he had been able to kill four men and wound ten others. Ming-lo, though somewhat less accurate, nevertheless had been able to inflict injury on seven of the guards.

The tong members were firing their muskets wildly in the direction from which they thought the attack had originated. Practically all of their shots went into the darkness toward the firecracker flashes, and only a few passed harmlessly overhead. Probably one or two tong members had seen Toby's and Ming-lo's gun flashes.

Their revolvers reloaded, they resumed their fire, and following the procedure they had established, they moved several steps closer with each shot they discharged.

The long strings of firecrackers were still going off, and tong members made the mistake of bunching together. Lacking knowledge of the essentials of a gun battle, they made themselves vulnerable from the outset. Thus, Toby and Ming-lo took a heavy toll of the defending force.

Musket fire remained heavy, however, spraying a wide area, but it was completely ineffective. Consequently, it was easy for Toby and Ming-lo to achieve a victory. Outlaws who had relied on terror to gain the upper hand began to give up the struggle.

Two or three surrendered, and suddenly an epidemic broke out. Men were throwing their muskets to the ground and raising hands above their heads in surrender.

Using lengths of thin but strong rope they had brought with them, Toby and Ming-lo forced each captive to loop a noose around the neck of the man in front of him and to tie his wrists behind him. In this way the entire group was made prisoner.

Only then, looking about for the army, did the members of the tong realize they had been defeated by just two foes. They were marched back to Peking with the now-happy peasants who had been taken into slavery. The gates of the city had just opened for the day when the long line entered. The tong criminals were promptly hauled off to jail and soon were sentenced by magistrates to long prison terms under harsh living conditions.

The unheard-of feat carried out by Toby and Ming-lo caused their fearsome reputation to spread even more widely in the country. Its effect on the tong's ability to wreak its will on the people was immediate. Toby's daring scheme had paid off handsomely.

Several other caravans of coolies were taken by units of the army, one in Shanghai and the other in Canton, acting on information Toby supplied to General Lin Lo-yuang.

Meanwhile, Toby's and Ming-lo's personal successes won them renewed praise from the empress. She increased the funds available for their war against the tong. This, in turn, made possible greater rewards for information, which soon began to filter in from many sources.

Toby was appalled by the full extent of the tong's activities. The small upper class was being systematically robbed of its most valuable possessions by professional thieves, who sold the items in an underground market.

And in every city, impoverished families sold the tong their daughters who had reached puberty, glad they no longer had these extra mouths to feed and using the ill-gotten proceeds to eke out a little longer their miserable existence. As for the unfortunate daughters, they were sent to brothels operated by the tong, where they came under the supervision of somewhat older girls, hardened "graduates" of the system. Sick and diseased by the time they reached the age of sixteen or seventeen, they rarely lived until the age of twenty.

Toby also discovered that opium parlors, or "dens," existed in every city and town of any consequence. A scant half-century earlier, most opium had been imported into the country from India. The demand for the drug was great among impoverished masses, who used it to induce a dreamlike trance that transported them from the miseries of their daily lives. It was now grown within China, particularly in the warm regions of the southwest, where rains were heavy. Every phase of the opium industry, from the growing of poppies to the drug's use, was under the tong's supervision.

"The more I learn about the tong," Toby said to Ming-lo, "the more closely it resembles the many-headed dragon of Chinese mythology you told me about. This organization is so evil that it continues to grow and flourish, no matter what we try to do to halt it."

"I know of only one way to destroy this tong," Ming-lo said solemnly.

"I know," Toby said. "We've got to drive our swords into its heart. And only when we've killed the core will the whole beast die."

Slowly, with painstaking thoroughness, the pair gathered information about tong activities. When they had gathered enough for an attack, they either struck at the source or turned the task over to a company of the army's elite troops.

Ming-lo had earned widespread respect when he had gone berserk and beheaded three of the tong's strongmen. The story of the brutal incident traveled to the more remote sections of China. If the number of his victims sometimes was exaggerated, that was all to the good.

The Chinese, particularly those who never had seen a foreigner, felt much more at ease with Ming-lo than with Toby, and as a result, most of the information about the tong was brought to Ming-lo. Almost every day new, vital data about the tong turned up, usually in the form of a complaint by a citizen victimized by the ruthless organization.

The task eventually became too much for the two-man team to handle. They almost foundered in the wealth of detail that poured in. The empress, reacting with unusual speed, gave them a new headquarters, situated in a building directly behind the imperial palace. A competent eunuch headed the administrative and clerical staff of sixteen persons, and a liaison office with the army's elite corps was established.

Never had Toby been so busy. He and Ming-lo gradually believed they were beginning to erode the tong's power. Their ultimate aim continued to elude them, however, and they knew that they would not succeed in smashing the tong until they found and eliminated the people who were directing it.

One morning Ming-lo came into Toby's office through the door that connected their respective private quarters. "We are spending too many days sitting here shuffling papers," Ming-lo said. "We need exercise."

By now Toby knew his companion well enough to realize that something of importance had materialized. "What's happening?" he inquired.

Ming-lo grinned. "For several weeks I have been hearing rumors of the existence of a den where any depravity is available. It is said to be a principal outlet of the tong's. And if my information is correct, it is right here in Peking. I just received corroboration of its existence this morning."

By way of response, Toby shoved aside the papers through which he had been wading and, rising, buckled on the belt that held his holster and Colt revolver. "I'm ready!" he exclaimed. "Let's go!"

In the outer city, they made their way through the densely populated slums. Ming-lo led the way. At last they reached a seven-foot-high stone wall. Entering, they found that it surrounded an enclave of about one hundred small buildings, closely resembling the hovels outside. But one significant difference existed between them. Just outside were a pair of sentries wearing the nondescript clothes of the poverty-stricken Chinese. Both were armed with old-fashioned, double-pronged spears. They stared hard at the intruders, but if they recognized them, they gave not the slightest indication of it. No attempt was made to keep the pair from entering the area. As soon as they were inside, however, Toby heard a metal gate close. They were trapped inside the walled village.

A broad-shouldered, middle-aged Chinese with graying hair approached. His eyes were riveted first on Ming-lo's scimitar, then on Toby's revolver. When he raised his head and started to speak, Toby was certain from the expression in his eyes they now had been recognized.

"How may I be of service to the brave lords?" the man asked deferentially in well-modulated Mandarin. "Every pleasure known to man is available here, and at prices so low one cannot afford to miss any of the joys."

Ming-lo looked down from his greater height. "If you

don't mind," he said flatly, "we will examine your village ourselves. When we reach a decision regarding our needs and our desires, we will let you know." Their "host" moistened his lips but merely bowed and gestured feebly toward a lane about twice as broad as nearby, narrower alleys.

Stepping around him, Ming-lo started off at a sauntering pace. Toby followed, casually resting his right hand on the butt of his pistol. His attention was first attracted to a double row of hovels. In the doorway of each, a young woman was posing seductively. Clad in short, snug-fitting *cheongsams*, they all had ripe figures. Even their heavy use of cosmetics could not conceal the fact that they were shockingly young; almost without exception they appeared to be in their early teens. A placard, its calligraphy in gold on a background of scarlet, was pinned to each hut announcing the specialties available there.

Toby's stomach turned over, and he felt ill. He realized that he was seeing the very worst of the Orient, that these girls had been sold into bondage by parents who could not afford to feed and clothe them. At fault, fundamentally, was the system in this region of the world. But the tong was taking shameless advantage of the situation.

Relieved when the miserable huts were left behind, Toby stood at Ming-lo's shoulder and peered into several other small buildings. In each of them, men were stretched out on crude beds of hard wooden planks. Each man loosely held a pipe in one hand. Some pipes were ornately carved, others were inlaid with mother-of-pearl or bits of ebony; all were three to four feet long. Occasionally, one of the men would puff reflectively. Pungent, sweet-smelling smoke filled the buildings.

Sprawled on their wooden beds, eyes closed, senses

completely dulled, the men were unaware of their surroundings. Sighing, breathing hard, and frequently weeping, they were lost in the opium dreams that removed them from the cruel realities of daily existence.

Again, Toby's stomach turned over. "I've seen enough," he said stridently. "What about you?"

"More than enough," Ming-lo replied in a grim tone. "But what do you say we do now?"

"I say we close down this rotting heap of garbage!" Toby answered angrily. "And we make damned good and sure it won't be used again!"

At that instant, they found their way blocked by three guards who stepped across the road. Each was armed with a bamboo club more than a foot in length. Filled with lead, the clubs could be very dangerous weapons, as Toby had been warned.

One of the trio started forward, his club poised above his head, ready to strike.

Ming-lo responded instantly, employing a variation of kung fu. His hands darting so rapidly their motion was blurred, he twisted his attacker's wrists, and the club flew up into the air. As it descended, Toby reached out and caught it. Smiling grimly, he, too, advanced, holding it perpendicular in front of his face as Commander Sterling had taught him. Ming-lo's full attention was centered on the guard who had launched the attack, so Toby faced the other two.

Outnumbered two to one, Toby knew he would need to prove himself more aggressive, more agile, and far quicker than his opponents. He was relying on the hope that they might lack experience in individual combat, having been hired by the tong for brawn rather than skill. In only one way could he find out.

One man, larger and looking more experienced, seemed to be the more dangerous of the pair. Toby decided to attack him first. Wielding his club as a sword, he feinted several times and then, instead of thrusting it home, bent his wrist and slashed downward onto the sentry's shoulder.

Toby struck again, unrelenting. This time, his blow caught the man on one side of the neck. The man dropped his own weapon to the ground as he clapped his hands to his neck.

"In this part of the world, the Anglo-Saxon sense of fair play has no place," Commander Sterling had told Toby. "When you have an opponent on the run, crush him completely. Otherwise, he may rise up again when you least expect it. And that could be the end of you."

Using all his considerable strength, Toby slashed the foe full across the face. The blow was harsh, smashing the man's cheekbone. He staggered and fell, unconscious.

Only one foe remained, but as Toby crossed his club with that man's, he realized he had grossly underestimated him. Although slender and much smaller, he used his club as though he had been wielding it expertly for years. Toby immediately backed out of range while he weighed the situation. At the very least, he ran the risk of having bones broken and being incapacitated. At the worst, he was in danger of his life.

Forced to alter his battle plan radically, Toby retreated swiftly instead of closing the gap between the Chinese and him. He reached for his pistol, drawing and cocking it. Without hesitating a moment, he squeezed the trigger. The sentry fell to the ground, an expression of surprise on his face as he died.

The pistol shot alerted other tong members in the

compound. Within moments, a dozen men, all armed with double pikes, were converging on Toby and Ming-lo. Six approached from one side while six more advanced slowly from the other. The intruders were surrounded.

The opium smokers' huts were useless as a means of cover, so Toby relied instead on a trick learned in his battles with Indians in the American West.

"We'll stand back to back, Ming-lo," he called softly, suiting action to words. "No matter what happens, we've got to hold these positions!"

The Chinese giant replied with a deep, reassuring chuckle.

Toby knew he had to open fire before his foes could throw their spears. Reluctant as he was to take advantage of primitive people with his modern weapon, he had no choice. If he permitted them to get any closer, he would certainly be overwhelmed and killed.

Shooting from the hip, he put a bullet into the wrist of one foe, knocking the spear from the man's hand. A second shot shattered the elbow of another sentry. A third lodged in the shoulder of yet one more guard, and his useless spear, too, clattered to the ground.

The three remaining sentries did not wait to be wounded but threw their spears away and fled. They disappeared through the now-open gate and vanished into the endless slums of Peking.

Suddenly Toby's blood congealed as he heard a sustained war whoop. Not even the Shoshone or the Arapaho had a cry as penetrating and as ferocious as Ch'ien Ming-lo's.

At the same time, his companion began to twirl his scimitar over his head. The long, curved blade moved so rapidly that no longer could it be seen clearly. He started moving forward slowly.

The six tong members who faced him stood rooted to the spot, too startled to move, too frightened to flee. Now, however, instead of grasping his blade by its handle and laying about him left and right, Ming-lo advanced toward the remaining guards.

Raising his voice in the local dialect, Ming-lo asked that someone bring him a long length of rope, for which he would pay handsomely.

Almost anything was available in the slums of China in return for money, and this district of Peking certainly was no exception. Within moments, two young men ran through the open gate and presented Ming-lo with a long coil of thin but sturdy rope. Twirling the scimitar lazily overhead now, Ming-lo grinned as he reached into his purse, withdrew a coin, and flipped it to the pair.

"I'll pay you double that amount," Ming-lo now told them. "Just knot the rope around the necks of these miserable wretches."

Chuckling gleefully, the two men fastened the rope around the necks of the six sentries, leaving a length of it for Ming-lo to grasp in order to lead them.

One more task remained. Again, Ming-lo bellowed. This time he promised a silver coin to every man who would help remove the wall that surrounded the enclave.

More than a score of men evidently heard, for within moments they rushed into the compound, bringing hammers and chisels. They worked furiously, pleased to be rid of the hated symbol of the tong.

Toby watched in fascination as the stone wall disappeared. As solid and forbidding as it had seemed, within a half hour it was gone. Even the stones had vanished. And they were not all that disappeared. Before long, the young prostitutes were gone, as were the signs advertising their specialities.

The opium smokers were no longer present, either. No pipes remained in the huts; even the wooden slabs that served as beds had vanished.

Presumably, those who had been forced into various perversions were now being given refuge by the slum dwellers. The entire poor quarter of Peking was united against the tong. When a home, temporary or permanent, was found for a refugee from the compound, no one in the area mentioned it. All eyes were closed, lips were sealed.

Toby and Ming-lo were in charge of a curious procession that made its way through the streets of outer Peking to the Imperial City and then went on to the Forbidden City. Now on horseback, Ch'ien Ming-lo led the parade, his scimitar in one hand, an end of the rope tied to his pommel, with the rest of the rope stretching out, wound around the necks of the tong members who had been made prisoner. Toby, also mounted, brought up the rear, carrying his pistol as a precaution. He had no need to use it, however; the prisoners remained docile.

At the gate that took them into the Imperial City, they picked up a squad of troops. The soldiers marched the captives in front of drawn bayonets until the prisoners were safely inside the Forbidden City, locked away in the dreaded imperial prison. There, Ming-lo conferred with General Lin Lo-yuang in low tones for some minutes.

When Ming-lo rejoined Toby, they went off together to their office. Toby glanced at the giant and found he was grinning broadly. "You seem very pleased with yourself," he observed.

"Indeed I am! We not only have done a very good

day's work, but other days at least equally good are sure to follow."

"How so?"

"It is agreed that General Lin will speak personally to each captive. He will assure them that if they cooperate with us and tell all they know about plans of the tong, they will not be executed. Instead, they will be granted complete freedom after they have spent a year or two in prison. They will not have much difficulty in choosing to cooperate rather than being put to death with a sword." He felt the blade of his scimitar with his thumb and chuckled aloud.

"I'd be grateful for any information that we may pick up about the tong," Toby said, "but I don't see how you can promise freedom to those who speak freely. The empress is very jealous of her prerogatives, as you know. I'm certain she would allow no one else to issue reprieves to prisoners."

"Oh, you have been informed correctly," Ming-lo conceded. "I would not dream of annoying the empress by asking her to extend mercy to any of our prisoners. Regardless of how much information we may get from them, they all will die. If the usual custom is followed, they will be executed in a public ceremony that will take place at sundown in three days' time."

Toby was confused. "But if General Lin promises the prisoners—"

Ming-lo interrupted with a loud laugh. "A promise to an enemy of the Chrysanthemum Throne has no meaning!" he exclaimed. "Whatever we promise the prisoners, we will suck them dry of the information they can give us. And then we will execute them without delay!"

Toby shook his head but kept his thoughts to himself.

The longer he remained in this strange land, the more acutely he realized that the ways of China and those of the West were very different. He felt homesick as well as heartsick, and he hoped with all his heart, soul, and mind that the prisoners would provide enough information for him and Ming-lo to smash the tong for all time. Then, at least, he would be free to return to the United States and to his wife and son.

The destruction of the *Amsterdam* and the captain's death ruined Kellerman's chance of receiving any more money from him or the tong. Bitterly, he reviewed how Kung Lee and Kayross had cheated him out of what he regarded as rightfully his from the importation of coolies and opium into the United States. With the money he had obtained now gone, he was desperate for funds. The answer was to set about acquiring money in the only way open to him. He staged two robberies, from which he obtained enough money to buy some clothes and to pay other expenses for a short time.

Determined to acquire a sufficiently large nest egg to leave New Orleans, he began his new scheming by entering a third-rate gambling club. There, by cheating at cards, he was able to win enough to finance himself in a higher-class gaming establishment the following night. Thanks to his expertise with cards, he won again. Now he had funds to make his boldest move yet: He would go the following night to a gaming establishment owned by his archenemy, Domino. And there he would play for high stakes. Though taking a chance that he might be recognized, he decided he had no choice. At no other gambling hall in town was betting for such high stakes permitted.

Kellerman did not know that the gaming house he

had visited on his second night of gambling was also owned by Domino. As he congratulated himself, he was unaware that his "winning streak" had been under constant observation for most of the evening.

Late that night, Domino sat in the library of his house, engrossed in his favorite game, playing it with a negligée-clad Martha, who looked far less glamorous with her makeup removed. She yawned frequently as she sipped hot chocolate, paying scant attention to the game. The atmosphere was relaxed, and the mild-looking gang leader, as always, blocked everything else from his mind to concentrate on winning the game.

Eddie Neff came into the room, controlling his excitement with an effort. "I've just come from the River Club," he announced loudly. "We've latched on to something there."

Hearing the tension in his voice, Domino looked up, the game promptly forgotten. "What is it?"

"A fellow was playing poker there tonight." Eddie paused, and though the night was cool, he wiped perspiration from his forehead. "He had a great streak of luck, and the fellows tell me they kept a close watch on him all evening."

"How much did he win?" Domino demanded gruffly.

"More than nine thousand dollars."

Martha whistled softly.

"The dealer, Sam, thought he was cheating," Eddie said, "but couldn't catch him doing anything wrong. If he was cheating, he apparently was a real expert. Sam overheard him make a remark that sounded as though he's intending to show up tomorrow night at the Cajun Club."

Domino sounded irritated. "Who is this man?"

"Believe it or not," Eddie said hesitantly, reluctant to be the bearer of news that would infuriate Domino, "but Tony, who saw him only from a distance as he was leaving, tells me that something about the man reminded him of Karl Kellerman."

Domino gripped the arms of his chair so tightly that his knuckles turned white. His mouth fell open. He was speechless for a full minute, and when he recovered his voice, it was strangled with rage.

"Impossible!" he exclaimed. "We finished him off. I swear, that man couldn't have gotten away. No survivors, they said!"

"I think that was true," Eddie told him soothingly, his need to quiet Domino's extreme distress exceeding his own feelings. "But do you remember when Pete came in to say that someone had climbed out of the water near the wreck and run away? I suppose there's always a chance—"

Domino interrupted angrily. "No one can be trusted, apparently, to do a job right. We destroyed a ship and its crew to get at him! Don't tell me he got away."

Neither Eddie nor Martha ventured a word.

"But just to be safe," Domino went on, calming slightly as he sought to think his way logically out of this newest dilemma, "we'll be ready for him at the Cajun. He'll be sorry—if it is Kellerman. We'll have so many guns on him he'll end up looking like a doily."

Martha intervened swiftly. "Don't go after him at the Cajun Club," she said. "It's too exclusive for any violence. That would ruin its reputation."

"Do you expect me to sit back and do nothing? Do you think I want to let Kellerman slip through my hands again?" Domino was red-faced. "That is, if this really is the rat."

"I think," Martha said quietly, "it's time for me to step into this picture. Spending hours each day sitting with Millicent as she recuperates, I've listened to her talking at length about Kellerman. I picked up what can be highly useful information. I think I understand him now. Perhaps I can be the key to cornering him for you."

"No!" Domino said explosively. Then, calming himself with an effort, he turned back to Eddie. "See me again first thing in the morning about this," he instructed. "I have another matter to settle tonight."

"Yes, sir," Eddie said, glad to be able to leave.

Domino turned to Martha, his eyes glittering. "Now," he demanded, "what's on your mind? Maybe you'll explain yourself?"

Martha faced him bravely. "Unfortunately," she said, "Kellerman has the qualities of a slippery eel. You've set three sure-fire traps for him, and he's escaped from every one of them. You know the police would close down the Cajun Club if there's a shooting and that the patrons would go elsewhere—for good. Any notoriety could ruin your best gold mine. As for Kellerman, I've learned from Millicent that sexy women are his greatest weakness, as you would expect. I'll make myself irresistible to him. Wherever he may go after he leaves the Cajun, I'll go with him, I assure you. He has no reason to suspect me of any connection with you. You and I should be able to keep in touch. It can be that simple."

"I'll be damned," Domino said with slow emphasis, "if I want you to become intimate with that slime."

"Really! Martha retorted. "You're forgetting that you informed me—long ago—that sex is best used as a weapon and that it's a far more potent weapon than the deadliest firearms. This is no time to become squeamish or start acting like a prude. You want Kellerman's head, and I'm the one who can bring it to you. I've worked closely with you, have performed a great many duties, and I've never failed in an assignment. I don't expect to fail now. I know how important the extermination of Kellerman has become to you, and I don't want you to be let down. That's the way it is, and I refuse to hear anything else."

Domino recognized with resignation that Martha always had her own way with him: He never had been able to refuse her anything she wanted. This occasion was no exception. His mind working rapidly, Domino had to admit that everything Martha had to say about Kellerman might make sense. He felt certain that she, of all people, would be able to live up to her promise and set Kellerman up so that Domino's men could kill him quietly and efficiently.

"All right," he said heavily. "Go after him any way you please. But take no needless risks. Anytime you think he may be on the verge of learning your identity, clear out. The sooner you're able to get in touch with me, the sooner I'll be able to breathe easily again!"

The next morning, after dressing for the day, Martha went to Millicent Gautier's bedroom for a cup of tea and their customary morning chat. Millicent, although thin and pale after her long illness, looked fit in a new full-skirted traveling suit that her husband had just bought for her. She smiled radiantly as Martha came into the room.

"This is the big day," Martha called out cheerfully.

"I can hardly believe it," Millicent replied. "I'm going home at last! I've been packed and ready to go since dawn. How soon do you suppose Jean-Pierre will come?"

Martha glanced at the clock on the mantel. "He said

he'd arrive between ten-thirty and eleven, so you have at least another hour to wait. Sit down and have some tea." She went to a teapot that rested on a tray and filled two cups.

"It's hard to realize I'm actually leaving," Millicent said and sighed.

"You've had a long road back to full health," Martha reminded her, "but you've made it. And, in the long run, you have lost nothing as a result of your experience."

"Thanks to you!" Millicent said. "I'll never be able to express my gratitude to you and Domino, not only for saving me, but for being so patient in nursing me back to health. You and I are going to see a great deal of each other in the months ahead."

"I hardly think that's too likely, my dear." Martha's voice was dry. "We really don't travel in the same circles, after all."

Millicent looked at her indignantly. "We're friends!" she exclaimed. "As you've demonstrated time and time again. I'd be a fine friend if I turned my back on you now. I'll be proud to be seen with you anywhere in New Orleans, at any time, in any company!"

Martha was touched. "Thank you, Millicent. You're very sweet."

"Come to think of it," Millicent said, "can you come to our house for dinner tomorrow evening? And don't tell me I'm not to overdo. We have a cook and a maid, so there will be no real work for me."

"I'd love to accept," Martha said, "but I'd better beg off and ask you for an invitation at some later time. I may be tied up tomorrow night with an old friend of yours."

Millicent raised an inquiring eyebrow.

"Karl Kellerman," Martha added, smiling.

Millicent's jaw dropped, and she stared at her friend in horror.

Martha explained that she planned to meet Kellerman that same night at the Cajun Club, and that thereafter, she hoped to isolate him where Domino's associates would dispose of him.

"Can't Domino find somebody else to take your place?" Millicent asked, wringing her hands.

Martha shook her head. "I'm sure that a dozen women could substitute for me, but none can do the job as well or as discreetly as I can. I know the habits of the police and could tell you where they're likely to be at any hour of the day or night. I can do a thorough job of isolating Kellerman. Frankly, Domino objected rather vehemently when I broached the subject. But it didn't take him long to see things my way."

Millicent continued to stare at her. "I beg you—be careful!"

"Oh, I shall," Martha replied. "Thanks to you, I know Kellerman well—"

"No, you don't!" Millicent cried, interrupting her. "He's the slyest, most treacherous, two-faced monster on earth, and nobody knows him well. If he thinks you represent a danger to him, even a slight danger, he won't hesitate to kill you—and without suffering regret or remorse. I realize you'll know what you're doing in dealing with him, Martha, but I implore you—watch your step and exercise great care!"

Thanks to Martha's dramatic and wise intervention, Jean-Pierre was far better able to understand his wife's mental state after she'd been kidnapped by Karl Kellerman. Nevertheless, the resumption of a normal married life was not easy for either of them. Perhaps the burden of guilt had been Millicent's or it may have been that her husband shared it. Whatever the reason, they were self-conscious whenever they tried to make love. Consequently, their attempts were halfhearted and always ended in failure. Both of them realized that something had to be done, but they were uncertain how to proceed.

Millicent spent hours alone, pondering the problem while her husband was off at work. Although many ideas occurred to her, she rejected them all as foolish or unworthy. Finally, one bold plan came to her, and she weighed it at great length. Either it would be enormously effective, or it would be catastrophic for both of them. The rift that continued to separate them might grow far wider and be impossible to bridge.

Uncertain, she weighed the matter for more than a week. Finally she decided to go ahead with her scheme. At this point she felt she had little to lose.

She spent all one afternoon primping and preparing. That evening, when Jean-Pierre came home from his office, she presented herself to him in the living room without saying a word. He was utterly shocked. She looked exactly as she had looked when she had returned from Madame Gayley's establishment. Her makeup, her hair, and her costume were identical to what she'd worn when she had been rescued from Kellerman's clutches.

He stared at her outrageous attire in astonishment, so frozen that he was unable to move or speak.

"Is this a-a masquerade?" he demanded, finding his voice at last.

She shook her head vehemently, her dark hair swaying, and held out her bare arms. "No," she said. "It's anything but a masquerade. I thought the time had come to let you know how I really feel and to share with you the intimacies that you imagined I'd shared only with someone else. The time has come to banish forever the ghost that separates and holds us apart."

Smiling at him, she curled her arms around his neck.

But he was still not entirely satisfied. He had a confession to make, and he wanted her to hear it. "There are ghosts that both of us know and recognize," he said, "and each of us has private ghosts about which the other knows nothing, ghosts that exist only within each of us."

She silenced him with a long, passionate kiss. "There are ghosts," she said, "that must be exorcised and sent packing for all time. Ghosts that neither of us wants to know and ghosts that neither of us has a right to know. These visions have no part of our relationship. They don't belong to you or me. They come from the times of our lives that we've lived separately, and they have nothing to do with us or our love for each other."

Jean-Pierre had heard enough. Sweeping her into his arms, he held her close. "Dearest," he said, "we're wasting our time with words. The time has come for us to act rather than talk!"

They began to make love in earnest, kissing and fondling each other as they stretched out on the divan in the living room.

Millicent, in spite of her bold attire, was reticent as always, and Jean-Pierre, encouraged by her innate sweetness, became that much stronger and more aggressive.

They swept aside all memories of the past. The intensity of their lovemaking burned up all the jealousy and bitter memories.

The experience more than satisfied them. It destroyed

all harsh memories of the past and enabled them to face the future, united, confident of tomorrow thanks to the love that both of them had shown. Their love was stronger and more secure because it had endured the fires of jealousy and suspicion.

As they were later able to agree, the phantoms of the past were buried in the love of the present, and in the promise of love for tomorrow.

XIII

If Domino had had a crown jewel, the Cajun Club would have been it. A superb restaurant, serving the finest food and the best vintage wines in New Orleans, it also attracted a glittering clientele of ladies and gentlemen who enjoyed games of chance. Gaming clubs operated openly under the city's liberal laws, and the Cajun was filled to capacity nightly with people in evening dress trying their luck at games of twenty and one, poker, baccarat, and roulette.

Most of the activity took place in the main salon, a large room with Louis XV furniture, mirrored, glittering walls, and a huge crystal chandelier. Here, those who chose to gamble for high stakes congregated. The click of chips and murmurs of voices formed a discreet background. Waiters noiselessly entered and left, carrying platters of succulent, huge Gulf shrimp and bottles of chilled champagne to the players.

In high spirits, Karl Kellerman entered the room, wearing a new suit of dark worsted wool that made him inconspicuous. Also, he had dyed his sandy hair black, which made him feel far more at ease than when he had worn a wig. Tonight the false mustache he wore was a solid black, and it drooped over his upper lip. As he sat down at a small table to play a game of twenty and one with the dealer, he smiled jovially. Casually he glanced around the room, and suddenly he swallowed hard, the game all but forgotten. A young woman had just entered the room, and she was one of the most entrancing women he had ever seen. Her shimmering red hair cascaded over bare shoulders. Her shining, moist lips were rouged to emphasize their contours, and her eyes, her most arresting feature, were enhanced with mascara and kohl. Her jade and diamond necklace seemed to bring out the creamy texture of her skin. Her walk, that of a patrician, was strangely disturbing. A full-length skirt seemed to be made of heavy fringe, and as she walked, it parted enough to reveal tantalizing glimpses of her long, shapely legs. The woman was wearing black silk stockings and exceptionally high-heeled evening slippers.

She seemed unconscious of the presence of anyone in the room as she walked across it and took a seat at a table near the one Kellerman occupied. As she seated herself, her skirt fell away to reveal a shapely leg. Kellerman began to feel an ache in the back of his throat.

She summoned a waiter and ordered a glass of champagne. Kellerman promptly did the same. The dealer seated opposite him handed him a deck of cards to cut, and he forced his mind back to the game.

Kellerman, who knew as much about the game of twenty and one as any professional, was thoroughly familiar with the betting odds for and against every hand. His natural instinct as a card player and his ability to keep mental track of the cards that had been played made it possible for him to win far more often than he lost.

After two hours at the table, Kellerman worked his stake of nine thousand dollars up to more than thirty thousand. Only then did he take a few minutes off. Lighting a cigar, he glanced at the beautiful woman to see how she was faring.

She was playing baccarat, and although he couldn't see the cards she was being served, he regarded her attitude as little less than magnificent. Her expression remained unchanged, regardless of whether she won or lost; her calm was monumental.

She, too, seemed to require a respite from her game. Signaling to the dealer, she declined to be served another card. She closed her large green eyes for a moment, and then, opening them again, regarded Kellerman. Her gaze was not coy, secretive, or flirtatious. Instead, it was candid, frankly curious, and searching.

Feeling as though he had been struck by lightning, Kellerman tingled as he returned her look with a steady stare of his own.

Still gazing at her, he summoned a waiter and ordered an expensive bottle of champagne taken to her. When the waiter uncorked it for her and explained, she looked over at Kellerman and dazzled him with a smile that was rich in promise. Suddenly, however, she drew back. Her face once again became expressionless, and her personality seemed to drain away. She lost interest in the man, as well as in her surroundings.

Returning to his game, Kellerman found himself unable to concentrate. In the next few minutes, he lost three thousand dollars. Realizing that his fascination with the woman would cause him to dribble away more of his earnings, he called a halt to the game and collected his winnings.

Rising, he wandered over to her table. "Do you mind if I watch?" he inquired politely.

"Not at all," she replied. "Thank you for the champagne. Please have a glass." Not waiting for his response, she signaled to a waiter, who approached and filled a glass for Kellerman.

He watched in approving silence as she won three bets in quick succession.

"I'd better quit while I'm ahead," she said, laughing.

He nodded gravely. "That's just how I felt." He pulled back her chair, and she stood.

"I'm Arnold Faberman," he said, offering her his arm.

"I'm called—Martha," she replied, lightly putting her hand on his arm.

They stepped out to a balcony overlooking the Mississippi. There, in the moonlight, they spoke at length.

Martha was so frank in her admiration that Kellerman's vanity expanded. He became an exceptionally easy mark for her. It was plain that he wanted her badly, and she fed his desire by casually brushing up against him, as if by accident, and then drawing back demurely.

Finally, unable to stand her teasing game any longer, he proposed that they leave the Cajun. Martha agreed instantly, and they went to the club entrance, where they hailed a carriage for hire pulled by a team of two horses.

Once they settled themselves in, Kellerman reached for her, but she moved away. Next, he proposed that she accompany him to his hotel.

"Ordinarily," she said distinctly, "I charge a very high fee for such visits. But I like you, and I'm willing to go with you at no charge."

Kellerman was elated. He had figured her correctly! She was a very high-priced prostitute but he was getting her services at no cost. As usual, his luck with women was phenomenal.

Martha was satisfied, quietly aware that they were being closely followed by one of Domino's carriages.

The couple spent the night in Kellerman's room at a large hotel, one sufficiently busy that he thought he would not be too noticeable there. Martha carried out her part of the mission with practiced aplomb, easily acting the role of an expensive courtesan, pretending that Kellerman was arousing her to a high pitch of sexual excitement.

They ordered fruit, rolls, and coffee sent to the room in the morning. Kellerman was so enthusiastic over their relationship that he asked, "Why don't you come with me? I'm shaking the dust of this town from my boots by noon. I'm heading north."

"That depends on where you're going and how you plan to get there, honey," she replied.

"I'm buying passage on a paddle-wheeler called the *Louisiana*. If you'll come with me, I'll simply get a double first-class cabin instead of a single. I'm going up to Cairo, Illinois, where the Mississippi and Ohio meet. I need to attend to some business there. We could make a number of stops in fine places on the way, where we could dine and rest, and then pick up reservations on later boats."

"That sounds good to me, honey," Martha told him, "but you'd have to buy me a new wardrobe. I can't go shopping dressed the way I am without creating a sensation. As a matter of fact, I'd attract too much attention now, if I go through the lobby in this evening dress."

Kellerman had no desire to call attention to himself in the hotel. "I'll take care of that for you," he said quickly. "I'll go out right now and buy you a wardrobe. Just tell me your size and what you'd like. I'll get you everything you'll need for a trip. I can be back in plenty of time for us to get to the waterfront and book passage on the *Louisiana*."

After seeming to ponder the idea further, Martha agreed, and Kellerman left to perform his errands.

Martha waited for several minutes, and then she went to a desk, where she found writing paper. Using a quill pen, she wrote rapidly, underlining various words for emphasis. Reading over what she had written, she added to it, then folded the letter and put it into an envelope. Placing it at the bottom of her reticule beneath some cosmetics, Martha settled back to await Kellerman's return.

He had found just about everything she would need for a trip by boat, including a smart coat to wear when they reached a cooler climate. Rewarding him with a prolonged kiss, Martha dressed quickly and touched up her makeup. After packing her new things in the valises he had bought, she was ready to go. Kellerman ordered their luggage placed in a waiting carriage. As soon as he paid their bill, they were on their way to the waterfront. He had no suspicion that they were being followed.

At the dock, while Kellerman went on board the *Louisiana* to buy their transportation if an appropriate double cabin was available, Martha stood quietly waiting beside the luggage.

A nondescript man in overalls and a peaked cap working nearby paid no attention to her as he appeared to oversee the loading of luggage and last-minute cargo on board the paddle-wheeler. Only someone who knew Eddie Neff extremely well would have known that it was he.

Martha, seemingly lost in thought as she stared out at the river, removed the letter from her reticule. Bending down, she wedged it easily between two boards in the dock. Then she drifted aimlessly to the far side of her luggage.

The duties of the "overseer" soon took him close to the spot where she had been standing. Quickly he bent down, and in a single, swift movement, he scooped the letter up and deposited it in the pocket of his overalls. He moved so rapidly that even someone watching him would have had difficulty in following his actions.

Still seeming to supervise the cargo handlers, the man moved to a place on the deck directly behind Martha. No more than six feet separated them now.

Coughing, Martha raised a handkerchief to cover her mouth, then began to speak quickly and clearly. The man gave the appearance of collecting his thoughts as he lifted his cap and slowly scratched his head. Then, when Martha stopped speaking and put her handkerchief back in her reticule, he called out what could have been considered orders to the workers. The work was finished just as Kellerman came down the gangplank, waving a ticket in triumph, to show Martha that he had succeeded in purchasing the cabin he wanted.

For a fraction of a second, Martha's eyes and those of the "overseer" met and held. A vital message was exchanged, unnoticed by Kellerman or any bystanders.

Just before the *Louisiana* moved into the current, a shabby man sleeping on a bench at the far end of the dock roused himself enough to scan the passengers who were lining the railing, waving to friends left behind or scanning the city's skyline.

The drifter was none other than Wallace Dugald. He gazed at the passengers, then suddenly narrowed his watery eyes to bring the scene into sharper focus. His vision fixed on a single face—that of his sworn enemy, Karl Kellerman. He would know the face anywhere, regardless of any disguise.

Frustrated by his failure to eliminate his former partner, Dugald had been driven to consume more and more of the wares of his saloon. Finally, he had been unable to operate the business successfully, and having lost it, he had sunk into a deep depression.

And now that bitter feeling of failure was heightened by the realization that the very man on whom he had sworn undying vengeance had just passed by him and was once more eluding his grasp. Wallace Dugald collapsed onto the rough timber of the dock, sobbing incoherently.

"The chief of sentries, captured in the walled village," Ch'ien Ming-lo reported cheerfully to Toby, "was eager to cooperate. He told all that he knew. In fact, he was so very helpful that I returned the favor—and executed him myself. Painlessly. It was the very least I could do for him."

Toby put out of his mind all thoughts of the cruelty and injustice practiced by the Chinese. He could do nothing to counter thousands of years of a way of life that was ingrained in them. Instead, he tried to concentrate on the information that the chief sentry had given Ming-lo. "What did you learn?" he inquired.

"He and two of his men had been ordered to report today to the tong headquarters. For the very first time, he had been told its location. They were scheduled to join numerous other members there, in order to receive and put away many cartons of opium scheduled to arrive from the south. The leaders have been using their places in Shanghai and Canton as storage depots to conceal supplies of opium. But apparently it was decided that, thanks to our efforts, they no longer are safe. They are going to use their headquarters for the first time. Apparently, all the major tong leaders will be on hand to receive the opium. It is worth millions of American dollars. We should make an appreciable haul when we capture them."

"Do you know the exact location of this headquarters?" Toby asked sharply.

Ming-lo grinned. "Of course," he said. "If you will accompany me right now, General Lin Lo-yuang will meet us in a building near the headquarters. From there, it will be safe to observe and make our plans of attack accordingly."

They rode at once to the Forbidden City, where they found General Lin waiting in an unoccupied office on the top floor of a government building. He stood at a window, looking at a nearby structure through binoculars. When he had greeted the newcomers, he handed them binoculars, as well.

Toby found himself examining a sprawling structure, three stories high, surrounded by numerous gardens and a half dozen outbuildings. All were enclosed within a high stone fence.

"This was a palace," General Lin explained, "built long ago for the illegitimate daughter of an emperor. According to the imperial records, which I just examined, the palace has been used in more recent times as a library. No one has lived in it for many years. At least, so the record books say.

"It appears," he added, "that the tong managed to gain access to the palace and is using the place for its own purposes. This was an exceptionally clever move. Who would expect a major criminal organization to use an establishment like this as its headquarters?"

Toby continued to study the palace. "It looks," he said at last, "like a relatively easy place to defend. If they have it as well guarded as you would expect, we'll find it very difficult to break in by the time their high command is on hand and the opium is delivered."

Ming-lo laughed. "Those who direct the destinies of the tong," he predicted, "will find it equally difficult to leave."

They began to discuss the mechanics of how to capture the leaders and at the same time confiscate the large quantities of opium that were expected to be delivered late in the day.

"I can promise you," General Lin said, "that by the time darkness begins to fall this evening, my troops just outside the city will have intercepted the opium wagon train. As soon as I have been informed that this has been done, I will then instruct a full battalion of elite guards to form a ring around the palace. They will be concealed in underbrush and in available entrances to buildings directly opposite the palace walls. We have more than six hundred soldiers in a single battalion, so we can set up a very tight cordon. The men know how to use modern weapons. They can be instructed to allow no one to leave the palace grounds alive. In that way, we bottle up the entire high command."

"Your suggestions," Toby replied, frowning slightly, "are fine as far as they go. But aren't you leaving several loopholes? If we delay too long, they might somehow learn of our strategy and prevent us from entering their walls."

Ming-lo nodded vigorously. "That's right," he agreed.

"How is opium packed, and how was it to be delivered?" Toby asked.

"Raw opium," General Lin responded, "is said to be packed much as it was many years ago, when India was the major source. It is described as heavily wrapped in oiled paper, to which beeswax is added. Then it is crated. A crate is about two feet in each dimension. Since each crate is so small, many crates at a time can be carried in wagons pulled by horses or oxen."

"It seems to me," Toby said, "that it will be necessary to send a party into the palace. Ming-lo and I ought to be members of that party."

Ming-lo instantly and heartily agreed.

One last major detail remained to be settled. "General," Toby asked, "can you loan me about twenty-five of your most exceptional younger officers? I would like them to be of the grades of lieutenant or captain, all under thirty years of age. And all skilled at handling knives and pistols, with a solid knowledge of martial arts."

General Lin assented, saying he would be pleased to provide the officers.

Without delay, they returned to the imperial palace, where each busied himself with his self-appointed chores. Ming-lo attended to the procurement of three very large wagons, pulled by teams of oxen. In them were piled tea boxes that resembled the opium packages. He also acquired cotton tarpaulins long enough to cover the load each wagon would carry.

General Lin's first task was identifying and assigning the young officers. With that out of the way, he named the elite guard battalion that he wanted to ring the Forbidden City palace and departed to brief the soldiers on their mission.

Toby first studied an old map of the compound. As he committed it to memory, noting especially the locations of various rooms and corridors, he began to feel confident that he already was familiar with the palace. *That can't be*, he told himself, but the idea lingered in spite of his determined efforts to erase it from his mind.

General Lin's personal aide-de-camp came to inform Toby that the young officers were at the military barracks behind the imperial palace awaiting his orders. He accompanied the aide to an assembly room, and there, behind closed doors, he inspected the men who would be his companions in the coming battle. He was heartened to note that they were lean and confident, and above all, intelligent. They handled pistols and knives expertly.

Swearing the young officers to secrecy, he explained their coming mission. He went into detail as to what he expected. "If you carry out your assignments successfully," he told them, "the power of the tong will be broken, and the forces of the empress will emerge triumphant. Remember that the members of the tong are vermin that must be exterminated, and it is your sworn duty to kill them. Obey Ch'ien Ming-lo and me as you would obey the empress. When called on to use your own initiative, think clearly and rapidly. Then act accordingly, always striking swiftly. You will face a ferocious enemy, so know that you must kill or be killed."

The officers filed out, and General Lin reappeared. He provided Toby with two belts filled with throwing knives. These knives, together with the gun belt holding his own repeating pistols, made Toby feel very much in command of the situation.

Shortly before sunset, while the troops of the elite guard battalion were slipping into place around the Forbidden City palace, Toby accompanied Ming-lo to the inner courtyard of the military compound, where only authorized persons were admitted. For the first time, he saw the wagons that Ming-lo had assembled. Each was very large, pulled by a team of four oxen. It was apparent they would be perfect for deception. At the rear end of each, tea boxes were stacked so as to appear to be containers of opium.

The young officers appeared from the interior of the barracks and dispersed to the wagons. Nine climbed into the first vehicle, while the remaining sixteen concealed themselves inside the other two. Then tarpaulins were drawn over them. Nothing could be seen except for an occasional glimpse of the carefully arranged boxes.

Ming-lo had Toby join him and the driver on the seat of the lead wagon. Like his friend, Toby donned a tattered coolie coat and a pagoda-shaped hat of blackened straw, which he pulled low on his head in order to conceal his features.

The three wagons started off promptly in single file, and it soon became evident that Ming-lo and General Lin had left nothing to chance. They departed from the military compound via a little-used exit. At the wall surrounding the Forbidden City, they used a gate where traffic was light. Once the convoy reached the Forbidden City, the drivers employed diversionary tactics, turning first left, then right, then left again on secondary roads. Toby was unable to follow the route well enough to know where they were.

A glint of humor appeared in Ming-lo's dark eyes. "We must appear to approach our final destination," he muttered, "from a direction opposite the one we actually took. We will convey the impression that we have reached Peking from the south, from Nanking."

Toby nodded and was grateful for his associate's attention to detail. Ming-lo thought of angles that had not entered his mind.

After a time, the caravan came to a relatively broad street, apparently a major thoroughfare, and proceeded down it. From a distance, Toby saw the turrets and towers of the small palace, behind its protective wall. Although he had glimpsed it only from the outside previously, he felt, once again, he had already been there.

The wagons were approaching the entrance to the palace. Ming-lo reached under the wagon seat and produced a small crossbow and steel-shafted arrow. It was the type used by outlaws in the countryside between Peking and Tientsin. At last they pulled to a halt in front of the gate, where a half dozen armed sentries, all in nondescript civilian attire, were grouped. Their weapons included knives, an ancient blunderbuss, an equally old rifle, and several types of swords. If necessary, they presumably could put up a thoroughly unpleasant fight with even these weapons.

As the lead wagon pulled to a halt, a sentry brusquely demanded that the tarpaulin be removed before he would open the gates.

To the astonishment of the sentries, Ming-lo leaped to his feet, brandishing his bow and arrow. In the crude accents of the southern interior, he bellowed, "I have ridden in this accursed wagon for so many weeks, all the way from Nanking to Peking, that my ass is so sore I find it difficult to sit down! I have been hounded by the army, by customs inspectors, and by stupid employees of a half dozen imperial viceroys. What, in the name of my revered ancestors, do you think is under the tarpaulins of these wagons? Do you think we are carrying contraband? Or perhaps," he added with deep sarcasm, "smuggling imperial troops into your precious palace? My crossbow itches. The itch is fierce and becomes worse second by second! You can see for yourselves that my wagons are loaded with boxes. Even you who have feeble minds certainly should be able to figure out what the contents of those boxes may be!" He worked himself up to a furious climax. "Either my wagons, all three of them, will be admitted to the grounds instantly, without delay, or I will be obliged to start taking lives with my arrows." He flourished the crossbow, nocked the arrow into it, and started to draw back the bow.

The chief sentry had heard and seen enough. He had always been told that anyone from Nanking was evil-tempered, if not totally mad, and this big man's conduct proved it. Rather than start a fight, which might cause some deaths and call the attention of the Peking authorities to the scene, he decided it was far better to allow the carts to enter and unload their precious cargo. Later, he could make a report complaining about the bad temper and insubordination of the giant from Nanking. His superiors in the tong would surely deal with the lout accordingly. Wearily, the chief sentry waved, and several of his men hurriedly pushed the iron gates open.

The first wagon pulled to one side, and the other two wagons entered ahead of it. Ming-lo's wagon now fell in behind.

Stowing away the crossbow and arrow, Ming-lo

breathed a deep sigh of relief. So did Toby. Thanks to his friend's inventiveness, the first obstacle had been overcome.

The convoy crept forward slowly. Two tong members stationed on the cobbled drive pointed out where the wagons were to go. Soon they rumbled into an inner courtyard. Again, Toby had the feeling that he had been here on some previous occasion.

Ming-lo seized the driver's whip and brought it down with all his great strength onto the top of the tarpaulin. As its loud, cracking noise echoed, he bellowed "Now!" at the top of his voice.

The officers, who had been awaiting just such a signal, threw off their tarpaulins and poured out of the three wagons into the courtyard, their weapons ready for use.

Toby and Ming-lo did not wait for the tong to strike the first blow. No sooner did the officers begin to emerge than they selected targets and began to hurl their throwing knives with their accustomed deadly accuracy.

Six tong members had been waiting casually for the wagons to halt so they could remove the boxes of opium. Now, scant seconds later, three of them were dead, and a fourth lay on the ground, seriously wounded. The two remaining tong strongmen, who had not yet been harmed, hastily fled. Two of the officers, waving pistols, fearing they would miss their share of the battle, went in pursuit and brought down the pair.

The sound of their gunfire, echoing through the old palace, alerted the tong's high command to their danger. They reacted swiftly.

Dividing the invaders' force, Toby took sixteen officers and headed for the main staircase, while Ming-lo went with the other nine toward narrower back stairs.

As Toby and his officers reached the staircase and

started to ascend, a thick shower of arrows poured down. No one was injured in the sudden assault, but Toby immediately called a halt to consider the situation. Though it seemed that men carrying modern weapons should prevail easily over men relying on a barrage of arrows, Toby had developed a healthy respect for arrows in his fights with Indians. He knew what needed to be done, but first he must find the necessary tools.

He sent several officers through the ground floor, foraging for small tables. They brought him nine, all approximately two feet in diameter. Toby noticed to his satisfaction that each of the tables was supported by a single pedestal rather than four legs. All were made of wood, yet the surfaces of all but two were covered by semiprecious stones, shells, jade carvings, and other ornamentation.

Grasping one of the tables by its pedestal and holding it as a shield in front of him, Toby told the officers to do likewise. He held the table by its base with one hand and drew his repeating pistol. So armed, he again started up the stairs. The officers were quick to use the other tables. The men who had no shields followed behind, bending over to get some protection from those ahead carrying shields.

The tactic Toby had devised so hastily proved far more effective than he had dared to hope. Several arrows bounced off the tiles glued to the table's surface and fell harmlessly to the floor. Several others sliced through the places where two tiles were joined and lodged in the table's wood, but not one got through.

When Toby reached the second floor landing at the head of the marble staircase, he saw, directly ahead in a doorway, a tall Chinese wielding a crossbow. Raising his pistol, he fired at the man. Then he quickly twisted to his right, where he saw another tong member with a raised crossbow. He shot again.

Both shots found their targets, and the two Chinese went down. Toby had singlehandedly established an opening for his men. He decided the most natural place for the tong to make its stand would be the one time audience chamber. Remembering the layout that he had so diligently memorized, he walked down the corridor toward it, staying close to one wall and still holding the table before him, as did the officers who followed in single file.

From the chamber's doorway, the tong leaders, who had no intention of giving up, opened fire with their pistols, blunderbusses, muskets, and knives. Toby was forced to halt frequently and hunker down behind his upraised table while he waited for the storm of missiles to lessen. To his intense regret, he saw two of the young Chinese officers fall, but he knew, too, that it was impossible to avoid casualties in such a battle. Both sides inevitably suffered. The tong now was giving as good as it received.

Forced to advance far more slowly and cautiously, Toby suddenly saw an extraordinary sight in the midst of the enemy's ranks. Firing a pistol at Toby and his officers from behind a pillar was a woman wearing a *cheongsam*. A mask of gold mesh concealed her face and hid her hair. She showed enough familiarity with her weapon to demonstrate that pistols were not new to her.

Toby was struck immediately by the idea that he had seen the woman previously. He could not remember where he had known her, however.

Erratic bursts of pistol fire sounded at the far end of the audience chamber. In spite of the gravity of the situation, Toby could not help chuckling. Somehow, Ch'ien

Ming-lo and the young officers under his command had managed to fight their way up the narrow secondary staircase and were attacking from the rear.

Pressed hard on two fronts, the tong discarded all caution and fought with concentrated fury. They used their weapons recklessly as they relied on the last of their ammunition to clear a path to safety.

Their efforts were successful, however. The young officers closed in from both front and rear, and the tong leaders, recognizing total defeat, began to throw down their weapons and surrender.

Toby left the surrender in the capable hands of Ming-lo. Aware that the woman in the gold *cheongsam* had vanished, he left the audience chamber in search of her.

She was nowhere to be seen. Guided by instinct, based on a past he could not quite recall, as well as on his memorizing of the palace map, he climbed to the third floor. After making his way down a hall, he pushed open the door of a suite. There, no more than ten feet from him, was Princess Ta-lien, exquisitely beautiful, as always, in her *cheongsam*.

Toby stopped short when he saw her.

Badly frightened, she seemed relieved when she recognized him. "I've been praying to the gods of my ancestors," she said, "that you would come and find me."

Toby was badly confused. *What is the princess doing in a building occupied by the leaders of the tong? Is she in some way involved with them?*

"Will you help me get out of this terrible place?" she asked, then hesitated for a moment. "I shall gladly give myself to you in return."

Sheer desperation was responsible for her offer, he thought. Naturally he would be glad to help her and would require no payment. He looked around to make sure the doorway and the hall were clear so they could begin their descent. But instinct caused him to swivel his head toward Ta-lien. She had a knife in one hand, raised high over her head, ready to strike.

Before she could move, a giant arm came over her shoulder, and a hamlike hand caught her wrist. The knife clattered to the floor. Ming-lo jerked her backward with his full strength. Ta-lien lost her balance, crashing to the floor and striking her head on the hard wooden surface. The blow knocked her unconscious.

Ming-lo contemptuously kicked her knife into a far corner and scooped her up off the floor, holding her in his arms. "In China," he said succinctly, "things are seldom what they appear to be."

Dazed by the sudden turn of events, Toby followed Ming-lo from the room. He looked from a window and saw a line of tong leaders, hands raised over their heads, being shepherded away by elite guard officers who had their pistols trained on the captives.

Toby and his forces had won a full victory over the tong.

The entire imperial court was in attendance for the ceremony in the audience chamber to honor the victors. The diplomatic corps was present, as were the officers who had participated in the defeat of the tong. Spectators stood eight and ten deep on either side of the heavy yellow rug that extended to the dais from the entrance.

General Lin Lo-yuang rose from his seat on the lower dais and announced the arrival of Toby Holt. Toby entered the chamber slowly. Pausing to bow formally to the dowager empress on the Chrysanthemum Throne, he was very much aware of the absence of Princess Ta-lien from her customary place on the lower dais.

Tong leaders had revealed her as the head of the organization, and Ta-lien's deceit had left Toby saddened. Until that day, his mental picture of her had been cloudy, and he had known only that he had liked her greatly. Now, however, as when the winds sweep down on Peking from the deserts of Mongolia and blow away the fog, he felt his mind was clear. He was able to see the princess for what she was, an inordinately clever, driven woman, whose ambition for power had led to her ultimate ruin. It was too bad, he reflected, that she had used her extraordinary intelligence for such evil purposes.

Toby walked to the foot of the dais, and there he bowed again to the dowager empress.

"Colonel Holt," she said in her harsh voice, "your deeds speak for themselves. Thanks to your efforts and those of our own Ch'ien Ming-lo, the tong has been crushed. Its powers are torn out by their roots, and they never will flourish again. Our citizens are now safe from the evildoers who sold them into foreign slavery, and the notorious trade in opium is halted. Let Ch'ien Ming-lo also come forward."

Ming-lo appeared out of the crowd, kowtowed before the empress, then stood.

Tz'u Hsi nodded to General Lin, who rose and approached Toby and Ming-lo, carrying two boxes. Each contained a chain of gold metal links with a "chrysanthemum sunburst" in a large medallion of pure gold. These he hung around their necks. Such high awards were rarely given. The entire assemblage cheered.

At last, after quiet was restored, the empress had one

more surprise in store. She beckoned to Toby, who mounted the dais.

"Colonel Holt," she said, "we have long pondered the question of how best to reward you for your services to us and to China. We have discussed you at length with those who know you best, and it is your own attitudes that have answered our question. Because of the constancy of your devotion to your wife, we give you this gift for her and request that you take it to her." She handed him a long, open box.

Toby glanced at the contents and saw a string of gleaming, matched black pearls. Even though he knew little about jewelry, he realized that the pearls were worth a fortune. He was thunderstruck by their magnificence, and had difficulty for a moment in collecting his thoughts and expressing his thanks suitably.

The audience had come to an end, and as the dowager empress left the chamber, everyone kowtowed, with the exception of Toby and the Western diplomats.

Clutching the gift box, Toby found himself standing beside General Lin Lo-yuang. After taking a deep breath, he plunged headlong into a subject that everyone at the imperial court had been speculating about.

"General," he asked bluntly, "what has become of Princess Ta-lien?"

The general's voice was bland, his face expressionless. "Her disgrace was overwhelming," he said, "so great that she knew she could never make amends. She borrowed scissors from one of the ladies in waiting who was assigned to keep watch over her. She cut her wrists open. May her spirit rest in peace beside those of her distinguished ancestors."

Was it true that she had committed suicide? Or had

she been executed on the order of the empress? Toby realized it was probable he would never learn the truth. The mystery of Ta-lien's passing would exist beside the mystery of why she had chosen a life of crime when she enjoyed such a high place in the hierarchy of her nation.

During his time in China, Toby had learned much about the world and about a people who had been almost completely unknown to him. Now the time had arrived when he had only one desire: to go home, to be with his own once again, to speak his own language, eat his own food, and wear his own clothes.

A company of elite guard officers would escort him to Tientsin, from where, he had been told at the American legation, a warship would transport him across the Pacific, another vessel already having been dispatched to carry the news of the completion of his mission. He was ready to go.

His one regret was that he and Ch'ien Ming-lo would part. They had fought together, taken grave risks together, and together had destroyed the most vicious gang of criminals in China. That was their joint monument.

Toby raised his head and squared his shoulders as he left the imperial palace. Tomorrow at this time he would be on his way to Tientsin, the first stop on his homeward journey.

XIV

Standing stalwartly by his mother, the little boy scanned the faces of the white-clad sailors who lined the deck of the warship. At last he centered his attention on the only man not in uniform. His deeply tanned face bore testimony to the long hours he had spent in the sun while crossing the Pacific. When he removed his hat, no longer could there be any doubt as to his identity. His shock of blond hair and his chiseled features spoke for themselves.

"There's Papa!" the little boy shouted, and waved so enthusiastically that he would have fallen into the water if his mother had not been maintaining a tight grip on him.

Toby Holt grinned and returned his son's greeting. Then his eyes met Clarissa's, and in that instant they both knew that their long, painful separation had come to an end. Their mutual longing gave way to the sense of peace that they knew only when they were together. Quiet smiles revealed the joy that both were feeling at that moment.

A few minutes later, Toby came ashore onto the San Francisco dock, followed by two sailors carrying his luggage. Tim threw himself at his father, who hoisted him onto one shoulder. Together, they approached Clarissa.

Time seemed to stand still as Toby deposited Tim on the ground and swept Clarissa into his arms. As they kissed, both were unmindful of the people around them. Then, releasing Clarissa, Toby lifted his son onto his shoulder again, and they left the dock for the entrance, where a carriage awaited.

"We have a suite at the hotel," Clarissa said. "The government made all the arrangements. In fact, your mother and the general are waiting there this minute to see you."

"They had some reason, I take it," Toby replied, "for not coming down to the waterfront to meet the ship."

"General Blake," Clarissa said, "has gone to great lengths to avoid notifying the press of your arrival. The newspapers know nothing of your return from the Orient."

He nodded thoughtfully. It was not very difficult to understand why his stepfather was taking pains to maintain secrecy about his arrival. He noted with approval that their driver was a uniformed army sergeant.

Eulalia and Leland Blake awaited Toby in the privacy of their hotel suite, and when he arrived they greeted him warmly. Toby had brought gifts for everyone: a bolt of silk for his mother, an ancient Chinese blunderbuss for his stepfather's weapons collection, and for Tim, a miniature flat-bladed version of Ming-lo's curved sword. A special gift for Clarissa was withheld until Toby had a chance to be alone with her, but he did present her with the pearls sent by the empress, which overwhelmed her. While she and Eulalia examined them and Tim ecstatically brandished his scimitar, Toby and the general retired to a small sitting room.

"I've relayed to Washington the report I received from you," Lee said. "President Grant has been kept fully informed of all developments. You'll find the entire correspondence in this file." He picked up a sheaf of papers and dropped the bundle onto a table again. "In brief, the President is enormously pleased with the results of your visit to China. You've paid off for him once again, and he's very proud of your accomplishments, and so is General Sherman. The President continues to hold the army responsible for getting rid of the tong in the United States. Its main body has been killed, but the limb continues to survive and flourish. General Sherman has delegated me as the officer to be responsible for cutting off that limb and killing it."

"I'm not surprised," Toby murmured.

"Since your mother and I arrived here two days ago, I've had conferences with the law enforcement authorities of San Francisco and of California. Frankly, they are very relieved that the army is in charge of smashing the tong. They doubt they would have the facilities for an operation that big, though naturally they offer help in anything that we may ask."

"If the American tong is at all like its Chinese parent," Toby said, "we'll need more than overwhelming, brute force in order to subdue it. We'll have to outsmart them. And I daresay we'll need some good luck, as well."

"I don't think luck played much of a part in the victories that you won," General Blake said, smiling. "If you agree, Toby, this will be your project. I'll give you all the help and support I can, but I want you to take complete charge and be in command."

"I'm honored by your confidence, and I accept, naturally," Toby assured him. "Cutting off the branches one by one can be a fruitless pastime. I propose that we take aim at the heart and head of the American tong, namely at Kung Lee. We should base our whole campaign on eliminating him from the picture."

"That makes sense—very good sense, Toby. I had something of the sort more or less in mind when I arranged to keep your arrival secret from the press. I wanted you to have a completely free hand to put your own plan into effect."

"Am I right, then, in assuming that Kung Lee is in the city at present?"

"He is, indeed. And what's more, he has been here for many months. I've had a full detail of plainclothesmen keeping a watch on his headquarters, which is also where he lives," the general went on. "He is being exceptionally cautious, and he maintains a very low profile. He seems to go nowhere and apparently sees visitors only at his headquarters. He's under siege, and quite obviously he knows it. He has been aware of your activities in China, we can be sure, so he undoubtedly knows you have destroyed the tong there. He has reason to feel threatened, and he's playing his cards very close to his vest."

"How many men can you spare for this operation, if you please, sir?" Toby asked.

The general grinned. "It isn't really a question of how many men I can spare. The correct answer, in any event, is—as many as you may need, regardless of whether or not you want troops by the hundreds or by the thousands. Ask, and they're yours."

Toby laughed and shook his head. "I don't believe in operating on such a large scale in a civilian community," he said. "Most residents of Chinatown are law-abiding people, I imagine, and I see no reason to upset the way they live. Give me twenty-four hours to look around, and I'll report back to you late tomorrow to describe my specific needs."

Not until later that evening, after a joyous family reunion at supper, did Toby and Clarissa have an opportunity to be by themselves. Then, after Tim, protesting, had been put to bed, they drifted into the sitting room of the suite.

Ceremoniously, Toby presented to his wife the special surprise he had been saving for this moment. It was a *cheongsam*, just as he had promised. Made of green silk and embroidered in gold, it had a slit on either side of the skirt to facilitate walking, and also featured a stiff, high-standing mandarin collar.

"How wonderful!" Clarissa exclaimed, holding the gown up to appreciate it fully.

Toby, pleased, grinned broadly. "I promised I'd bring you one," he said, "but it took more doing than I anticipated. Why don't you try it on?"

Clarissa retired to the bedroom and returned wearing the gown and smoothing its skirt. "I love it," she exclaimed. "Look!"

He examined her with great pride. "You look absolutely perfect," he told her. "I didn't see any woman in China who wore one with the flair that you show."

"What amazes me," Clarissa said, "is that it fits perfectly. How in the world did you ever manage that?"

Toby reddened and muttered, "It wasn't easy."

When his wife persisted in her questioning, he relented and explained. "I created something of a sensation at the Chrysanthemum Court when I mentioned to the empress one day that I wanted to have a *cheongsam* made for you," he said. "It seems the whole court became busy on the project. Two ladies in waiting selected the materials, which the empress approved personally. The royal dressmaker was called in, and the wife of the British ambassador translated your measurements into the measurements used in China. All in all, it was a project that lasted for weeks, and I was surprised when they actually handed me the finished gown."

Clarissa regarded him with glowing eyes. "This is the nicest present I've ever been given. In fact, it overwhelms me. I much prefer it to the gift from the empress, or anything else I've ever had from anyone in the world—even from you!"

Toby checked with the army intelligence officers who had the tong's headquarters in San Francisco's Chinatown under constant surveillance. His own investigations were sufficient to assure him that Kung Lee was still in town and doing business from his old address. He could see only one way to handle the problem: He would force a direct confrontation with the tong chieftain.

As a first step, Toby enlisted the aid of intelligence agents stationed at San Francisco's Presidio. He threw a cordon around the tong's building, with the agents unobtrusively dressed to resemble Chinese as much as possible. A few were, in fact, of Chinese descent. All carried concealed weapons and received only one order: Under no circumstances was Kung Lee to be permitted to leave the building. If he tried to escape, he was to be apprehended instantly.

Next, Toby wrote a short communication to Kung,

informing him that he would appear at his office in twenty-four hours and demanding that the tong leader surrender at that time. Thereupon, he would face trial in the federal courts on numerous charges. Kung was advised to have his attorney accompany him when he surrendered to the government.

Rather than put on a show of force, Toby decided he should be accompanied by only two intelligence officers.

General Blake was moved to protest. "Toby," he said, "you're taking a very grave risk. You face an opponent who is ruthless and tough. You ought to reduce to a minimum your chances of being hurt."

"I don't expect Kung Lee to do anything to harm me," Toby replied. "The more obvious the pressure I might apply to him, actually, the more violently he is likely to respond. If I show up at his office with a large, armed contingent, his loss of face would be so tremendous that he'd have to fight it out with us. That's just what I'm trying to avoid."

"You've learned a great deal about the mentality of the Orientals," the general said, smiling. "I defer to your judgment."

Kung Lee sent no reply to Toby's letter. Exactly twenty-four hours after dispatching it, Toby strolled through the narrow streets of Chinatown with his two companions. They slowed their pace when they drew near the insignificant two-story building that was the tong headquarters. All were armed with six-shooter pistols concealed beneath their suit jackets.

No greetings were exchanged with the intelligence agents on duty near the building, but the word was passed quietly that the climax was at hand. The agents were alert, ready for any sudden, unexpected development.

The middle-aged Chinese woman on duty in the curio shop on the building's ground floor blinked innocently behind thick spectacles when Toby informed her that he had come to see Kung Lee. Her lack of surprise betrayed her, so Toby was sure his arrival had been anticipated.

The woman went through the motions of climbing the staircase behind the curio shop, and when she reappeared a few minutes later, she bowed to Toby and murmured, "You may go up."

He mounted the stairs slowly, his two companions following closely.

Two heavyset Chinese, each with a long, wicked knife protruding from his belt, were stationed at the head of the stairs. They stared impassively at the approaching trio.

Toby astonished them by speaking in faultless Mandarin. "There is no need to disturb yourselves," he told them. "I know where to find Kung Lee's office."

The two guards stared at him openmouthed as he led his companions through the tong offices.

The establishment was humming with activity. At one desk a man was adding up columns of figures with an abacus. Another, a younger man, was writing letters in flowing Chinese calligraphy. Several others were conferring in a small group, where one of their number was busily taking notes. To the credit of the tong employees, none reacted in any way to the appearance of the three white men.

The door to Kung Lee's private office was closed. Toby halted in front of it and rapped authoritatively twice, then opened the door without waiting to be asked to enter. He stepped across the threshold.

Kung sat behind his large, polished mahogany desk, smoking the last of a cigarette that he had affixed in a long, ivory holder. He showed the strain of recent events but brazenly had dispensed with the guards Toby had anticipated. About sixty years of age, he looked at least a decade older. His cheeks were sunken, and deep hollows showed beneath his eyes. His face had a skull-like appearance. As always, he remained in firm control of his emotions. Only the burning look in his dark eyes betrayed the intensity of his feelings. He inhaled smoke, then busied himself extinguishing his cigarette and removing the butt from the holder.

"Good afternoon," he said, electing to speak in Mandarin. "You are punctual, Colonel Holt, which does not surprise me. In fact, nothing that you do surprises me any longer."

"We are here to demand that you surrender yourself to the authority that we represent, the United States of America," Toby said firmly.

"I regard it as a crime," Kung said softly, "that I have been hounded for many months by representatives of a government that does not understand me or my people. You who claim that this tong engages in evil practices fail to recognize the good that this benevolent brotherhood accomplishes. You have no understanding of the people of the East, nor of the motives that inspire them."

He suddenly stopped speaking in Mandarin and switched to English. "I wish it plainly understood," he said, "that I consider myself the victim of a personal vendetta. I hold you personally responsible for hounding me, for making my existence untenable, and for trying to destroy me!"

Putting the mouthpiece of the cigarette holder between his lips, Kung quickly aimed the instrument at Toby's face and blew hard on it. A tiny, metal-tipped arrow flashed in the afternoon sunlight as it sped toward its target.

Only Toby's unparalleled instinct for survival saved him. Not stopping to think, he jerked his head several inches to one side. The arrow missed, burying itself in the wood panel of the wall, where it quivered delicately. In the same swift motion, he drew his pistol, cocked it, and pointed it at Kung.

Instantly the two army captains drew their pistols, too. If Kung made one false move, he would die instantly.

His eyes burning with undisguised hatred as he stared at Toby, Kung Lee removed the cigarette holder from his mouth, spread his hands on the top of his desk, and sighed gently. "Just as you have wanted to rid the world of me, Holt, so I have been eager to dispose of you. You have succeeded, and I have failed. Very well, I accept whatever fate is in store for me. I am your prisoner."

Toby's capture of Kung Lee made headlines all over the country. He was once again subjected to the steady glare of the limelight.

Distressed by the publicity, Toby was glad to escape into relative obscurity as soon as he and his family went home to Oregon. He began to relax as soon as they reached their ranch on the Columbia River.

He and Clarissa quickly settled into old, familiar routines, but the rhythm of daily life was interrupted several days later. The family was summoned to Fort Vancouver on the Washington side of the Columbia. General Blake had received orders from the President commanding him to honor Toby in a suitable ceremony. Toby gritted his teeth to prepare for going through the motions of being a hero.

Standing outside his headquarters, General Blake formally tendered Toby the President's Medal, first issued by George Washington to honor outstanding services rendered to the United States by a civilian, and employed only infrequently by later presidents.

Toby's face burned as he stood in the bright sunlight hearing his stepfather read the President's laudatory message. But as his eyes met Clarissa's, he felt calmer. She was reminding him silently how much she loved him, and he realized that nothing else really mattered.

After the medal was pinned to Toby's lapel, a military review was held in his honor, and he took the salute of the entire garrison. A parade ended the ordeal, and Toby was glad to adjourn to the Blake home, where a buffet supper was held in his honor. Most of those in attendance were military officers with whom he was on friendly terms, the governors of Oregon and the Washington Territory, and a number of other highly placed officials.

Talking informally with them, he made light of his exploits in China and of the capture of Kung Lee, but those who were familiar with his modesty were not deceived by his attitude. After the guests departed, Toby and Clarissa withdrew to the general's private den to read the many messages that had been received throughout the day.

Toby, tired of the praise, barely scanned the messages, but Clarissa read each of them thoroughly. President Grant, several Cabinet officers, and General Sherman were prominent among those who sent congratulatory telegrams and letters. One telegram in particular captured her interest, and she became engrossed in it.

Toby noted that the message was far longer than most, and when he became aware that his wife had become exceptionally preoccupied, he asked, "Have you run across something unusual?"

"I think you'd better read this yourself," she said. "It's from New Orleans, from the man I've heard you talk about, named Domino."

First scanning the message, then absorbing it more fully, Toby learned that Domino was desperately seeking his help. Karl Kellerman, he said, had escaped from numerous, seemingly impenetrable traps. Currently, Kellerman was heading north on the Mississippi.

The next sentence of the telegram struck Toby with the impact of a bomb: "Martha is traveling with him."

Domino offered no explanation for Martha's presence with Kellerman, and Toby could not imagine how so intelligent a woman could have fallen into the clutches of such a depraved being.

The message ended with a long, heartfelt plea by Domino, begging Toby to join him in New Orleans as soon as possible and to accompany him in pursuit of Kellerman.

The communication ended on a desperate note: "I urgently need your help."

Toby sat in silence, staring at the telegram for a long time. Finally, Clarissa broke the spell. "I think you should go," she said quietly.

He shook his head, half in anger, partly in resignation. "That's impossible!" he exclaimed. "You don't need me to remind you that I've been gone for many months, nor that affairs at the ranch need attending to. What's more, my promise to you is doubly binding. Now that I'm back, I feel obligated to stay. I cannot imagine anything that could persuade me to leave you again."

"Domino says that he badly needs you," she declared.

"Somebody always is claiming to need me," Toby objected. "I can't seem to get away from it. I can't pay any attention to such claims. I must think of my family before I go charging off to help other people."

Clarissa was quietly contemplative. "You told me a great deal about Kellerman before you went to the Orient. And I've read several newspaper articles about him. Remember, he was the scoundrel who dragged poor Millicent off to New Orleans and mistreated her so badly there."

"That's typical of the fellow," Toby agreed.

"Kellerman was in partnership with Kung Lee," Clarissa said forcefully, "when a freighter they owned together burned up in New Orleans and the captain and crew lost their lives. I saw speculation in the press that Kellerman was killed, too, but this telegram from Domino certainly rules out that possibility. You destroyed the tong, here and in China. It seems to me that it's wrong to leave your task unfinished. Since Kellerman was closely associated with the tong, you should go after him, too, and not rest until you've turned him over to the authorities."

"I *am* tempted to pitch in and help Domino," Toby admitted. "I'd like to see this business through to the end and have Kellerman eliminated from causing trouble, once and for all. But if I go down to New Orleans, there's no telling how long I might be there. Perhaps days, but it could turn into weeks, apart from the travel time. I owe it to you and Tim to stay here and start assuming my obligations."

"I hardly need to remind you," Clarissa told him, "that you have an even broader obligation to the people of this country. When a man like Kellerman is free to roam where he pleases, he's a menace to every decent, law-abiding citizen. You're capable of seeing to it that he falls into the hands of the authorities. You've already done so much for our country that I think you and I would be selfish if you fail to accomplish this last task. In the long run, it doesn't really matter if we're separated again for a short time. We've demonstrated that we're capable of surviving months of being apart. Tim seems no worse for the experience. What's more, the ranch hasn't suffered, either. Stalking Horse has a first-rate crew, and the place is still running at a very healthy profit."

Toby was struck again by her selflessness.

"If others could take your place, find Kellerman, and arrest him," she went on, "I would say by all means, let them do it. You have done more than your share. But I know of no one who is capable of taking your place. I know that you're thinking of your promise to me, and I'm grateful for it. At the same time, I must try to think of the America that Tim's generation will inherit someday. For such a reason, I think your duty is plain. You need to set an example for all Americans to follow now, one that will serve to guide that later generation."

Almost never had Toby heard her speak so convincingly or with such depth of feeling. He weighed the matter for a time and at last said, "I'm afraid you're right. I'll send Domino a telegram telling him that I'll be in New Orleans as soon as I can get there."

The small, one-horse carriage crept along a nearly deserted street in San Francisco. The Chinese driver eased the vehicle forward slowly as it neared the city's main jail. The driver was obviously taking his time.

In the backseat a slender man named Chong was deliberately ridding himself of his weapons. He took a knife from the calf of one leg to which it was strapped and deposited it beside a pistol that he had taken from a pocket. Then he checked his clothes and briefcase to make certain that he had no other weapons hidden away. When he was ready, he rapped on the little glass window that separated him from the driver's box.

The driver turned, nodded almost imperceptibly, then flicked the reins to increase the horse's pace. The animal responded, continuing at a slow trot until the carriage had reached the main entrance of the jail. There Chong climbed out and, taking his briefcase with him, went inside. "I'm attorney Chong," he announced to the attendant in charge. "I've come to speak with my client Kung Lee."

He submitted without protest as guards searched him and examined the interior of his briefcase, which contained only legal papers. Then was he admitted to a small, barred conference room in which a heavyset guard, with his arms defiantly folded, was stationed. Neither he nor the other man spoke to each other.

A few moments later, Kung Lee was led into the room. He was his customary debonair self except that he wore no necktie. He and Chong exchanged bows, and the smaller man spoke at once in one of the provincial dialects of China, a tongue that few people in the United States could understand or speak.

"I have come here as your attorney," Chong said. "Therefore we will first devote ourselves to legal matters."

Kung Lee inclined his head in a bow that seemed subservient. This, of course, was nothing but a pose to impress the guard, who looked at him curiously. The man obviously had no idea that Kung Lee considered no man his superior.

"I have been assured by the real attorneys working on

your case that you will be free later today," Chong said. "They have succeeded in raising the very high bail that was set. It seems a number of wealthy friends and associates have stepped forward to make contributions. Others have been 'persuaded' by the usual means."

"That is good," Kung Lee replied briefly, a faint smile touching the corners of his lips.

"What is it that you may want done between now and the time when you are released?" Chong asked.

Kung Lee glanced sideways at the guard, who was paying no attention to the chatter in the foreign tongue, and replied succinctly, "I want virtually nothing done. I'll take care of almost everything when I am released. However, you might get in touch with the man called Graat and tell him to wait for me at my headquarters with his woman. I'll see them and give them orders when I'm free."

"That is all?"

"That is more than enough," Kung Lee said wryly. "If Graat and his woman are prepared to do their customary job for me, that's all that I want."

A long line extended through the streets of Chinatown to the modest second-floor headquarters of the tong. People from every walk of life were waiting to greet Kung Lee, who once again—for the time being at least—was a free man sitting in his own headquarters. The wealthy businessmen of the area, innkeepers, restaurant owners, and other men of substance—many of whom had contributed to Kung's bail—were present to pay their respects, as were those of more humble station, such as shopkeepers and laborers, who lived in fear of the gang leader and dared not fail to make an appearance.

Kung Lee stood in his office with several of his heavily armed bodyguards, discreetly watching from the corner of the room as people filed by him. The other room was filled with yellow chrysanthemums, ordinarily the imperial flower used for imperial occasions. The people of Chinatown needed no reminder that Kung Lee was equal to the empress.

Those of his guests who were recent immigrants and were unfamiliar with the American legal system assumed that Kung's return to his headquarters signified his total victory over his adversaries. They had no way of comprehending that he still faced a protracted trial or deportation proceedings.

Others who were more knowledgeable understood the seriousness of the gang leader's situation. They were therefore amazed at his ebullience and optimism in the face of his coming legal battle, and they could only attribute his mood to his confidence in his well-paid attorneys.

Some speculated that Kung might attempt to go into hiding to escape the legal consequences of his actions. Others doubted that he would take this step, believing that he would prefer to meet his adversaries face to face.

Whatever the future held, none could deny that the gang leader seemed determined to celebrate his release from jail, and he was clearly enjoying this evening's festivities.

As was customary in a Chinese celebration, a great deal of business was accomplished. Two of the leading merchants had a dispute that needed to be settled, and they made an application to Kung Lee to mediate their differences. He agreed to see them both early the following morning. The son of a Chinese cleaning woman, a boy in his teens, was seeking his first job, and his mother won

Kung Lee's promise of support in finding him employment. On a somewhat more serious level, two cardplayers who had accused each other of cheating finally agreed to leave the settlement of their dispute in the hands of the tong leader. Kung Lee graciously accepted the role of mediator; clearly, he was all things to all people.

At last the line of well-wishers petered out. Kung Lee had shaken hands with the last of his callers and sent them on their way. Now, finally, he was ready to get down to business.

His bodyguards cleared the few remaining visitors from his office. At this moment Chong came in and bowed deeply, all pretense of his being Kung's equal having been dropped the moment the two men left the prison.

"Graat and his woman are here, my lord, and await your pleasure," Chong said, bowing again.

"Show them in," Kung replied abruptly.

Chong bowed his way out and returned shortly, leading an American couple. The man was wearing a well-tailored and obviously expensive suit, a handmade shirt, and a silk cravat. Otherwise, he had no distinguishing marks or characteristics. His features were drab, and his complexion was slightly sallow. That was his strength as well as his weakness: He could appear anywhere and not be recognized. He was difficult for witnesses to recall or identify, so he could come and go freely, without fear of discovery.

The woman, on the other hand, was as spectacular as Graat was nondescript. Her hair was the color of pale wheat, and it tumbled down her back, hanging almost to her waist. She was not young—perhaps between twenty-five and thirty, with heavy makeup emphasizing her sultry features. What made her stand out, however, was her body, which was as light and supple as that of a girl in her late teens. She moved with a sinuous grace and seemed to be quite aware of her assets, which gave her an air of superiority. Unlike most of those who were meeting Kung Lee for the first time, she displayed neither respect nor fear, and she eyed him boldly as she sat down in the chair he indicated. She seemed to be daring him to say or do something that would cause her to react. She looked as though she alone had the right to decide to respond.

"I daresay you're familiar with the history of Toby Holt and of the opposition I have faced from him over a long period of time," Kung Lee said.

Graat smiled, and the woman nodded. "We've read the accounts of his exploits in the daily press," Graat said, "and whatever details we may have missed have been supplied by Mr. Chong. It's quite a story."

"The story is just beginning, not ending," Kung Lee said. His voice became hard. "I've been told on good authority that you people are unique, that there's no one in the business who compares with you."

Graat nodded modestly. The woman studied her blood-red fingernails and made no reply.

"He has caused me no end of trouble," Kung Lee went on. "It is he who is responsible for my present circumstances. His pursuit of me is as though it is personal in nature, rather than as a law officer pursuing a . . . a criminal as part of his job. Very well, I accept it as personally as he seems to wish—and I expect to turn it against him. Now, here is where you come in. . . .

"I expect that Holt will be returning to his home in Oregon very shortly. I want to hire you, effective immediately, to go there and keep your eye on him. For the moment, at least, do nothing. Simply keep watch on him and discover where he's vulnerable and where he's strong. When you have enough information to recommend a plan of action, let me know, and I'll decide on the next step. Keep your own identities absolutely secret, of course, and proceed with great discretion."

Graat seemed to come to life, and a dull glow appeared in his eyes. "You can depend on it, Mr. Kung," he said. "No matter what you want done about this fellow Holt, it will be done."

Kung gave the flicker of a smile. "Satisfactory!" he exclaimed. "In about a week, you will leave for Portland. Holt has a large spread not far from the city. You'll have no trouble in finding it. Keep in touch!"

The paddle-wheeler eased out of the center of the Mississippi River and edged toward the docks of the port of Memphis. Most passengers already were gathered on the deck, waiting to go ashore for several hours during the layover in Memphis. But two among them, intending to disembark for a longer stay, were the objects of intense scrutiny. The couple's luggage was piled in front of them near the gangway.

The man was tall, ruggedly good-looking, and wore his clothes with a careless, debonair air. His companion, a strikingly beautiful redhead, clung to his arm and looked up at him with adoring eyes. Her heavy makeup emphasized her classical features and the lustrousness of her green eyes. Her traveling costume, a two-piece suit, was both conservative and daring. When she moved, the slit in her ankle-length skirt revealed one leg above the knee. The fit of the outfit emphasized her slender yet well-rounded figure.

Martha knew exactly what to expect. She and Kellerman, traveling by easy stages from New Orleans, would be making the third stay of their northward journey. They would engage a carriage at the docks and undoubtedly would be driven to one of the town's fancier brothels, where they would obtain a room and stay for two or three days before resuming their journey on the next north-bound paddle-wheeler.

This stop, however, was different from the others that had preceded it. Only the night before Martha had learned the exact destination Kellerman had in mind, and she was eager to report to Domino at the first opportunity. Her journey was going according to plan, and she wanted to take no risk in upsetting it. She had Kellerman fooled, but she knew he would become vicious if he realized what she was up to.

The ungainly passenger-cargo ship maneuvered into her berth with surprising ease. As soon as she was moored, Kellerman and Martha followed their luggage ashore.

Kellerman hired an open carriage, and after they were seated, he rearranged Martha's dashing, feather-trimmed hat, tilting it forward rakishly over one eye. Sitting proudly erect, she attracted much attention as they drove through the downtown business district. She realized that Kellerman must be showing her off for a purpose.

If he followed his usual custom, as soon as they settled in at the brothel where they would stay, he would suggest that she entertain one or more of the establishment's patrons while he attended to private business elsewhere. He always refrained from questioning her when he returned, and she knew that he assumed she had followed his suggestion. Furthermore, she understood what motivated him: He figured that by earning her own money on their journey, he wouldn't need to keep her supplied with money.

It suited her purposes to let him believe what he wished. Therefore, as they drove along, she smiled steadily and occasionally nodded her head when she passed a well-dressed gentleman who might be taking an interest in her.

They came to a neighborhood of upper-class homes, large dwellings set on well-tended lawns amid numerous trees. Most of the houses were surrounded by high fences. They drove past the front gates of one such property, a house with a broad portico supported by Greek columns. When they were pulling up to the main entrance, Martha recognized it for what it was, an exclusive bordello.

After a liveried servant removed their luggage from their carriage, they were greeted by a handsome, dark-haired woman.

"I hope I can rely on you, Mrs. Myers, to return the favors I have done you in the past—at least to some extent," Kellerman said. "Can you provide my friend and me with quarters for the next few days?"

The woman's dark eyes darted from Kellerman to Martha. At last she said, "I don't see why not, Karl. It's a reasonable request."

She led them to a handsome bedroom suite on the second floor of the mansion.

"It may be," Kellerman told her, "that we can repay your kindness sooner than you think. If you have any special clients who don't mind paying big-city prices for their pleasures, it may be you can persuade Martha to entertain them."

As Martha smiled brightly, Mrs. Myers examined her

critically and at length. "Martha and I can discuss the situation," she said, "provided she's willing."

"I would be glad to oblige you, ma'am," Martha said demurely.

"I'm going out shortly, and I'll leave you ladies to your own devices," Kellerman said jovially.

Mrs. Myers attended to placing their luggage, then withdrew. As soon as they were alone, Kellerman insisted on fondling Martha, which she allowed with good grace, never losing her dignity. She understood well what an innocent person like Millicent had suffered at his hands and felt a deep, burning loathing for him.

Kellerman finally departed, promising to return in about six hours, in order to take her out to supper.

When alone, Martha removed her hat and, seating herself at a large, well-furnished dressing table, began to repair her makeup. She was not surprised when a tap sounded at the door, and as she applied a fresh coating of mascara to her eyes, she called, "Come in!"

"I provided Mr. Kellerman with a horse when he went off into town to attend to his business," Mrs. Myers said as she came into the room. "I suppose you know we have several gangs here in Memphis, and they compete with one another actively."

"So I've been told," Martha replied as she took from her handbag a small change purse. She opened it and removed her necklace, absentmindedly fingering it.

"That's a fascinating necklace," Mrs. Myers said casually.

Martha matched her tone. "Yes," she replied, "it *is* interesting." She paused for a fraction of a second. "Would you care to examine it?"

"I'd love to."

Martha handed the necklace to the woman, who examined it critically, paying particular attention to the two diamond-encrusted dominoes. "I wonder," Mrs. Myers said lightly, "whether this piece of jewelry has any special significance."

"It may have," Martha admitted as she applied rouge to her lips.

The woman sighed and dropped the necklace onto the dressing table. Martha scooped it up and returned it to the small change purse, which she then carefully placed at the very bottom of her large handbag. "This has served its purpose in Memphis," she said distinctly. "I shall have no cause to wear it again here."

The woman studied her. "Do I gather that your current companion is unaware of the significance of this particular item of jewelry?" she inquired, her eyes bright, her manner cautious.

"You're right," Martha replied. "Kellerman is badly frightened by Domino, and with good reason. He double-crossed Domino on more than one occasion. He must know that sooner or later he's going to pay with his life for his mistakes."

"Obviously," Mrs. Myers said, "Kellerman was mistaken when he told me you would be pleased to entertain any special customers of mine."

"He sometimes becomes too enthusiastic for his own good," Martha answered calmly. "He sees it as a way of saving himself money. If customers pay me a good fee, he feels he doesn't need to supply me with funds as we travel."

"That," the woman remarked succinctly, "sounds like the Karl Kellerman I've known for years."

"I sympathize with you, Mrs. Myers," Martha said unexpectedly.

The woman was startled. "What do you mean?"

"If I understand the Memphis situation correctly, and I'm sure I do, three separate gangs are fighting for superiority here. Not only are you forced to walk a tightrope among them, but you undoubtedly must pay them all large bribes from time to time to keep their approval."

Mrs. Myers nodded bitterly. "So many people think I run such a glamorous business," she murmured. "If only they knew! It's a losing race, that's what it is!"

"Suppose all three of the gangs knew you were under Domino's protection," Martha said. "Would that make a difference?"

"All the difference between day and night!" Mrs. Myers exclaimed. "Domino's influence, like his reputation, is as great here as in New Orleans. He has a long, long reach. He doesn't hesitate to strike swiftly and surely. If one of his lieutenants passed the word here that I enjoy his protection, not one of the gangs would dare come near me. They wouldn't threaten me, they wouldn't take a penny from me, and they'd leave me alone. Their lives would depend on it!"

"I can arrange for such protection for you," Martha assured her. "I can't do it immediately, but I give you my word that it will be done as soon as I go home. That should be within the next month to six weeks, if things work out as I expect them to. I give you that pledge on behalf of Domino, and I think you know us sufficiently well to know that once we pledge our word, we never break it."

Mrs. Myers was ecstatic. "I never thought I'd enjoy

such good fortune," she said. "Tell me what I must do to earn it! No matter what it is, you can consider it done!"

"All I ask in return," Martha said, "is a very minor favor. If you will, please write a letter to an address in New Orleans that I'll give you. Say in the letter that a certain couple arrived in Memphis today. But mention no names and be sure you say nothing about the length of time we plan to spend here—I don't want Domino organizing a rescue expedition prematurely. Say further in the letter that our destination has become known. We expect to reach Dave's Warehouse in three weeks or less."

"Two to three weeks," Mrs. Myers repeated dutifully, and then she raised an eyebrow. "Dave's Warehouse. Isn't that in Cairo, Illinois?"

"That's right," Martha told her. "It's located at the north side of the junction of the Mississippi and Ohio. I just learned today that that's where we're going, and I want to pass it along to Domino with all possible speed. Tell him, finally, that if there's any change in plans, he'll be notified, but I doubt very much that any change is contemplated. Tell him that my companion seems to have some purpose in going to Dave's Warehouse, but I haven't yet learned it."

"Every word that you've told me will be repeated in the letter," Mrs. Myers promised fervently. "I swear it!"

"Good!" Martha said. "Then we've made a deal."

When the train from St. Louis pulled into the newly built railroad station in New Orleans, Toby Holt was the first passenger to descend from the sleeping car to the platform. Several reporters were on hand to interview any celebrities who might be coming into town on the train. But before they had a chance to identify Toby, a young man detached himself from three other men and hurried to him.

"Eddie Neff, of Domino's staff," he said, extending his right hand in greeting. "Welcome to New Orleans." They were now surrounded by the other young men. One picked up Toby's baggage, and the group moved swiftly along the platform into the station.

"You'll be staying with us while you're in town," Eddie told him. "Domino believes we can hold the press at arm's length far better that way than if you stay at a hotel. It's imperative that nothing leak out about your presence. We're anxious not to give Kellerman any inkling that you and Domino are about to descend on him."

"Has he reached his destination?" Toby inquired. "He hadn't when I received Domino's telegram."

"Domino will explain the present situation in detail to you," Eddie replied.

His escorts were clever, Toby thought admiringly as the young men maneuvered him into a carriage, followed him into it, and instantly started out the driveway onto the cobblestoned streets. They moved so swiftly that if any reporters had been following, they would have been left hopelessly behind.

A short time later, they arrived at Domino's home, where the gang leader eagerly awaited his guest. Domino, who had gained widespread notoriety for his operations outside the boundaries of the law, shook hands warmly with Toby, who had achieved international fame for upholding law and order. Once again the unlikely pair were united by a common bond, the mutual desire to catch Karl Kellerman.

Toby declined a predinner drink, and as they waited to be called to the dining room table, Domino launched into a discussion of the business at hand. "A few hours ago," he said, "I received indirect word from Martha. She was in Memphis at the time with Kellerman."

"Before you bring me up to date," Toby said, "I'm curious—more than curious. You mentioned in your telegram that Martha is traveling with Kellerman. How does it happen that she's formed a relationship with him? She's far too intelligent to have fallen for his crude approach to women."

"Martha developed a scheme to induce Kellerman to form a relationship with her," Domino explained soberly. "She did it in full consciousness of the risks. She wanted to make certain, beyond any question or doubt, that we were able to back him into a corner where he would find it impossible to escape. He has escaped us more often than I care to recall. Martha was willing to make a sacrifice to make sure that he couldn't escape again. So far, she has clung to him, and he appears to have no idea of her real identity."

"That's good to hear," Toby interjected. "She wouldn't live long if Kellerman learned about her connection with you."

"Well," Domino said, "I've been worried about her safety ever since she began her deception. Frankly, this latest move has me more concerned than ever. According to the messages she sent, she and Kellerman are on their way to the town of Cairo, in Illinois, and expect to arrive there about two weeks from now. What do you know about Cairo?"

"Very little, I'm afraid, except for its strategic location, and its general reputation."

"In spite of underworld activities that flourish there," Domino said, "Cairo is basically a quiet place. Almost every major city gang is represented there, and we have an unspoken agreement to keep the peace. Our people never attack the gang representatives from New York and Chicago, let's say, and they, in turn, leave us in peace, too. Troubles are caused largely by independent operators, men like Karl Kellerman, who intentionally go to Cairo just to share in the spoils. When they become greedy and reach too far, they often meet a swift end."

"It sounds," Toby commented, "like a very rough community."

"It is," Domino agreed. "It's rougher than you can possibly imagine, but I haven't yet told you the worst. The biggest of the local operators in Cairo is a fellow named Dave Hammersmith. A number of the big city gangs have their own outlets, but none can compare in size with a place called Dave's Warehouse. Dave owns a building that dominates the whole waterfront district. He uses the bottom floors for a bar, a gaming house, and a bordello. The upper floors are a storage warehouse where he has loads of stolen objects for sale to any comer. Buyers come there from New York, Cleveland, Detroit, Chicago, and St. Louis, and I don't know how many other major communities. They know what they're getting, and Dave makes no bones about it as he sells his merchandise for whatever the traffic will bear."

"You don't make it sound very appealing," Toby said with an unamused laugh.

"It isn't, I assure you." Domino rose from his chair, mixed himself another drink of whiskey and water, then sat down again. "Unfortunately, Dave's Warehouse is Kellerman's destination with Martha."

"Why?" Toby demanded. "Can you imagine the reason?"

"I wish I knew." Domino shrugged wearily. "All I can do is assume that Kellerman must have business of some sort with Hammersmith. I've been acquainted with Dave for years. I know he's amenable to every type of deal under the sun. My guess is that Kellerman wants to make him an offer of some kind. And, knowing Dave, if it's at all reasonable he's sure to accept it. What really worries me is Martha."

"I can certainly understand that."

"Dave keeps the warehouse closed to all women except for the women who work in his bordello. He has unbreakable rules on that. Even a wife who comes with her husband to buy stolen furniture must cool her heels in a first-floor waiting room and is allowed nowhere else in the building. I don't know how Martha might try to get around Dave's rules. But I can say that if Kellerman tries to force her to enter Dave's brothel, I won't shoot him—I'll strangle him with my bare hands!"

XV

In a room off a side corridor in Dave's Warehouse, Martha gazed incredulously at her reflection in a full-length mirror. Kellerman had insisted on her outrageous getup, citing Dave's rules for women in the bordello, and Martha had gone along because it fit in with her own plans. But now she didn't know whether to laugh or cry. Cosmetics, applied so lavishly that she seemed barely recognizable to herself, caused her expression to resemble a grimace when she smiled back at the apparition. She touched a velvet beauty spot pasted on one cheek and examined a black velvet ribbon around her throat. Long rhinestone earrings, falling almost to her shoulders, swayed as she moved. Her shoes had such high heels that she teetered when she tried to walk and was forced to take tiny steps so she would not fall.

Never had she appeared in such revealing undress. Her knee-length dressing gown was of exceptionally thin silk with a plunging neckline. Ordered to rouge her nipples, she could see that they became visible even beneath their covering of sheer black silk.

But around her neck, Martha wore her jade and diamond necklace of dominoes, which stood out even more prominently than usual against the background of the black throat band. She had put on the necklace only after Karl left.

After rapping at the door, a man immediately opened it. "When you came in, you was saying that you had to see Dave Hammersmith right away." He spoke belligerently, but whistled approvingly under his breath. "Well, Dave will see you right now. Come with me, babe."

Teetering precariously, Martha minced into the corridor. The man was waiting beside the doorway. He put one arm around her waist and with the other hand caressed her breasts. "All the girls give samples," he leered. "How about you?"

Martha drove a heel into his instep with as much force as she could command. Tears came to his eyes as he hastily dropped his arms.

"Touch me again at your peril," Martha warned.

In a surly silence, he led her into an office at the far end of the floor. He rapped on a door, opened it, and said, "The dame who 'had to see you' is here, boss."

"Send her in," Hammersmith commanded.

Entering, Martha saw that he was a corpulent, graying man with a bushy, handlebar mustache.

Chewing on an evil-smelling cigar, he scrutinized her carefully, taking in every aspect of her appearance as she stood at his desk. At last, he waved her to a chair and grunted. "For once in his life, Kellerman was absolutely right," he said. "You're one mighty hot sketch, and you can make a couple of fortunes. One for me and one for yourself."

Martha deliberately raised her hand to the miniature dominoes at her throat.

Dave followed the motion of her hand, and his eyes narrowed. Squinting, he stared at her throat and then asked hoarsely, "Do I see what I think I see?"

"Indeed you do," Martha told him quietly.

Dave clenched his cigar between his teeth. "Damn Kellerman for not telling me the whole story!" he muttered.

"He didn't tell you," Martha explained, "because he doesn't have any idea of my identity. As far as he's concerned, I'm just a girl he picked up in New Orleans."

He shook his head and, trying to cover his confusion, put a match to his cigar, though it was still lighted. "Do I take it that you don't really want to work in my house?"

"That's correct," Martha said. "Kellerman, of course, doesn't know that. Just as he has no idea I haven't worked at our various stops along the Mississippi. He thinks I've been earning money for things I've needed, instead of using my own funds the entire time."

"Let me get this straight," Dave Hammersmith said, removing a bandanna from a pocket and mopping sweat from his forehead. "You're willing to dress—or I should say undress—so that you look like one of my girls. But you won't go through with the rest. You'll be satisfied to make Kellerman and others think you've become one of my girls. Am I right?"

"That's more or less accurate," Martha agreed. "I can think of ways I'd rather dress. But I realize you have house rules, so I'm prepared to go along with them, while I bide my time here."

"Let me think a minute," Dave said as he pressed his

hands to his temples. His dilemma was a simple one, as he saw it. In business for many years, he had earned an exceptionally good living by obeying one cardinal rule: Under no circumstances antagonize one of the big city bosses, whose enmity could end his business overnight, and perhaps end him, too. Domino was vastly more important to him than Kellerman, and it was imperative that he do nothing to incur Domino's anger.

As for this enchanting woman, he had many unanswered questions, but he had no intention of prying. It was enough that she came from Domino, and whatever her relationship with Kellerman was, it was her own business. Why she was pretending that she was a prostitute he did not know. But he recognized that it was important that she be satisfied with her situation and not find a reason to complain to Domino. Dave realized he would be well advised to go along and allow her to carry out her charade.

He grinned at her ingratiatingly. "Anytime I can give Domino a helping hand," he said, "I'm glad to oblige him." His manner now completely jovial, he hoisted himself to his feet. "Come on along to the bar downstairs. We'll have a drink on our little deal," he told her, beckoning. "Get acquainted here, and the less gossip there's likely to be."

As Martha accompanied him down the stairs to the long bar, she shrank inwardly, deeply embarrassed by appearing in such skimpy attire. She realized, however, that her safety depended on her ability to convince everyone who might have contact with Kellerman that she was a prostitute. Whatever was necessary to pave the way for Domino to follow her and Kellerman, she would do. And she must do nothing to arouse Kellerman's suspicion.

Although it was early in the day, in the bar were

several men and a half dozen young women dressed much as she was. *At least,* she thought, *now I can feel somewhat less conspicuous.*

Most of the men were alert, tense, and hard-eyed; Martha was sure they were gangsters. The undisguised lust in their faces disturbed her. She would have to try to keep them at a distance, without angering them. It was going to be harder than she had anticipated.

To Martha's surprise and relief, Dave came to her rescue with a single, simple gesture. He called for drinks, handed her one, then encircled her shoulders with one brawny arm and held her firmly. "Here's to you and me, honey!" he called out in a distinct, loud voice.

Martha immediately understood the significance of his gesture and responded by smiling steadily as they clinked glasses and drank.

Introductions were hardly called for. Notice had been served that Martha was Dave Hammersmith's girl. Every man in the Warehouse knew that a fence surrounded her. The word would spread rapidly enough, and every man who came to the Warehouse would know Martha was to remain untouched by anyone whose attentions she herself did not solicit.

After they finished their drinks and mounted the stairs together, Dave's arm continued to encircle her shoulders until they reached the second floor, out of sight of those at the bar.

"Thank you!" Martha exclaimed gratefully.

"Don't mention it." Dave rolled his cigar to the opposite side of his mouth and smiled at her. "Just remember to let Domino know that I took good care of you while you were here."

Her spirits continued to improve as she returned to

her room. Dropping into a chair, she picked up a book, *Oldtown Folks*, by Harriet Beecher Stowe, which she had purchased at the last of their stops on the northward journey. When Kellerman returned, she was still engrossed in its stories of life in New England.

Looking weary, he dropped heavily into a chair. It was evident to Martha that, however he had occupied himself all day, he had not had an easy time of it. He was far less than his usual, buoyant self.

Martha rose and, taking a bottle of gin from his supply, mixed a drink. As she placed his glass on a table beside him, she could see his lethargy was disappearing. He was staring at her, drinking in every detail of her appearance. In Kellerman's eyes, her eroticism very plainly was overwhelming.

He reached for her, and she hastily took a backward step. In recent days he had not made any advances to her. She could see that he was following a pattern: As she became increasingly familiar to him, he began to lose interest. Now, thanks to her appearance, he had become aroused. But she expected that feeling soon would pass and he would fall back into his old patterns.

With no intention of becoming intimate with him, Martha decided to use his own game to turn the tables. "I'm tired, very tired," she said. "I've been busy all day while you've been running around town."

Kellerman desisted immediately. As Martha watched his ardor cool visibly, she knew she had struck precisely the right note. He would not expect her to yield to his own lovemaking when, at the same time, he was requiring her to play the role of a prostitute. "I knew you'd have no trouble here," he said, taking some credit for what he gathered was her immediate success. "That's why I recommended you to Dave without restrictions."

"I thank you for that," Martha said. "And I'll begin to pay off my debt to you someday when I've been less busy."

His vanity prompted him to chuckle indulgently.

For the moment, Martha was in a better position than she had enjoyed in weeks. Not only was she relatively safe in the Warehouse, but also she had found a way to spare herself intimacy with Kellerman.

She could ask for little more—other than to hope fervently that Domino would reach Cairo quickly. She had kept her promise to him, and now it was up to him to carry out his end of the daring arrangement.

The climactic move to capture Kellerman was under way. In a sleek fifty-foot launch, the hunters were making a steady seven knots against the Mississippi's current.

No expense had been spared to make the launch efficient and comfortable. Her coal-fired engine activated a screw propeller as efficient as those in modern navy ships. Quarters were ample for the owner, Domino, and his passengers, Toby Holt and Eddie Neff. There was adequate room for the three members of the crew, as well.

Two of them, known as Red and Eagle, alternated at the controls and kept the boiler fed with fuel. The third, known as Cook, prepared meals and attended sketchily to the housekeeping. All three, Toby noted, carried knives and repeating pistols, as did Domino and Eddie. No one would take the launch by surprise.

Red, in charge of buying coal and food when they halted at a port every other day, seemed to know everyone of consequence on the Mississippi. He alone went ashore to make his purchases of food and fuel, and he returned as soon as possible so that they could sail again without delay. Eddie Neff never went ashore or even appeared on deck at the stops, but Toby knew better than to question him. He obviously had reasons for staying out of sight.

In the many hours that Toby spent with Domino sitting on the fantail deck of the launch, he came to know the gang leader well and was surprised by his humanity and erudition. "I make war," Domino said, "only on the greedy, the cheats, and the two-faced of the underworld. Of course, I sometimes operate in defiance of the law, but that's because the public demands what I can provide. We may have to wait a long time for this, but I predict the day will come when gambling will become legal throughout the United States. So will brothels, because the public demand is there. I don't tolerate white slavery in any bordello, but aside from that, you bet I'll operate them. The women earn a profit for themselves under safe conditions, customers are never threatened or cheated, and I earn a profit. I try never to hurt the interests of an honest man in any business deal, nor do I willingly cause them harm—unless, of course, I'm forced to do so by circumstances."

He was sensitive, interested both in politics and the arts, and his temper appeared to be always under control. Toby realized, too, that much of Domino's thinking was far ahead of other people's. Toby found it difficult to believe that this apparently gentle, mild-mannered man was the same man who inspired such terror among criminals.

"I've noticed," Toby said one afternoon as he sat with

Domino and Eddie on the deck, "that this launch has no name printed on her. I assume there's a particular reason for that?"

Domino chuckled. "I might have guessed that you'd notice that, Toby," he said, "and you're absolutely right." He laughed again. "This launch is used for various purposes, some other than legal. So it's appropriate that she shows no name. Witnesses would have a terrible time identifying a nameless ship. It can be a convenience, too, to give her a temporary name one day and then wipe it out."

For the next few days, nothing occurred to vary the pattern of daily calls at river ports, during which Red went ashore to obtain supplies and conduct other business. Domino was always eager to be on his way after each stop, but Memphis proved to be an exception, for here he made a point of going ashore, taking with him both Red and Eagle.

He went first to the house of Mrs. Myers, the madam who had arranged to send a message to him from Martha. After a brief but cordial visit with her, he called on each of the three warring gang leaders of the city, informing them that Mrs. Myers's establishment was to be above the struggle, under his personal protection. It would no longer be a pawn in the incessant fighting among the gangs.

While Domino was thus occupied, Toby went off to visit the commissioner of police. The commissioner listened to Toby's questions and seemed to become apprehensive. "I shouldn't be offering advice to someone with your vast experience, Mr. Holt," he said, "but I think you're about to take a bigger bite than you can digest. Kellerman is a ruthless man. Like a rat, he's most dangerous when he's cornered. I can't do much officially to help, but I could assign a couple of experienced detectives to assist, if you wish."

"I don't believe that'll be necessary, Commissioner," Toby answered. "Thanks anyway, but I'm relying on Domino to provide whatever backup I may need."

The commissioner looked at him in astonishment. "I find it amazing," he said, "that a man of your stature associates with a criminal like Domino, much less depends on him. I trust you know what you're doing, and I wish you luck in tracking down Kellerman."

"You haven't heard anything new about affairs in Cairo, then?" Toby asked.

The commissioner shook his head. "The only way I'd hear anything would be if one of our citizens got hurt or was abused in Cairo. But our people have the good sense, generally, to stay away from the town."

Back at the launch, Domino joined him a short time later. "What have you learned?" he asked.

"Nothing." Toby laughed painfully. "I received a little lecture and was told I should stop associating with people like you. Otherwise, I accomplished nothing."

"Well, I learned plenty," Domino said grimly. "Kellerman and the redheaded woman—obviously Martha—reached Cairo a week ago and took up residence at the Warehouse." He sighed, frowned, and clenched his fists. "I know Dave Hammersmith's operation there fairly well, and I know no woman could live at the Warehouse unless she's working in his bordello. If that's the case, Martha's gone too damn far, and she's going to have to account to me."

"Don't judge her prematurely," Toby advised. "She has a good head, as you know better than I do."

"That's true, at least until recently," Domino conceded, "so I'll wait until I see her before I make any real judgments. What's important is this: Martha is at least posing as a prostitute. I'm sure to be recognized in and around Dave's and so would Eddie. That pretty much leaves you, Toby, to get to Martha, possibly as a patron, and find out Kellerman's whereabouts. Then, and only then, can we strike! We'll be ready, but I must ask you to get inside that place first."

With a nod of his head, Toby accepted the unsavory assignment.

Toby strolled along Cairo's Mississippi River waterfront. His gaze impersonal, he raised his eyes and looked at the massive building above him. As he walked up to it, he could see how nondescript the Warehouse was; only a small sign advertised its saloon and gambling facilities.

Toby was particularly concerned by the absence of balconies and fire escapes above the ground level. On the ground floor, the doorways seemed to be centered in a small front area. One pair of large double doors off to the side apparently could be used for moving large furniture in and out. Toby committed the location of every entrance to memory before moving on.

He paused at the saloon entrance just long enough to make sure that his suit jacket was fully buttoned, concealing the holster that held his repeating pistol, and covering his belt and knife. Then he pushed open the door and went in. Although two hours of daylight remained, the gas lamps were lighted in the bar, which was crowded. All the women were clad in transparent, knee-length silk gowns. Toby was shocked by the air of lewd permissiveness, but he showed none of his feelings as he made his way to the bar and ordered a tall drink of whiskey and water.

No sooner was he served than a husky female voice sounded softly in his ear. "Do you suppose you could spare the money to buy a thirsty girl a drink?" she asked.

Toby turned and was startled to see Martha, cosmetics heavy on her face, her body as uncovered as that of any of the other women. No sign of recognition registered in her face.

He took care not to reveal that he knew her. "I reckon that can be arranged," he said, and beckoned to the bartender, who slid a glass of colored water across the bar to her and charged Toby exorbitantly for it.

Martha raised her glass. "Here's to ya, honey!"

Toby was determined to play his own role faultlessly. "Here's to you, sweetie," he replied, and raised his own glass. They sipped in silence, and Martha edged closer and linked an arm through his. Toby realized, to his surprise, how much Martha, with her red hair and green eyes, resembled his own wife. Her height added to the illusion, which persisted, despite her makeup and strange garb.

"You're new in town, huh?" she asked.

He nodded. "Just got in."

"You've come to the right place, honey," she told him. "Nobody here ever gets lonesome. You want to have a little private chat?"

"Why not?" he countered. "Sounds pretty good to me."

They finished their drinks quickly, and then Martha led him out of the bar, clinging to one arm as she guided him toward the staircase. She flirted as they mounted the stairs, and anyone who might have glanced in their direction would have taken them for a typical couple making their way up to one of the bedrooms.

Not until they entered Martha's room did her attitude change. Her manner became crisp as she dropped his arm, picked up a dressing gown from the bed, and wrapped the garment around her. "Are you alone?" she asked briskly.

He shook his head. "Domino and four of his men are waiting for my signal right now."

"Good! You don't have much time, though. If Kellerman follows his customary routine, he'll be back by sundown."

Toby went to a window, raised the shade, and looked down onto the street. He stood plainly revealed. After no more than a moment, he saw a flicker of light as someone in Domino's party lighted a long sulfur match and held it for a count of ten, the prearranged signal.

Only then did Toby step back to the center of the room, where he took the precaution of opening the flap on his holster.

Struck by Martha's attractiveness, he realized how strongly drawn to her he had been ever since they first met, many months earlier. Seeing her in such an intimate setting aroused him, much to his distress. A happily married man, he was also a healthy male animal, and he could not help responding to Martha's erotic appearance.

She became aware of his increased interest, which immediately sparked her own. Instinctively drawn to him, she had on one occasion offered herself to him. She was therefore pleased by his response to her now.

In the inner recesses of his mind, Toby was relieved that the time he must spend alone with Martha was limited to the period before Kellerman's return and the much briefer time before Domino could make his way into the building and up to her room. In that short a time, he could not become involved with Martha.

"I gather you've encountered no serious difficulty in deceiving Kellerman."

Martha smiled broadly. "It's been easy, almost absurdly easy," she assured him. "He believes that any woman who meets him falls in love with him. It doesn't occur to him that a woman might resent his treatment and try to even the score."

"Now that we're about to strike, Domino will want you out of harm's way. Are you able to get your hands on a change of clothes?"

"Of course," she said. "I have my own clothes in the closet." She gestured toward the far side of the room.

"Domino will be here in the next few minutes, so I urge you to change now," he said. "Not only will you upset him if he sees you looking like this, but he'll want you out of here before Kellerman arrives. He'll send one of the men with you as a bodyguard. You may have forgotten what Kellerman did to Millicent when he believed she had double-crossed him, but I haven't. I assure you that Domino hasn't, either. He wants you well out of the way."

Martha pushed up the sleeves of her robe and rubbed her bare arms briskly. "I haven't forgotten," she said, "and I certainly have no intention of making Millicent's mistakes. The last thing I want is to become a hostage in Kellerman's hands. But I have no time to dress before Domino arrives. In fact, there's probably just enough time for me to thank you, Toby, for all you've done."

He felt he had done no more on her behalf than he would have toward any woman in her precarious situation, but he had no opportunity to demur. Martha was standing close to him, her scarlet lips parted, her enormous green eyes raised to his, and he was conscious only of her overwhelming sexuality.

Toby had to draw upon all his willpower to prevent himself from taking her into his arms and kissing her. He knew she would offer no resistance. He hesitated momentarily, not only through loyalty to Clarissa, but also because he realized that his relationship with Martha might become complicated beyond his ability to handle.

A warning bell sounded in Toby's mind, but he was beyond caring. A faithful servant of discipline all his life, ordinarily obeying and heeding the sharp demands that it imposed, he was now ready to deliberately cast aside all caution.

Martha, innately aware of his desire, knew it perfectly matched her own. She, too, was in the grip of emotion stronger than her common sense. She took a half step closer to Toby, her face raised to his; at the same moment, he moved to her.

The real world intruded. A soft, insistent tapping sounded at the door. They instantly moved apart.

With a single broad gesture, Toby swept Martha behind him, and facing the door, he drew his pistol.

"Come in," Martha called.

They breathed more easily, and Toby lowered his pistol when Domino entered, followed by his men.

Domino embraced and kissed Martha, then held her at arm's length and frowned at the dressing gown, which could not entirely conceal the strange garb she still wore underneath it. "What a way to dress!" he exclaimed. "What a disgusting masquerade!"

"Dave Hammersmith has been very good to me," she said. "Strictly for your sake, naturally. He warned everybody in the establishment that I was his girl. And as a

327

result, no one has come near me. Kellerman has been off somewhere every day, attending to business that he never mentions to me. I've been totally untouched here, believe it or not!"

"That would be hard to believe from anyone but you—but I do believe it," Domino assured her. "However, now we're wasting time. We'll talk about such things later. Where is Kellerman?"

"I've urged Martha to get dressed," Toby said, "so she can be out of here before Kellerman shows up."

"That's right," Domino said, and added to Martha, "Do it!"

Martha hurried to the wardrobe, removed several items, and took them into her dressing room.

Domino turned to his men and began to issue orders. "Eddie," he said, "you and Red go out and wait in the corridor and find a place to hide until Kellerman shows up. I don't want him to see you and be scared off. Don't show yourselves until after he's come into this room. But I expect you to use every means to prevent him from leaving the place alive. Eagle, you and Cook are to escort Martha out a back door and take her to the launch. Keep her out of harm's way until we return. Have you got it straight?"

The men nodded affirmatively, and Eddie and Red left the room immediately.

Domino drew his repeating pistol, assured himself that it was in good working order, and continued to hold it.

Martha emerged from the dressing room. She had not taken the time to remove her makeup, but she wore a hat with a large brim that cast her face in shadows. A coat of dark gray wool covered her from neck to ankles.

"Eagle and Cook will take you to my launch," Domino told her. "Leave by one of the back doors so you don't run into Kellerman on your way out. We anchored the launch a short distance down the Mississippi, where it's quiet. Put yourself in their hands and take no risks. We'll join you as soon as our business here is finished," he concluded, looking grim.

"Good luck," she said as she kissed Domino. Then she turned to Toby, and a tender note crept into her voice. "Take care of yourself, too, Toby."

"Don't you worry about me," he replied.

Martha left without a backward glance, Eagle on one side of her and Cook on the other, both with their hands in their pockets, their guns gripped, ready for action.

Domino closed the door, and Toby moved to the window. After a time he called, "Martha and her guards are on the street now. They're heading to a side street in the direction of the river. They shouldn't run into Kellerman."

"She's safe now, and for the first time since she left New Orleans, I can breathe easily," Domino said. As he looked around the room, he shook his head. "I don't really like this layout," he announced. "It's too cramped for our purposes." He went to the door and beckoned to Toby to follow. "Eddie, Red," he called softly, "stay where you are. We're going to wait until Kellerman shows up, and when he goes in the room, we'll get behind and block him off on the stairs heading down to the main floor. In that way, we'll have him well sealed off from escape." Beckoning again, he led Toby around a corner. Keeping themselves concealed close to the wall, they settled down to await Kellerman's return. Domino and Toby exchanged no further words, and as their silence lengthened, the tension increased.

Slow footsteps sounded on the stairs, and Domino's grip on his pistol tightened. Then they heard a soft peal of feminine laughter. The gang leader raised his head in confusion.

A moment later, Toby caught a glimpse of one of Hammersmith's women mounting the stairs arm in arm with a befuddled man. She had a firm grip on his arm and, paying no attention to Toby and Domino, guided her escort past them to a room down the corridor.

Toby smiled and shrugged. Domino responded by shrugging in return. Then both gripped their pistols anew and resumed their wait.

After another interminable wait, the woman and her companion emerged and returned to the staircase leading down to the bar. Neither paid any attention to the two men. As they disappeared from sight, Toby glanced at his watch and found that a half hour had elapsed since they had first appeared.

More footsteps could be heard now ascending the stairs. They were heavy and sharp, those of a man who knew where he was going. Kellerman came into view, his expression arrogant, and as he opened the door of Martha's room without bothering to knock, Domino and Toby slipped from their hiding place to the staircase and took up positions there. At the same moment, Eddie and Red came into the open on either side of the door.

Kellerman had left the door ajar. By craning his neck, Toby could make out his figure inside the room.

"Martha?" Kellerman was calling. "Damn you, Martha, where are you?" Some instinct impelled him to reach into his double holster and draw one of his six-shooters.

"Damn you, Martha!" he said again in annoyance. "If you're playing some kind of trick on me, you'll regret it!"

He turned, and seeing Red, he shot from the hip as he dashed into the corridor. Red collapsed onto the floor and lay still in a growing pool of blood.

Kellerman desperately broke into a wild run, taking the stairs to the third floor two and three at a time.

He took his three surviving pursuers completely by surprise. They had not expected him to run up the stairs. Before they could aim and fire, he had turned a corner at the stairwell.

Toby and Domino followed. Toby was sure no exit from the floors above was possible.

Eddie stayed behind long enough to check on Red, but once he dropped to one knee beside him, he knew nothing could be done. Muttering under his breath, Eddie followed up the stairs. Now he had one more score to settle.

Toby mounted the steps cautiously, crouching low, with Domino close behind. The older man's jaw was clenched, and a single look convinced Toby that he did not intend to allow Kellerman to escape. One way or another, he would kill him before nightfall.

Certain precautions were necessary, and Toby gestured sharply. Domino nodded assent and moved to the far side of the staircase. Together, they made too tempting a target.

Only silence greeted them when they reached the third floor. Toby could see no sign of Kellerman. He almost surely was lying in wait, Toby thought, hoping to catch them in an ambush.

The windows on the third floor were unused and consequently were smeared with grime. The light that filtered in was murky so that seeing anything was difficult. Objects that loomed up ahead could not be readily identified. Motioning again to Domino to follow, Toby crept forward into the first of the large rooms in which furniture was stored. Some bulky objects were covered with sheets, while others stood uncovered. Toby moved, inch by inch, blinking until his eyes became accustomed to the dim half light. He realized he would have to depend on his extraordinary eyesight and hearing in order to find Kellerman.

The floorboards creaked alarmingly beneath Toby's weight, so he moved closer to a wall and soundlessly continued to advance.

Each room was three times the size of an ordinary parlor, and Toby, Domino, and Eddie scoured each, looking into every corner and searching behind every bulky object, but they found no sign of Kellerman.

Toby realized that a prime requisite in stalking a human being, as in hunting a wild animal, was patience. He progressed methodically, going from room to room, taking no risks as he crouched close to the floor.

At last his patience was rewarded. Suddenly, as he came from behind a long couch, a pistol shot reverberated, and a bullet sang above Toby's head. Using the couch as a shield, he peered around the end of it. No one was in sight.

There were two possibilities, Toby reasoned: One was that Kellerman was lying in wait, and as soon as Toby made a clear target, he would be shot at; the other was that Kellerman had fled after taking the single shot. He pondered briefly and came to the conclusion that, based on what he knew of Kellerman, the man would choose to bolt and run, rather than to make a firm stand and risk a gun duel. If that was actually the case, the way again was clear to continue the search.

Toby decided to take the chance, so he stepped into the open, nevertheless crouching low. He resumed his advance very cautiously. He could hear Domino's labored breathing, but he did not turn to look, assuming that he could take care of himself and assist in whatever might develop.

The bark of Domino's pistol suddenly broke the silence. The sound was so close that it almost deafened Toby's right ear. He glanced back over his shoulder. Domino was pointing excitedly at a far corner of the room.

Still exercising patience, Toby smiled wryly as a rat scurried out of the corner.

Resuming his advance, Toby went from room to room, traveling in a U-shaped route, following the rooms down one side of the Warehouse and intending to double back to his starting place up the other arm. When he reached the turning point at the bottom of the U, he heard a sudden exchange of pistol fire from the stairwell at the far end of the corridor.

He broke into a run, with Domino at his heels, and again two shots were fired. When Toby finally burst into the open at the end where he had started his search, he found Eddie Neff, smoking pistol in one hand.

Eddie jabbed a finger in the direction of the stairs to the fourth floor. Once again, Toby was surprised. He had thought that Kellerman would try to force his way down, but instead he was drawing the noose tighter around his neck. No escape was possible from the fourth floor. He had no way of getting to the roof, and even if he could manage somehow to pull himself up onto it, he had no place to go from there.

Domino struggled to keep up the pace as Toby mounted the stairs two at a time. At the top, he crouched as he advanced into a room with five piles of furniture.

A pistol blazed. Three shots smashed harmlessly into the wall. Kellerman had decided to make his final stand here. Ducking behind the nearest pile of furniture, Toby saw that Domino had arrived to his right, and had crouched behind another pile of furniture.

Toby carefully scanned the far side of the dimly lighted room. Finally, he came to the conclusion that Kellerman was in either of two places, hiding behind furniture. In order to determine Kellerman's exact location, Toby devised a plan. Reaching into a pocket, he removed a bandanna and then took a silver dollar from another pocket. He wrapped the coin in the handkerchief. Then, gripping his pistol firmly with his right hand, he threw the bandanna-wrapped coin into the air a short distance ahead of him.

As the handkerchief began its descent, a pistol blazed at the far end of the room.

At last, Toby knew Kellerman's location! Instantly taking aim, he waited for a second shot to be fired. Kellerman did not disappoint him but sent another bullet toward the area where the handkerchief had been visible.

The second flash of his gun was all Toby needed. He squeezed his trigger, aiming at the flash. His second shot brought a cry of agony from Kellerman.

In the next instant, his pistol clattered to the floor. It was apparent that Toby's shot had caught him neatly in the hand.

Kellerman bolted through a door into the adjoining room. As Toby followed a dozen yards behind, Domino lingered to scoop up Kellerman's pistol and drop it into his pocket.

Kellerman carried no firearm now, but he had no intention of surrendering. Instead, he leaped onto the dusty sill of one of the windows. Using his heavy boot, he kicked out the glass.

Toby, reluctant to shoot the fleeing man in the back, shouted across the room. "Halt!" Domino raced up to join him.

But Kellerman paid no attention to the command. To Toby's horror, he threw himself into space.

The room became very quiet as the men stared at each other wordlessly. They walked over to the window and stared down into the dark, swirling waters of the river almost directly below.

"My God!" Domino murmured. "I don't see how anybody could survive a fall like that."

"Even if he lived," Toby replied, "he'd have to be an expert swimmer to navigate those waters. The current is ferocious."

They could see no sign of Kellerman anywhere from their high vantage point, so after several minutes they descended and, taking Eddie Neff with them, went around the building and scrambled down to the riverbank.

"It appears to me," Toby said, "that he would have landed out yonder, far from shore. That would have to be the end of him."

They searched the muddy banks of the river but found no traces of a man's having come ashore.

"I hated Kellerman as I've hated few other people in my life," Domino said, "and I guess he's finished. I only wish I could have killed him myself. But if he's drowned out there, he's paid for his sins, all of them, today."

Despite their apparent victory over Kellerman, the death of their companion had left all three in a somber mood as they made their way to the place on the Mississippi where the launch was moored.

A few days later, when the launch tied up at New Orleans, Toby stood on the deck, his valise beside him as he shook hands with Domino.

"It's just as well, I think, that Kellerman jumped to his death," Toby said. "Certainly it's better this way. If we'd taken him prisoner and turned him over to the authorities, well, not that I'd mind seeing him in jail, but I think justice probably was served better this way."

Domino gripped his hand. "I'd feel much happier if we knew for a fact that Kellerman is really dead," he said, "but I don't suppose we'll ever find out any more than we know. I don't see how he could have survived that leap, but he escaped so many times that it wouldn't surprise me if he showed up somewhere. Don't ask me how, much less when or where. I hope," he went on, "you can stay put on your ranch for quite a while now. You and your family deserve the time."

"Who knows when we'll meet again," Toby said, "but until then, I wish you good luck in everything. And I hope that you'll stay out of trouble."

"I never cause trouble," Domino told him. "It just seems to follow me. And every now and then it catches up with me." They grinned at each other, shook hands again, and Toby turned away.

Martha stood at his elbow. "I'll go ashore with you, and we'll say good-bye there," she told him.

Toby picked up his valise, and she preceded him onto the dock. When he dropped the suitcase to the wharf, they faced each other.

"Our paths crossed only briefly during this episode,"

Martha said in a low voice. "The next time we meet, we'll see more—a great deal more—of each other."

Her eyes were bottomless pools of green as Toby gazed into them, and for a moment he felt as though he were drowning. He tried, feebly, to joke about their relationship. "You seem very sure that our paths are going to cross again."

"I'm quite certain of it," she replied. "We can't have come this far, only to have it end in nothing." She curled one arm around his neck, drew his head down, and kissed him full on the lips.

Their kiss lasted a brief moment—or was it an eternity? Toby didn't know.

Then Martha turned on her heel, and making her way to the launch's gangway, she boarded without a backward glance.

Toby picked up his valise and slowly walked to the far end of the dock, where he could hail a hansom cab that would take him to his train. Soon he would be home again.

The reality of Clarissa and Tim awaited him there. That was far preferable to the dubious promise of high adventure with a woman as mercurial as Martha. Yes, he was glad his mission had come to an end and he was going home—where he belonged.

READ THIS THRILLING PREVIEW
OF A BOLD NEW SAGA
FROM THE CREATORS OF WAGONS WEST

AMERICA 2040

BY EVAN INNES

As the author of WAGONS WEST, I love to write about the conquering of the American West and the good folks who brought law, order, and civilization to the unknown wilds. In America 2040, I've found a mixture of all the qualities of WAGONS WEST, but set in the future—courageous men and women forced to flee to the far planets to settle and live, while the Earth teeters on the brink of nuclear war. AMERICA 2040 tells about men and women like you and me, who are determined to carry on American morality and love of freedom and family on uncharted lands light years away. AMERICA 2040 is a terrific exciting book!

Dana Fuller Ross
Author of WAGONS WEST

To American President Dexter Hamilton, entering Greater Moscow in the spring of 2033 was a fifty year leap into the past, an enigmatic separation from his familiar, changing, bustling world. The impressive modernity of Gagarin Airport, the city's newest civilian and military aviation facility, had not prepared him for the real Moscow.

There was snow in the city, grayed, trodden, piled. Along the motorcade route he and his entourage caught glimpses of real antiques: diesel-powered trucks spouting the contaminants of burning fossil fuel to cloud the chill air. People swaddled in animal furs. Drab, stern, slab-sided apartment buildings that had been built shortly after World War II.

Under a lowering, slate sky, the Kremlin loomed redly beyond the frozen Moskva River. To Hamilton, and to millions, the triangularly shaped fortress housed most of what was evil in the world. The relationship between Russia and the United States remained tense, hostile, suspicious, and dangerous, but Dexter Hamilton wanted to be the American President who halted the eternal arms race and delivered the world, forever, from the threat of nuclear incineration. To that end, he was to meet with the Soviet leader, Premier Yuri Kolchak.

The President was young to be serving in that office, only forty-six, having been born in 1987. His silvering hair—a tight, curled mass that clung to his well-formed head—seemed to be a tacit signal that, although young, here was a wise, experienced man.

Behind the smile-crinkled blue eyes, the classic nose, the upturned mouth, there was the strength that had given him the governorship of North Carolina, then a seat in the Senate, and finally the Oval Office.

When the limousine hummed through guarded gates, past heavily armed and stalwart men handpicked for Kremlin duty from the huge Red Army, Dexter Hamilton was guided from the car by a woman general. He walked with long, quick strides, eager to begin the summit meeting with Premier Yuri Kólchak.

Premier Kolchak was waiting for him behind a wide, gleaming table in a conference room. The Premier was a darkly handsome man, but there was something in his eyes that bothered Hamilton, a quality he'd seen before. Then the memory came back to him: When he was quite young he'd owned a little dog that had wandered into a field and been swept up in a tomato picker. The dying, mutilated dog lay stunned and shocked. In Kolchak's eyes were those same qualities—a pain that seemed to approach madness. Was there truth to the rumor that the Premier was seriously ill?

Several minutes after the meeting has begun, Yuri Kolchak rises abruptly from his seat, obviously taken ill. He is led away hastily, without explanation or apology. Hamilton is escorted back to his suite, where, except for a serving girl bringing dinner, he is left alone for the night.

The next morning there was a knock on the door of his luxurious suite in the Kremlin, and a smiling, dark-haired serving girl in livery appeared. Pleasant aromas of coffee, real eggs, and ham came from the serving cart she was standing behind. A great number of covered serving bowls were on the cart, certainly enough for more than one man.

Just then he heard a deep, resonant voice coming from behind the girl.

"Good morning, Mr. President. You slept well?"

Premier Kolchak was dressed informally in tunic, trousers. At forty-seven his slightly Slavic face was smooth, and his dark and bristly hair showed no hint of gray. He extended a hand. Hamilton took it. Each grip was firm.

"Forgive me for surprising you," Kolchak said as the serving girl disappeared out the door. "But if I had taken time to warn you that I was coming, we'd have to invite our aides and observe protocol." There was no explanation of the previous meeting's cancellation.

"I understand," Hamilton said. Kolchak took a seat and Hamilton sat across the table, and they began to eat.

"My people don't understand your real purpose here," the Premier said.

"Well, Yuri," Hamilton began, "you like straight talk, so here it is: I'm here to talk peace. I want to talk about what we have in common. We're all passengers on a small, increasingly overcrowded planet. It is time we took down the bombs from the space stations and junked the missiles and the space weapons. The men who bring peace to the world will be sung in history down through the ages. Let's make those men you and me."

"I could learn to like you," Kolchak said. "I will give you anything you want from this conference."

The statement seemed simple enough, direct enough, but there was something wrong.

"Because you see," Kolchak said, his dark, hard

eyes boring into Hamilton's, "whatever you achieve in this present conference does not matter." The Premier had finished eating. He leaned back, wiped his lips on a linen napkin, let it fall to his knee. "What matters is what you and I say here in this room." He smiled. "I hope you will be receptive and reasonable."

"I'll do my best."

"For centuries," Kolchak said, "elitist and imperialist countries have delayed the destiny of the masses. We can no longer allow that. Soon, Mr. President, the downtrodden of the world will be free to share in the fruits of their own labors. Within my lifetime, the revolution will be total." He paused. "With one single exception. We will allow the continued existence of the United States as a governmental entity. In time, with the rest of the world's workers freed from their masters and living in equality with their fellows, you will see reason and work with the rest of the civilized world." Ever since the use of the first atomic bomb on Japan, men had dreaded that someday, in some country, a madman would be in a position to push the button. This, Hamilton felt with a despair that made him want to strike out, was the man.

"Mr. Premier, this must be the first time in the history of my country that a President has been so threatened."

Kolchak shrugged. "We can no longer allow you to prevent the legitimate aspirations of the peoples of this world. We have liberated many countries. We will liberate more."

"Are you speaking of South America?"

"That, first."

South America was dominated by the emerging

imperialistic giant Brazil, whose armed forces had overwhelmed Cuba, ending Communist rule there. However, Communist insurgents continued to rebel against Brazilian authorities in the Caribbean and South America. An American fleet was stationed in the Pacific, but as of yet there had been no direct confrontation with the Russians.

"Are you declaring war?" Hamilton asked. "For we will fight you over that continent."

"There will be a war only if you choose to interfere. If both our countries let loose all our military power there will be little, if any, life left on Earth. But that doesn't really matter."

"What, in God's name, does matter?"

Kolchak leaned forward, his face pale, his lips twitching in obvious pain. "The triumph of right."

"Your brand of right, of course?"

"Of course. There is no other. Now will you pull out of South America and let events take their course?"

"No."

Kolchak leaned back, sighed. "Then, Mr. President, prepare yourself for some very difficult decisions."

"We've faced tough decisions before," Hamilton said. "I'll admit that you're scaring the living daylights out of me, but we won't stand aside and let you gobble up what's left."

Kolchak smiled. "Understand this, Mr. President. Before I die, the world will be Red or dead, and quite frankly I don't give a"—he used a Russian obscenity unfamiliar to Hamilton—"which it is."

Hamilton heard himself saying words, inane words. "May you have a long life, Mr. Premier."

"No, my friend, you will not escape the responsibility in that way."

"You *are* ill," Hamilton said softly.

Kolchak, with a cold smile, nodded.

"Perhaps we could help in some way. Our medical research—"

"Is no better than ours."

"How long?" Hamilton asked.

"Fewer than nine years."

"I'm sorry," Hamilton said. "But we have time to think about it, to talk. Yuri, there's no winning a war. My God, man, we've both got enough warheads in space to do the job twice over. If you push the button I'm dead, but I'll have time to push my own button and you're dead."

"But I'm dead regardless of what happens," Kolchak said. With a wicked gleam in his black eyes, he added, "All I care about is that the world is ours . . . or else it does not exist at all."

President Hamilton returns to Washington, where he briefs the head of the CIA and orders him to make the assassination of Yuri Kolchak a top priority. Then Dexter Hamilton and his scientific advisor, Oscar Kost, explore other ways to avert annihilation of the American people and their way of life. Their search takes them to Vandenberg Air Force Base in California, to learn about Project Lightstep, a top-secret operation.

Dexter Hamilton and Oscar Kost were introduced by a two-star general to Harry Shaw, a small, dark man, with a wide forehead and thin mouth that was, nevertheless, capable of a wide smile.

"This is a genuine pleasure, Mr. President, Mr. Kost," Shaw said.

"The pleasure is mutual," Hamilton said. "I have

to confess that I know absolutely nothing about this project. Please start at the beginning."

"I'll try to make it brief," Shaw said. "When I was an undergraduate I worked with platinum metals and their ability to store heat and energy, but it wasn't until I got my hands on a supply of rhenium that I began to make any progress. I decided to hit a few molecules of rhenium with antimatter, and as a result we almost obliterated Los Angeles. The reaction was contained, but just barely," Shaw added.

Hamilton didn't see the significance. A bigger and better bomb would not make Yuri Kolchak take his finger off the button. Nuclear bombs could already destroy all life on Earth, so why bother with something else?

"Harry," Hamilton said, "just tell me rhenium's other applications."

"It's currently the energy source for an experimental space vehicle disguised as a simple planetary probe. It's out beyond Pluto right now. If we've succeeded, that vehicle, propelled by rhenium, has made a round trip to within a few million miles of the star closest to our system, Proxima Centauri. That's thirty trillion miles in a billionth of a second."

Hamilton felt a sudden surge of joy. He glanced at Kost. Oscar's hooded eyes were gleaming. For the first time since his meeting with Yuri Kolchak, Hamilton felt a swelling of hope in his breast. As the countdown clock jerked its second hand closer to the critical moment when the experimental space vehicle's computer-screen transmission would be received by Vandenberg, a fantastic and exciting dream grew inside Dexter Hamilton: If Yuri Kolchak sent the whole world up in smoke and dust and fire, there would be still one last hope for the human race.

"One minute and counting," an amplified voice said, breaking the tense silence.

Hamilton's eyes were on the clock.

"Thirty seconds . . . twenty—"

Screens came to life, flickered, were blank. There was an air of supreme tension in the room, a breathless hush except for the counting voice.

"—five, four, three, two, one—!"

A large screen flickered, static lines flowering, diminishing, and then the screen was filled with fire—harsh, golden, roiling, boiling fire.

"Oh, God, no," Hamilton said. Seen close up, a sun is an awesome furnace, the golden fires of thermonuclear reaction forming slowly roiling masses on its curved surface.

"Wait," Harry Shaw said, his voice cracking with excitement. "We're not on the scopes. We're on radio telemetry."

And slowly, slowly, the screen changed, the fire gradually becoming more distant.

"The camera is changing lenses!" Shaw yelled. "We were too close!"

A cheer went up.

"It worked! Thank God, it worked!" Harry Shaw yelled, doing a little dance. It worked! Man could travel faster than light. With some luck, and some tricky, very secret planning, there could be people, Americans, out there traveling through the far reaches of space.

Now there was hope. At least some would survive. Hamilton would see to that. He could not trust Yuri Kolchak to leave the United States alone. Kolchak would want total world domination, and Dexter would never bow down and live under Communism. There'd be a part of the United States of America alive, out there in space. And if the missiles began to lance down from the orbiting space stations, at least a seed stock of humankind, if the form of Americans, would be alive.

The colossal rhenium-powered spaceship, secretly constructed under the Utah desert over a period of six years, is ready for lift-off. In the interim, Yuri Kolchak's health and the international political situation deteriorate. President Hamilton addresses the nation and the world, on the brink of nuclear war, disclosing at last history's best kept secret, the **Spirit of America.**

From cameras outside, a view of the White House was flashed upward to satellites, and a band played the "Star Spangled Banner." The anthem was being fed to the sound monitors in the Oval Office. As the last notes of music died, the director stabbed a finger toward Hamilton, who sat immobile, his calm, kind, distinguished face in repose, his eyes looking directly into the cameras. At last his drawling voice broke the almost unbearable tension.

"My fellow Americans. Today, December 24, 2040, this great nation of ours is about to embark upon humankind's greatest adventure.

"Even as I speak, while hundreds of thousands of our servicemen and women are massed in South America because of that age-old curse of mankind—war—other brave men and women are preparing to leave behind family and loved ones, their homes, their native country, even the planet of their birth.

"Today, one thousand Americans will leave Earth to open a new frontier among the stars.

"We Americans have a history of facing and

overcoming the unknown. Our forefathers dared a great ocean and overcame great obstacles to establish this nation, under God, and in freedom. They came to face the fierceness of a raw, vast land, and they established a nation that is unique, a nation wherein each and every individual has equal rights.

"Today our freedom faces its gravest test. Even now, our avowed enemies in South America threaten to overwhelm us, and the largest battle fleet ever to be assembled is massing off the western coast of the South American continent.

"I cannot tell you, my fellow citizens, what tomorrow will bring. But I can tell you this: The spirit of America will not die. The force and the dream that made this country great will live on in those brave pioneers who today will leave Earth to venture into the unknown.

"America now offers hope to the billions of people, citizens of every country. For the great ship that will journey to the far stars can, with international cooperation, bring the blessing of plenty back to our wasted world. American science, American genius, and the American dream have opened up a vast new empire, which can provide us with badly needed living space, a safety valve for our overpopulation, a source of rich, new raw materials to quiet our hunger and restore to us, and to the world, the standard of living we once knew.

"As President of the United States and as your spokesman, I extend the hand of cooperation and friendship to our enemies. The destiny of humankind cannot continue in bitter warfare until there is nothing left but ashes and cinders. No, we have a higher destiny. Our destiny lies among the stars."

Hamilton's face was seemingly at peace, his eagle's eyes looking straight into the camera.

"And now, my fellow Americans, let us experience this great moment together."

The first view was from a distance. Desert. Low mounds in the background, and then, from a hovering helicopter, the first view of the ship. It looked like some fantastic toy buried in a round hole in the ground. Only when the airborne camera pulled back to a long shot and it was possible to see vehicles, antlike people, the temporary town, was it possible to gain an idea of the ship's vast size.

From the top it looked like a huge wheel and had been painted red, white, and blue. On a blank expanse of metal near the core were Old Glory and the words *UNITED STATES*. And on the outer wheel, proudly, in huge letters that gleamed in gold against white, *Spirit of America*.

It came to life slowly. First a billowing rush of smoke pouring up from the circular pit around its sides, obscuring it, and then tongues of flame.

Was it merely illusion or did that impossibly huge mass move?

Smoke. Flames. Rocketry had reached its zenith. Fuels of high mass-to-bulk ratio had been developed during the space-station-building epoch. Combustion times had been extended. But never before had such a mass been lifted from Earth's gravitational pull. Never before had so much fuel been expended in so short time.

The ship crawled upward, and the flames decreased, and *Spirit of America* emerged from them, huge, round, lifting slowly, slowly, and that sound familiar to all Americans was rumbling and roaring, the awesome power sound of bellowing rockets as it had never been heard in such intensity. And now it was accelerating slowly, slowly, too fantastic to be anything but trick photography, and yet it was real.

The ship bellowed straight up for long minutes, and then, as the cameramen began to switch to their long lenses, it tilted slowly and angled off toward the east. It was so big that the longest lenses could follow it into orbit. True, the ship was but a bright speck of reflected sunlight when, after the rockets had ceased firing, it swam through the darkness of near space, a bright star to be seen with the naked eye, but it was there, and after the long tension of watching the takeoff, a billion Americans cheered.